Y0-CZM-317

DANCING WAS MERELY
AN EXCUSE TO HOLD HER

The music flowed over them, around them, and they made patterns together on the dance floor, oblivious to everything except each other.

He feels so good, Summer thought helplessly.

She feels so good, Ryder thought, and nearly groaned.

It's been so long.

It's been too long.

He could hurt me, came the warning whisper.

I could hurt her, his conscience muttered.

I'm crazy, she thought helplessly.

This is crazy! he thought, and groaned.

Ryder pulled back slightly and looked down at Summer. Her expression was as dazed as he felt, and it was his undoing. When he spoke, his voice was thick. "Let's get out of here."

ABOUT THE AUTHOR

Louisiana native Suzannah Davis has always loved books. The daughter of a newspaper family, she worked as a librarian after finishing college. However, it wasn't long before she was writing books instead of cataloging them. *Airwaves* marks Suzannah's debut with the Superromance line. She wrote her story after visiting Chattanooga with her family and confesses she's always had a secret desire to be a deejay, just like Jubilee!

Suzannah Davis

AIRWAVES

Harlequin Books

TORONTO • NEW YORK • LONDON
AMSTERDAM • PARIS • SYDNEY • HAMBURG
STOCKHOLM • ATHENS • TOKYO • MILAN

FORTY YEARS OF
Romance

Published June 1989

First printing April 1989

ISBN 0-373-70359-7

Copyright © 1989 by Suzannah Davis. All rights reserved.
Except for use in any review, the reproduction or utilization
of this work in whole or in part in any form by any electronic,
mechanical or other means, now known or hereafter invented,
including xerography, photocopying and recording,
or in any information storage or retrieval system, is forbidden without
the permission of the publisher, Harlequin Enterprises Limited,
225 Duncan Mill Road, Don Mills, Ontario, Canada M3B 3K9.

All the characters in this book have no existence outside the
imagination of the author and have no relation whatsoever to
anyone bearing the same name or names. They are not even
distantly inspired by any individual known or unknown to the
author, and all incidents are pure invention.

® are Trademarks registered in the United States Patent and
Trademark Office and in other countries.

Printed in U.S.A.

For my favorite radio personalities:

Florence Bethard
KRRP, Coushatta, La.

and

Jeff and Melinda
KITT, Shreveport, La.

With sincerest thanks and appreciation.

CHAPTER ONE

"DON'T FORGET, GUYS AND GALS, send in those snapshots. We'll pick Chattanooga's ugliest kitchen next week for a complete make-over, courtesy of Downtown Plumbing and Supply. Now stay tuned for the latest WCHT news update on the stabbing death of Councilwoman Cleva Wagner. Until tomorrow's edition of the Coffee Club, this is Jubilee Jones wishing you two sugars in every cup!"

Josephine Summer Jones punched a button on the massive radio control board and WCHT's upbeat news lead-in filled the cluttered little room. Stretching, Summer stifled a wide yawn and pulled off her headphones, absently throwing her sun-streaked blond braid over her shoulder with a flick of her wrist. Her eye caught her own petite reflection in the glass control booth windows and she grinned at herself.

It was quite an advantage working on the radio. Nobody knew or cared if you came to work in overalls and a pink T-shirt, just as long as your voice was top form. After a year and a half of the six-to-ten morning shift, Summer had thrown fashion out the window in favor of comfort. Not like some people she could name. Her grin widened as WCHT's news anchor, Vanessa Lauden, slipped into the adjoining console.

"Morning," Vanessa piped, gingerly settling the bulbous headphones over her spiked punk-rocker hairdo. "Good show."

"Thanks, pal." Summer grinned again. "Hot news this morning?"

"Yeah, and it's hard as the dickens to get anything substantial out of the police." —

"It's awful about Ms Wagner. Have they got a suspect?"

"Not yet, but they've really got the lid on this one." Vanessa shrugged philosophically. "Can you make lunch today?"

Summer shook her head. "Sorry. I told Beryl I'd bring Lizabeth and her troupe out to play."

Vanessa laughed. "You're just a kid at heart, aren't you? You spend a lot of time volunteering at the Foundation. Haven't you got enough to do?"

"I enjoy it." To Summer, the time she spent with the speech- and hearing-impaired children, entertaining them and motivating them with her songs and puppets, was rewarding and precious.

"Well, if you keep forgetting to feed the inner woman, you'll never grow up," Vanessa warned with a twinkle in her eye.

"That's Aunt Ollie's line," Summer pointed out. "You're supposed to tell me that I'm going to shrivel away to nothing unless I do something about my nonexistent love life."

"Aren't we all?" Vanessa sighed. She propped her chin on her fist. "Where did all the nice men go?"

Summer feigned surprise. "You mean such an animal exists?"

"Well, sure."

"Name two," Summer challenged.

"How about your uncle for one."

"Uh-uh, disqualified. Uncle Burt's married *and* close to retirement age."

"What about Merl?" Vanessa demanded, referring to WCHT's station manager. "Now you have to admit, he's a thoroughly nice man." Her voice held a note of triumph.

"Sure, I'll admit it. And I'll tell him you said so, too," Summer teased.

"Don't you dare, you wretch!" Vanessa giggled, but her cheeks were flushed as she shuffled through her notes with unusual clumsiness.

Summer's curiosity was piqued, but she automatically glanced at the large wall clock. The red second hand swept steadily toward the top of the hour. No more time to chat this morning.

"See you later," Summer mouthed silently to her friend, pointing to the clock.

Vanessa gave Summer a jaunty "thumbs up" signal, punched a button, and launched into the morning's news, her black and white triangular earrings dancing a jig among her brunette curls.

Summer gathered up several empty coffee containers and let herself quietly out of the control room. Ron Kerry, the beefy, red-haired deejay whose show followed the Coffee Club, raced by to join Vanessa, giving Summer a brief, harried grin and trying not to spill a drop from yet another cup of coffee. Summer watched the two of them settle in.

Vanessa was fashion conscious to an extreme, but this morning her black and white polka-dotted suit, topped with the massive headphones, reminded Summer of a giant, but very feminine, Martian beetle. In fact, that might be a good idea for an animated cartoon. Maybe she should send it to Clancy. Summer paused in the green-carpeted corridor and tossed her own empty cups into a nearby wastebasket with more force than necessary.

No, bad idea, she admonished herself firmly. She owed nothing to Clancy. She'd spent too many years, wasted too many dreams out in Clancy's fantasy land, Los Angeles, California. Besides, Clancy wouldn't be interested in what he'd call a penny-ante idea now that he'd made it to the big time. Why, you could turn on the TV every Friday night and see him shooting up the bad guys as America's sexiest private eye. Clancy had gotten what he wanted—and it hadn't been Summer Jones.

Aunt Olivia and Uncle Burt had never quite understood why she'd stuck it out as long as she had. After all, her only claim to fame in Hollywood had been a few commercials and a stint as the voice of Lizabeth Lizard, the pouty Mae West of Saturday morning's cartoon hit, *Animal Alley*. Not that they hadn't been proud of her in their own way. But the niece they'd raised as their own daughter had always been something of a mystery to such straightforward and unpretentious people as they were. A not-so-glamorous job singing and playing piano in a west L.A. nightclub and Clancy's false promises hadn't been what they'd wanted for Summer. So they'd been relieved when she came home to the mountains and the family-owned radio station where she belonged.

Summer had learned the futility of loving an ambitious man the hard way, but at twenty-eight she was finally getting her life in order. If she occasionally felt a sharp pang in the region of her heart for all the wasted years, the mistaken loyalty to one Clancy Darrell, well, she could now tell herself it was only nostalgia and not a broken heart. Oh, she might be glib with Vanessa on the subject of men in general, but experience had taught her caution. Her life was full and rewarding, and if she sometimes felt a little lonely, she'd hardly stop long enough to admit it. After all, the last thing she needed in her life right now was a man! Not when she was finally learning to stand on her own two feet.

Summer walked toward her office, pausing at the wall of cubbyholes to retrieve her stack of mail. Flipping through the letters addressed to Jubilee, she felt a sense of satisfaction. She was finding her own success, right here in Chattanooga. The fans loved Jubilee Jones. Her morning show had the highest ratings. Well, almost—except for flip-flopping one and two with WROC's Gulliver. Drat that newcomer, anyway!

She wrinkled her nose. Gulliver! A lot of deejays used assumed names, herself included, to be more memorable to the listening audience. But Gulliver? The next thing one knew, he'd be broadcasting from Lilliput! On second thought, Summer decided with an impish smile, maybe that wouldn't be such a bad idea. At least he'd be outside of her listening area.

She tucked the mail under one arm and ripped open the first letter, then paused, frowning. Not that she wasn't up to a little healthy competition. She could take the heat, after all. But there certainly was no accounting for taste, as Aunt Ollie liked to say. Summer supposed some people would find Gulliver's off-the-wall humor amusing, but the few times she'd managed to catch a snippet of her rival's performance, she hadn't been impressed.

Sure, he had a mellow baritone voice that was easy on the ears, but then so did two-thirds of the other deejays in the city. She could almost hear his voice, practically oozing with self-confidence and charm.

. . . going to be another hot August night, but first go for some fun in the sun with that special someone, maybe a romantic boat ride . . .

No, she amended hastily, make that arrogance. Maybe that's what got to her about Gulliver. He sounded too cocky by half.

. . . or a scenic drive and end up holding hands at one of the overlooks . . .

No human had a right to be that self-assured, Summer thought, even if his professional voice was a mixture of Walter Cronkite, Peter Jennings and Bruce Springsteen. What a combination. Solid and reliable, urbane and intelligent, and downright sexy!

. . . atop Lookout Mountain. I'll bet you can see three states from there today, if you can take your eyes off each other long enough . . .

Summer came out of her daydream with a start. That was Gulliver all right, and he wasn't just coming from inside her head! She followed the sound of his deep voice out into the reception area.

Carol Thompson, WCHT's receptionist and secretary, fiddled with the dial of the small portable radio sitting beside her typewriter. A recent graduate of business school, she had the fresh-scrubbed, all-American cheerleader looks that Summer would have killed for at eighteen. Carol ran a hand through her perfectly disheveled blond locks and inserted a new sheet of paper into the typewriter, humming softly to herself as Gulliver introduced the next song.

Mischievously Summer reached in the can of pens and pencils sitting on the desk corner and grabbed a plastic letter opener. She stuck the opener under the bib of her overalls and groaned dramatically, clutching the "knife" and staggering as if mortally wounded.

"Et tu, Carol? Then fall, Jubilee!" she choked, draping herself across the other woman's desk.

"Eek! Summer, what on earth?" Carol squeaked in alarm.

Summer opened one long-lashed eyelid and peeked at Carol. "Slain, killed, destroyed—by my own loyal secretary! Oh, the treachery! Oh, the deceit!"

"You're crazy, do you know that?" Carol asked, giggling.

"Oh, yeah? So how come you're listening to *him*?" Summer stood up and tapped the little radio with the point of the letter opener.

"Oh!" Carol blushed, and hurried to twirl the dial on the offending instrument. "Oh, I'm sorry. I—I didn't mean...that is... Oh, Summer! You won't tell Mr. Pierson, will you?"

Summer propped herself on the corner of the desk. "Of course not, you goose!" She began to use the letter opener on the rest of her mail. "Although it's something of a shock to find our competition being played in the front office."

"I won't do it again," Carol said with a gulp. "I didn't mean to, really. I was just playing radio roulette and kinda got sidetracked."

"Don't worry about it. For curiosity's sake, what made you stop on Gulliver?"

Carol looked slightly nonplussed. "I don't know. I guess I liked the song that was playing then. Of course, that Gulliver's got a really sexy, bedroom voice and he's awful funny sometimes." She saw the stiff look on Summer's face and blurted, "But you're still the best, Summer. Jubilee's tops!"

"Thanks," Summer said. Her voice was dry. "So what's the difference between our two shows? Which would you choose if you didn't work here? Be honest, my ego can take it."

"Well..." Carol chewed thoughtfully on her lower lip. "Jubilee's like sitting at the breakfast table having a cup of coffee with your best friend. With Gulliver, it's not so much what he says as how he says it. He makes me go all shivery sometimes." She laughed uncomfortably. "I'd choose you, of course."

Summer couldn't contain a self-deprecating grin. "Right. You'd pick your dull old best friend over Mr. Wonderful? Tell me another one, Carol."

"That's not fair, Summer. Here," she said, poking a sheaf of logs and scripts in Summer's face. "There's your new promotions. Ed said to get those Bagel Beanery spots recorded as soon as possible. They want to start them the day after tomorrow."

"Hmm, okay," Summer murmured, flipping through materials. Was she wrong or had there been a decrease in the number of advertising spots lately? She shrugged. Must be some kind of temporary slump. "I'll record these tomorrow afternoon. Today I've got an appointment at the Speech and Hearing Foundation with a group of Lizabeth Lizard fans." She stood up, gingerly balancing her load of mail and scripts. "And Carol, I didn't mean to tease you. I'm really interested in your impression of Gulliver. After all, I need all the help I can get to keep that rascal out of first place!"

"Oh, you don't need to worry about that," Carol scoffed. "Jubilee Jones is a winner. Only..."

Summer paused. "Only what?"

"Only I wonder what Gulliver's really like? Have you met him?"

"No. You know most deejays move around like a band of gypsies. He's new and I haven't run into him anywhere yet."

"But don't you wonder?" Carol persisted. "I mean, that voice of his. All sexy and rumbly. Do you suppose he lives up to it in person?"

"I can wait to find out." Summer flashed a grin. "Haven't you noticed? The rule is: the deeper the deejay's voice, the more like a gnome he'll be."

Carol chuckled. "I won't believe that until I see it."

"A buck says I'm right."

"You're on," Carol agreed and turned back to the type-writer. "And I'll expect to be paid off in real money, not postage stamps!"

Summer chuckled and retreated down the hall to the tiny cubicle she called her office to finish sorting through the mail. Thirty minutes later, she set the final letter aside with a relieved sigh and let her gaze move to the small square window. Between the line of glass and concrete buildings forming Chattanooga's skyline, she could catch a glimpse of the Tennessee River curving through the city like a silver ribbon. A boat ride on this steamy August morning was, indeed, appealing. Summer made a small sound of disgust and turned away from the window.

This darned Gulliver was beginning to prey on her mind! Well, she had worked too hard to let success slip through her fingers now. She had to think of something fresh to recap-ture listener interest, some new angle that would nail down that number one spot for Jubilee for good. Maybe Merl Morgan, WCHT's volatile and creative station manager, could come up with an idea to put Jubilee back on top and keep her there. She glanced at her watch and picked up the large duffel bag that was home to Lizabeth and the rest of her puppet friends. She'd have time to pick Merl's brains before she had to leave for the Foundation.

When she poked her nose into Merl's office a few moments later, Summer found her friend leaning over a filing cabinet drawer, muttering to himself. Sunshine flooded the small room, highlighting the piles of tape cartridges, leaning stacks of professional publications, overflowing boxes of promotional materials, extra mikes, black coils of lead-in wires, and towers of records and compact discs. Actually the office looked better than it normally did. Summer knocked on the door facing.

"Merl? Got a minute?"

Merl raised his shock of corn-yellow hair and flashed a smile. His bright blue eyes shone behind his permanently askew aviator-style glasses and his red "Roll Tide" T-shirt hung on his angular farm-boy frame. He straightened, absently flinging a rubber snake back into the file drawer. "For you, doll, I got two."

"Lost something?" Summer asked with a hint of mischief.

"Contracts. Your uncle wants them. They gotta be around here someplace."

"Knowing your filing system, I'll bet they're under something like 'Slave Labor' or 'Fantasy Island.'"

"Now, wait a minute... Hey!" He snapped his fingers and his countenance brightened. He dug back into the drawer, pulling out a manila file with a triumphant grin that split his face and bobbled his Adam's apple. "You were right. I put it under 'Star Wars.'"

Summer groaned and rolled her eyes. She plopped into a bright orange, molded plastic chair, set her duffel between her feet, and waved a small, well-groomed hand in defeat. "Spare me the explanations, okay?"

"Sure, doll. Actually, I'm glad you're here. I could use some cheering up, seeing how my social life's totally in the toilet these days."

"Geez, Merl! What a welcome," Summer groused.

"No offense intended, doll. But you see before you a man rolling gutter balls in the bowling alley of love." Merl perched, storklike, on his chrome-edged desk.

"What about that cute young thing you were seeing?"

He made a gesture with his hand like a jet nosediving into the earth, and supplied appropriate sound effects. "Crashed and burned."

"Gosh, you, too? What's with everyone lately?"

"My bunions tell me winter's coming. It starts you thinking about who you'll be cuddling up with on those long, cold nights."

"Take my advice," Summer said, smiling. "Buy an electric blanket."

"Woman, you got no romance in your soul," Merl accused, aggrieved.

"Sure I do, but I know you don't find a meaningful relationship without a little work. Especially at your age."

"Ouch." Merl winced. "Low blow, Summer. You don't have to rub it in that I'm pushing thirty. Look, you know I'm a country boy. I was raised in a big, happy family with eight brothers and sisters. There's nothing I want more than to find the right gal, settle down, buy a Suburban, and have two-point-four kids. But I'm running out of places to look."

"How about right under your nose?"

"Huh?"

"Golly, your vocabulary is phenomenal, Merl."

"Don't try to side track me with compliments. Give, Summer."

"Well," she said airily, "I have it on very good authority that a certain stylish news anchorwoman thinks you're 'thoroughly nice.'"

"You mean..." His Adam's apple bobbed convulsively and his expression was stupefied. "Vanessa?"

"Uh-huh."

Merl's face fell. "Nope. Classy babe like that couldn't possibly see anything in me."

"She said nice."

"Nice is vanilla pudding and a Ford pickup." He shook his head. "Now if she'd said handsome, or sexy, or talked about caviar and a Lamborghini..."

"Don't sell yourself short. You like her? Go for it. You can't be any more miserable, can you?"

"That's what you think," Merl muttered. He held up his hands to stem her protest and firmly changed the subject. "Like I said, I'm glad you're here. We've got things to discuss."

Summer gave him a skeptical look. She'd heard that line before—just before one of his more outlandish promotions. Merl was definitely an idea man, and the stunts she'd had to pull in the name of station publicity had been memorable, to say the least.

"Oh, yeah? You're not going to perch me up on another billboard for three days and nights, are you? Or have me officiate at the All-City Turkey Shoot again. I'm all for anything that'll keep Gulliver out of my number one spot, but I swear, Merl, one of these days..."

"No, nothing like that."

"Well, why not?"

"Huh?"

Summer grinned and toyed with the tail of her braid. "There's that dynamic vocabulary again. I'm feeling a little desperate, Merl. I need a new promotion. Something original that will capture everyone's attention and leave Gulliver eating my dust in the ratings race."

"I thought the ugly kitchen contest was fairly original." Merl tried to look affronted.

Summer sighed and tugged at the green sequined puppet peeking out of her duffel. "It's okay, but hardly exciting."

"Honey, you've got to realize your public isn't looking for excitement. People feel comfortable with Jubilee. That's your charm."

Summer grimaced, and set Lizabeth Lizard on her lap, fondly smoothing her multicolored, plumed topknot and pink ostrich feather boa. "Well, they're starting to feel more comfortable with Gulliver, and that's what's bothering me. Can't you think up something that'll make me more visible?''

"Sure. How about a raffle? Or maybe a trivia quiz. Trivia's still big. I'll bet we could get a sponsor in a snap.''

"It might work, but I need something with more clout. I was thinking about expanding my Friday call-in show. You know, tackle subjects with a little more weight or interview controversial people and get the audience's opinions. What do you think?''

"I'd be willing to give it a trial run, if your uncle approves.''

"Good. Is there anything else I could do?''

"Well, how about some personal appearances? Once the public gets a load of how button-cute you are, everyone will tune in. Don't you get requests to emcee fashion shows and charity bazaars and stuff?''

"All the time. I'll bet I got half a dozen today alone. But I can't do them all.''

"Why not? You could make quite a bundle if you charged a fee.''

"Not to a charity!'' she objected. "My time is a donation, and I like to choose the organizations that I have a particular interest in, such as the Speech and Hearing Foundation. Isn't that right, Lizabeth?'' She shoved her hand into her puppet's body and Lizabeth winked one long-lashed bulbous eyeball at Merl. "That's right, handsome,'' the puppet said huskily.

Merl laughed. "Okay, but the key is picking at least a few that will get you some television and newspaper coverage, as well. I'll go through them if you like and let you know what I think.''

Summer felt relieved. "I'd appreciate it a lot.''

Merl studied her through his smudged and slanted glasses. "Say, you really are worried about this, aren't you?''

"I know Uncle Burt isn't going to fire me if Jubilee slips a little, but I want to do my best for the station. The Coffee Club means a lot to me, Merl."

"It does to all of us, believe me, Summer." Merl's homely features took on a worried appearance. "I hate to mention this, but have you heard your uncle say anything about the radio station changing hands?"

Summer's jaw dropped and Lizabeth went limp. "What are you talking about? No, of course not!" She shook her head firmly. "Where'd you get a crazy idea like that?"

"Grapevine."

"You should know better than to believe office gossip, Merl. Uncle Burt has been running this station since I was a little girl. It's a family operation and always will be."

"You're positive?"

Summer grinned and Lizabeth came to attention. "Would we lie to you?"

Merl still looked doubtful. "Maybe you don't know everything."

Summer gave a sigh of exasperation. She swung the strap of her duffel over her shoulder and headed for the door. "Look, I'll go talk with Uncle Burt right now if it will make you feel better. We'll scotch this rumor before it goes any farther."

"I hope you're right. You and Lizabeth come back and see me real soon, hear? She's about the only female I've seen lately who turns me on, green skin and all."

Summer ducked into the hall and stood behind the door, allowing Lizabeth to take center stage in the open doorway.

"You're not so bad yourself, sugar," she purred. "You can crawl under my rock anytime. Ta-ta!" Blowing kisses in time to Merl's muffled chuckles, Lizabeth made her exit.

And Summer turned around and ran right into a chest.

It was a very broad and solidly male chest, and her nose crunched painfully into the granitelike wall. She rocked back abruptly on her heels. Large hands cupped her shoulders for a moment to steady her.

"Whoops! Sorry," he said in a voice glinting with amusement.

Flustered, Summer felt the heat rise in her cheeks. She clutched her throbbing nose and received a brief impression of dark hair and eyes, but she was too embarrassed to register anything more.

"Could you direct me to the business office?" he asked, a note of suppressed humor coloring his deep voice.

Wordlessly, her eyes on the tips of her pink and white Nikes, she automatically pointed down the hall. Her flush deepened as she realized Lizabeth was still on her outstretched arm, and appeared to be ogling him. "Beg pardon, mister," she said in Lizabeth's voice, batted the puppet's eyelashes at him once, then fled.

"You're always getting me in trouble, Lizabeth," Summer muttered, scurrying toward her Uncle Burton's office. "Why can't you be good?"

"'Cause it's more fun to be bad," Lizabeth quipped. "And wasn't he yummy?"

"I didn't get a good look at him," Summer said virtuously.

Lizabeth sniffed at that downright lie.

"All right, so what I noticed was pretty okay," Summer admitted, remembering the broad chest under his casual tweed sports coat and the long, lean jean-clad legs. He stood just under six feet which made him tall to her five-foot-nothing. She wished she had paid a little more attention to the details, then stifled a laugh.

I'm losing it, Summer thought, gingerly feeling her nose but finding nothing broken. *Talking to yourself is bad enough, but answering, too! They'll certify me for the loony bin for sure!*

She wiggled her fingers and slid the recalcitrant puppet off her arm, laughing softly. What must that guy have thought? Shaking her head, she dismissed him from her mind. She was more concerned with having Uncle Burt refute Merl's rumor.

Burton wasn't in his office. She still had a few minutes before she needed to leave for the Foundation, so she decided to wait. She carefully packed Lizabeth back into her duffel bag, then wandered around the shabby office.

A quartet of photographs lined the cabinet behind Burton's desk. Summer touched the brass frame of one picture, her expression wistful. There she was at age four, sitting on Aunt Olivia's lap with Uncle Burton beaming behind them. That photograph had been taken shortly after her father, Olivia's brother, had been killed in an auto accident. Since her mother had died only a year before that, the little girl stared out of the picture with eyes that reflected her bewilderment.

But Olivia and Burton, childless themselves, had struggled to replace that look with self-confidence and the knowledge that she was completely loved and cherished. Summer's lips curved upward as her gaze traveled over the other photos. Seven-year-old Summer with two pale braids, no front teeth, and a Whitey Ford glove the year her team won the district championship. Summer in her high school cap and gown. Summer in a one-shouldered evening dress at her first college formal. Olivia and Burton had given her everything that her two natural parents would have—love, discipline and a sense of family. Though they were apt to be a bit overprotective of her, she loved them both with all her heart and would do anything for them.

Summer's eyes traveled over the wall of plaques and certificates that recognized Burton's thirty-five-year career in radio. She was proud of the number of public service awards he'd received. There had been a lot of ups and downs since he'd taken over in the wake of Summer's father's death, but all in all it had been a substantial contribution, she thought, and they weren't done yet.

The door opened and her uncle appeared, a frown pleating his brow. His expression cleared when he saw her.

"Summer! Good morning, sweetheart." He gave her a hearty squeeze and bussed her cheek. He'd lost most of his hair since the first picture had been taken, and his waistline was as round as Santa's, but he was still capable of warming Summer's heart with only his smile. She kissed him back.

"Hi, Uncle Burt. What's got you going so bright and early?"

"Just business, as usual. Listen, I don't mean to rush my favorite girl, but could you come back a little later? I've got an appointment." He gave her shoulder a pat and moved behind his desk.

"No problem. I'm on my way to the Foundation, anyway. I just wanted to ask you something. Merl's got some crazy idea that we're planning to sell the station and I—"

Burton's expression froze and Summer broke off, disconcerted. He sat down heavily in the leather swivel chair, his shoulders slumped with disappointment and regret.

"I didn't want you to find out this way," he muttered.

A tremor of premonition made Summer catch a painful breath. "Uncle Burt, what is it? What's the matter?"

"I'm sorry, my dear," Burton Pierson said. A sorrowful expression wreathed his round, ruddy face. "But I'm afraid it's true."

CHAPTER TWO

JOHN RYDER BOWMAN PAUSED before Burton Pierson's half-open office door, his hand raised in a knock he never completed. There was no mistaking that sultry voice on the other side of the door. For a moment, he ignored the sense of her words and simply enjoyed the sexy cadences.

Jubilee Jones. No wonder she had two-thirds of Chattanooga's population tuning in every morning. Who could resist that husky, intimate voice? It conjured images of candlelit dinners and sweet surrender with its dulcet tones and smoky, provocative nuances. And that little laugh of hers. It could melt a man's spine. All that from just a woman's voice. Amazing.

Not that Ryder would let himself be affected by the voice of an unknown female. He'd learned the hard way about a woman's tricks. And often the body behind a luscious voice was a real disappointment. But that didn't mean he couldn't appreciate Jubilee's talents—and take advantage of them. And it didn't make him any less curious about the owner of that voice.

Ryder frowned. She certainly wasn't laughing now. In fact, it sounded as though she would like to flay a strip of hide off some unfortunate soul. Maybe the purring kitten was really a wildcat in disguise. He pushed open the door.

He didn't know what he'd been expecting, but it certainly wasn't the petite lady standing with her back to him, her waist-length braid flipping back and forth in agitation like a feline's tail. Good God! The little puppeteer who'd tried to mow him down in the hall! This half-grown kid couldn't be Jubilee Jones!

His eyes narrowed slightly and he examined her more closely. Despite the enveloping covering of a pair of overalls, there was nothing childish about the womanly curves beneath the faded blue denim. In fact, she had positively the cutest tush he'd seen in some time. He felt an involuntary grin tug at the corners of his mouth. Who said the gods weren't kind?

"It can't be as bad as that!" she was protesting.

"I'm afraid it is." Burton Pierson sank lower into his chair behind the expanse of his desk. "I suppose I was wrong not to tell you before. We've been teetering on the verge of bankruptcy since before you went to California. It was just a matter of time..."

"But the Coffee Club has the highest ratings. I don't understand!" she wailed.

"You're splendid, my dear, but one successful show can't carry this station any longer. The competition, you know. This offer comes just in the nick of time. I don't have to tell you how bankruptcy would affect your aunt. I've tried to keep all this from her, but if we lost the house, everything—it would kill her."

"But the station's always been in the family! My dad started it. Isn't there anything we can do?"

"Accept the inevitable," Ryder advised from his position in the doorway. Burton Pierson glanced up with an expression of mixed relief and apprehension, but Jubilee whirled on her heel, piercing the intruder with a hostile gaze. Ryder froze, stunned by a pair of pansy eyes.

Her face was pretty, small-featured and heart-shaped, with sculpted cheekbones and a dainty nose. But those eyes! How had he managed to miss those eyes? Deepest, darkest blue-violet. Hyacinth eyes, rimmed by the longest and lushest of sooty black lashes. Eyes a man could gladly drown in, framed by finely arched brows lifted now in recognition and haughty inquiry.

"Can we help you?" she demanded stiffly.

"Summer, my dear," interjected Burton, "this is the gentleman who's made the offer for the station, Mr. Ryder Bowman. Mr. Bowman, my niece, Summer Jones."

"I believe it's considered polite to knock, Mr. Bowman, before you barge in on a private conversation," she said with icy hauteur.

Ryder's lips twitched. "Hardly private. I could hear you down the hall."

He let his gaze roam from the crown of her sunlit head to the rubber soles of her jogging shoes, then back to the soft, sweet curve of her rosy mouth, compressed now in antagonism. His male appraisal was frankly, unabashedly appreciative. Jubilee Jones was quite a pleasant surprise. Yes, indeed, things were definitely looking up.

He walked over and offered his hand, gazing down at her with a half-smile. She studied his hand a fraction of an instant, then determinedly shook it, her chin thrust out at a feisty, belligerent angle.

"Jubilee Jones," he murmured. "How do you do?"

Their brief collision in the hall hadn't prepared Summer for the impact Ryder Bowman made upon leisurely inspection. She guessed he was somewhere in his mid-thirties. His tanned face was all planes and angles, and a strong, rather hawkish nose bisected dark, straight brows. He had thick black hair, a square jaw and, most fascinating of all, a slash that indented his right cheek. In another, weaker face it might have been called a dimple, but here it was far too devastating for such a mundane term. She found she hadn't been the only one using this moment to make an assessment.

"What a combination," Ryder said in admiration. "A Lauren Bacall voice and Elizabeth Taylor eyes."

Summer bristled and jerked her hand free. "Yeah," she drawled sarcastically in her best Mae West imitation. "Too bad they come in a Shirley Temple body."

Ryder's deep, generous laugh caught her off guard. There was something familiar about it, but she was too busy shoring up her defensive position to concentrate on that. He jammed his hands into his front pockets and grinned at her.

"Who'd have guessed all that wattage came wrapped in such a tidy package? It's a pleasure, Summer."

His hazel-brown eyes laughed at her, tiny sparks of emerald-green taunting her from the depths of his knowing, mocking glance, and her hackles rose. Ryder Bowman was too certain of his own considerable attraction and ruthlessly ambitious. Red flags and warning bells went off in Summer's head. He was too much like Clancy, and just exactly the kind of man Summer had sworn never to have anything to do with again. And worse, he had come to steal a radio station right out from under Uncle Burton's nose!

"I was just about to tell Summer about the merger, Mr. Bowman," Burton said with a nervous gulp.

Summer's head snapped back to her uncle, dismay making her voice squeak. "What merger?"

"With Mr. Bowman's other station, my dear, WROC. Our AM band with his FM band, isn't that right?" Burton sent Summer a pleading look.

"That's right. We'll begin broadcasting as a single station on both bands—a simulcast—as soon as the FCC okays it," Ryder explained. "With an adult contemporary format and a beefed-up news schedule, I believe WCHT-WROC will do very well."

She should have realized WCHT was in trouble, Summer thought, swallowing painfully. Nothing like being gobbled up by the newest, most aggressive station in the city. But what would become of old-fashioned service and tradition? She doubted very seriously if Ryder Bowman thought about the listeners in any terms other than dollars and cents.

Ryder blessed Summer with a smile that said her mutinous thoughts were all too easy to read. She reflected sourly that his parents had no doubt spent a fortune in orthodontia and glared back at him.

Burton cleared his throat nervously, mopping his balding pate with a crumpled handkerchief. "Well, Summer, what do you think?"

Summer's expression was troubled and she moved to stand protectively at Burton's side. Her fingers gripped his shoulder. "I don't know what to think. I can't believe it's come to this. If I'd only known..."

"Mr. Bowman's offer has been most generous," Burton said, patting Summer's hand in an awkward gesture of reassurance.

Summer turned and leveled a stare at the tall man. "How generous?" she asked bluntly. Ryder named a figure and Summer sucked in an indignant breath. "This station is worth twice that!"

"You won't get a better offer," Ryder replied equably. "Not with practically zero accounts receivable, obsolete equipment and the amount of outstanding indebtedness."

"I'm afraid he's right," Burton said with a sigh.

Summer felt a helpless frustration. Why had Uncle Burton kept all of this from her? After all, she owned a small percentage of WCHT in her own right, and this situation hadn't developed overnight. She knew it wasn't a deliberate conspiracy on Burton's part, but a misguided effort to protect her. He hadn't realized that in doing so he'd denied her an opportunity to help.

Her tone was pleading. "Can't we go over the books with the accountant? Maybe we can refinance or..."

"It wouldn't make any difference," Burton said. "It's too late. The fact is we've run out of options."

"But..."

"There's no other alternative, my dear. Unless you want me to declare bankruptcy. Then WCHT would really be dead, and you don't want that, do you?"

Summer felt a hot prickling behind her eyes and blinked to keep the shaming moisture from betraying her before an unsympathetic stranger. She shook her head. "No, of course not. Are you certain this is what you want?"

"It's what's necessary, Summer."

"I understand, Uncle Burton," She forced a wobbly smile for his sake and drew a shaky breath. "Well, I guess that's that."

"Not quite," Ryder said. He lifted one dark eyebrow and watched Burton expectantly. The pudgy older man grew pink and flustered.

"Mr. Bowman would like...that is, uh...he expects Jubilee Jones to continue as a staff deejay."

"Wh-what?" Summer's jaw dropped. Ryder Bowman was going too far. She might have to agree to sell the station, but she couldn't pretend nothing had changed! Loyalty to Uncle Burt made her give the only answer possible.

"No, I don't think so. Thank you just the same."

"Summer, stop and think," Burton pleaded. "It means keeping your job."

She shrugged. "I'll find another. I've started from scratch before."

"Might I ask your objection to continuing here?" Ryder asked mildly.

"Call it personal, Mr. Bowman." She glowered at him. "You might take advantage of our financial situation, but I have no intention of letting you take advantage of me."

For a fraction of a second, Ryder's confidence faltered. Jubilee Jones was crucial to his plans for WCHT-WROC. He hadn't counted on finding a stubborn little shrew on the broadcasting end of that voice, nor had he been prepared for the sparks they shot off each other. But Ryder was accustomed to having his way. Chattanooga's most popular air personality or not, it seemed this lady deejay was a tad too big for her sassy little britches!

"There's no way I can convince you to change your mind?" His baritone voice was silky with challenge.

"No."

"Summer, please! I promised our cooperation," Burton said, wringing his hands. "I knew I could count on you."

"I'm sorry. It just wouldn't work."

Ryder straightened. "Well, as the lady says, that's that. If she won't be swayed, I'm afraid our deal is off, Mr. Pierson. Thank you for your time."

Two voices echoed in dismay. "What!"

"Mr. Bowman, please wait. I—I'm sure some arrangement can be worked out," Burton gabbled. He shot clumsily to his feet as Ryder took a step toward the door.

Summer saw the panic in Burton's face. She wished with all her heart he'd stand up and tell this joker Bowman where to get off, but she knew it wasn't in his nature, and had never been. Bowman had them in a corner and he knew it.

"Just what are you trying to pull, Mr. Bowman?" Summer demanded in a tight voice.

Ryder paused, his gaze speculative on her. "I'm a businessman, Miss Jones. Without Jubilee, all I'd be getting for my money is a little goodwill. If I can't have you, then I have no need for the rest of WCHT.'

Burton's voice was placating. "I'm sure as soon as Summer understands that you intend to make provisions for the rest of the staff, the terms will be a bit more palatable."

Summer's attention focused on her uncle's sweating countenance. Did *everything* depend on Jubilee? It wasn't just her job, it seemed, but those of her friends, Merl and Vanessa and the others, as well as Uncle Burton's chance to sell the station, that was contingent on her agreeing to work for this odious Mr. Bowman. She looked at Burton's anxious expression and felt guilt weigh her down. What right did she have to let her personal feelings override the welfare of others? She wasn't so selfish that she'd sacrifice her friends' jobs, and her aunt and uncle's retirement just because she couldn't take a little heat. She'd probably never see Bowman much, anyway.

She cleared her throat. "How long would you want Jubilee?" Burton's face swelled with a conspicuous relief.

"A yearly contract is appropriate, I think," Ryder replied carefully. He knew enough about negotiations to understand when to take the pressure off. He'd pushed her hard, but as usual, he'd gotten what he wanted. It was very gratifying.

"All right." Summer felt rather than heard her uncle's release of tension on a silently exhaled breath. Ryder's expression of complacent satisfaction made her grit her teeth. "I don't like it," she muttered, "but all right."

Ryder stiffened, his mood punctured by her bluntness. He nodded. "Very wise of you."

"I still get the morning drive-time." She could make a few demands of her own, even in defeat.

"Of course." He could afford to be gracious in victory. "One other thing..."

"Yes?" Her eyes were cloudy, a dark purple thunderhead of suspicion.

"I'm going to team you up with Gulliver."

"What!" Never in her wildest dreams had such a possibility crossed her mind. Jubilee co-hosting with her biggest rival? No way! She shook her head, slinging her braid from side to side. "Uh-uh. I work alone. The Coffee Club's *mine.*"

"Trust me on this one," he said, smiling slightly.

Her heated retort was smoothly cut off by Burton's unctuous words.

"Don't you have to get to the Foundation, my dear? If you'll excuse us, Mr. Bowman and I have a lot to discuss. Let us get the preliminaries out of the way and you can work out the details later."

Summer shot a hasty glance at her watch. Damn! She was already late! "You're right. I've got to go. I—we'll—" She broke off, then dropped a swift kiss on her uncle's plump cheek.

"Your aunt still expects you for dinner tomorrow night," Burton reminded her. "Don't forget."

Not trusting herself to reply, Summer nodded. She grabbed her duffel and stalked past Ryder Bowman, giving him a look that told him more clearly than words that this battle wasn't over. The smile he gave her said he'd be ready.

SUMMER JAMMED HER KEYS into the door lock of her blue vintage Mustang and cursed. The multilevel parking garage was a cavernous gray concrete structure and her words echoed hollowly up and down the dimly lit angled driveways.

"Damn! Damn. Damn..."

She struggled futilely for a frustrating moment until the stubborn lock clicked free. It didn't help her feelings to notice that her hands were shaking. The sappy grin on her lemon yellow happy-face key ring wished her a nice day. It was the final insult. She scowled, wrenched open the door, and flung herself into the seat and sagged in weary defeat.

There was so much to absorb: WCHT to be sold, finding Ryder Bowman her new boss; and teaming up with Gulliver. She blinked, fighting a sudden rise of salty tears. She'd always prided herself on being a flexible person, but in the space of just a few minutes, her neat, ordered life had been turned topsy-turvy by a man with a cool, logical disposition, and green-flecked eyes. She couldn't help feeling a little sorry for herself. Sniffing, she rubbed her fingertip over her eyelids, took a fortifying breath, and determinedly started the engine. The car radio blasted her eardrums.

"... break it to me gently..." begged the singer.

She twisted the dial.

"... weather outlook for..."

"... Wagner murder connected to last spring's unsolved..."

"... I got you, babe..."

Summer flipped off the radio in disgust. *He's got me, all right,* she thought morosely, *right between a rock and a hard place. Now what am I going to do about it?*

She pushed the stick shift into reverse and backed out of the parking spot, made a turn, then headed down the ramp toward the exit. She slowed momentarily at the black and yellow swing-arm barricade at the base of the ramp where a young sandy-haired attendant stood guard in a glassed-in booth. The embroidered oval on his starched uniform shirt said "Bud." She flashed her parking permit and the swing-arm slid smoothly upward.

"Thanks," she called, waving, then pulled out into the congested Chattanooga traffic.

What she needed, she decided, was a long walk, a hot bath, a large pot of herbal tea, and plenty of time to sort all this out. Instead, in short order she'd be surrounded by a bunch of special kids enrolled in the Foundation's summer program, expecting her to be her usual cheerful, perky self, not this teary mass of jangled nerves! But Ryder Bowman was enough to drive anyone around the bend. All right, so he had magnetism that scorched the air and was devilishly good-looking, but blackmail didn't place him very high in her estimation. Still, he seemed to be Uncle Burton's last hope. She stifled a dejected sigh and forced herself to concentrate on her driving.

The imminent demise of WCHT meant more to her than just the loss of the family business. Her show was her identity. Her life had revolved around the Coffee Club ever since she'd come home from L.A., battered and heartsore. The unseen listeners had been her lifeline back to self-confidence and purpose. She'd developed the interview and call-in portion of her show to repay the loyalty of her fans by giving them information and referrals that could benefit them in their day-to-day lives. What would become of that if she and Gulliver had to share their airtime?

Summer pulled into the parking lot in front of the Speech and Hearing Foundations's rangy, brown brick building, parked, and reached for her duffel. A worried frown pleated her brow. There were so many unanswered questions, but the most frightening aspect of this situation was that she seemed to be losing control of her own destiny again. And the prospect of that chilled her to the bone.

An hour later, Summer sat at the old upright piano pounding out the last chorus of "The Ballad of W-Wallace, the Prince of W-Whales" for an appreciative and enthusiastic group of young singers. A large black and white whale puppet took pride of place atop the piano, while the children sang of the trials of a gentleman whale with an unfortunate stutter. Summer struck the final chord and swiveled around on the stool to take a bow.

"Thank you, that was great!" she exclaimed, then exchanged Wallace for a droopy-jowled puppet sporting a star and bandana. Duke the Bloodhound, was always her Master of Ceremonies. With a flourish, Summer made Duke doff his cowboy hat and prepared to wind up the day's activities.

"Wa-a-l, 'lil pardners," Summer had Duke say in a gruff voice that was suspiciously reminiscent of John Wayne, "I guess we showed those bad guys it's not polite to make fun of the way others talk. Isn't that right, Gabby?"

The grizzled gopher puppet with a perpetual bucktoothed grin and a broken-brimmed cowboy hat nodded vigorously, manipulated by a winsome little volunteer with brunette pigtails and hearing aids.

The group of seven- and eight-year-olds sitting cross-legged on the carpeted floor of the classroom laughed in agreement. They looked just like any group that age, except for a few hearing aids and the occasional use of sign language.

"So remember this advice from Ole Duke and Gabby," Summer concluded, "you have to be a friend to make a friend. *Adios*, pilgrims, until next time."

The children clapped and shouted goodbyes, then got to their feet at their teacher's urgings. Some of their speech was garbled and monotoned, but they were typical kids otherwise, energetic and noisy.

"Thanks, Amy," Summer said, retrieving Gabby from the little girl. "You did a fine job as this week's assistant." Amy beamed and blushed, then raced off to join the others.

"Bye, Mizz Zummer," a toothless, red-haired Tom Sawyer type said. He sported two large white hearing aids.

"See you next time, Silas," Summer called. Her smile was genuine and involuntary, a reflection of the affection she felt for her small fans. Despite herself, she felt a lot better.

She was stuffing Duke into his place next to Lizabeth when a curly brown head peeked in the classroom door.

"Hi, J.J. Want some lunch? I'm buying," Beryl Hatcher offered.

"Is that supposed to be a bribe?" Summer asked, giving an exaggerated shudder. "You remember I've dined here before."

Beryl wrinkled her puckish nose at the insult to the school cafeteria. A portion of the Foundation's students came for individual therapy after classes at public school, but the clinic conducted its own full-time accredited kindergarten and grade school on the premises. Students as young as two and three came here to learn lipreading and other skills necessary to function in a hearing society. They were justly proud of their modern facility, including the lunchroom. "Oh, come on," Beryl said with a grin. "I guarantee the fruit cocktail and Jell-O are fresh."

Summer laughed, looking at her plump friend with amusement. Only Beryl had the nerve to call Summer "J.J." They'd grown up on the same street, bosom pals even though Beryl was a couple of years older, and by virtue of superior years she was the only one Summer never threatened with a "licking" for using the shortened version of her hated first name, Josephine. That was allowed because Summer never called her "Beryl, the Barrel" to tease her about her weight as the other neighborhood children had done. It was an unwritten pact between friends, which had withstood the test of time.

When Summer had returned from California, it had been Beryl's suggestion that she volunteer at the Foundation. As co-director, Beryl was as enthusiastic and bubbly as she'd always been, even with a husband and two school-age children of her own to keep her busy, and she'd refused to take no for an answer. Next to the Coffee Club, it had been the best thing that had happened to Summer. Beryl's prescription of hard work and the tonic of some appreciative kids had pulled her out of the doldrums following her collapsed romance with Clancy faster than she'd expected. Maybe they'd help her deal with the newest daunting developments at WCHT in a similar manner.

"Okay, bring on the Jell-O," Summer said with a quirk of her lips. She slung her duffel over her shoulder and the two of them headed down the hall toward the cafeteria. They joined a group of teachers waiting to pass through the serving line. The air was filled with murmurs of conversation and the clash of cutlery. The warm odor of fresh bread and stewed chicken tickled their noses while Beryl chattered about school activities.

"You haven't forgotten about giving our Brownie troop a tour of the radio station when the regular school session begins, have you?" she asked.

"It's on my schedule for next month," Summer answered. *If I'm still around,* she thought glumly.

"Hey, what's the matter?" Beryl asked. She cocked her head to examine Summer, her bright brown eyes and rounded figure giving a fleeting impression of an inquisitive hen. "You look a little blue all of a sudden. And don't tell me it's the food."

Summer smiled weakly and reached for a red plastic tray and a rolled napkin of utensils. "Is it that noticeable?"

"Only to me. What's going on?"

Summer sighed and pushed her tray down the chrome pipe railing. "I found out this morning that Uncle Burton's going to sell the station."

"Hmm. Well, why not? I guess it's time he started thinking of retirement. What's the problem? Don't you approve?"

"No—yes—I don't know," Summer hedged. "It was a shock, that's all. I didn't realize the station was in such dire straits as it appears we're in. Uncle Burton is accepting an offer that I'm sure is too low. *And* my new boss wants me to co-host the Coffee Club. I don't know what to do about it. I don't know if there's anything I *can* do." She sighed. They took their loaded trays to an empty table. "The Foundation wouldn't happen to need a full-time music director, would it?"

Beryl's round-cheeked face was rueful. "We'd love to have you, but the funds just aren't there. There are so many deserving children, and our paid tuitions don't really cover everything. That's why we have to depend on donations and on volunteers like you. Why, one of our best therapists is leaving at the end of the month for more money, and I don't really blame her."

"I'm sure you could get a larger salary elsewhere, too, Beryl. Why don't you?"

"Are you kidding?" Beryl stuck a spoonful of cottage cheese in her mouth and swallowed. "Where else could I work eighty hours a week for slave wages?"

"In other words, you love it." Summer toyed with the cubes of red gelatin swaying on one section of her plate.

"Right. Just like you love doing the Coffee Club. What will happen to Jubilee if the station changes hands?"

"It looks as though I'm part of the package deal. I get a partner I don't want, and Uncle Burton gets his sale. I suppose I should be flattered." She toasted Beryl with her spoon and nibbled at the gelatin.

"So, why should anything be really different?" Beryl asked.

An oppressive sense of apprehension made the cherry Jell-O clog in Summer's throat. She swallowed painfully. "I have a feeling that *everything* will be different from now on."

CHAPTER THREE

RYDER BOWMAN STOOD OUTSIDE the door of the WCHT recording room and watched Summer Jones at work. He could hear her faintly through the glass window, touting the merits of a place called the Bagel Beanery. He wasn't certain whether one purchased bagels or beans at such an establishment, but he bet a lot of folks would be stopping by to find out, just as soon as these advertising spots hit the airwaves.

He shoved his hands into the pockets of his jeans and grinned. What a powerhouse that woman was! And worth every penny he'd have to pay to get her. Her uncle was doing him more of a favor than he realized.

The meetings he'd had on an informal basis this morning with Burton Pierson and his staff had gone well. With the proper management, Ryder would be able to weld them into a cohesive team. WCHT-WROC could be the brightest star in his growing network of radio and television stations. It always gave him a deep sense of satisfaction to take an organization and turn it around so that it could meet its greatest potential. His ideas and innovations were earning him a reputation in the industry, too. They might call him a rogue, but they couldn't deny that he made things happen. The Bowman Network was a growing, viable entity, and it was making him a very rich man.

Ryder smiled to himself. He'd come a long way since he was busting his tail and risking his neck chasing stories on the streets of Atlanta. He'd paid his dues with interest. It had been a black time, but he'd been able to build some-

thing out of the ashes of Elise's betrayal and Bill's death.
And he intended to keep on building. It was all he had.

He watched Summer slam a tape cartridge into the machine, slap a timer, punch a console button for background
music, and then start another spiel into the orange foam ball
covering the microphone. She was such a half-pint she had
to stretch to reach some of the controls. Ryder's lips
quirked. She ought to appreciate the state-of-the-art equipment he planned to install in the new studios of WCHT-
WROC more than anybody. Between the reel-to-reel and
compact discs, things would be a lot easier on her physically.

And a lot harder on me.

The thought came unbidden, unwelcome but unavoid-
able. His gaze concentrated on the gentle swell of her breasts
under the black sweatshirt she wore over black acid-washed
denims. She might be small, but she was all woman in all the
right places. Her fair hair was pulled back from her face in
a businesslike French braid that displayed her delicate features like an old-fashioned cameo. She ought to be quite a
knockout when she took the trouble to get dolled up. But
she wasn't a no-brain Kewpie doll, no matter what her
looks. She'd proved that yesterday. He admired the way
she'd stood up to him. Of course, it had been a futile gesture, but then she was an amateur and he was a pro.

But becoming involved with an employee spelled disaster
with a capital *D*. Summer Jones was an attractive nuisance,
and if he expected to get WCHT-WROC off the ground,
he'd better put aside the notion, no matter how desirable he
found her. He was a mature man, and didn't have to act on
every impulse, however compelling. Business came first.
Still, those incredible eyes...

Ryder stifled a faint sigh of regret. He raised a fist and
tapped quietly against the glass. Summer glanced up, her
eyes wide and startled. Ryder again felt the power of her violet gaze.

God! How was he going to keep things on a professional basis when all she had to do was look at him to tie him up in knots? His scowl of derision pulled his features into a harsher line than he intended.

"Can we talk?" he asked through the glass. "Whenever you're finished."

She nodded in comprehension. A flicker of trepidation made her expression waver for an instant before she carefully composed her features. Ryder stared at her and she met his regard unflinchingly.

Damn it all! he thought, turning away.

For a fleeting moment he'd seen a flash of vulnerability. He was taking advantage of her in a lot of ways. It didn't help his conscience to find there was softness beneath the steel of her personality. Their first meeting had been a mistake, in more ways than one. Now he was going to have to offer some concessions to keep her in line. Yeah, he'd better back off, and fast, if Gulliver and Jubilee Jones were going to accomplish anything together in this town. From now on, everything was going to be strictly business.

He hoped.

COWARD. WIMP. FRAIDY-CAT.

Summer scowled. Calling herself every name in the book wasn't doing her ego any good, but it wasn't making her move, either. Ryder Bowman wanted to talk. She'd put it off long enough, re-recording the Bagel Beanery spots until they were letter-perfect. Reluctantly she gathered up her notes and her purse, knowing it was now or never. Maybe she'd delayed so long he'd given up and gone home. It was a heartening thought.

She peeped out of the recording room door, but the hall was empty. So far so good. If she could just leave the station unobtrusively, then their "talk" would have to be postponed. She made it halfway down the hall.

"Hey, doll!"

"Merl!" Summer jumped and looked sheepishly at the station manager. "I'm on my way home."

"Long day, huh?"

Summer gave a deep sigh. "You said it."

"At least those rumors have been put to rest."

"Now we just have speculation to fall back on, right?" Summer said. Her expression was sour.

"I think Mr. Bowman's been up-front with us. I'm not apprehensive. Let's face it, Summer, things could stand to be improved around here."

Another door opened down the hall and Vanessa appeared. She clicked toward them on her stylish high heels. Her smile wavered slightly on seeing Summer with Merl. "See you tomorrow," she said as she passed.

Summer nudged Merl with an elbow. "Now's your chance," she whispered.

"What?" Merl looked startled.

"Go on. Offer to buy her a cup of coffee or a drink or something."

"Uh-uh, I couldn't," Merl demurred, flushing. "I'd step all over my tongue. Vanessa's sort of unapproachable."

"Well, I have to admit she's something of a mystery woman around here, but I think she's just naturally quiet and reserved. Shy, even."

"Who, Vanessa?" Merl was incredulous.

"Sure. It was quite a while before she opened up with me and you know what a chatterbox I am. I still don't know much about her background, just that she's basically a very private person. But with a little persistence, who knows?" Summer grinned encouragingly. "Go ahead. You've got the perfect excuse. What could be more natural than two co-workers talking over what's happened?"

Merl's expression was doubtful, then he brightened. "Yeah. Sure. Hey, Vanessa! Wait up," he called. He cast Summer a crooked smile and then loped after the retreating brunette.

Well, Summer thought, *at least something's going right.*

"Is office matchmaker part of your job description, too?" Ryder Bowman asked, appearing suddenly at her side. His deep voice was tinged with humor.

Summer stifled an inward groan and cursed her luck. Just when she thought she'd made a clean getaway! She turned, forcing a polite, banal smile and ignoring his question. "Mr. Bowman."

He casually hooked the collar of his sports coat on one finger and slung it over his shoulder in a typically male stance. The cuffs of his shirt had been rolled back, revealing hard, muscular forearms lightly dusted with dark hair. He studied her thoughtfully. "Call me Ryder. We're going to be working closely together, Summer. There's no point in getting off on the wrong foot."

She stiffened. "It's too late for that."

A slow grin tilted his mouth. "You think I'm a bully, don't you?"

"Actions speak louder than words." Her tone was sugar-sweet.

He made an irritated sound. "Get off it for just one moment, will you? We need to iron out a few things."

Summer bit her lip and glanced away. She knew instinctively she wouldn't like anything he had to say. "I—I'm tired. Surely it can wait?"

"No, it can't. How about a walk? I'll buy you a drink." His hazel eyes glinted. "Humor me. After all, I am going to be your new boss."

She forced herself not to grind her teeth. "Only under protest. Believe me, Mr. Bowman, if Uncle Burt wasn't counting on me, I'd have never agreed to stay on."

"I think you've made that clear. But a year from now you'll be thanking me, Summer. Jubilee and Gulliver will be an unbeatable team."

"Look here," she said, punching the center of his broad chest with her finger to emphasize her words. "I never agreed to share the Coffee Club. I work alone and you can tell Gulliver I said so." His deep laughter startled her. "What's so amusing?" she demanded.

"Well, darlin'," he drawled, "if you've got anything to say to Gulliver—you're looking at him."

Summer's eyes widened with shock. *Oh, no!* she thought. *It can't be!*

But she knew it was. Recognition clicked, memory merged. That deep resonant voice! Gulliver and Ryder Bowman, one and the same man! No wonder he'd sounded familiar. She had a sudden, horrifying vision of herself locked in a control booth with this all-too-unnerving individual. She was woman enough to acknowledge his masculine attraction, fool enough to be affected, but not dumb enough to voluntarily walk into this hungry lion's den!

"Uh-uh. That's it," she said. Shaking her head, she stomped off down the hall, muttering. "No way, José. Forget it. *Finis*. End of discussion."

Disconcerted, Ryder strode after her, catching her by the arm. "Wait a minute, lady!"

"No, you wait a minute, buster! Or Gulliver or whoever you are!" she spluttered. "If you think that I—that you— that *we*—" She broke off, totally at a loss for words.

Ryder's lips twitched and his hazel eyes shimmered. "Boggles the mind, doesn't it?" he asked softly.

Summer couldn't repress the bubble of incredulous laughter that escaped her. "You've got to be certifiably insane if you think this will *ever* work!"

"I've been accused of it on more than one occasion," he admitted. He shoved a long-fingered hand through the dark hair falling over his forehead, tilted his head back to study the ceiling for a moment, and blew out a long breath. Then he looked at Summer again. "Will you hear me out? Come on, I'll buy you that drink and we'll talk. What do you say?"

Summer hesitated. This was the closest thing to a polite request she'd seen. Perhaps they could communicate if they tried. At least, he'd stopped *ordering* and was offering to listen to her point of view. She gave him a hesitant smile. "All right."

His grin was boyish and electric—devastating to Summer's over-stressed nerves. "Great!" He placed a firm hand against the small of her back, and guided her expertly through the reception area past Carol toward the main entrance. "I know this little place down the street..."

"Just a second, Ryder," Summer said. She dug into her purse and walked back to Carol's desk, placing a one-dollar bill in front of the mystified girl. "I believe I owe you," she murmured.

Carol shot Ryder a startled glance and her eyes rounded to the size of half-dollars. "Him?" she asked, sotto voce.

Summer nodded ruefully and Carol mouthed a silent, appreciative "Wow!"

"What was that all about?" Ryder asked a moment later as they walked toward the bank of elevators.

Summer shrugged. "I just found out there's no such thing as gnomes."

"A TERRIBLE WASTE."

Ryder tossed the evening paper on the small table between them. It was still too early for the happy-hour crowd in the Amaryllis Lounge, but a few lone customers leaned against the oak and brass bar talking desultorily to the bartender. A beer sat at Ryder's elbow and Summer toyed with the stem of her wineglass. A wicker basket of tiny fish crackers filled the management's requirements for hors d'oeuvres.

She glanced down at the blaring headlines. Outrage over the fatal attack on Cleva Wagner poured off the newsprint in rivers of black ink. A picture of the slain blond smiled up from the paper.

"It's a vicious crime." She gave a disbelieving shake of her head. "Who could do such a terrible thing?"

"Some maniac. It says here she was out jogging."

"It doesn't seem right," Summer said, her tone thoughtful. She took a cautious sip of her Chablis. "I interviewed her once. She didn't strike me as the careless type."

He shrugged and popped a couple of crackers in his mouth. "Maybe you're right. As councilwoman, she was highly visible, and outspoken. Maybe she'd made some enemies."

"But knifed!" Summer shuddered. "Every woman in Chattanooga will have the jitters now."

"Including you?" His lips curved slightly. "I could have sworn you're absolutely fearless."

Summer met Ryder's gaze directly. "I'm no fool."

"No. I can see that." He pushed his beer aside and leaned his elbows on the synthetic marble tabletop. "At any rate, you can bet the cops will be putting in plenty of overtime. Something like this can paralyze a city."

"You sound as though you've been through it before."

His gaze danced away. "Yeah. Something like that."

"Where?"

"Atlanta." His expression was sardonic. "Trying out your interview skills on me, Jubilee?"

She studied him, her brow furrowed. Something in her memory banks whirred and clicked and she made an intuitive leap with a certainty that was common to her nature. "You wouldn't happen to be the same Bowman who did that exposé of organized crime in Atlanta a few years back?"

"You're very quick."

His face had taken on a closed quality and Summer shivered. He had such odd, changeable eyes. Not a warm brown, but a cool, calculating hazel with an ability to shoot an occasional flash of frigid green right through you. Now they appeared neutral, almost a non-color, and they gave away nothing. She stirred uneasily.

"The newspapers in Los Angeles played it up because there was something similar going on there at the time.

That's why I remember it. Political corruption and murder-for-hire, wasn't it?''

"Yeah." He took a sip of beer. "They called District Attorney Joe Simitall's death a suicide until my partner and I proved it was murder, arranged by a couple of high-ranking police officers with the help of the mob organization. He was heading an investigation that was getting too close to the truth and they eliminated him. It wasn't pretty."

"You came out of it something of a hero, as I recall."

"My partner came out dead." His voice was flat.

"Oh. Sorry." She bit her lip. "It must have been awful for you."

"Sure. I never quite got over having someone trying to blow my head off. The book I wrote afterward was supposed to be my catharsis. Instead, it did so well I bought my first radio station."

His tone was cynical, but somehow Summer knew that those facts bothered him. Making money on his partner's death was something that probably went against his grain. "You could have dropped the story."

"No, I couldn't. I always finish what I start."

Summer could believe that. He was decisive and determined. He'd never let personal feelings or fears interfere with any goal he set. But it had cost him, she could tell. Maybe the scars left by such a harrowing experience were still too tender to touch, even though those responsible were now behind bars.

"Do you mind if I ask you one more question?" Summer asked.

"Not if you don't mind if you get an answer."

"How did you get from there to here? And what are you doing jocking on WROC?"

"That's two questions."

Summer repressed a smile. "Did anyone ever tell you you're a wise guy, Bowman?"

"Often. But usually the language is a bit more forceful."

"I was brought up to be a lady," she said primly. Ryder's soft laugh sent goose bumps down her arms.

"Did they finish the job, half-pint?" He held up his hands in mock surrender at her aggravated expression. His smile faltered and he reached out to gently cup her chin with his fingertips. His voice went low and husky. "You really have the most gorgeous eyes I've ever seen."

Summer blushed and sat back farther in her chair to break the disturbing contact. "You didn't answer my question."

Ryder reached for his beer. "All right, to make a long story short, I invested my book profits in a little radio station in Atlanta and found I had a talent for reorganization. I've picked up several ailing enterprises and managed to turn them around. Then I go on to the next challenge. And I like deejay work. I started out there and I find it the best way to put my finger on the pulse of a station. Satisfied, Ms Interviewer?"

"For the moment."

"Then perhaps we should get to the business at hand."

"Which is?" she challenged.

"The social event of the season—the wedding of Jubilee Jones and Gulliver."

At that moment a smiling cocktail waitress in black heels and hose and the abbreviated tuxedo glided past, asking if they needed anything. Ryder shook his head and his gaze followed the waitress, checking out her shapely legs. When he turned back, he found Summer measuring him with the light of battle in her eyes.

"Relax, Summer. I'm not the Big Bad Wolf come to gobble you up."

She shot him a dubious look, wary as a boxer sizing up an opponent. "Right."

Ryder's jaw tightened. It was clear he wasn't accustomed to resistance in any form. "Look, male-female teams for the morning drive-times are what's hot right now. Combining our shows when we go to simulcast makes perfect sense."

"For you as the owner, perhaps," she argued. "But not for me."

"Is it money? The salary will be more than you're making now." He named a sum that made Summer gasp softly, but she shook her head.

"I'm not trying to gig you for more money. I've never worked as a team, and frankly, I'm not sure I want to try."

"With me, you mean."

"Whatever." She tried for nonchalance, but was afraid he could feel her tension.

"I thought you had more guts than that," he goaded.

She frowned. "I've made it clear that I don't approve of your methods. You backed me into a corner, but I won't fight the sale of the station for my uncle's sake. But insisting we work as partners when I feel the way I do is asking for trouble!"

"Let me be the judge of that."

"Well then, use your head! Surely you can see—"

"That together we'll corner the early-morning market, particularly with the advertising campaign I've planned."

"I see." Her pansy-colored gaze was thoughtful. "You've got it all mapped out."

"Of course. I leave nothing to chance. So don't blow it in a fit of artistic temperament."

She drew herself up to her full but still insignificant height, indignant. "I'm a professional, Mr. Bowman, not some prima donna, despite what you may think. I've built the Coffee Club into something I'm proud of. I'd hate to think I'm throwing it all away."

"You won't be. I'm counting on it. Within our new format you can stretch your talents and increase your listenership to the fullest. You're not going to shirk a challenge like that, are you?"

"It won't work," she said stubbornly. She rubbed the aching spot between her finely arched brows. "I don't know why you can't see it. Either let me work alone, or let me off the hook altogether."

"And have you end up as my competition again? Forget it."

"But . . ."

"I'm paying for Jubilee, remember? I'm not going to do anything that'll jeopardize her, am I? She represents quite an investment on my part. All I'm looking for is a proper return on it."

"Like some kind of stock portfolio?" she muttered sarcastically. "How very flattering."

"Don't look so glum, Summer." His smile was almost kind. "I'm impressed with the interview portion of the Coffee Club. How would you like to expand it?"

She eyed him suspiciously. What kind of carrot was he dangling now? Did he know how important her interview and phone-in program was to her? Sitting back, she crossed her arms defensively, her perusal evaluating. "You aren't above a little bribery, either, are you?"

His deep chuckle acknowledged her thrust. "Not if it keeps you sweet, Jubilee."

She chewed her lip. Despite herself, she was intrigued. "Expand the program how?"

"The frequency, the subject matter. You can do something you can sink your teeth into for a change. Perhaps start with a self-defense expert in the wake of this Wagner murder, for example."

"That might have . . . possibilities," Summer hedged, reluctant to admit that such an idea had already occurred to her. "What if it cuts into your airtime?"

"I'm going to have my hands full beefing up the advertising sales and the news department. That's part of the reason the team format seems like such a good idea right now. And don't forget, Summer, I have stations in Atlanta, Birmingham and Knoxville. You play your cards right, and we just might syndicate your program. Think of that. Your own segment, produced and directed by you, airing throughout the region."

Summer's heart thumped with growing excitement. "You make it sound very attractive," she murmured.

"But you still have reservations?"

Reservations hardly described it, Summer thought ruefully. Working with him would be like trying to walk a tightrope blindfolded. One misstep and . . .

She took a deep breath. "Do you honestly think we can work together without the hostilities turning into open warfare?"

"Hmm, good point." His smile was slow, but he knew she was nearly ready to capitulate. "Personally I think a few fireworks will only add to the show's appeal."

"What if these fireworks turn out to be the atomic bomb?"

Ryder laughed. "I'm willing to chance it. Once WCHT-WROC is solidly based, I'll be moving on to other things. In all probability, within a year or so you'll be back on your own again. Doesn't that make you feel better?"

"If I survive," she said dryly.

Humor crinkled the corners of his eyes. "We're professionals. Surely we can handle it—for the good of our respective careers."

Summer wasn't so sure, but what choice did she have? And the chance to expand her interview show was really too good to pass up. If Ryder could put aside their differences and ignore the occasional twinge of physical attraction, then so could she. After all, as he'd pointed out, it wouldn't last forever. Except at work, she could avoid him like the poison he was.

And, Summer thought with sudden mischief, things could be hurried along. Gulliver might decide to bow out even sooner than he expected if Jubilee made things too uncomfortable for him. Maybe she'd been coerced into this decision by a set of circumstances she couldn't control, but he'd soon find she wasn't going to be a pushover all the time!

"All right, then." She held out her hand. "It's a deal. You've got yourself a partner."

Ryder took her hand, feeling the firmness of the grip and the softness of her skin. "Welcome to the team, partner."

"Just so long as we understand each other," she said.

"Now *that* I'm not so sure of."

She withdrew her hand and allowed herself a small, feline smile. "Then perhaps you're smarter than I thought, Ryder," she purred.

Somehow, the look of calculating determination in her pansy-colored eyes didn't reassure Ryder. He'd gotten what he wanted. Why didn't that make him feel better?

A FEW HOURS LATER SUMMER STOOD in front of her aunt's kitchen sink peeling potatoes. One of Aunt Olivia's gingham aprons covered her comfortable crinkle-cotton skirt and blouse. Through the window over the sink, Summer watched the small backyard slip deeper into twilight, throwing the long shadow of the swing set she'd played on as a child across the neatly tended grass. The modest house was a mate to the others lining the streets in this older neighborhood. A few late roses bloomed unobtrusively against the cedar board fence in the corner of the yard. Their faint, sweet odor wafted through the open window and mixed with the cooking aroma of pot roast. She could see Uncle Burt puttering about the toolshed, the shaft of yellow light from a single bulb pouring from its open door. Nostalgia wrapped soft fingers around Summer's heart. It was good to be home.

"I'm glad you're home tonight." Olivia Pierson echoed Summer's thoughts while spooning rich brown gravy over the succulent roast bubbling on the stove. She put the lid back on the pot and turned to Summer with mild reproach in her blue eye. "You don't come often enough."

"You're right, Aunt Ollie." Summer wiped her hands and pressed a kiss on her aunt's soft, wrinkled cheek. She inhaled the familiar scent of attar of roses and talcum powder. "And being busy isn't enough of an excuse. I'm sorry. I'll try harder from now on."

"I'm not complaining, honey," Olivia replied. "A young woman like you needs a life of her own. Are you still seeing that young man? What was his name? The TV man."

"Tony Keatchum." Summer shook her head. "Not recently. He's just a friend. There's no one special right now."

"Oh? I had hoped that after Clancy—" Olivia broke off, flustered. "Well, never mind about that."

Summer smiled as her aunt busily placed the potatoes in a casserole dish. "I can talk about Clancy, Aunt Ollie," she said.

"No, no, I didn't mean . . ." Olivia's silver gray curls bobbed around her flushed face. Summer dropped her arm around Olivia's shoulders in an affectionate clasp. Her aunt's small stature made Summer feel tall.

"It's all right—really. I'm over Clancy Darrell."

"I knew he wasn't the man for you."

"No, he wasn't," Summer said quietly. How easily the words came to her lips, and how hard they came from her heart. It wasn't easy to admit to an emotional blunder of such magnitude. Her only hope was that it had taught her a lesson about love she wouldn't soon forget. The next time she fell in love, she promised herself, it would be with a nice, safe man with middle-class goals, someone who could promise stability and faithfulness and mean it.

Olivia sighed. "I suppose it's foolish of me, in this modern day and age, with all the career women making successful lives, but I can't help wishing you'd find someone really special to share your life."

"It's not foolish for you to care, Aunt Ollie." Summer's eyes clouded. "Someday I'd like to have what you and Uncle Burt have together . . ." She shrugged and smiled. "All in good time, I guess."

"Of course, you're right. And you've certainly got your hands full with Jubilee." Olivia sliced pats of butter on top of the potatoes and slipped the casserole dish into the oven.

Summer's glance strayed to the open window. Had Uncle Burton told Olivia about the sale of the station yet? Despite her talk with Ryder, Summer was tormented by doubts. Wasn't there any way they could hang on to the station? Perhaps there was still time for a last-ditch effort. "I think I'll go see what Uncle Burt is doing."

Summer found her uncle in the shed fussing over a new fishing fly. He was winding a piece of nearly invisible nylon filament over a bit of fluffy yellow feather, his actions neat and fastidious as he peered through the reading glasses perched on the end of his nose. Somehow he never had the harried air here in his private domain that seemed to follow him like a small black cloud at work.

"May I disturb you, Uncle Burt?" she asked from the doorway.

"Summer. Come in." He frowned in concentration, his shiny pink scalp gleaming under the yellow light. He carefully clipped the thread and stepped back to admire his handiwork.

"Will it catch a whale?" Summer teased.

Burton chuckled. "I'll settle for a rainbow trout."

"Uncle Burt..." Summer sighed. "Can we talk now?"

Burton gently set the fly in the neatly arranged tray of his tackle box and removed his glasses. He looked at his niece with a mixture of rueful regret and little-boy reluctance. "About the station?"

She nodded. "Do we really have to let Bowman have it?"

"It's the only way, I'm afraid. I—I haven't done very well with the business, I'm sorry to say. Maybe I'm taking the coward's way out, but frankly, I'm glad to be getting out from under the pressure."

Summer's throat felt thick and she swallowed with difficulty. She knew how hard it was for her uncle to admit this failure. Uncle Burt seemed so defeated. When had he begun to look so old and worn? she wondered suddenly.

When the radio station had been merely a small country enterprise, he'd been able to cope—barely. And Summer had to accept a portion of the blame for their financial difficulties. She'd turned a blind eye in recent times to their

sliding popularity and the decrease in revenues, content to
let him handle the business details as he had in the past. But
Burton wasn't able to deal with the demands of a cutthroat
competitive market any longer, and for an old man, tired of
the game, selling WCHT was a way out. Could she deny him
that on the basis of a personality clash?

"Mr. Bowman's offer is quite fair, Summer," her uncle
continued. "After the debts are cleared away, there will be
a tidy sum for you from your father's portion and sufficient for your aunt and myself to take an early retirement."

"I don't want anything!" Summer protested. "You raised
and educated me. Whatever the sale brings, I want you to
have it. You're entitled to a comfortable income."

"Thank you, my dear, but I want you to have some security, too."

"I'm well able to work and take care of myself, Uncle
Burt. I want what's best for you."

"Then you'll agree to the sale? You'll have to sign, too,"
Burton said anxiously.

Summer studied her uncle's apprehensive face a moment
and knew that she wouldn't contest his decision. No matter
how unsettling she found Ryder Bowman, he was Uncle
Burt's salvation.

"Yes, I'll sign," she said.

"I'm sorry that you had to find out about everything in
such a shocking way."

"It was a surprise, that's all."

"I hope his insistence on having Jubilee continue on the
station didn't put you off," Burton said. His glance shifted
away uneasily and he latched the tackle box with fussy,
nervous movements. "I certainly won't go through with it
if you have any reservations, Summer."

There was that word again, Summer thought. It could
hardly describe the sinking feeling she had in the pit of her
stomach every time she thought of working side by side with
Ryder. But that was a problem she was just going to have to

deal with. She shrugged and tried to smile. "It's nice to be wanted, I guess."

"He's very astute in the business. Started out as a reporter, I think, so he knows the industry from the ground up. Seems to have the Midas touch when it comes to the broadcast media. He's got a string of radio and TV stations all thriving under his management." Burton's short laugh was humorless.

"You've done your best," Summer said warmly and gave him an affectionate hug. "That's all anyone could ask. Have you told Aunt Ollie yet?"

"We'll tell her together over dinner."

Olivia Pierson calmly passed the platter of sliced beef and vegetables and listened carefully as Burton broke the news. She didn't seem surprised.

"I knew you were up to something," she told her husband. "You've been working too hard. This seems a sensible solution."

"I could never put anything over on you, could I?" Burton asked, his relief at her easy acceptance evident. He clasped his wife's hand under the table and squeezed it.

"You continue to try." Olivia's blue eyes twinkled. "When does this Mr. Bowman want the sale to go through?"

"As soon as possible. He's got a big promotion planned to introduce Gulliver and Jubilee as a team when the stations merge."

Olivia's lips pursed. "I like Summer's Coffee Club the way it is."

"So do I," Summer muttered. She pushed her plate aside. "You realize Mr. Bowman *is* Gulliver."

"Oh, no, really?" Olivia asked. She frowned. "That could be a bit awkward for you, Summer."

"Well, at least she still has a job," Burton said, his voice too jovial.

Summer sent her uncle a sharp glance, then rose from her place. She returned with the coffeepot and poured three cups in a familiar, family routine.

She realized that Burton was feeling guilty about her having to accept Ryder's terms in order to complete the sale. She loved her uncle too much to dwell on her reluctance. It was time to face reality, and she owed him too much to make him feel uncomfortable. She realized now that to oppose the sale would be the ultimate selfishness. No matter what it cost her personally, it was the best thing for Olivia and Burton. For their sakes, she could make the best of things and show a cheerful front. And yes, put up with Ryder Bowman for a year.

She returned to her seat and sipped her coffee. "Actually, the more I think about it," she said casually, "the better I like it . It will be very exciting to be in on the opening of a new, top-flight station."

As exciting, she thought wryly, *as going over Niagara Falls in a barrel every morning!*

"That's right, Summer," Burton said, his enthusiasm a bit forced. "You'll be using the latest technology. Working with Gulliver will be quite an educational experience."

Like taking a postgraduate degree in Living Dangerously, Summer mused, smiling weakly. "I'm sure I'll learn a lot."

"And I'm sure that you'll teach Mr. Bowman a lot," Olivia said staunchly. She patted Summer's hand. "Our Jubilee's the best."

"Thanks, Aunt Ollie."

"If you ladies will excuse me, I've got a few things to do," Burton said. He wandered off toward his study while Summer and Olivia quickly cleaned up the meal.

"Bowman." Olivia frowned in thought as she ran hot water into the sink. "Now why does that name seem familiar?"

"You remember that scandal in Atlanta about police corruption and some sort of underworld connection? Ryder Bowman broke that story,'' Summer said, drying each dish as Olivia handed it to her.

"I remember. It was in the news for weeks. But that was quite a few years ago, wasn't it?'' Olivia dismissed the subject with a wave. "Speaking of news, wasn't that awful about Cleva Wagner? I want you to be very careful, Summer, with some madman loose in the city.''

"I'm careful, Aunt Ollie. Don't worry.''

"I can't help but worry, honey. A single girl like you, living alone. And do you realize that it's still pitch-black when you go to work some mornings? I don't like it. No, ma'am, I don't like it at all.''

Summer hid a smile at her aunt's clucking. "My town house is well-located, I park in a garage with an attendant, I don't walk in dark alleys, and I stay out of rough neighborhoods. I'm perfectly safe, Aunt Ollie.''

"Well, you can't be too careful these days,'' Olivia muttered.

"Don't worry,'' Summer repeated, dropping a kiss on her aunt's wrinkled cheek. "Nothing's going to happen to me.''

CHAPTER FOUR

"DON'T LOOK AT ME like that."

Ryder Bowman paused with his sandwich halfway to his mouth, glaring through the wide, sliding glass doors fronting his chrome-and-glass breakfast area. A small, bedraggled creature peered back hopefully. Muttering underneath his breath, Ryder dropped the roast beef and sourdough poor boy back into its wrapping paper, pushed away from the sleek white Formica countertop where he'd chosen to snatch dinner standing rather than disturb the pristine order of the sterile dining area, and stalked toward the doors. In the background, the compact television positioned on the cabinet droned with another shoot-'em-up chase scene from *Bayside Beat*, the hottest new fall detective series.

"Didn't I tell you I'd call the pound if you came around here again?" Ryder demanded of the scruffy white and black dog waiting in the darkness on the flagstone patio. He slid open the door and gestured threateningly. "Go on. Scat! Shoo! Beat it!"

The little animal retreated a few judicious paces, then lay down with his black nose nestled on his front paws, his big, melting brown eyes filled with reproach. Irritably, Ryder slammed the door and went back to his sandwich. He picked it up, glanced toward the door, and groaned in defeat. How could he eat with that sad, ugly little face pressed against the glass?

"All right, you win," he muttered. He grabbed the remains of his meal and moved toward the door. Immediately the dog's ears perked up, and his tail began a slow side-

to-side undulation whose tempo increased in proportion to
the decreasing distance between Ryder and the door. Ryder
stepped out onto the patio and set the sandwich down.
Shoving his hands into his pants pockets, he cocked a mid-
night-black eyebrow at the canine interloper. "Well, what
are you waiting for? Come and get it."

The stray scrambled up with a clatter of toenails on stone,
gave a deep, polite doggy bow, then sniffed Ryder's offering, tail high and waving like a flag. He was an appealing
little mutt, Ryder thought with reluctant admiration, and
what a panhandler! He knew how to look just pathetic
enough to get past even a hardened case like Ryder Bowman.

"If you ever tell anyone I'm a soft touch I'll deny it," he
warned sternly.

The little dog looked inquiringly at him, then grabbed the
sandwich, and disappeared into the bushes at the edge of the
patio with his prize in his jaws. Ryder ran a hand through his
shower-damp hair and laughed softly.

It wasn't often that he let himself be taken advantage of
like that, but the stray was becoming a regular visitor. He
wore no collar, and besides, you wouldn't often find a Heinz
57 variety pooch like that in this exclusive neighborhood
atop Lookout Mountain. No, the neighborhood dogs were
all well-mannered poodles or Shih Tzus who only made it to
the streets on the end of a leash, not a freebooter like that
little tramp. The buzz of the telephone cut through the cool
September evening.

Ryder turned back toward the house, a straight-lined
modern arrangement of natural stone that clung to the steep
lot like a part of the mountain itself. Its open rooms and
uncluttered spaces appealed to his need for order, and it had
been decorated by one of Chattanooga's most prestigious
firms with modular furniture in grays and mauves and navy,
with big, cushiony pieces that fit a man, and with an abun-
dance of cubes and mirrors. Not that he noticed it with any
regularity as long as he was comfortable. It was a place to

eat and sleep and think about business. He didn't even take advantage of the spectacular view of the city from his sloping backyard very often. There was too much to do to indulge in such a luxury. He grabbed the phone hanging on the kitchen wall on the third ring.

"Bowman," he said into the receiver.

"What'cha say, Tex?" drawled a familiar voice.

"Hey, Kent."

"You must be losing your touch, sitting home alone on a Friday night. You're going to shatter all my illusions about hotshot tycoons."

"Who says I'm alone?"

"Whoops! Sorry, pal. I'll call you back—"

Ryder grinned. "As a matter of fact, my guest just left. Wolfed down what was left of my dinner and disappeared on four feet. You want to use your great sleuthing ability to track the culprit down?"

"Four feet?" Kent Ogden's deep voice resonated with laughter. "I knew you'd been out with some real bowwows before, Tex, but I'm a cop, not a dogcatcher!"

"Sometimes it amounts to the same thing, doesn't it?"

"Yeah. Suppose it does at that."

There was a silence on the wire for the span of a memory. Lt. Kent Ogden, Chattanooga P.D., had been on special assignment to the Atlanta police when Ryder had been pursuing his underworld investigation. Together they'd tracked down the human dogs who'd murdered Bill Norred, Ryder's fellow reporter. Their friendship had been forged under fire, and there was a strong bond between the two men.

"Actually," Ryder said, breaking the quiet, "I'm on my way to a retirement party down at the new station." He grabbed the tie draped over the back of a steel- and cane-backed chair and pulled it under the collar of his starched shirt.

"Out with the old, in with the new, huh, Tex?"

"It's the way of the world." Ryder held the receiver between his jaw and shoulder and struggled with the top button on his shirt.

"So everybody's happy to have the Bowman Network in place?"

A memory of angry violet eyes made Ryder's mouth quirk. His voice was dry. "Not exactly. But she'll get over it."

"Hmm. Planning to use that famous Bowman charm on the lady, are you? Tex, if you could distill that stuff, you could make a million."

"Thanks for the vote of confidence," Ryder said with a laugh. He expertly adjusted the silk tie into a perfect knot and flipped his collar into place. "So what's going on? Did you draw the graveyard shift?"

"Something like that. Surveillance. We're busting our butts trying to nail that Wagner killer. I'll have to pass on our tennis date in the morning."

"Excuses, excuses," Ryder ragged his friend. "You're just afraid I'll whip your tail again."

"You and what army? Besides, you cheated."

Ryder chuckled into the receiver. "Then you'll have to give me a rematch to find out for sure."

"You're on. Soon as I can cut loose from this case."

"Tough one, huh?"

"A real bitch," Kent agreed solemnly. "The guy's got to be a psycho."

"I know the city's finest will take care of that nut in short order," Ryder said. He glanced at his watch. He'd have to hurry to make the party on time. "Are we on for racquetball next week, as usual?"

"As far as I know." There was some background noise and a muffled reply from Kent, then he spoke to Ryder again. "Look, I got to run. Duty calls."

"Yeah, me, too. I hate these things."

"I know it's a tough, dirty job, Tex—" Kent laughed "—but someone's got to do it. See you."

"Yeah. Hey, Kent?" Ryder's bantering tone became one of concern. "Take care of yourself out there, buddy."

"Always, my friend. Always."

"SAY CHEESE," SUMMER SAID.

The camera flashed, capturing her beaming aunt and uncle and the enormous cake that wished them a "Happy Retirement" in pink and yellow icing. Friends and well-wishers crowded into the WCHT offices, filling the rooms with loud conversation and laughter.

For Summer the occasion was filled with a certain bitter-sweet poignancy, but she couldn't wish that circumstances were different—not when Uncle Burt looked more relaxed than he had in fifteen years and Aunt Ollie couldn't stop smiling. She slipped the lens cover back into place and smiled at her subjects. "That'll do it."

"Thank you, Summer," Olivia said. "Vanessa, will you cut the cake now?"

"Be glad to, Mrs. Pierson," Vanessa replied. She sliced the cake with efficient movements and handed the first piece to Burton. Her attire was a bit more subdued tonight, as befitted the occasion, but she still turned heads with her striking Indian tunic and dramatic silver and turquoise jewelry. Summer felt positively dowdy in her tailored linen dress and Gibson Girl hairdo.

Olivia linked her arm through Summer's. "I'm so glad you talked Burton into having this party."

Summer quickly kissed her aunt's soft, lined cheek. "You both deserve so much, it was the least I could do. Besides, everyone wanted to wish you *bon voyage*."

"When Burton waltzed in with those cruise tickets to Alaska, you could have knocked me over with a feather. Who'd have believed that man could come up with such a romantic idea? I thought for certain I'd be spending our first official vacation cleaning fish!"

"Don't speak too soon," Summer warned laughing. "There's a lot of salmon in Alaska, as I'm sure Uncle Burt knows. You might still get your chance."

Olivia joined in the laughter, but as her blue eyes sought her husband on the other side of the table, her expression softened with tenderness.

"Since we signed the papers, he's been a changed man." She glanced at Summer and squeezed her hand. "I know your part in all this, and I just wanted to say thank you."

Summer flushed slightly, knowing she didn't deserve her aunt's gratitude, not when she'd been torn by conflicting desires, wishing at one moment that the sale would fall through, praying the next that it wouldn't. But everything had gone off without a hitch and the station now officially belonged to Ryder Bowman. And, as he so indelicately put it, so did Jubilee, since Summer had signed her contract as well.

"I'm happy for you and Uncle Burt," she said awkwardly. "It was an opportunity too good to pass up."

"Yes, I know. Bankruptcy would have crushed Burton." Olivia smiled at Summer's surprised expression. "Don't look so shocked, darling. Of course I knew about it. I'm not a ninny. But he didn't need to worry about worrying *me*."

"You're quite a woman, Aunt Ollie."

"No, dear, just a wife who loves her husband, and who's glad we'll finally get to enjoy some time together. Oh, there's Agnes and Harry! I must go speak to them. Have some cake, dear, while I visit."

"Yes, ma'am," Summer grinned and watched Olivia bustle over to greet her friends. Despite her aunt's denials, Summer knew her strength and kindness, and for the first time was truly glad about selling the station if it brought such happiness to the two people in her life who loved her unconditionally.

"Hey, Summer!"

Merl Morgan waded through the crush toward her. His tie hung askew and his hair stood up on the back of his head, but his wide grin was infectious. "Nice shindig."

"Thanks. Well, how's WCHT-WROC's newest program director?"

"I'm just great!" he said enthusiastically.

Merl had been offered and accepted the position shortly after the sale. He and Vanessa had chosen to remain during the transition. At least they'd had a choice, Summer reminded herself sourly, whereas Jubilee...but it did no good to dwell on that.

"Wait'll you get a load of all the high-tech equipment, sound systems and computers in the new studio!" Merl continued.

"I'm sure it's downright marvelous," Summer drawled with a twist of her lips. "Am I the only one who's going to miss this old place when we make the move?"

"Probably." Merl shrugged apologetically. "Besides, the new studio's just around the corner from here, anyway. It's still familiar territory."

Merl couldn't be more wrong, Summer reflected. Although the new office and production complex near the Convention and Trade Center was in close physical proximity, the studio was uncharted terrain as far as she was concerned, as unfamiliar as the valleys of the moon. And Ryder might as well be an alien invader for all the nervous anxiety he evoked in her when she thought about working with him, a day that loomed closer with each breath. Summer shook off the feeling of foreboding and returned her attention to Merl.

"You're not sorry to lose the position of station manager?" she asked.

"Not a bit. Programming is right up my alley. You know I prefer the creative end of things. This could be my big chance! If things go right, I can work my way up in the Bowman Network. The growth potential is tremendous. This is just what I've been waiting for."

"I'm glad somebody's happy," Summer muttered. She forced a smile. "How about a piece of cake?"

Merl shot a glance in Vanessa's direction, blushed, then shook his head. "Maybe later." His voice dropped conspiratorially. "Vanessa and I are going out after this for a late supper."

Summer's eyebrows lifted. "You don't say. Well done, slick."

Merl shrugged, his expression diffident. "We'll see. Say, have you seen the ad layouts on Jubilee and Gulliver yet?"

"Not yet. Should I have?"

"You're going to love 'em, doll! By the time I get finished we'll have the whole city howling to hear Jubilee Jones and Gulliver. A new dynamic duo!" Merl gestured vigorously. "Hot property! Chattanooga's sizzling singles!"

"For God's sake, Merl," she protested, a bit taken aback. "Just what are you trying to sell?"

"Sex, of course," he replied cheerfully. "Everybody loves a lover, y'know."

"What?" Summer croaked, aghast. "You mean the campaign is slanted so that people will think that I...that he...that *we*...?"

Merl nodded, his glasses bobbing on his long nose. "Well, at least they'll wonder. And that'll keep them listening. Isn't it great?"

"Great," Summer echoed, her voice dripping with sarcasm. "So, Merl? How's it feel to be a pimp?"

"Aw, Summer!"

"Don't 'aw Summer' me!" She waved an imperious finger. "I don't want to project that kind of image."

"Ryder approved it."

Summer drew an indignant breath. "Well, I haven't. And if my name's on it, then I have the right to say something. I'm entitled to my privacy."

Merl lifted his hands helplessly. "Look, I just follow orders. Maybe you should take this up with Ryder."

"You can bet I will!"

"Look, ah, I'll see you later, okay?" Merl said, doing his best to retreat.

"Sure." Summer was too busy grinding her teeth to mind. She stomped over to the table and took a position by Vanessa's side.

"What's the matter?" the newswoman asked, her dark eyes curious.

"He's going to give me an ulcer," Summer groaned. She stacked used cake plates with a ferocity that threatened to shatter the crystal saucers. Gathering up discarded paper napkins, she twisted them together as though she were wringing someone's neck. "That man!"

"Who, Merl?" Vanessa asked in amazement. "What can Merl have done? He's the sweetest—"

"Not Merl."

"But you were talking to him just now." Vanessa carefully slid her finger down the icing-coated cake knife, cleaning it with too-obvious unconcern.

Summer chuckled. "Don't worry, I'm not going to commit mayhem before he's able to buy you dinner. How'd you manage that, anyway?"

Vanessa's smile was a bit rueful. "I asked *him*."

"You didn't!"

"He gets so tongue-tied, I finally just blurted it out," Vanessa admitted. She sighed. "Now he'll probably think I'm too aggressive."

"Well, make sure he takes you to an expensive place," Summer said, her brow creasing again with her thunderous thoughts. "Between him and that new boss of ours my stomach acid is reaching an all-time high. Sizzling singles— phooey!"

"Careful! You're going to drop those!" Vanessa cried.

Summer grappled with the leaning tower of plates threatening to topple onto the floor. Just as she got them under control a deep voice made her jump.

"Having trouble, ladies?" Ryder asked. In a dark suit, pale blue shirt, and carefully understated tie he looked every inch the powerful executive.

"Not at all, Mr. Bowman," Vanessa said brightly. She held out a plate loaded with a generous chunk of cake and a multitude of pink and yellow sugar posies. "Cake?"

"Thanks." Scooping up a blob of icing with a long finger, he popped it into his mouth, savoring the sweetness with a grimace of pure pleasure. He gave Summer a lazy smile. "Nice to see you, Jubilee."

Summer swallowed and clutched the plates even tighter. She was upset about the proposed ad campaign, but what really made her mad was her involuntary response to Ryder's dark good looks and unconsciously sensual actions. In another situation, she'd have been more than willing to pursue the physical awareness that only grew stronger each time she saw him. It was really too bad that so far everything he'd said and done had made her hopping mad. She didn't want to be in a constant battle with him, not if they were going to have to work together, but linking Gulliver and Jubilee romantically for the sake of publicity was going too far. Her words were tight when she spoke. "We need to talk."

His eyebrows lifted, and he glanced around at the crowd. "Now?"

"Now." She picked up the stack of dirty plates and jerked her head in the direction of the small kitchenette.

"Certainly." He dazzled Vanessa with a smile and sauntered after Summer's retreating figure.

Summer set the plates in the sink and turned as Ryder carefully closed the kitchen door behind him, shutting out the party sounds. She lifted her chin, her attitude pugnacious.

"Merl told me about the ad campaign," she said.

"Uh-huh." He pushed a bite of cake into his mouth, chewed and swallowed. A crumb remained on the corner of his mouth, and his tongue flicked out to capture it in a move that made Summer faintly breathless. "Did he tell you we have an appointment with the photographer on Monday?"

Summer tore her gaze away from his lips. "Photographer? What for?"

"Billboards, newspaper ads. Oh, and we'll make the TV commercial next week."

"Now wait a minute," she protested. "Nobody asked my opinion about this. I don't want my name and face plastered all over town."

"Not yours, honey—Jubilee's," he said softly. "And you gave permission for 'reasonable use.' Didn't you read the fine print in your contract?"

"Reasonable? It's an invasion of privacy! Linking us together like we're . . . an item or something!"

He laughed. "Grow up, Summer. The public is going to eat this up. Wondering do they or don't they? Will they or won't they? Our ratings will go right off the charts." He reached out, and his fingers lightly brushed the soft tendrils of fair hair at her temple. "Just because you're accustomed to a certain anonymity doesn't mean I'm not going to take advantage of that gorgeous face of yours."

The breathless feeling was back. Summer took a step backward, and the edge of the sink pressed against her waist. Ryder took the last sugar icing flower from the edge of his plate and ate it slowly, his eyes never leaving Summer's mouth.

"How can you eat that?" she asked, grasping at the first thing that came to her. It was difficult to form the words. Her lungs wouldn't draw enough air. "Don't you know that stuff will kill you?"

Ryder set the plate in the sink behind her, and his hands caught the counter's edge on either side of her waist, trapping her between the cabinet and his body. Sparks of green humor glinted in the depths of his hazel eyes. "Yeah," he agreed huskily, "but what a way to go."

"I—I don't find anything funny about this," she said stiffly. "I never agreed to expose my private life to every curious Peeping Tom." There was a note of desperation in her tone. Ryder leaned closer. His warm breath fanned her cheek, and she could smell a trace of vanilla flavoring.

"You're getting all worked up over nothing. The ads are just insurance, taking advantage of the public's natural curiosity," he said. His voice grew very deep and husky. "I must admit I have a certain amount of curiosity myself. And there are lots of better things to get worked up about."

He lifted his hand and lightly traced the curve of her lower lip. Something elemental arced between them, surprising and potent and eloquent, and Summer jerked, as though flicked by an electrical shock.

I don't need this, she thought wildly. *I don't want any more complications.* Ryder's fingers moved from her lips and gently stroked the tender underside of her jawbone, his expression one of intense concentration. There was a trace of panic in her breathless protest.

"Don't..."

"Don't what?"

His voice was low, and his eyes reflected the deep green of a forest glade. She was so soft, he thought, so delicate and utterly feminine in that simple dress with her pulse fluttering in her throat and her eyes shooting amethyst fire. He was nearly hypnotized by the feel of her and the faint, flowery scent she wore.

"Just...don't." She arched her neck away from his questing strokes.

"Be honest, Summer. You feel the chemistry, too. Aren't you the least bit curious?"

"You've got a hell of a nerve," she whispered shakily, undone by his touch and the lambent flicker of his gaze.

"There's something there, all right. We can use it to our advantage on the air, or we can enjoy it privately. What do you say?"

"I'd say that there's no way I'd get involved with a man with a hotel heart."

"Hotel heart?" His expression was quizzical.

"Like my Aunt Ollie says, always room for one more." Summer's chin lifted, but her tone was an unconscious mixture of false bravado and old hurt. "I checked out of that particular resort for good a long time ago."

"You've got a smart mouth, lady," he growled, amused. His narrowed gaze latched on to the quivering outline of her lips. "But I can think of several satisfactory ways to shut you up."

Her eyes sparkled with temper. "Not without a fight on your hands, buster!"

Ryder shook his head in reluctant admiration. When had he ever met such a stubborn, infuriating, *desirable* hellion? He hadn't mishandled an employee this badly since he went into this business. But then, he'd never met a female who'd gotten so quickly under his skin. Somehow, Summer Jones made him forget that logic and control was everything. The last time a woman had ruffled him to this extent he'd made the biggest mistake of his life. Was he on the brink of making the second biggest one? He forced the tension out of himself, then took a step back and favored her with a lazy smile.

"Yeah, I guess you're right." He rubbed his jaw thoughtfully. "Neither the time nor the place. But someday soon..."

"As Aunt Ollie says, don't count your chickens!" Summer snapped, infuriated at his smug assurance. How could he be so calm when she was a mass of molten nerves? But she'd be damned if she'd let Ryder Bowman get the better of her, now or ever! "And for the record, I heartily object to advertising that insinuates a relationship between us. And if you don't like that, you can take your job and go straight to hell!"

"You stubborn little shrew!" Ryder raked a hand through his hair. "By God, I ought to let you go. If I hadn't promised your uncle—" He broke off.

But Summer had heard enough to make her feel cold all over. "Promised him what?"

"Nothing. Forget it." Ryder maintained an inflexible silence, only the muscle in his jaw working to indicate any inner tumult.

And he calls me stubborn, Summer thought as realization washed through her in humiliating waves.

"Never mind," she said tightly. "I can guess. In return for the station you promised Uncle Burt to keep me employed, isn't that it? Security for a lifetime for me, but nothing but a peck of trouble for you."

She turned away, pressing a trembling hand to her mouth and feeling like a total fool. She was embarrassed, abashed, mortified—there weren't enough words to describe the feelings that swept through her like chills and fever.

Everything was a sham: Ryder's determination to keep Jubilee on the air, his arguments to overcome her reluctance, even the offer to expand the interview portion of the show! It was humiliating beyond belief to realize he'd made concessions to something that had never been his idea in the first place! How could Uncle Burt have done this to her?

Strong hands closed over her shoulders, and Ryder turned her around to face him. "Don't jump to conclusions," he said.

"Don't bother to deny it." Her lips twisted. "It's so typical of Uncle Burt, I can't understand why I didn't realize it before. I'm very sorry. I won't expect you to honor my contract under these conditions."

"Well, I expect *you* to honor it."

"Good grief, Ryder! What's the point?" Tiredly she rubbed the furrow between her eyebrows with two fingertips.

Ryder gave her a gentle, reproving shake. "Come on, Summer, think. I'll admit Burton made a couple of stipulations before he agreed to sell, but I'm a businessman. I don't do favors of that magnitude unless there's something in it for me. If you think you're backing out on me now, lady, you've got another think coming."

"You're not just saying this to salve my pride?"

"I don't allow emotion to interfere with business. Your uncle meant well, but it suited my purposes, too. You're a dynamite jock, and together we're going to take this burg by storm. That's all I'm concerned about. Now how about another piece of that cake?"

Somewhat mollified, Summer allowed Ryder to escort her out of the kitchen. Perhaps what he said was true, but under the circumstances he was entitled to more from her than the headaches she'd given him so far. Unknowingly Uncle Burt had taken her position of strength away from her.

Swallowing her chagrin, she vowed that from now on she'd cooperate with whatever Ryder wanted. She guessed she owed him that much, at least. She would be docile, easygoing, amenable—the very picture of accord and harmony if it killed her. And, knowing Ryder's ability to rile her, it very well might.

THE STRIDENT BEEP of the alarm clock insistently pierced the early-morning darkness. Summer rose from the wicker rocker and crawled over the rumpled quilts of her brass bed to thump it into silence. She'd been awake, unable to remain in bed, sitting next to the sliding door that opened from her bedroom into the small enclosed backyard of her town house.

Today was *the day*, though the sun wouldn't be up for another hour, and now the clock demanded that she get up and get on with it.

She walked, surefooted in the dark, through her tidy home, automatically flipping on the VCR as she passed by the oak shelf unit in her country-decorated living room. Listening to the taped broadcast of the previous night's late news, she went into the kitchen to brew her first cup of coffee. She sipped it slowly, perched on the tall Windsor-backed bar stool at the kitchen island. Postcards from her aunt and uncle decorated the refrigerator door with scenes of the Alaskan coastline, a herd of moose and a yellow-billed puffin. In the background, the newscaster droned on, and

Summer noted the state legislature was at it again, and
there'd been a three car pileup on the interstate highway.
Maybe she could work some mention of one or the other
into her show this morning. It paid to let your listeners know
you were up on the latest news. She hoped Ryder felt the
same.

Ryder. She quivered with trepidation. He'd been all business the few times she'd seen him over the past weeks, at the
photography session, publicity shots, and when she went to
familiarize herself with the new facilities of WCHT-WROC.
She'd fought hard to keep her dignity and to be as cooperative as possible, and there was a kind of unspoken truce
between them. But they hadn't been sitting side by side in a
ten-by-ten control booth for a four-hour stretch, either.
Well, it was too late for second thoughts now. She grimaced as she headed for the shower. It was time for Jubilee
and Gulliver to face the music—in more ways than one.

Summer drove through the empty streets of downtown
Chattanooga while the first faint rays of morning crept like
golden fingers over the eastern ridges. She scowled as she
passed the oversized billboard touting "Chattanooga's
hottest new couple—Gulliver and Jubilee Jones." For over
three weeks, promotion after promotion had hyped the new
partnership of Jubilee Jones and Gulliver, and Summer was
thoroughly sick of it. Whether she wanted it or not, even
before their debut as a team, she and Ryder were an "item"
in Chattanooga's consciousness. It remained to be seen if the
publicity would live up to the reality of the new Coffee Club.

She drove into the cavernous parking garage, parked and
locked the Mustang, waved in passing at the slight figure of
the attendant inside his glassed-in booth, and walked briskly
around the corner, her heels tapping rhythmically on the
sidewalk. She used her new set of building keys to let herself into WCHT-WROC's newly renovated but now deserted lobby, pushing through the massive double doors just
as the sun's first beams turned the tall windows into panels
of pure gold.

The quiet entrance was tastefully decorated in the same
tones of teal and gray that flowed throughout the three-story
building. Summer paused and drew a deep breath for courage. She didn't really know what had prompted her to dress
up today, she thought, then scoffed at her own foolishness.
Of course she did. Clothes gave a woman confidence, and
she knew she'd need all of that scarce commodity she could
get. So she'd put on her highest heels, her sheerest stock-
ings, a sophisticated sweater dress that flowed over her figure, and pulled her hair into a heavy, elegant knot on her
nape. Jubilee was ready to hold her own with Gulliver.

Heels clicking, Summer walked into the waiting elevator
and punched the third-floor button. Business offices occu-
pied the second floor, but the third was the working portion of the station. The doors opened, and she walked down
the long corridor, passing the tape library and production
rooms for news and commercials, heading for the heart of
the WCHT-WROC, the control room. She found Ryder
loitering in the hall with a cup of coffee in one hand and the
latest copy of *Billboard* magazine in the other.

Why did he have to be so attractive? she wondered, her
mouth going dry. Just the sight of him in his dark slacks and
crisp plaid shirt was enough to make her breathing erratic.
She knew for certain that she was going to have enough
trouble with her new boss and teammate without these
dangerous stirrings to complicate matters. Unbidden, she
recalled the feel of his strong hands gently stroking her neck.
The memory provoked a shiver that made her greeting a bit
tremulous.

"Good morning..."

Ryder's automatic reply lodged in his throat at the sight
of the luscious little woman walking toward him. God, she
was a knockout! And the way she'd fixed her hair made him
wish he could remove the pins and bury his hands in that
long, golden cascade. He smiled to himself, amused at the
primitive urge to claim what he wanted. The caveman wasn't

so very far underneath his civilized facade. He tossed the magazine aside.

"Hello, yourself," he drawled. He gestured toward her, his smile teasing. "Very nice getup. Is it all for me?"

Self-consciously, she smoothed the aqua knit over her hips, then pushed the cuffs up her forearms. "I'm trying to look like a professional for a change," she said lightly.

Ryder frowned when she didn't rise to his bait. Where was the feisty wench who was always ready to cross verbal swords with him? This subdued version of Summer Jones had been around since the Piersons' party, and he found a polite and pallid Jubilee didn't suit his taste nearly as well as the firebrand he'd first met. He glanced at his watch. "You're early."

"So are you."

He shrugged. "We had a little last-minute trouble with the transmitter. It's okay now. Ready for the big moment?"

"As ready as I'll ever be."

He was surprised at the shaky breath she drew. "Not nervous, are you, Summer?"

"A little." She smiled gamely. "All your high-tech equipment gives me the willies."

"I'll handle that part of it today. You'll pick it up easily enough, anyway. Sure that's all it is?"

She frowned. "Of course. What else?"

He rubbed his jaw, and his cheek creased into a wicked grin. "Are you afraid Jubilee will come off second-best head-to-head with Gulliver?"

"I can hold my own," Summer stated, her chin lifting to meet the challenge in his eyes.

"That's what I'm counting on, sweetheart."

Disconcerted, she licked her lips and looked away. "Is there any more of that coffee?"

"Sure." He led the way into the staff lounge and poured her a cup, black, the way she liked it, without asking. It pleased her that he should remember such a little thing, but then he was a man who made it his business never to overlook the slightest detail. She murmured her thanks, then wandered aimlessly around the lounge, slowly sipping the hot brew and battling a case of first-timer's nerves.

"Merl scheduled your Coffee Club interview for nine-thirty," Ryder told her. "Who's coming in today?"

"A local hang glider. Did you know they actually jump off Raccoon Mountain?"

"Sure. I've even done it a time or two myself. It's great fun."

She made a little sound of disbelief. "Sounds suicidal to me."

He laughed easily. "So how long do you plan to interview this maniac?"

"Ten minutes ought to do it, then I'll follow up with a few phone calls until the top of the hour, if that's okay."

"Sounds good. Production's got everything rigged for delay taping. Can't be too careful, you know. The FCC frowns on obscene phone calls going out over the air."

"I know," Summer said, smiling. "I'll be careful."

Ryder glanced at his watch again and set his cup aside. "It's about time. Ready to knock 'em dead?"

Summer nodded and placed her own cup on the table next to his. She walked toward the door, infinitely conscious of Ryder's hand in the small of her back.

"Oh, and Summer?" Ryder said, as if something important had suddenly occurred to him.

She paused, glancing up into his face. "Yes?"

"This."

Ryder lowered his head, expertly fitted his mouth against hers, and took her breath and her sanity in one fell swoop.

CHAPTER FIVE

SUMMER WAS TOO SURPRISED to resist. And then she was too overcome by pure pleasure to do anything but kiss Ryder back. His lips were mobile, warm and demanding, and the earth vanished from beneath her feet. When he finally lifted his head, she was surprised to find she was clinging weakly to him, her hands laced around his neck.

"Well, what do you know?" he murmured.

Drawing back slightly, Summer fought for equilibrium, though her head was spinning and her breath was dangerously short. "Wha-what was that for? Good luck?"

"Just testing."

"Testing?"

"To see if you were still alive."

"I—I don't understand."

That fascinating slash appeared in Ryder's cheek. "You've been so compliant recently I thought I'd better check to see if we could still stir up some fireworks together before we hit the airwaves."

Summer stiffened, blinking and shaking off the lingering aftereffects of his kiss. "Fireworks?" She raised a small fist and brandished it at him. "You try that again, and you'll be seeing stars, Bowman!"

"That's more like it."

Disconcerted, Summer moved away from him. "More like what?"

"I'm paying for a living, breathing deejay with a head on her shoulders and a ready wit, not that mealy-mouthed

Southern belle who's been tiptoeing around me for the past couple of weeks, afraid to say boo.''

Indignant, Summer drew herself up to her full height and glared at him. She carefully ignored the lump of feminine hurt centered deep in her chest. She should have known Mr. Ryder Bowman wouldn't stoop to something so *emotional* as a good-luck kiss! No, indeed, that kiss had been carefully calculated for maximum effect, but she wasn't going to let that hurt her feelings. She was made of sterner stuff, and if Ryder wanted fireworks, he'd get a lot more than he'd bargained for!

"I thought I was being a cooperative employee, Mr. Bowman," she said sweetly. "There's no need to try to deliberately stir up a hornet's nest of trouble." Pivoting on her high heels, she stalked toward the control room, flinging one last challenge over her shoulder. "Get ready to eat my dust, Gulliver."

She marched into the electronic heart of the radio station, waving to Jack "Mack the Night" Maxwell, the late-night deejay. The wiry young man made his final adjustments and left it to her, stifling a wide yawn. She sat down at the boards, pulled her microphone into place, and automatically checked the daily log. Reaching for her headphones, she ignored Ryder as he took the seat beside her.

"You're really cooking now, aren't you, Jubilee?" he asked softly, his lips twitching.

Summer longed to slap that smug look of blatant satisfaction from his face, but she wasn't about to let him know that one kiss could have such an effect on her. "You'll let me know if you need me to show you the ropes, won't you?" she offered, her voice saccharine with sarcasm.

Ryder grabbed his own headphones, laughing softly. "What, and give you the opportunity to lynch me with them? No, thanks, I'll take my chances."

"Swell." Summer glanced at the large clock on the wall, then held one side of the headphones against her ear to monitor the song currently playing. "You tend to your business, and I'll tend to mine."

"Just one more thing . . ."

"What." She wasn't in the mood for any more shenanigans, and the belligerent tilt of her chin spoke volumes about her frame of mind.

Ryder's smile broadened into a wide, wicked grin. "Just what would it take to get you to kiss me like that again?"

"Chloroform," she snapped. Without missing a beat, she situated her headphones and pushed a button. Instantly her voice modulated, took on that throaty, warm-in-bed tone that was Jubilee's trademark. "Good morning, Chattanooga. This is Jubilee Jones—"

"and Gulliver—"

"—telling you to rise and shine—"

"—for this morning's edition of—"

"—the Coffee Club!"

"GO AHEAD, CALLER. Would you like to take up hang gliding as a sport?" Summer asked. There was a moment's hesitation on the telephone line, then a reedy voice replied over the static.

"That w-would be too exciting for me, Jubilee. I like tamer things."

"Like what, for example?"

"Reading poems," he said shyly. "Taking long w-walks in the w-woods. I'd like to show you my flowers someday."

"Oh, that's so sweet," Summer bubbled.

"You mean a lot to me, Jubilee. I don't think I like sharing you with that fellow, Gulliver."

"We're all still adjusting," Summer said honestly. "Give us some time. Oops, and speaking of time, that's what I'm running out of. Thanks for calling in."

"Can—can I call again sometime?"

"Absolutely," Summer said warmly. She looked up as Ryder slipped back into his place at the boards. "It's been good talking with you. Bye now."

"Shall I cue that one up?" Ryder asked, pointing to the replay system.

Summer shook her head. "No, it was nothing special. Sounded like a kid with a crush on me."

"Okay, let's wind this up and give Vanessa her lead-in." Ryder hit the mike button, all business as his deep voice repeated the station's call letters. "This is WCHT-WROC, coming to you in simulcast with the best in adult contemporary music. Thanks to Jublilee's guest, Mr. Phil Lucas, and all those who called in. Stay tuned for Vanessa Lauden with this morning's headline news. Until tomorrow, this is Gulliver—"

Summer held up a finger, indicating her turn. "—and Jubilee, wishing you two sugars in your cup!"

Ryder keyed up the snappy new station jingle, leaned back in his chair, and reached overhead in a bone-cracking stretch. His mouth quirked with a wry grin. "Well, Jubilee? That wasn't so bad for a first time, was it?"

Summer finished tidying her work area, shuffling tape cartridges and log sheets. She had to admit it had gone smoother than she expected, but she wasn't going to give Ryder any kind of satisfaction by saying so. She was still smarting over the audacious kiss. "One down, three hundred sixty-four days to go," she quipped.

"Hey, you're not still sore, are you?"

She cast him a scathing look and headed for the door just as Vanessa hurried into the booth. The newswoman wore a short suede skirt and bulky, hand-knit sweater and held a mass of notes in one hand and a trio of fat mylar balloons in the other.

"Here," Vanessa said, pressing the multicolored ribbons attached to the balloons into Summer's grasp. "Carol says these came for you."

"Thanks." Summer couldn't help but smile at the fat orange cat on one balloon. The logo above him stated: "It's another hurts-to-move morning." Another balloon said "Congratulations," and the third wished, "Good Luck."

"Vanessa, I want to talk to you after the break about some ideas for the news department," Ryder said. "I'm considering a satellite news network, and I want to get your input."

"Sure thing, Mr. Bowman." Vanessa flashed a confident smile and seated herself at the microphone, just as Ron Kerry, the next deejay on deck, appeared with a cup of coffee in his hand. Summer took the opportunity to step out in the hallway. She paused to open the small card dangling from the balloon bouquet, and smiled as she read the message.

Good luck on your first day wrestling with the tiger.
                                    Love, Beryl

Leave it to Beryl to put her finger right on the heart of a matter, Summer thought wryly, warmed by her friend's thoughtfulness.

"Secret admirer?" Ryder asked, coming up behind her.

Summer hastily slipped the card back into its envelope. "A friend of mine. Some people know how to start a person's day off right."

"I thought that's what I did," he replied, favoring her with an engaging grin.

He looked almost boyish, and dangerously attractive, but Summer wasn't fooled. He couldn't cajole her with charm into forgetting he'd kissed her just to fire up her temper to suit his purposes. She was secretly afraid that it would be quite some time before she forgot that devastating kiss at all, but she resented being manipulated like one of her own puppets. He didn't want her cooperation, so they were back to square one. She could revert back to her original plans with a clear conscience, giving him plenty of reasons to turn the Coffee Club back over to her alone. She'd see how well Gulliver could take the heat, and if he didn't like it, then he could get out of her kitchen!

"Some people have more finesse than others," she told him haughtily. She headed toward her new office with the balloons bobbing behind her. He kept pace with her until she paused outside the door.

"I've never been accused of lacking in that department," he said, chuckling. "Maybe I caught you on a bad day. We can give it another go in the morning. In fact, it might even become a kind of tradition with us."

Summer's teeth came together with a snap. "When hell freezes over, and I'm invited to the skating party! I'm warning you, Bowman, you'd better not try anything like that again."

Ryder leaned against the wall, crossing his arms and regarding her with more than a hint of challenge in his eyes. "Why's that?"

"Because this isn't just fireworks anymore, Gulliver. This is all-out war."

THE NEXT FEW DAYS consisted of a series of skirmishes that left Summer wondering just exactly what she'd chosen to get herself into. Thankfully Ryder didn't repeat that well-remembered kiss, but every morning he had a way of looking at her, of studying her mouth with a certain intensity that left Summer a jittery bundle of nerves. The worst part was the silent laughter she saw glinting in those changeable hazel eyes.

Summer was no sloucher in this battle, however. On-air repartee and off-air bickering were her only defenses against Ryder's undeniable masculine appeal, and she often had the pleasure of seeing him disconcerted by a rapid rejoinder or a bit of off-the-wall humor that left him out in the cold. On the other hand, Ryder's notions of high-tech radio management kept Summer constantly hopping to keep up, and that, coupled with a liberal dash of drawled comments about her talents and skills, or apparent lack of them, had Summer's irritation level at an all-time high. Merl wasn't the only one to notice the tension between the boss and his number-one jock, but he was the only one brave enough, or foolhardy enough, to comment on it.

"You must like living dangerously," Merl said, passing Summer a list of the new lineup of pop songs scheduled for airtime.

Summer pushed aside several stacks of accumulated clutter on the corner of his wide oak desk and parked her jeans-clad bottom on the cleared space. Merl's new office was fast becoming a replica of his old one. The amazing thing was that Merl was always able to put his hands on exactly what he needed. She flipped idly through the typed pages of hit singles and shot him an inquisitive glance.

"Could we schedule a few more oldies? And what do you mean dangerously?"

Merl took the sheets back again and frowned at them. Taking a pencil from behind his ear, he made a few notations in the margins. "Oldies, it is. And I mean the way you and Ryder start on each other at the drop of a hat. You got a death wish or what?"

"It's called keeping an edge on things."

"Well, be careful you don't fall off that edge. Ryder Bowman doesn't seem to be the forgiving type. You keep pushing him, and he could slice a little thing like you into teeny-tiny ribbons." Merl pulled a finger across his protruding Adam's apple and made a ripping sound. "Julienned Jubilee."

Summer laughed in spite of herself. "Don't remind me."

"Then why risk it, doll? Don't you cherish your paycheck at all?"

"I'm hoping our esteemed boss will get the picture that the hassle is just not worth it, and put Jubilee back on the air as a solo act."

Merl pursed his lips and gave a low whistle. "You don't mind high stakes, do you?"

"I think it's worth it. Gulliver and Jubilee haven't lit any real fires with the public. The mail has dropped off, too.

Why, all I've gotten lately is a couple of flowery love letters from a secret admirer."

"Well, count your blessings," Merl retorted. "That's more than some of us. Seriously, it's early days yet. You have to give your listeners time to adjust. You two haven't really hit your stride together, but I don't know if you ever will as long as there's this much hostility floating around."

"I wouldn't call it hostility exactly," Summer said slowly. "More like a healthy respect. You know, I'm gunpowder and he's a lighted match, that kind of thing."

Merl gave an exaggerated shudder. "Oh, boy. Just let me know when to take cover, okay?"

"You've got it, pal. Say, how goes it with you and Vanessa?"

"I don't know. You tell me." He fiddled with his pencil, then dropped it in disgust on his blotter.

"Scuttlebutt says you've been seen together quite a bit lately," Summer commented. "Come on, give."

"All I know is that I haven't worn a tie this often in years," Merl grumbled. "We've hit every string concert and modern art gallery in the city. Why, I'm even taking her to the opening of an art exhibit at the Hunter Museum tonight."

"So what's the problem?"

"I'm boring her to tears, that's what! I don't know what to say about that stuff."

"She must enjoy your company, or she wouldn't keep going with you," Summer pointed out. "Maybe you should stop trying to impress her with all these highbrow activities and do something you'll enjoy, too. Be yourself for a change."

"She'll drop me like a hot potato."

"Well, you don't have to go so far as a tractor-pull competition, but how about a day in the country? Show her who you really are." Summer reached over and patted his hand. "Give the lady a chance, Merl. She might surprise you." She glanced at her watch. "Yikes! That last six-in-a-row must be just about finished." Her voice dropped into the Western drawl she affected with her Duke the Bloodhound, character. "I'd better skedaddle before my partner sends the posse out a-lookin' for me."

She let herself into the control room scarcely a minute before the last song finished. Ryder wore a white shirt and navy slacks today, and his tie was loose. He looked up at her with a grimace of irritation and ran a hand through his dark hair. "Where the hell have you been? I can't find the Vincent's Deli spot."

"Right here." She slipped a typewritten script from beneath a crystal paperweight and passed it to him.

"Why can't you keep things where they belong?" he demanded sourly. "I've spent the past ten minutes looking for the thing!"

"I knew where it was." Her tone was mild, and she carelessly flicked an imaginary speck off the sleeve of her emerald silk blouse. She wore her hair loose and flowing today, and she tossed the shimmering golden mass back as she took her seat. "Can I get you anything else?"

"How about a partner who won't try to drive me crazy with childish tricks?" he growled, then turned toward the microphone. "That was Phil Collins with his newest hit..."

Summer frowned, stung by Ryder's accusation. She wasn't playing games with him. The ad script had been there in full sight all the time, if he'd only looked. They were having a contest of wits and wills, that was true, but she had abided by their unwritten rules. She wasn't about to stoop to petty tactics to get her way, not when there were more satisfactory methods to accomplish her ends.

"Gulliver, I've been in the back trying to defend you," she said into the mike. She caught Ryder's eye and gave him an innocent smile. "Some of the other deejays say you're just about the biggest goof-off they've ever seen."

"Are you calling me lazy?"

Summer smiled into her microphone. "Not me. I only said the only exercise you get around here is when you occasionally walk in your sleep. But I know you're not too lazy to walk on over to Vincent's Deli and pick up one of their hot pastrami sandwiches..."

Ryder stifled a groan and joined in on the rest of the advertising spot, lauding the new menu at Vincent's Deli with Jubilee chiming in with prices and locations.

"And don't forget," Summer finished, "they also have those wonderful kosher dill pickles, and that alone is worth the trip. Nice folks over there, aren't they, Gulliver?"

"The very best—"

"And speaking of pickles, here's a tip for you from my Aunt Ollie, who's currently catching salmon in Alaska," Summer rambled. "Have you ever made pickles, Gulliver?"

"Not that I recall."

"Well, if you ever get around to it, instead of scrubbing those bushels and bushels of cucumbers by hand, what you do is load them all up in your washing machine."

"Give me a break, Jubilee!"

Summer smiled at Ryder's increasingly ominous expression. He had obviously failed to see the humor in her little joke. She cued up the next pre-taped advertisement and shoved it into the appropriate slot while she continued to give her folksy tip.

"No, really. You put those dirty green veggies in the washer, no soap, of course, and use cool water, so that they'll come out all clean and ready for the canner. Try it and see if I'm not right. And now here's a word from the people at Shannon Car Dealers."

The Shannon jingle hummed through the control room. Ryder stood up so that he could see Summer fully. His voice was tight, and a betraying muscle throbbed on the angle of his faintly blue-shadowed jaw.

"Just what the devil are you trying to pull with all this rubbish?" he asked.

"Jubilee's fans are accustomed to a homey approach."

"Well, Gulliver's aren't, so spare us both, okay?"

Summer made a tick mark on the log beside the Deli and Shannon spots to indicate they'd been played, then gave Ryder a measuring look. "What's your gripe, Gulliver? Are you afraid you're being outclassed?"

He rolled his eyes. "Lord spare me from feeble-witted women jocks who think they're *funny*, for God's sake! Just do your job, okay, and leave the ambience to me."

Summer sat up straighter, a fine bloom of rosy color staining her cheeks. "That's what I'm doing, only you're too dense to see it."

"Dense!" He glowered at her in disgust. "Just once I'd like to work with a woman whose IQ is greater than her age."

Summer sprang to her feet, her eyes flashing violet-blue. "If I'd known you wanted to work with someone on your intellectual level, I'd have introduced you to something I found growing on the bottom of my shower curtain."

"Lord help the man who ends up with you, lady," Ryder retorted, an angry glint of green in his eyes. "If you were my wife, I'd have to feed you poison."

"If I were *your* wife," she shouted back, "I'd take it!"

Eyes locked in angry combat, they both became aware at the same instant that there was nothing in the control room but the faint, raspy breathing of two angry people and—utter silence. They lunged as one, hitting the waiting cartridge with the next set of songs with one accord, one intention—to fill that bane of every radio station's existence: dead air. The funky beat of the Pointer Sisters' "Automatic" jumped onto the airwaves.

Ryder rapidly checked the console, muttering curses under his breath. Summer stood rooted in place, totally appalled and horrified.

"Did—did all that go out?" she asked hoarsely.

"Looks like it. Damn!"

"But I punched in the cartridge, I know I did," she wailed.

"But you didn't bypass the mikes. I've told you a hundred times!"

"And I've told you I don't understand all this high-tech junk yet!"

"Well, you've really done it this time, Jubilee. We'll never have any credibility after this. The sponsors will be screaming! What a job of sabotage! You've torpedoed the Coffee Club with that witch's tongue of yours!"

"Me! You're the one who started this!" she said. Her lip trembled, and moisture welled in her eyes.

"Don't start crying on me!" he roared, shaking his index finger in her face. "I can't stand that."

She sniffled valiantly. "If you weren't so mean to me, I wouldn't have said all those nasty things. What are we going to *do*?"

"Hell, I don't know!" He raked agitated fingers through his thick black hair, then his eyes narrowed, and he went into his logical, calculating mode, assessing the situation. "I suppose we could just apologize." He glanced at the timer on the series of songs. "But whatever, we've only got two and a half minutes to decide."

"They'll never understand," Summer mourned. "What have I *done*?"

"What have you two done?" Merl burst into the control room, his sandy hair sticking up on his head, his fists full of yellow memos.

Summer fell into her chair, burying her face in her palms. "It's started already," she groaned in abject misery.

Ryder sighed in defeat and awkwardly patted Summer's shoulder. "Don't take it so hard, honey. We all make mistakes."

"What are you two talking about?" Merl demanded.

Ryder shook his head, and his grimace was rueful. "We know we blew it, Merl. We'll just have to go on..."

"Blew it? Are you crazy?" Merl shook both hands, showing the crumpled memos. "The phones are ringing off the hooks! Whatever you two did, Chattanooga loves it! And they want more!"

"MAN-OH-MAN, YOU'RE KILLING ME!" Kent Ogden groaned, puffing for breath. He flung himself down on the locker-room bench and blotted his sweating face with a towel. "When am I gonna learn?"

Ryder pulled his own soaking wet T-shirt over his head and tossed it and the rest of his racquetball gear into his sports bag. "Learn what?"

"Not to mess with you when you're in this kind of mood." Kent flashed a crooked grin that balanced a nose that had been broken more than once. "It isn't good for my ego to get my butt kicked like that."

"Sorry." Ryder rubbed the back of his neck, his expression rueful. "I guess I was trying to work off a little steam."

"A little! Tex, you pulverized me." Kent shoved his hands through his thick blond hair, dark now with perspiration, and his slate blue eyes crinkled at the corners with wry humor. "Something tells me you've got woman trouble."

"Yeah, I guess you could say that, but not the way you think." Ryder shook his head as he recalled the past two weeks since his and Summer's almost-disastrous on-air quarrel. What began as an accident had turned into a running joke. The hell of it was: how could you argue with success?

"I caught your show this morning," Kent said. "Pretty funny stuff. That Jubilee loves to take a chunk outa your hide, doesn't she?"

Ryder made a sound of disgust. "I never figured I'd wind up playing straight man to a pint-sized comedienne, that's for sure."

"Then why are you?"

"Hell, the listeners love it!" Reluctantly he laughed. "How do you figure that? I spend months and months on market research, test the waters for every foreseeable eventuality, and in two minutes Summer Jones throws everything out the window, and I'm left playing Abbott to her Costello."

"And that's what bugs you, isn't it?" Kent guessed. "She comes flying in on the seat of her pants, going on pure instinct, and all your highfalutin' notions didn't stand a chance."

Ryder tossed a bar of soap at Kent, who deftly fielded the object one-handed. "Anyone ever told you you're a real pain in the—"

"Careful, Bowman," Kent warned, with a glint of mischief in his eye. "Or I'll have to run you in for verbal assault."

Their laughter echoed off the tiled floors and walls of the health-club locker room. Kent was as fair as Ryder was dark, but Ryder's wiriness contrasted to Kent's brawnier form. The blond man's deceptively lazy demeanor hid a razor-sharp intellect that made him one of the police department's most valuable detectives. As always, Kent had an uncanny ability to read his friend Ryder like an open book.

"I'd give a month's overtime pay," Kent drawled, "to know exactly why that little lady's got your chitlins all in an uproar."

"For crying out loud, will you can the good-ole-boy routine?" Ryder complained. "I know they taught you English at Georgia Tech."

Kent shrugged his brawny shoulders. "Must be the company I'm keeping these days. But don't try to change the subject. I've got a feeling you've developed a hankering for a certain dishy little blond deejay. Am I right?"

"I'd sooner handle nitroglycerin."

"Ho boy!" Kent hooted, slapping his thigh. "This gal I've got to meet!"

Ryder's expression darkened, and he slammed the locker shut. "I learned my lesson in Atlanta. No way am I getting involved with a woman I have to work with."

"Hardly the same situation," Kent objected. "You couldn't know that bitch set you up."

"Well, if I hadn't been so willing to believe every lie Elise was feeding me, if I hadn't seen myself as her white knight, protecting her from Grigorio and his bunch, then Bill might still be alive today."

"Hey, man, sometimes the heart overrules the head. It was a dangerous game, but you had no way of knowing she was Grigorio's mistress. There's something about a damsel in distress that just naturally brings out a man's protective instincts. But we busted them all, Elise included. Ten to twenty in the Women's Correctional Institute as accessory to murder is no small price to pay."

"It was an error in judgment I have no intention of repeating," Ryder said in a stony voice.

"Hard as nails, ain't you, Tex?" Kent goaded with the temerity of an old friend. "You're not fooling anybody but yourself. Anyway, you and Jubilee get high marks on pure entertainment value, plus this self-protection interview series of hers is making people down at the station sit up and take notice. It's good stuff."

"Yeah," Ryder admitted, sprawling on the bench beside Kent. "We've had a good response from the public. She's got talent, but then I never said she didn't."

"It just comes in an explosive package, right?" Kent laughed, thumping Ryder's back heartily. "Well, we all have our frustrations. So what else is new?"

"How's the Wagner case coming?"

Kent grimaced. "Slowly, very slowly, as my captain reminds me daily. It's hell just waiting for the psycho to strike again. That's why Jubilee's educational programs are so important right now. The women of this city have to remember not to take chances."

"No leads at all?"

"Very few. I'm flying to Phoenix tomorrow night to work a cooperative investigation for a few days. They're looking into a similar case, and we're going to compare notes."

"Can I quote you?"

"Just call me a 'reliable source,' okay?" Kent grinned.

"Sure. And while you're taking your joyride at the tax payer's expense, I'll be back here letting Jubilee flay the hide off me every morning," Ryder said sourly.

"My advice is to give her a little slack. I know you like to be in control, but you can't halter a spirited filly like that and not expect her to put up a fight. Loosen the reins a little, Tex, and I'll bet she comes around."

Ryder's eyes narrowed in consideration. "Hmm. You could be right. For a flatfoot who can't win at racquetball, you can still score occasionally."

"There's a method to my madness." Kent chuckled as he rose and headed for the showers.

"What's that?"

Kent grinned over his shoulder. "The winner buys the beer!"

CHAPTER SIX

"YOU MEAN ALL THAT BICKERING is intentional? You plan that stuff?" Beryl Hatcher asked in amazement.

"Yup." Summer nodded and stole a cucumber slice from the salad her friend was preparing. Dressed in cotton shorts and a T-shirt, her hair in a casual ponytail, she didn't look much older than Beryl's kids, a ten- and eight-year old brother and sister who were busily carrying cookout supplies through the back door. Summer leaned against the butcherblock counter in Beryl's spacious kitchen and nibbled at the cool green and white round.

"We block out at least part of our routine every day." She shrugged and managed a rueful smile. "Other times it's spontaneous combustion between Jubilee and Gulliver. That man can make me 'madder than a wet hen,' as Aunt Ollie says."

"Well, sometimes I laugh so hard I cry," Beryl said, liberally sprinkling olive oil and vinegar over the assorted greens. "Even the other teachers at the Foundation have been talking about you. They don't want to miss a single episode. You should be pretty proud of that."

"The whole thing backfired on me," Summer admitted. "I thought I'd drive Gulliver out of my slot, but now it looks as though I'm *really* stuck with him."

"Honey, you must be out of your mind," Beryl nodded outside toward the wooden deck where her middle-aged husband was adjusting a smoking barbecue pit. "Don't tell Larry, but I wouldn't mind being stuck in a control booth with a fellow who's that mouth-watering! Is he really as sexy in person as he looks on those TV commercials?''

"The man is definitely centerfold material," Summer replied, morosely digging into the wooden salad bowl for another morsel. "But it's hard for me to appreciate that since he's usually growling at me."

Beryl playfully slapped Summer's wrist. "You can't tell me working with a hunk doesn't have its compensations."

"Maybe, but it's too bad his disposition doesn't match his looks."

"You're still holding a grudge against him because he bought your uncle's station," Beryl surmised.

Summer munched slowly, looking thoughtful. "No, I don't think so. At least not anymore." She made a face. "The whole thing knocked me off balance. I guess I threw such a tantrum because I was scared."

"But it hasn't turned out so badly, has it?" Beryl asked.

"I'll reserve judgment on that," Summer replied dryly. "But I know it was the best thing for Aunt Ollie and Uncle Burt."

"Have you heard from them?" Beryl set the salad bowl on a tray loaded with paper plates, napkins, and flatware with red, white, and blue plastic handles.

"They called last night. The cruise was such a success, they've decided to extend their trip. They're renting a car and driving down the Pacific coast to California. Aunt Ollie says she wants to see the giant sequoias."

"Good for her," Beryl enthused. "It's about time they had a chance to feel carefree again."

"You're right. And despite my reservations, Ryder has already managed to turn the station around. At least I think he has. Tomorrow's Judgment Day. He's called a staff meeting to give us the preliminary verdict."

"You're not worried, are you?" Beryl's glance was sharply inquisitive.

Summer gave a little sigh. "Mr. Ryder Bowman is a businessman, as he is so fond of reminding me at every opportunity. He's made his office into a regular command center to run his not-so-little broadcasting empire. It's a reminder that we're just a portion of his business interests, and a small one at that. If the bottom line doesn't suit him . . ." She shrugged. "Let's just say that I'm glad the condemned woman will eat a hearty meal tonight."

"That is if Larry doesn't incinerate our steaks!" Beryl shoved the loaded tray into Summer's hands and grabbed a casserole of baked beans from the stove. "Let's get out there before he does any more damage."

Later, replete on salad and beans and despite Beryl's apprehensions, perfectly grilled T-bone steaks, they sat out on the deck, listening to the children chatter and watching the September sky darken.

"This is my favorite time of year," Beryl said with a sigh.

"Every season's your favorite," Larry retorted affectionately, propping his feet on the deck railing, and lacing his hands over his portly middle.

Beryl wrinkled her stubby nose at him and laughed. "All right, but this is my *most* favorite, when the summer heat is over, but it hasn't gotten cold yet. I can even wait for the leaves to change when it's like this."

Summer took a deep breath of balmy air and had to agree. "There's no place like Chattanooga in the fall."

"We'll probably drive over to the Smokies in a few weeks when the season hits its peak to take our annual leaf-looker's tour," Larry said. "Want to come with us, Summer?"

"Sounds lovely, but I'd better see how things go at the station before I commit myself," she replied.

Plump, brown-haired Allison, a miniature version of her mother, piped up from her seat on the deck's steps. "Aunt Summer, you haven't forgotten my Brownie troop is coming Thursday, have you?"

"No, ma'am, I haven't. And you can tell your friends if they're very good, I'll even take everyone out for ice cream afterward."

"Awright!" Allison chortled and cast a gloating look toward her older brother, Rich.

"The Boy Scouts already went there last year," he sniffed with the hauteur of superior age, but Allison was unperturbed.

"Will we see Lizabeth there?"

"Probably not," Summer replied with a laugh. "My boss doesn't think I should play at work. Besides, Lizabeth is an awful tease. She gets me into all kinds of trouble."

"Will you show us again how to make those sock puppets?" Rich asked.

"Sure. Run and get the socks."

The children galloped into the house with Beryl reminding them to bring back only *old* socks. She shook her curly brown head, giggling. "The last time you started this, for weeks Larry couldn't find any socks that didn't have eyes."

"Got some pretty strange looks around the boardroom, let me tell you," he drawled.

"Sorry," Summer said, her eyes twinkling. "Kids just love to make puppets. Even the smallest ones down at the Foundation really get into it."

"By the way, we're planning another fund-raiser for the Foundation," Beryl said. "I just thought I'd warn you. We'll be looking for a mistress of ceremonies to host a rather unusual auction."

"You know you can count on me."

"I'll get back to you when the committee firms up the details. You're going to love this."

"I am?" Summer asked, lifting one finely arched eyebrow. "What's up for bid? Vacation trips? Antiques?"

"No." Beryl smirked. "Better than that."

"How much better?" Summer asked suspiciously.

"The answer to a working girl's prayer." Beryl's brown eyes sparkled with mischief. Larry gave a disdainful snort, and his wife pulled a face on him. "Oh, hush up, you! It's all in good fun and for a worthy cause."

"What is?" Summer demanded, baffled.

Beryl's puckish face lit up, and as she leaned toward Summer her voice was conspiratorial. "We're talking beefcake, honey. Mega-hunks and heartthrobs. We're going to auction off lots and lots of gorgeous, single *men*."

"You're going to help me with the Brownies, aren't you?" Summer asked.

Vanessa hesitated as they filed down the teal-carpeted hallway toward the station manager's office the next day. She glanced down at the body-hugging, multilayered brown and purple knits she wore. "You must be kidding. You know I'm always on a diet."

"Not that kind of brownies!" Summer laughed, shoving her hands into the deep pockets of her khaki bush pants. Her matching top sported brass buttons and epaulets, and her hair was tied back with a leather thong. "Beryl's Brownie troop will be here tomorrow. I'll need some help keeping them corralled."

"I'd be glad to."

"You're certain it won't interfere with anything you and a certain program director have planned?" Summer teased.

"No, of course not." Vanessa's olive complexion flushed a delightful peach shade.

"I wish my two good friends would let me in on how things are going," Summer announced to no one in particular.

"They're...okay." Vanessa glanced away, hiding the expression in her coffee-brown eyes, and bit her lip.

"Gee, such enthusiasm."

Vanessa turned quickly to Summer, touching her shoulder. "Oh, no, I don't mean for you to think...that is..." She paused and drew a deep breath. "I think Merl's just the sweetest thing. He's always considerate. We're getting along very well now that he's stopped trying to impress me with his sophistication. Did you know he was practically an authority on modern art?"

Summer's jaw dropped. "He is?"

"Oh, yes," Vanessa replied solemnly. "He adores it. He's such a special person, everything I've ever wanted, so good-hearted and kind. If I appear cautious, it's just that...well, I don't want to make a mistake again. He loves kids, too. Did you know he has *eight* brothers and sisters?"

"He mentioned them once or twice," Summer said with a smile. "And I think caution is fine. It takes time for two people to develop a relationship."

"Yes, I agree, only—" Vanessa broke off with a little nervous laugh.

"Only what?" Summer asked curiously.

The newswoman cast a swift glance up and down the hall. They were bringing up the rear of the group going into Ryder's office, but she still leaned toward Summer and answered in a whisper. "Only I wish he'd quit treating me like a china doll and *kiss* me, for goodness sake!"

A bubble of incredulous laughter escaped Summer, and her eyes widened. "You mean he hasn't..."

Vanessa sighed. "Not a move. I love a gentleman, but really."

"Hmm. I see your problem. Maybe you're not the only cautious one. He's an old-fashioned kind of guy, very conservative underneath that country-box exterior. Maybe you're going to have to make the first move."

"I already have."

"Huh?"

Vanessa gave a sheepish smile. "I've invited him to dinner at my place tonight. If French cooking, candlelight and a bottle of wine don't do it, I give up."

"Thatta girl!" They reached the open doorway of Ryder's office, pausing at the crush of bodies blocking their path. Summer mouthed the words, "good luck," and gave a thumbs-up sign.

"If you ladies would be so good as to join us?" Ryder's deep voice carried over the subdued mumblings. "Come on up front."

Faintly irritated at having everyone's attention called to them, Summer shrugged and led Vanessa through the assembled staff of WCHT-WROC. Merl gestured and made room for them beside a bookcase, giving Vanessa an especially warm smile. Ryder cleared his throat, and Merl tore his gaze away from the brunette, pushing his glasses up the bridge of his nose. The rumble of conversation died away, and everyone came to attention.

Ryder sat on the edge of his desk, arms folded loosely, the pale yellow cotton of his dress shirt stretching across his muscular chest. His piercing hazel gaze traveled over the station employees one by one. There was a sudden charge of tension in the crowded office.

"You all know why I've called you here today," Ryder began abruptly. "A station lives or dies on its ratings. Good ratings mean we're doing it right. Bad ratings mean fewer sponsors, re-evaluations, probably a staff shakeup. The bottom line for WCHT-WROC is . . ."

He paused ominously, and barely a breath could be heard in the room. Summer's hands clenched into fists at her side, and she licked dry lips, watching Ryder's serious expression for a hint of the verdict as anxiously as everyone else. His eyes locked with hers, and suddenly the slash in his cheek appeared.

"We're a hit," he said softly.

Summer felt her stomach go weightless at the sheer sensual charm of his smile. Amazingly she smiled back at him. Gasps and cries of delight and congratulations swirled around the room, but she was oblivious to everything but the fierce, proud light in Ryder's eyes. She felt his pleasure and his pride as though it were all her own, as though they were connected on an empathetic level that transcended conventional understanding. Ryder, mellow with success, was a force almost too potent to resist. He tapped a thick folder on the desk.

"It's all right here," he said. "Birch rating polls say we're neck-and-neck with our competition. They call us the fastest-growing adult contemporary station in two states. That's outstanding for a station that just changed formats."

An undercurrent of murmurs moved around the room, and Summer studied the faces of the other deejays, the news team, the clerical staff. There was relief in their expressions, now that their jobs were apparently secure, and pride, too.

"You've worked hard," Ryder continued, letting his regard include everyone, "and I'm damned grateful. I know I've been rough on some of you, but I knew if I demanded your best, you'd give it to me. You didn't let me down." He pointed to Merl. "I think we all owe a debt to our P.D., for some excellent programming. Thanks, Merl."

There was a smattering of applause. Merl stepped forward, lifting clasped fists in a typical boxer's cocky victory salute. "Anytime, boss."

"And Vanessa," Ryder went on. "We're getting a reputation for serious journalism around here, and I'm pleased to announce she'll be coordinating all our news broadcasts as our new news director."

There was more applause and congratulations as Vanessa blushed and ducked her head to acknowledge the accolades. Summer grinned and patted her friend's shoulder while Merl looked proud enough to pop.

"Not to mention that she's got a helluva cute wardrobe," Ryder quipped, evoking appreciative laughter. "And then there's my own Jubilee, keeping Gulliver on his toes and making people sit up and take notice with her interviews."

"I'll say!" teased Jack Maxwell from across the room. "She gets more phone calls than the Bell System, especially from one guy. Think he's in love with you, Jubilee?"

Summer vamped a limpid look over one upraised shoulder, her voice Mae West's throaty warble. "Umm, what's not to love, sugar? A girl needs know-how to handle those gentlemen callers, and brother, do *I* know how!"

Laughter erupted from the group, but Ryder's glance was sharp. "Is this a problem?"

Summer shrugged. "No way. He's a sweet kid with a bit of a stutter, sort of a human Wallace the Whale. Nothing I can't handle."

"Okay." Ryder nodded. "Good work, Summer."

Summer took a curtsy. "Thank you, kind sir."

Ryder's mouth twitched, and he looked away. "I want the rest of you to know I'm pleased with what you're doing, too, but we can't rest on our laurels—or our ratings. Next ratings review, I want us to be clearly on top, and if we keep on the way we're going, that's certainly a goal we can reach. Now," he mock-growled, "get back to work!"

The meeting broke up with cheerful chatter and relieved laughter. Summer congratulated Vanessa on her promotion and turned to follow the others out of the office. She felt a warm hand close around her elbow.

"Can I have a word with you?" Ryder asked.

"Of course." She walked back with him to the broad mahogany executive's desk. "Do you want to go over the clippings and bits for tomorrow morning's show?" she asked. "I found a new book that ought to be helpful, *1001 Insults for All Occasions.*"

"Oh, Lord, I'm in trouble now," he groaned.

"No, it's for *you*," she said saucily. "I thought I'd give you a fighting chance."

"You're all heart."

Summer laughed, then sobered. "I have to admit, that was deftly done just now."

Ryder was temporarily nonplussed. "The meeting?"

She nodded, and her expression was reluctantly admiring. "I didn't know you had it in you. You handled it very well, just serious enough, but with sufficient humor to let them know you're human and approachable."

"Since when haven't I been approachable?"

"Oh, you must know they hold you in awe," she scoffed. "The mover and shaker in our little world."

He thumbed his bottom lip, his eyes gleaming with humor. "But not you, huh?"

"That's because I had your number from the very first," she replied airily. She picked up a pen off the desk and twirled it between her fingers.

"Numbers are the name of this game. Come here, I want you to see something." He flipped open the folder, pointing to a column of figures.

Curiously Summer bent over the desk, tossing the pen aside. Her breath caught in a little gasp. "Is that us?"

"Uh-huh."

"Oh, Ryder!" Summer grabbed his hands and beamed up at him. Her pansy-colored eyes sparkled, and she fairly bounced with delight. "That's the highest rating the Coffee Club has ever gotten!"

He laughed as she nearly danced a jig. "Pretty proud of yourself, aren't you?"

"Of us!" Her lips tilted. "You did it, too. As much as I hate to admit it, I guess this proves you were right all along."

He was a bit disconcerted at her unabashed honesty. "Well—thanks, sweetheart."

Summer realized suddenly that she was holding his hands and hastily pulled away. "You know me," she babbled, inexplicably nervous. "I'll give the devil his due. It looks as though the team approach was the best for the morning show."

"Not just any team. You and me. You'll pardon me while I gloat at this magnanimous admission of yours?" he asked, humor twisting his mouth. "You've given me some uncomfortable moments, so it's damned nice to see my theories proven, even if the particular slant of our airtime relationship isn't quite what I'd envisioned."

Her laughter tinkled gaily. "Be my guest."

"You have to admit it's been kind of fun so far."

"Fun? For whom?" She shook her head ruefully. "Sometimes I think the only thing holding me together is static cling."

Ryder's bark of laughter startled her, but no more than the companionable arm he draped over her shoulders or the affectionate squeeze he gave her. "You're one of a kind, little lady. Truly an original. Do you think we can keep up the Coffee Club banter but drop some of this mutual antagonism?"

Her reply was strangely breathless. "I think maybe we can try."

The faint spicy scent of his after-shave made her dizzy. She felt disoriented, her perception of Ryder undergoing rapid alteration. The professional way he dealt with his employees, his fairness and willingness to listen, how he went out of his way to praise and encourage, all made him less the tyrant of her experience, and more the capable and astute businessman. But underneath the cool hard-as-nails executive was a man who cared about his employees and not just the totals in a ledger.

Summer blinked, fighting to assimilate these varying impressions. She had to admit she'd enjoyed meeting the challenge of Ryder's ready wit. Yes, it was fun. Working closely with him, planning the "bits," she'd realized he was the consummate professional. He'd do his best for her, even when she was being her most difficult, for the good of the program, for *her* Coffee Club. The realization made her take pause, for when it was all said and done, the thing she'd been most determined to do was insure that the Coffee Club survived. And he'd seen to it, not to spite her, but *despite* her. She felt ashamed of herself, and resolved to keep sight of that larger goal, no matter what she felt personally for Ryder Bowman.

"I knew from the moment I heard that dynamite voice of yours that we'd complement each other," Ryder said.

"Is that what we do?" She made her eyes wide and little-girl innocent. "I'd have called it something else—sniping, low blows, potshots."

"All right, I get the picture," he said with a chuckle. "Whatever it is, you have to admit it works. Whenever you start coming out of left field I provide a steadying influence—"

"—and whenever you become too pompous I take you down a peg or two, and teach you how to lighten up."

He hesitated a moment as if he'd never considered what she could teach him, and his dark lashes lowered, hooding his green-speckled gaze. The slow unveiling of his dimple as he smiled down at her was devastating. "You know what this means, don't you?"

A wary suspicion colored her reply. "What?"

"It means there's a possibility we may come out of this thing friends."

Friends? Summer thought. Yes, she could believe it. She'd found a lot to admire in him. But if the way his nearness made her heart hammer was any indication, liking Ryder Bowman was potentially a hundred times more dangerous to her peace of mind than hating him had ever been.

"Friends would be nice," she managed.

"Then what do you say we start over?" Very gently, he brushed his knuckles down the curve of her cheek. "The boss shouldn't play favorites, and I'm not the kind of guy who sends flowers anyway, but if things were different, I'd send you roses for making the Coffee Club such a hit."

"Oh? And what would the card on this mythical bouquet say?"

"Hmm." His gaze traveled over her sunlit hair, and his voice was deep and suddenly serious. "Maybe something about false starts and second chances. What do you say?"

She bit her lip, gave a mischievous smile, and slipped out from underneath his arm. "I'd say the boss is always right."

"That'll be the day, Jubilee!"

She paused at the door, her fist cocked on her hip. "Well, as Aunt Ollie says, 'Every dog will have his day.'"

Ryder folded his arms and grinned. "Don't you have anything better to do than stand here and insult your boss?"

"I believe that's my job," she said with a smirk. "All right, I'm going! There's a stack of commercial spots on my desk that need doing anyway."

"So get busy."

She wrinkled her nose. "Nag, nag, nag."

The sound of his deep laughter followed her down the hall. Staff members bustled to and fro, and the clacking of typewriters and ringing of telephones punctuated her bemused thoughts. When Ryder Bowman decided to turn on the charm it was wise to be wary. *Keep your head, gal,* she warned herself. A tiger was fascinating and beautiful, but you didn't willingly throw yourself into his lair.

She turned the knob on her office door and pushed inward, vaguely puzzled by the spongy resistance it met. Pushing harder, the door suddenly gave way.

Hundreds of balloons descended in a multicolored cascade, falling over her head, bumping her surprised nose, spilling past her legs into the corridor in a runaway rainbow of galloping globes. Gasping, she stepped backward, popping one rubber bubble with her heel. Laughter rang out behind her, and she whirled around.

"What? Who...?"

A host of amused faces peered out of every doorway, and at the end of the long corridor, Ryder, Vanessa and Merl were doubled over with mirth.

"You clowns!" Summer threatened, laughter in her voice. "I'll get you for this!"

A single helium balloon drifted by just then, and Summer made a grab for the attached note. She scanned the missive and gave a hoot of laughter.

"Congratulations, partner. Love, Gulliver," it read. "P.S.: Gotcha!"

THE INTERCOM BUZZED on Summer's desk late the next day. She set aside a rather mushy and flowery adoring fan letter, the latest in a string of anonymous romantic tomes to reach her desk. Her secret admirer extolled her beauty and virtue to an embarrassing extent. Still, she wouldn't be human if the strokes to her ego didn't feel good. With a laugh, she discarded the letter into "File 13" before she got a swollen head. Kicking a stray yellow balloon from under her chair, she flicked a trio of green ones off the intercom as it buzzed again, and punched a button. "Yes, Carol?"

"Mrs. Hatcher is here with her Brownies, Summer," said Carol's disembodied voice.

"Thanks, I'll be right down." Wading through the ankle-deep flood of balloons, Summer decided to see that each Brownie got several to take home. She cleared a space by the door, then quickly slipped into the hall before any more could escape. The entire third floor was dotted with colorful globes. Ryder's stunt had made a hit with everyone. Now, Summer was busily engaged in plans to retaliate. She knocked on the door of the newsroom and peeked in.

"Vanessa? Our visitors are here."

"Fine. I've just finished," Vanessa said, pulling a sheet of paper out of her typewriter. She wore a denim skirt, a billowing crimson blouse, and dangling starburst earrings. Her dark hair was pulled back today, with little-girl bangs framing her wide forehead. Summer glanced down at her own hot pink, butterfly-appliquéd sweats and gave a shrug. As usual, Vanessa looked the chic adult, and Summer appeared to be one of the kids.

They headed for the elevator. Station security required visitors to check in with the receptionist, then be escorted upstairs to the control rooms and business offices by a staff member. Summer tapped the call button on the wall and gave Vanessa a teasing look.

"So? How did it go last night?"

A soft, slow smile appeared on Vanessa's lips, and her expression became far away and dreamy. "Just fine."

Summer stepped into the elevator, holding the door open for Vanessa. "I take it the wine worked?"

Vanessa looked thoughtful. "You know, we never even uncorked it."

"Oh, ho! That sounds promising." Summer touched the numbered buttons and the door slid shut.

Vanessa blushed and smiled. "He's wonderful. And I've got it bad."

"And that's good?"

"It's very, very good," Vanessa admitted. Then she giggled. "Oh, Summer, I like him so much! And if last night was any indication, the feeling's mutual."

"That's great!"

"Maybe sometime we could all go out together."

"Love to, but you're the one with the new boyfriend, not me," Summer pointed out wryly.

"Couldn't you call your friend Tony? The one that's in television?"

Summer leaned against the rear wall of the elevator and tugged on her long braid. "You know, I just might do that. Tony wouldn't mind doing something just as friends, and I haven't been out in what Aunt Ollie calls 'a coon's age.' It might do me good."

"Let's plan something soon then," Vanessa urged.

Summer agreed just as the elevator door opened. In seconds, they were surrounded by a noisy group of eight Brownies in brown and orange dresses, knee socks and beanies. The little girls were of assorted shapes and sizes, including Allison and the dark-eyed charmer with the long, black pigtails and double hearing aids who'd been Summer's helper at the Foundation. The one thing they all had in common was an excess of energy and high spirits.

Beryl, in her matching leader's uniform, herded her group together and shouted at Summer over the tumult. "I hope you're ready for this!"

Summer grinned, grabbed Allison and a friend by the hand, and motioned Vanessa to do the same. "I'm always ready for a challenge!"

It was that and more, escorting the group through the facility and answering innumerable questions about life on the radio. Vanessa gave the tour of the newsroom, looking a bit harried by all the turmoil. Ryder even took a few minutes to come out in the hall and work his masculine charm on the little girls. Summer couldn't help noticing how the girls took to him, and he answered all their questions with great patience. Afterward, Beryl shot Summer a significant, if slightly dazed, look that said she had not been immune to Ryder's considerable magnetism, either. Then they all went into the control room where Ron Kerry allowed each Brownie to say hello on the air. At the end of the tour, at Allison's insistence, Lizabeth Lizard even made an appearance, and each girl was duly presented with a balloon from Summer's office. The group then adjourned to the ice cream parlor located in the neighboring block.

Summer paid for the ice cream and chatted with Beryl, who sipped a diet drink and tried not to notice the sinful concoctions being consumed on all sides of her. Summer noticed Vanessa in a booth at the rear of the group, deep in conversation with the dark-haired, hearing-impaired Brownie. There were enormous ice cream sundaes in front of both of them, and little Amy Brown had polished off her own and was doing considerable damage to Vanessa's untouched confection.

"I can't thank you enough for this," Beryl was saying. "It's been the highlight of our year, so far."

"It was fun. Vanessa even enjoyed it," Summer replied. "Look how she's taken to Amy."

"That's sweet of her to take so much time with her," Beryl agreed. "Amy's one of the Foundation's best students. She's a whiz at lipreading and attends public school. Unfortunately, I don't know whether she'll be able to continue coming to the Brownie meetings much longer."

"Oh? Why's that?" Summer idly licked the last glob of melted ice cream and butterscotch sauce from her long-handled spoon and futilely scraped the bottom of her dish for more.

"Her mother is quite ill."

"Oh, that's a shame. I hope she gets better soon." Summer licked the spoon dry and set it down at last.

"I want to thank you for torturing me with every bite of that sundae," Beryl complained, then prophesied darkly. "One of these days you're going to have cellulite, too, and I'm gonna love it!"

"You know we all love you the way you are, barrel—er, Beryl," Summer retorted with a grin.

"All right, Josephine! Don't start anything you can't finish!"

"Shh. I take it all back!"

"You'd better," Beryl said fondly, then glanced at her watch. "Look at the time! All right, girls, let's go."

Amid much laughing and cries of thank you, Beryl escorted the troop out to her waiting van. Summer felt limp. She saw Vanessa still sitting in the rear booth in a similar stage of exhaustion and went to join her.

"Whew!" Summer slid into the seat opposite Vanessa. The newswoman was unconsciously snapping and unsnapping the clasp on her billfold, and she looked as totally drained as Summer felt. Summer gave a loud sigh of relief and flexed her tired feet. "I never realized what a chore being a mommy was," she said playfully.

Vanessa sucked in a painful breath and went white around the mouth. Startled, Summer reached across the table.

"Vanessa, what is it? Are you all right?"

"N-no." Vanessa's voice cracked on the word.

"What's the matter? Can I help?"

There was pain in Vanessa's coffee-colored eyes, but she shook her head.

"For goodness sake, Van! Something's upset you. Let me help." Summer touched Vanessa's trembling fingers, and the contact or the sincerity of her concern made Vanessa hesitate, then suddenly flip open her billfold to the plastic snapshot holders.

Her voice was a ragged thread. "Look."

Frowning, Summer craned her neck, studying the picture of a small dark-eyed girl whose face was very familiar. "I don't understand. What are you doing with Amy Brown's picture?" she asked, puzzled.

"That's not Amy." Vanessa's lips quivered. "That's me, on my mother's porch when I was seven."

"But that's amazing," Summer said, studying the photo again. "The likeness is uncanny—" She broke off as Vanessa suddenly pressed her hands to her mouth and curled over as though pierced by a fiery pain. "Vanessa?"

"Oh, God, Summer," she moaned, and her dark eyes filled with tears. "I think Amy's my little girl!"

CHAPTER SEVEN

"I WAS BARELY SEVENTEEN and as green as grass," Vanessa said.

She sat on Summer's camel-back sofa and stared out the window at the leaden October skies. A soft, sad rain fell steadily, puddling on the brick patio and bedraggling the last of Summer's potted petunias and pink geraniums.

Vanessa had been too upset to make much sense at the ice cream parlor following her startling disclosure, and Summer had done the only thing she could think of by bringing her home. She poured another cup of herbal tea from the pot on the butler's tray coffee table and said nothing, sensing her friend's need to talk. Vanessa's eyes were red-rimmed with weeping, but her voice was low and calm.

"I know it sounds corny, but I thought he loved me." She gave a bitter laugh. "I found out very quickly he cared for no one but himself. Not me, not our baby, no one."

"What did you do?" Summer questioned softly.

Vanessa shrugged and drew a deep shuddering breath. "When I told my mother, she kicked me out. Called me . . . terrible names."

"Oh, Van!" Summer whispered, appalled. She couldn't conceive of Aunt Ollie treating her like that. No matter what, her aunt and uncle would have found a way to help her and support her. Hadn't they understood about Clancy? Summer imagined Vanessa's despair and desperation and felt sympathetic tears prickle her own eyes.

"We lived in Knoxville then, and I had nothing, no job, no husband," Vanessa continued dully. "How was I going to support a baby? I wanted something better for her than what I could give her."

"So you put her up for adoption?"

Vanessa's fingers clenched, lacing and unlacing. Her dark brown eyes were tortured. "What else could I do? I came to Chattanooga and stayed at a home for unwed mothers. After my baby girl was born, they made the adoption arrangements and I went back to Knoxville, got a job, started night school. I was determined to make something of my life, to prove them all wrong, to show them I *was* something."

"I wondered," Summer murmured. "You've never said much about your home or your family."

"I never had either one, not like you did," Vanessa said. "I know I did the right thing, both for myself and my little girl, but there was never a day, not even an hour, that I didn't think about her. I think that's why I came back here to work. It made me feel closer to her. And now—" Her voice caught on a sob. "Oh, Summer! She's *deaf*! Did I do that to her?"

"Now wait, Vanessa," Summer said, setting her empty cup down and leaning forward earnestly. "You can't be sure that Amy Brown is your daughter. I admit there is a resemblance, but there are lots of dark-eyed brunettes. You're probably just jumping to conclusions, and worrying yourself needlessly."

"Oh, no," Vanessa denied, shaking her head. "I know it's her. I know it *here*." Her fist covered her heart. "And she told me her birthday is April the third. That's the same day my baby was born, the same year. Summer, it's her. It's got to be!"

Summer lifted her palms in a placating gesture. "All right, just for the sake of argument, let's say that Amy Brown is your daughter. What do you intend to do now? You gave up your rights to her a long time ago."

Vanessa surged to her feet, restlessly moving around the living room. She stroked the wooden neck of the carved goose resting on the shelf unit, toyed with the blue ribbons of a grapevine wreath, then paused in front of the old wedding-ring quilt hanging on the stark white wall above the small brick fireplace. Her face was a pale contrast to the brilliant crimson of her blouse.

"I don't want to do anything to hurt her."

"I know that," Summer said softly.

"If I could just be sure she was happy, it would be enough. If I'm sure her parents take good care of her, if they love her..." Vanessa swallowed and blinked rapidly. "Summer, I have to know!"

Summer frowned thoughtfully. "Beryl did mention Amy's mother is ill right now."

"Could you find out for me? Could you ask Mrs. Hatcher about Amy?" Vanessa sat back down, her dark eyes never leaving Summer's face. "Please, Summer. I swear I'm not going to disrupt her life. I won't try to see her or anything. I just have to know she's really all right!"

"I suppose it wouldn't do any harm to ask," Summer began, chewing her lip. "Are you sure? Can't you just let it go?"

"I can't."

Summer sighed. "No, I didn't think so. All right, I'll talk to Beryl."

"You won't say..."

"No, of course not." Summer smiled. "It won't seem out of the ordinary for me to ask about Amy. Beryl's accustomed to my curiosity. I'm touched that you felt you could tell me all this, Van. I won't betray your confidence."

Vanessa stood and gave Summer a brief, fierce hug. "I know. Thank you, Summer. I don't know what I'd do without you."

"What are friends for? Say, how about grabbing a bite to eat? I'm famished, and I know this great barbecue place."

"I just think I want to go home—" Vanessa broke off, groaning. "I forgot. Merl and I are supposed to go out tonight. I don't think I'm up to it."

"Do you want me to call him?"

Vanessa plopped back down on the sofa with a grateful look on her face. "Oh, would you?"

"Sure. I'll tell him you ate too much ice cream or something."

"I'd really appreciate it."

Summer hesitated on the way to the phone. "Van? What about Merl?"

Vanessa glanced down at her hands, her fingers working nervously. "I—I think I'm in love with him."

"Oh." That brought Summer up short. "I mean, ah . . ."

"Will I tell him about my past?" Vanessa shook her head. "I don't know. If things work out between us, someday. Maybe. I don't know," she repeated in a whisper.

"You can cross that bridge when you come to it, Aunt Ollie always says," Summer answered. "Look, I'll make your excuses to Merl, but you don't need to be alone just yet. We'll get something to eat, then you can take me to that boutique you like so much."

"Oh, Summer, I don't think—"

"Please. You've got to help me find a really knockout dress for the Foundation's Bachelor Auction. You never can tell. I might find the man of my dreams there, and I want his eyes to jump right out of their sockets when he sees me. Say you will," she urged. "It'll be fun."

"You know I can never pass up an opportunity to go shopping," Vanessa protested with a weak laugh.

"Good." Summer beamed, pleased that her ploy to take Vanessa's mind off things was going to work. She again headed for the phone. "I'll call Merl and then we'll go."

"Who can resist Jubilee in her bulldozer mode?" Vanessa asked wryly. "And Summer?"

Summer looked up from her dialing. "Hmm?"

Vanessa's dark eyes were eloquent with gratitude. "Thanks."

"IT'S TWENTY BEFORE THE HOUR of eight o'clock and a crisp and fallish fifty-five degrees," Ryder said into the mike. His fingers moved deftly over the control board, pulling levers, while he watched the dials and judged the eighteen-second lead-in on the next song. "And that's the time and temp from WCHT-WROC, AM/FM. Chattanooga's favorite radio station."

The music swelled, then muted as he touched a control. The door to the soundproof booth opened, and Summer breezed in, a stack of mail clenched under one arm and two full coffee cups in her hands.

"Black, two sugars," she said, setting his mug, an electric blue affair with an "I love NY" logo, on the edge of his side of the control table. "Mail came."

"Anything?"

"You check," she said shortly, oddly preoccupied. She slipped onto her high stool and set aside her own steaming cup without tasting it. The mug was a crockery version of an old blue, tin speckleware pattern with a crowing rooster on the side.

Ryder eyed her, his dark brows lifting in mute inquiry. *What's eating her this morning?* he wondered, reaching for the first envelope. Since the staff meeting and the balloon incident, he'd thought there'd been a meeting of minds. But he'd learned the hard way about changeable women. It didn't pay to assume too much. The phone buzzed, and Summer grabbed it.

"Coffee Club. Oh, hello," she muttered, hitting the button that cut off the speaker-phone system and piped the caller directly through the receiver.

Ryder scanned the letter, a request for a public-service promotion, and half listened to her murmured "uh-huhs" and "Is that so's?" He watched her from the corner of his eye, giving her points for the fuzzy pink sweater that subtly outlined the jut of full breasts and the faded denims that fit her sweetly rounded bottom like a second skin. She was small but womanly and lusciously perfect, and he hastily tore his gaze away.

"Duty calls. I'll have to let you go," she said, then paused. "Oh, isn't that sweet? Why don't you mail them to me here at the station, and maybe I'll read them on the air. Yes, thanks. Bye now."

"Boyfriend?" Ryder asked as she hung up.

"Fan. He's writing a poem for me. How about that?"

Ryder pulled a face, and his voice was dry with sarcasm. "Really nifty. Why don't you get us a weather update from the National Weather Service?"

Summer stuck out her tongue at him, but flipped on the small black box that was the station's link to the NWS, dutifully noting the forecast and scrawling it onto a scrap of paper pinned to the board in front of them. She cut it just as the song was ending, checked the log and reached for the typewritten sheet with the next scheduled advertising spot.

"Well, Gulliver, have you heard the latest from the folks down at County Security Systems?" she asked, beginning the spiel. They worked their way through information about portable burglar alarms for homes and apartments, then finished with the address and telephone number.

"And that will about do it for County Security Systems," he concluded and reached for his mug. "Jubilee has just brought in my morning tonic. I knew that woman would be good for something." Summer raised her own forgotten cup to her lips just as he took a deep swig of the hot brew. "Umm," he began, then, "Ya-uck!"

He spluttered, grimacing at the bitter taste of unsugared coffee, while Summer made a face at the cloyingly sweet mixture in her own cup.

"Woman, are you trying to poison me?" he demanded. "You didn't put any sugar in my coffee!"

"So I made a mistake," she said into the mike. "So sue me, Gulliver."

"I want my java!" he mourned comically.

"Such a big baby," she scoffed. "Here, just change cups with me."

"Can't even keep a pair of coffee mugs straight," he teased, exchanging mugs. "Folks, she's a nice girl, but sometimes there aren't any tenants in the penthouse."

He took a cautious sip from her rooster mug, and Summer felt a strange weightless sensation in the pit of her stomach as his lips rested on the place where hers had been just seconds before. The powerful memory of that first morning together, of his mouth on hers in a mind-shattering kiss, sprang full-blown into her mind. It was vastly unsettling. Hastily, almost so fast she sloshed it, she set down his mug, unwilling to taste where he had tasted in a mimicry of that intimate ritual.

"The boss man didn't hire me to be your personal waitress, Gulliver," she returned, scowling fiercely at him and reaching for the announcements list. "From now on, sport, you can fetch your own coffee." She began reading. "The Chattanooga Speech and Hearing—"

"Lord, I've done it now," Ryder interrupted. "You should see the look I'm getting."

Her frown became even darker, and she tried to concentrate on her reading. "—will sponsor an auction next week—"

"If looks could kill," Ryder interrupted again, laughing, "I'd be on my way to a funeral. Hey, Jubilee? Don't you know that it takes more muscles to frown than to smile?"

"So leave me alone," she snapped. "I'm exercising!"

Ryder chuckled and punched a cartridge for the next commercial message. The strident Jitney Grocery jingle trilled in the background. "You're on a roll this morning, sweetheart."

"Quit picking on me, Ryder," she warned, shuffling her papers. "I'm not in the mood for it today."

"Aw, what's the matter, 'lil pardner?" he drawled in an imitation of Duke the Bloodhound. "You got a burr under your saddle blanket?"

Summer glanced away, looking out the oversized, smoked-glass window that gave them a view of downtown

Chattanooga. She could see the river and the corner of her parking garage, as well as a piece of the Convention Center, but it wasn't the view that preoccupied her this morning.

Vanessa's sad revelations of the previous evening worried her, and she was anxious about her promise to probe Beryl for more information about Amy Brown. She wanted to help Vanessa, but what if Van's good intentions failed her? Summer didn't want to be part of anything that hurt an innocent child by dredging up old scandal. And what about Merl? If his heart was involved deeply in his and Vanessa's budding relationship, didn't he have a right to know? But Summer had no right to tell him, to betray Vanessa's confidence, not even to protect Merl. Still, she had promised Vanessa to investigate Amy's background, and she had an appointment to take Lizabeth and her troupe to the Foundation this very afternoon. That didn't give her much time to decide exactly what she was going to do. Caught between loyalty to two friends, she felt in a quandry, and she wasn't up to fielding Ryder's sallies.

"Just leave me alone, if you know what's good for you," she muttered darkly.

The ad finished, and Ryder pushed the On button to his mike. His deep voice was mockingly humorous. "Jubilee's still 'exercising,' folks. But you should see her, she's cute as the dickens when she's what her Aunt Ollie calls 'flustrated'—which unfortunately for ole Gulliver is most of the time."

Summer ground her teeth. Why couldn't that confounded man ever do anything she wanted? She glanced down at the announcement slips, and inspiration struck. Her lips curled into a sly, feline smile.

"Well, now, Gulliver," she purred. "You might ruffle my feathers, but looking at a handsome fellow like you all morning is quite, er—rewarding. In fact, sometimes I feel so-o-o guilty that I'm keeping you all to myself up here at WCHT-WROC."

Ryder's eyes narrowed. What was the little cat up to now? "You don't say?"

Summer leaned toward the microphone, and her deep violet eyes focused on Ryder's face. "Yes, indeed. Billboards and television commercials are fine, but it's not like being in the actual presence of a man who's so..." She paused, and her voice went breathy. "...stimulating."

"Why, Jubilee! Are you trying to lead me on?" Despite the teasing jocularity in Ryder's voice, tiny shivers of sensation feathered along his spine and he shifted uncomfortably.

"Really, ladies, you have no idea what it's like to sit here day after day with this man." Her hyacinth gaze drifted over his features. "Today he's wearing a red flannel shirt that's terrific with his black hair. And he's got the cuffs rolled up halfway—you know the way I mean, showing off those tight, muscled forearms just made for holding a woman close."

"Gee, Jubilee," Ryder drawled. "I had no idea..."

"Girls," Summer said, lowering her voice to a confidential aside. "I have to tell you this man is built. Whipcord lean, and shoulders to die for. Is it any wonder I get all flustered?"

Ryder frowned, wondering just how many citations they could get for this from the FCC. He made a slashing motion across his throat. "Moving right along—"

"And you should see this man move in a pair of jeans," Summer interjected with a deep sigh. "Oh, and those eyes! They're shooting green sparks at me right now, ladies, and I swear I can hardly catch my breath."

"So inhale!" Ryder growled. She was scorching him with her suggestive words, her searching looks, and he felt a familiar tightening in his loins. The little witch! She knew exactly what she was doing to him. Gritting his teeth, he plunged ahead. "It's coming up to the top of the hour, and we'll be having news—"

Summer saw the growing desperation in his eyes and went in for the kill, ignoring her own racing heartbeat.

"The best news is you'll never find a sexier man than Gulliver—except at the Chattanooga Speech and Hearing Foundation's 'Man of Your Dreams' Bachelor Auction. So it's only fair that I offer to share him with the female population of the city."

"What?"

Summer sat back with a triumphant grin. "That's right, ladies. Don't you think Gulliver should participate in this worthy event to benefit the Foundation? Call us up right now at 555-2121 and cast your vote."

"Now wait a minute!" Frantically Ryder reached for the mike's Off button, but Summer simply hit her own controls, overriding manually when he tried to cut her off.

"Ladies, you could buy a night on the town with our very own Gulliver—if the price is right! So phone in right now!" She reached over and hit the toggle that started the next song.

Ryder stared at her in stupefied frustration, then pushed back his chair and stood up, towering over her. He was coldly, furiously angry. "Just what the *hell* do you think you're doing?"

"Volunteering you for a worthy civic cause. It's a great idea, don't you think?"

"Not only no, but *hell no!*" he roared. "Lady, you have blown a fuse! Popped your cork! Hit the wall at Mach Five! If you think I'm going to get up before a bunch of howling females and parade myself around like a stud bull up for sale, you've really lost all your marbles!"

She ignored his tirade, picking up the phone, punching buttons, and speaking quietly into the receiver.

"Are you listening to me?" he shouted.

She placed the receiver face down against her shoulders and smiled sweetly up into his furious face. "Don't you know you can't fight city hall?" she said conversationally.

"What is that supposed to mean?"

She nodded toward the phone. All the lights on its long panel were lit and flashing. "They all want you, Gulliver. Do I have to go back on the air and tell your fans that you're too selfish to have a little fun for the sake of some deserving children?"

"I—you—" He ran his hands through his dark hair and groaned.

"I thought you'd see it my way. The auction is two weeks from today, and you'll need a tux. Oh, and you're to foot the bill for the dream date of your choice. Make it something special, okay?"

"You'll pay for this." He muttered violently under his breath, something about boiling oil and torture racks.

"Don't be such a poor sport," she chided. "Oh, and Ryder?"

"What now!"

Her smile was merry. "Gotcha!"

"THANKS FOR MEETING US," Summer said the next day.

Beryl slid into the bench opposite Summer and Vanessa at a popular Chattanooga pancake house, and smiled as a waitress plopped a plastic-coated menu and glass of water down in front of her.

"Are you kidding? It's not often I get to 'do' lunch with the ladies. And besides, Larry needed some quality time with the kids, otherwise he'd spend the entire Saturday watching the football games on TV."

Summer laughed at Beryl's triumphant attitude. "So we're actually doing you a favor."

"I'll say! East Gate Mall is just across the street, I've got the credit cards, and no kids! It's time to shop 'til I drop."

"Vanessa's motto," Summer groaned in mock despair. "She's determined to find me the right pair of shoes to go with my new dress, even if it kills me."

"You've got no stamina," Vanessa said with a wry tilt of her crimson-painted lips. "From now on consider yourself in training."

"In that case, let's eat!" Summer replied.

They gave the waitress their orders for gourmet hamburgers. Beryl took a long drink from her iced tea, then fixed her bright, inquisitive eyes on the other two women.

"So, what's all this about Amy Brown?"

Summer glanced at Vanessa, then plunged into her spiel. "Ah, there's someone who'd like to help Amy stay in the Brownies, and—"

"Actually," Vanessa interrupted, "it's me. I was so taken with her the other day, I wanted to know more about her. And when Summer told me her mother was sick—"

"Really, her foster mother," Beryl interjected.

Vanessa's dark eyes grew wide and startled. "She's in foster care?" she asked carefully.

"Oh, yes. Has been for years. The Oateses are lovely people, and they've raised a series of foster kids, but they're getting on now. Amy's 'Nanny Barb' is more like a grandmother, I'd say."

"I—I thought she was an adopted child." There was a painful edge to Vanessa's voice.

Beryl tore open the cellophane wrapper of a pack of crackers and munched thoughtfully. "No, as far as I know, she's always been a foster child. A handicapped child is so much harder to place in a permanent home, you know."

"Her hearing...how bad is it?" Vanessa asked tightly. "Has it been...from birth?"

"No. I'd have to check the records, but I think it was the result of a high fever as an infant. She's about fifty percent impaired. It happens sometimes that way. It's no one's fault, of course."

Vanessa made a small pained sound, and Summer hastened to ask a question. "Is she in a good home, Beryl? I mean, is Amy happy there?"

"I'd say so. She's smart and well-adjusted. Of course, a younger couple might be able to offer more time and involvement with a lively eight-year-old, but her circumstances are no different from many other kids'."

"You mean because of the Oates's age, they can't do as many things with Amy?" Vanessa asked. "What if someone . . . what if *I* wanted to spend some time with her? You know, doing the things her foster parents can't."

"I see no problem with that," Beryl replied. "The social-service people encourage Big Sister and Big Brother programs in the community. But it's a commitment, Vanessa," she warned. "These children grow to depend on you. It's not something you can just stop when the novelty wears off."

"I understand. I'm willing to take that responsibility."

Summer chewed her lip. Being privy to Vanessa's real reason for wanting to be close to Amy gave her an uncomfortable awareness of her own responsibility in this. Any number of things could happen, and some of them might be disastrous for Amy.

"I think you should think this over carefully," she said to Vanessa.

"But I really want to do it," the brunette said.

Beryl nodded in approval. "If you're determined, I'll give you the social-service number and Mrs. Oates's number, as well. It's an opportune moment. Mrs. Oates admitted she'd felt too bad to take Amy shopping for school clothes like she wanted. She probably wouldn't mind a little help."

Vanessa's high laugh was frenetic, her eyes too bright. "Well, that's one department I can certainly handle!"

"I'm sure you'll make a terrific Big Sister," Beryl said. She dug in her purse for a ballpoint pen, and scribbled the phone numbers on a scrap of paper. Vanessa accepted it as if it were made of gold.

"I hope you know what you're doing," Summer muttered.

"For the first time in a long while, I think I do," Vanessa said. She carefully folded the piece of paper away. Her dark eyes were liquid with gratitude. "Thanks, Beryl. You'll never know how much I appreciate this."

"You're welcome. And while we're being so polite, I have to thank you, J.J., for getting Gulliver to participate in the bachelor auction. I can't believe you talked him into it."

"Neither can he, but anything for a good cause," Summer said with a smile.

The waitress appeared with their orders and began unloading their plates onto the table. Beryl reached for the catsup bottle and splashed a pool of the thick red stuff onto her French fries.

"Well, I don't care how you did it," she said, popping a fry into her mouth. "Just as long as he shows up."

"Don't worry," Summer replied, determination and mischief glinting in her eyes. "He'll be there."

"WHERE IS HE?" Beryl hissed.

"Don't worry. He'll be here!"

I hope, Summer thought. Snagging a glass of white wine from the circulating waiter, she sipped the crisp Chablis and crossed her fingers. Ryder's reluctance to participate in the "Man of Your Dreams" Bachelor Auction hadn't abated during the past two weeks, but she could have sworn he'd show up tonight. Backed into a corner or not, he was a man of his word—at least she'd thought so.

"We'll have to adjust the program if he doesn't," Beryl said in a worried tone. "Thank goodness he's last, but I'm afraid half of the women here came just to have a chance to bid on Gulliver!"

Summer scanned the Convention Center's ballroom. Scores of beautiful, well-dressed women had paid admission to the event for the opportunity to rub elbows with some of Chattanooga's most eligible bachelors. Circulating among the guests at this pre-auction cocktail party were a city councilman, a motorcycle racing champion, a plastic surgeon, a handful of assorted executives, a football player, a TV anchorman, and several more debonair and exciting men-about-town. But no Gulliver.

"He knows I'll wring his neck if he doesn't come through for you," Summer said to reassure Beryl. "He'll *be* here."

"If you say so." Beryl looked pretty in aqua chiffon, but her attitude was harried. "I swear I'll never get involved in anything like this again. From now on, it's bingo and cake sales. This is too nerve-racking!"

"You've got a great turnout, and the Foundation is going to make gobs of money. Now quit fretting and enjoy."

"Easy for you to say. Although you look like a dream. Where did you find that dress?"

Summer glanced down at the wide, floor-length skirt of her black and white pin-dotted gown. Strapless, it sported a tiny bolero jacket of reverse fabric. It was an old-fashioned dress made in an eighties fabric, and she felt extremely feminine in the rustling petticoats she wore to make the skirt stand out. She'd twisted her hair into a loose knot on top of her head and curled wispy tendrils at temples and nape. Aunt Ollie's pearls were her only ornament.

"Vanessa took me to a shop she knows. Do you like it? It's not too much?" she asked.

Beryl shook her head, her bright eyes admiring. "It's super. In fact, we may have trouble keeping the bachelors away from *you*."

Summer laughed. "Flatterer. But keep it up." The mention of Vanessa sent her thoughts skittering away on another tangent. "By the way, thanks for helping out with Vanessa's questions the other day."

"I wish there were a hundred more like her. She's really taking this volunteer thing with Amy seriously, isn't she?"

"I—I think she's very fond of Amy already," Summer hedged. Her conscience gave a guilty twinge.

"Mrs. Oates mentioned how kind she'd been when I went by to get Amy for Brownies. She hadn't been feeling well, and Vanessa's help really means a lot to her. Mrs. Oates said Vanessa took Amy shopping twice, and then to the Confederama so Amy could do a school report. They're getting along so well Mrs. Oates said Amy was disappointed Vanessa had to go out of town this weekend."

"Yes, she'd made plans with Merl to visit his parents in Alabama," Summer murmured. Her next question was cautious. "You don't think she's spending too much time with Amy, do you?"

"No, of course not. I think her interest is lovely. Oh, praise the saints!" Beryl said suddenly. "There he is!"

Summer turned and caught her breath, all her worrisome thoughts immediately banished. Ryder, resplendent in an inky black tux and spotlessly white pleated shirt, paused near the entrance. He was a sight to behold, his handsome features dark and hawklike, the stance of his lean body emanating sheer maleness, an untamed virility that his civilized garb merely emphasized. He briefly scanned the crowd. When he spotted Summer standing with Beryl, he started threading his way through the crush and turning quite a few inquisitive, feminine heads in the process.

"Mr. Bowman," Beryl gushed. "We're so glad to have you here tonight."

"My pleasure, Mrs. Hatcher," Ryder said smoothly. His hazel gaze flicked to Summer in a swift assessment. The corner of his mouth twitched. "Jubilee Jones, as I live and breathe! And on your way to the ball, I see."

"Hello, Ryder," she said, smoothing her full skirts self-consciously. She was acutely aware that his gaze had scored her flesh where the flaring lapels of her bodice revealed the soft curve of her bosom. The sudden wish that she had swathed herself with black burlap from throat to ankles made her voice tart. "It appears Gulliver is in inimitable form tonight. Just be careful you don't turn into a pumpkin."

He laughed, then surprised her by catching her upper arms, leaning forward, and planting a tiny kiss of greeting beside her ear, just as though he hadn't seen her only a few hours earlier at the station. "When is this cattle show supposed to start?" he murmured. "I'm ready to get it over with."

Summer pulled back, striving to keep the breathless note from her voice. "I—I'm sure you're very eager for the festivities to begin, Ryder, but first you're supposed to mingle."

"Well, considering all the local talent I see," he said, letting his gaze slide across the feminine throng, several whom were even now waiting expectantly just outside their little circle, "that shouldn't be a hardship. Excuse me, ladies. I'll see you on the block."

"Golly, what a heartbreaker." Beryl sighed.

Summer took a hasty gulp of her wine and fumed. Darn it! Ryder wasn't supposed to *enjoy* this. She set her empty glass on a table and snagged another from a passing waiter. "Don't tell me you're smitten, too, with that—that Gulliver!"

Beryl gave Summer a shrewd look, then began to laugh.

"What?" Summer demanded.

Beryl continued to giggle, waving her plump hands in a deprecating gesture. "Oh, nothing. Just that Jubilee seems to have met her match."

"That'll be the day!" Summer snorted. She linked arms with Beryl. "Come on, introduce me to those other gorgeous guys. I want to mingle, too. I didn't spend all that money on this dress to waste a chance like this!"

She made the rounds with Beryl, laughing and talking, checking out the bachelors, whom she had to admit were all they were supposed to be, charming, witty, urbane and sexy. Why, then, did none of them excite her like that infuriating Ryder Bowman? His deep laughter raked across her nerve endings more than once, and she was always faintly aware of his position in the room, and of the blonde, or brunette, or redhead who was invariably clinging to his arm and listening breathlessly to his every word.

Beryl went to check on things backstage, and Summer went to the refreshment table to find a drink.

"Well, hello, stranger," a voice said beside her. "Long time no see."

Summer turned with a smile for an old friend. "Tony! How have you been?"

Tony Keatchum ran a hand over his expertly coiffed blond hair and favored Summer with one of the brilliant white smiles that had made him such a favorite of local television viewers. "Just fine. Busy."

"I can tell." She gestured at his briefcase with the TV station logo on the side and the tall black cameraman who accompanied him. "How did they miss a good-looking bachelor like you? You should be parading in front of the camera tonight instead of behind it."

"Thanks, but these guys have got more guts than I do! I'll stick to reporting the action tonight, if you don't mind. It ought to be quite a show, though."

Summer laughed. "That's what most of the participants are afraid of. Oh, there's Beryl signaling me. I've got to go."

"Listen, I'll call you sometime. We'll go out and have a few laughs," Tony offered.

"Fine," Summer said vaguely, knowing it was one of those things people said to each other that they had no intention of pursuing. She and Tony were friends and nothing more. In a way, she thought, as she moved through the crush toward the stage, it might have been better if she could have had some feelings for Tony. Then she wouldn't be so fuddled by everything Ryder said and did!

As Summer went backstage, she saw Ryder out of the corner of her eye, gently disentangling himself from a statuesque, titian-tressed beauty. Summer took an instant dislike to the brazen hussy, and turned away in a bit of a huff, her expression sour that Ryder's discomfiture hadn't lived up to her mental images when she'd conceived this prank. A sudden thought occurred, and she smiled to herself. Ryder might have been able to handle a throng of fawning lovelies with great aplomb, but marching around onstage while they shouted bids was bound to make him uncomfortable. She flipped through her cards containing the biographical information on each bachelor and considered the prospect with a smidgeon of malicious glee. This she had to see!

The auction went smoothly, and with a great deal of hilarity. It was Summer's duty to introduce each candidate up for bid, and explain his dream date. Then a professional auctioneer, Sam Greenberg, would conduct the bidding. Beryl had thought the auctioneer's singsong chant would keep the excitement up and induce the women to bid higher, and her expectations were certainly met.

The plastic surgeon who offered himself and a weekend in Bimini went for top dollar to a sixty-five-year-old grandmother. A sleek real estate agent came away with the brawny football star, and the politician who promised a romantic tour of the state legislature was snapped up by a bespectacled but voluptuous senior law student who offered, in return, to let him examine her briefs. Finally it was Ryder's turn.

"...one of Chattanooga's most popular air personalities," Summer read. "A dynamic deejay, Gulliver!"

Ryder took his place onstage, grinning easily into the spotlight. He turned to Summer and winked, then began the mandatory stroll around the protruding ramp. He sauntered around in his usual, long-limbed gait, but Summer wasn't fooled. She was suddenly cheerful. He was hating this! Her voice sounded perky and teasing over the public-address system.

"Actually, it's nice to see all of Gulliver's fans in one room." There was a round of appreciative laughter, and Summer grinned. "Meet John Ryder Bowman, award-winning journalist and presently CEO of the Bowman Network. He lists his hobbies as hang gliding and jogging. He likes all kinds of love songs, getting up early, and anything sweet. Gulliver won't disclose the destination of your date, but says it will be a trip straight up to heaven."

The last evoked a chorus of hoots, and Summer slapped down her card on the podium and grinned at the audience. She gestured toward Ryder, whose ears were turning a bit red, the only sign that he wasn't as cool as he looked. "I can't vouch for that, but let me tell you, ladies, you can believe this rascal about as far as you can throw him! So if you like living dangerously, get ready to bid on the famous—or infamous, as the case may be—Gulliver! Over to you, Mr. Greenberg."

"Who'll gimme ten, who'll gimme ten..." The auctioneer's melodic drone started fast and picked up pace.

Summer's eyes darted back and forth over the crowd, catching the signals and shouted bids from a flattering assortment of women. The bidding skyrocketed, and one by one they began to drop out as the ante got too high. Finally it was down to a petite brunette in a blue-spangled miniskirt and the titian-haired beauty, and a battle royal ensued, with Mr. Greenberg egging the combatants on with his energetic chant. Ryder looked a bit lost center stage, as if he didn't quite know what to do with his hands. The lights of the Minicam warred with the stage lights as Tony's assistant recorded the heated bidding for the late news.

"Got six, gimme six-fifty," Mr. Greenberg offered, pointing to the brunette. She hesitated, then reluctantly shook her head, declining the bid. Greenberg focused on the redhead, who smiled like a cat lapping cream and arched her milk-white shoulders in an attitude of victory.

"Six hundred dollar bid for Gulliver," said Greenberg. He looked over the crowd, and Summer did, too, but all the faces were silent and expectant. Out of the corner of her eye, she saw Tony instruct his cameraman to move closer. She shot a quick glance at Ryder, only to find all his attention diverted to the redhead. His eyes were hooded, smoky slits, and his mouth quirked with humor and anticipation.

"That's six hundred going once..."

The sultry redhead pursed her carmine-painted lips and puckered an imaginary kiss at Ryder. There was a curious tightening in Summer's stomach. Her face felt hot, and her hands felt cold.

"Six hundred going twice . . ."

Ryder began a slow smile, revealing that devastating dimple for the redhead's perusal. Summer's throat worked. Greenberg lifted his gavel to close the bid.

"One thousand dollars for Gulliver!"

Greenberg's gavel hung suspended in midair, and a stunned silence hung over the amazed crowd. The redhead scowled in astonished defeat, but no on was more surprised than Summer.

Incredibly *she* had shouted that outrageous bid!

CHAPTER EIGHT

"GOING ONCE, going twice, sold!"

The auctioneer's hammer fell, sealing the bid and Summer's fate with its decisive knell.

Summer's stomach tumbled in a series of acrobatic flip-flops punctuated by the audience's approving applause. Whatever had possessed her to make such a crazy bid? She took one look at the growing thundercloud on Ryder's brow and knew she would have to brazen this out or look the fool. She leaned toward the microphone on the podium, her mouth curved into a mischievous, unrepentant smile.

"Sorry, ladies, but Gulliver's gotten the best of me so many times on the air, I couldn't resist having him obligated to do my bidding at least for one evening. Get ready to sweep me off my feet, Gulliver!"

The crowd laughed and clapped, all except the fuming redhead. Summer glided across the stage toward Ryder, a smile plastered on her face and her heart tripping double-time against her chest.

"What are you up to now?" he murmured suspiciously as she drew near.

Summer took his arm, waving at the audience and the television camera trained on them. "Smile," she ordered between clenched teeth. "You're spoiling the image."

"Right."

The grin that split his face should have warned her, but she was unprepared when he scooped her up and slung her over his shoulder as if she were a sack of chicken feed. Summer yelped in surprise, and the audience roared. Ryder

gathered her voluminous skirts with one arm and gave
Summer a playful swat. "What's the matter, Jubilee?" he
asked over his shoulder. "Didn't you tell me to sweep you
off your feet?"

Hanging upside down, Summer batted her eyelashes at
the crowd, and feigned an adoring sigh. "I just love a man
who follows orders, don't you?"

She felt Ryder's involuntary snort of laughter, the massive shoulder beneath her stomach jouncing her and making her own giggles disjointed and breathless. Ryder
marched offstage to thunderous applause, waving trium-
phantly while Summer threw kisses with both hands.

"That was great!" Backstage, Beryl was laughing so hard
her cheeks looked like red rubber balls. She wiped tears of
mirth from the corners of her eyes. "What a finale! You two
are terrific together. Why didn't you tell me what you had
planned?"

Ryder eased Summer to her feet. She blinked as the blood
rushed out of her brain and half leaned against him for
support while her head cleared. Hastily adjusting her dress,
she gave thanks that the strapless design hadn't failed her
during this bit of shenanigans.

"Planned?" she echoed. "I'm as surprised as you are!"
Ryder's hand was firm and disturbing against the small of
her back, and she stepped away to retrieve her jacket and
bag from Beryl. "What I have to know is—will you take a
check?"

"Well, er, sure," Beryl stammered, casting Ryder a tim-
orous glance. "Yours was the top bid tonight, but are you
certain..."

Summer made swift mental calculations and decided a
depleted bank account for a worthy cause was a small price
to pay for the evening's fun. Opening her bag, she pulled
out a pen and her checkbook and scribbled the amount of
the donation. "Of course I'm certain. I needed a tax de-
duction, anyway. Besides," she added, casting her partner

a wry look as she handed Beryl the check, "it was worth every penny to watch Ryder squirm!"

"You have a warped sense of humor, Jubilee," Ryder returned. He jammed his fists into his pants pockets and thoughtfully tongued the inside of his cheek. "Expensive, but twisted."

"You're just pouting because you had your heart set on that imitation Ann-Margret."

"And now I'm stuck with Shirley Temple again, right?"

Summer placed her forefinger under her chin and dipped a wide-eyed curtsy. "Welcome aboard the *Good Ship Lollipop*." She broke off as Beryl dissolved into another spate of giggles, and her own smile quirked mischievously. "Relax, Ryder, you're off the hook. It's great publicity, that's all, and isn't that what you're always telling me we need? Don't worry, I won't hold you to the date."

"Not so fast," he drawled. "You paid for me, lady, and now you're going to get me!"

Summer's smile died by degrees, and a tiny chill of premonition made her shiver. "That's not necessary. I'll let you buy the doughnuts next week if you feel obligated."

"Uh-uh. I've already got everything arranged, and you're going."

"You mean right now?" Summer squeaked.

"Oh, go ahead," Beryl interjected. "You might as well take advantage of it as long as he's being a good sport."

"That's right," Ryder agreed, his voice a husky challenge. His eyes sparkled, seeming more green than hazel. "I just want to make certain you get your money's worth. Besides, this way I don't have to spring for the tux rental twice."

"Spoken like a true gentleman," Summer retorted. She studied him warily. "Do you plan to feed me?"

"But, of course."

"Arsenic, I'll bet," she muttered.

Beryl giggled, and gave Summer a nudge in the ribs with her elbow. "Go on. Double-dog-dare-you. Don't be a sissy."

"That's right, Summer," Ryder taunted gently. "I promise the hot dogs I've laid on don't have a grain of poison. Of course, the nitrates and preservatives will do the job eventually, anyway."

"Sounds delightful."

Knowing she should stick to her guns, positive she ought to have her head examined for even considering a "date" with Ryder Bowman after what she'd pulled on him, Summer nevertheless found herself tempted. Curiosity warred with caution. She wondered exactly what he'd planned for the dream date he would have been sharing with the statuesque redhead this very moment if she hadn't stepped in. She was certain it wasn't hot dogs. It might be interesting to see Ryder in a new environment. Besides, she was starving.

"All right," she said. "You're on. Let's see if the fabulous Gulliver knows how to treat a lady." She knew she'd left herself wide open with that one and pointed a swift, cautionary finger at his nose. "Don't say it!"

Ryder pretended to be affronted. "You play dirty, lady."

"Well, you can't. Not tonight."

"Very well, Cinderella." Ryder assisted her into her short jacket and tucked her hand into the crook of his arm. "Your carriage awaits."

"Have a good time, kids," Beryl said.

Summer shot Beryl a dubious glance, then allowed Ryder to guide her through a maze of halls and out the rear door of the building. The pale yellow glow of a streetlight illuminated the empty alley, and the air was crisp and cool with a faint whisper of wood smoke and fall. Summer lifted her skirts to save them from the damp concrete and gazed curiously at Ryder.

"Is it midnight already?" she asked.

"Even Cinderella has to have a little faith." He tugged her forward until they reached the opening of the alley. Wait-

ing beside the curb was a uniformed chauffeur and a long
white limousine.

Summer's eyes grew wide. "Wow. I take it all back."

"Good evening, miss," the driver said, opening the car
door. "I hope you'll have an enjoyable time."

"Why, thank you," Summer murmured, allowing him to
hand her into the spacious interior. She sank into the deep
leather seat and looked around, fascinated.

"Thanks, Carlisle," Ryder said, climbing in beside Summer. "We'll proceed to the first stop now, please."

"Very good, sir. Just sit back and enjoy the ride." Carlisle slammed the door and went around to the driver's side.
Summer noticed that the smoke-gray privacy panel was in
place. She was certain the back seat, with its own small refrigerator, stereo system and bar, took up at least a quarter
of an acre.

She caught Ryder's eye and smiled. "What, no Ja-
cuzzi?"

"In the trunk," he said, chuckling. Opening the refrigerator, he removed a small plate. "Hors d'oeuvre?"

Summer's eyebrows arched. "Caviar?"

"Russian."

"Hmm." She chose a small morsel and nibbled deli-
cately. "I can see you've put some thought into this date."

"Most assuredly." Ryder poured a blush wine into a
crystal goblet and offered it to her. "Wine?"

"Why not?" She sipped and didn't try to stifle a sigh of
pleasure. "Lovely."

"I'm glad you like it."

Summer laughed delightedly. "Ryder, I'm amazed. This
is fun!"

"It can be."

An involuntary sigh escaped her. "I suppose I should
apologize. I know you'd much rather be sitting here with
that long-legged redhead. I really put a spoke in your wheel,
didn't I?"

Ryder shrugged. "Let's just say I found the entire experience fascinating." His tone grew low, and his gaze touched her face, her lips. "But things have turned out satisfactorily. Quite satisfactorily, indeed."

He touched a button and soft music flooded the car. Stretching out his long legs, he sipped from his own glass. Their shoulders touched. The interior of the limo was a quiet oasis of luxury, and very intimate.

Summer felt a curious mixture of pleasure and wariness. Did he really prefer her company over a knockout redhead? It was probably only so that he could have her close at hand when he decided to take his revenge, she thought dryly, then scoffed at her own suspicious nature. Maybe she should take things at face value. Perhaps for once they could shelve any lingering antagonism and merely enjoy each other's company. She knew Ryder could be charming when he cared to, but there was danger in that. It was best for her peace of mind to keep things light. She took another sip from her glass, then made a point of examining the floor, the ceiling, even under the seat.

"What are you looking for?" he asked.

"Just checking. After caviar, wine and music, I wondered where you were hiding the heart-shaped bed."

He smiled. "You know, I failed to ask if that was an optional or standard feature." The vehicle slowed, turned, came to a halt. "But I guess we'll have to wait until later to explore the possibilities."

He reached for her glass, and their fingers brushed. Hazel eyes delved deeply into pansy-colored ones. Her pulse jumped nervously at the intensity of his gaze, and she pulled away. "Where are we?"

Deliberately he set aside their glasses. "First things first," he said, sliding his arm over her shoulders.

Startled, Summer's eye widened fractionally. "First?" she croaked.

"Yes." He paused, and his smile was devilish. "First, we have dinner."

The atmosphere of The Loft restaurant was a subtle blend of candlelight and elegance. The food was superb, the service excellent, and Ryder the perfect companion. They talked about everything except the radio station. Gulliver and Jubilee had been left behind, and it was only Ryder and Summer who ate prime rib and discussed books and music and the news. Ryder told her some of his more amusing experiences as a reporter. She talked about her family and her puppet troupe, and about growing up with Beryl as a neighbor. The conversation never languished, and they lingered over their coffee, reluctant to break the easy camaraderie.

"That was a marvelous meal," Summer said with a sigh. She sat back in her chair and smiled across the table at Ryder. "And nary a hot dog in sight."

His lips twitched. "Disappointed?"

"Maybe just a tad," she teased. She liked to see him smile, enjoyed provoking that wonderful dimple. When it appeared, as it had now, it did funny things to her insides.

He'd never known a woman with the temerity to tease him so audaciously, he thought, watching her. She might be impulsive, tempestuous, even occasionally foolhardy, but she met life with such joy, such vitality, such *feeling* that he couldn't help but feel a bit envious. He distrusted emotion in himself, but in her it was all light and fire and energy. More than her physical beauty—and in the soft glow of candlelight that was enough to take his breath away—it was her inner vibrancy that intrigued him. He hadn't expected to spend the evening with her, but then when had she ever done as he expected? Insisting they follow through with this romantic evening had been his way of regaining control of the situation. Outmaneuvered by a feisty sprite of a woman, he'd broken his own resolve to keep their relationship on a professional footing for the chance to pay her back in kind. Now he wondered if he'd made a strategic error.

What the hell! he thought, struck by an uncharacteristic recklessness. *One evening together won't do any harm.*

And, he had to admit, for once it was very pleasant to be with her without their continual verbal sparring. She was an entertaining and eloquent lady when she let down her prickly guard. Her pale gold hair was haloed by the flickering illumination, giving her an ethereal, almost angelic appearance, but her smile was enough to tempt the devil in any man. He suddenly realized that if he didn't touch her soon he was going to go crazy. He held out his hand.

"Dance with me?"

Something flickered behind her amethyst eyes. She bit her lip and glanced toward the lounge where a small combo played softly. "You don't have to keep up the pretense. It's not like this is a real date or anything, and besides I really should be getting home..."

"Summer." His deep voice was like a caress across her bare skin. "When are you going to realize that I *never* do anything I don't really want to do?"

"Oh." She blinked. "But I practically forced you to participate in the auction."

"True. But if I hadn't decided it was a good idea, there wouldn't have been a snowball's chance in hell of me showing up. The night's still young, and I intend to make the most of it. So come dance with me. Or are you afraid?" Her chin went up at the challenge, as he'd known it would.

"You have an inflated opinion of yourself, Bowman. I'm not afraid of anything." She smiled sweetly and placed her hand in his. "I was merely having some consideration for your advanced age, but if you think you're up to it, let's go."

Brave words, she decided moments later, and an utter lie. Pressed close to Ryder's hard lean strength, swaying slowly to the evocative tempo of a love song, she was deeply afraid that she had made a major miscalculation. At arm's length, she could deal with this enigmatic man, but with the warmth of his large hand pressed firmly against the small of her back and the clean scent of starch and spicy after-shave and man permeating her senses, she was dizzily aware of her vulnerability. A secret yearning began to unfold deep within her.

It was a mistake, he admitted to himself. Dancing was merely an excuse to hold her, and everything he'd remembered about the brief embrace he'd stolen the morning of their debut was merely a shadow of the reality. The delicate floral perfume that tantalized, the expanse of bare, creamy shoulders that begged to be stroked, the way she fit against him, so small and womanly—everything combined to produce an ache that couldn't be denied or ignored.

The music flowed over, around them, and they made patterns together on the dance floor, oblivious to everything except each other.

He feels so good, she thought helplessly.

She feels so soft, he thought and nearly groaned.

It's been so long.

It's been too long.

He could hurt me, came the warning whisper.

I could hurt her, his conscience murmured.

I'm crazy, she thought helplessly.

This is crazy! he thought and groaned.

Ryder pulled back slightly and looked down at Summer. Her expression was as dazed as he felt, and it was his undoing. When he spoke, his voice was thick. "Let's get out of here."

It was the cool night air and Carlisle's polite presence that jolted Summer from the sensual spell of Ryder's nearness. For a while she'd indulged in a fantasy, but it was just that, a bit of unreality sparked by the night magic and an awareness she could not control. She knew better than that! she chided herself, and drew a cooling breath into her overheated lungs. The wine had muddled her head, she decided. She must bring the evening to a speedy conclusion before she made a fool out of herself. Not waiting for Ryder, she scrambled into the limousine and plunked down in the far corner, nervously adjusting her billowing skirts.

"Does Carlisle know my address?" she asked as Ryder joined her, and the limo purred through the still-busy Chattanooga streets.

"I'll take you home. After the surprise." He took her hand and twined his fingers with hers.

"It's late," she said, trying to ignore the warmth of his touch, and failing miserably. "I should be getting home . . . what surprise?"

His low chuckle made her breathing uncomfortably short. "You'll see."

And that was all he'd say, except to smile and absently stroke her hand with the callused edge of his thumb. By the time they reached their destination, St. Elmo Station, Summer was breathless and her pulse was erratic. Thankfully he released her to assist her from the vehicle.

"Here we are," he said.

Puzzled, she looked around at the darkened buildings, the white columns and fences shining dully in the glow of a turn-of-the-century gaslight, the cross ties and steel rails dark silhouettes against the gray rock of the rail bed. Behind the station rose the dark bulk of Lookout Mountain sporting a faint, fairy-dusting of lights across the distant ridge that was barely discernible from the star-studded, midnight sky.

"The Incline Railway?" she asked. "But Ryder, it's closed."

"Not for us."

Like magic, the lights came on all over the station and inside the red car waiting to make its nearly vertical climb. An attendant poked his head out of the station house door and waved to them.

"Come on." Ryder took her arm, and they climbed the ramp that wound around to the entrance of the car. Built like a staircase, the seats inside were arranged on descending levels. "Be careful," he warned, helping her down the steep grade to the lowest level that faced tall glass windows. Glass surrounded them on all sides of the car, including the roof above.

As a Chattanooga native, Summer had ridden the Incline Railway many times. Proclaimed the steepest and safest passenger railway in the world, many residents on the mountain used it to commute into the city, especially during the icy winter months when the winding highway that scaled the mountain was at its most treacherous. But Summer had never ridden it without a crowd of tourists as companions, and certainly never in the middle of the night!

"I'm impressed," Summer said, sitting down on the front seat amid a billow of skirts. Ryder slid in beside her, his arm resting on the tubular steel handrail behind her shoulders. "How did you manage it?" she asked.

"Let's just say that I am not without influence in this town." Reaching behind the seat, he came back with a single long-stemmed red rose tied in silver ribbons and presented it to her with a flourish. "For a lovely lady."

"Oh, how beautiful." She buried her nose in the velvety petals and drank in the rich perfume. But her pleasure was tempered by a taunting inner voice that reminded her he'd already admitted he wasn't the kind to send flowers. The romantic gesture was merely window-dressing, a detail not to be overlooked when planning a dream date for an unknown companion, and not specifically intended as an emotional statement to one Summer Jones. Her lips curved in a wry smile. "You don't miss a trick, do you?"

Ryder frowned, but the lights suddenly went out, and with a screeching lurch, the car jerked into motion. Startled, Summer made a grab for the handrail, missed, and came up with a handful of Ryder's lapel.

"Oops, sorry." She let go, shifting uneasily on the slippery seat, bracing herself with her high-heeled shoes to prevent herself from sliding forward as the car creaked and swayed.

"Here, get comfortable," Ryder said, putting his arm over her shoulders and pulling her against him. He tugged loose his black bow tie and shoved it into his jacket pocket, and released his collar button. "We've got about a twenty-minute ride, so relax and enjoy the view."

Moving up the mountainside, away from the glare of street lights and surrounded on both sides of the track by a dense growth of tall trees, the interior of the car was nearly black. Perhaps the womblike darkness gave her courage, but she found herself doing his bidding, enjoying the man-warmth of his chest against her shoulder.

"This seems so atypical of you," she said as they rose higher and higher, and the lights of the city unrolled beneath them. "When was the last time you stopped to admire the view?"

"About thirty seconds before the lights went out. I was looking at you."

For a long moment, Summer was struck silent, then she laughed softly, a tremulous sound in the noisy railcar. "Compliments, too? You've really done your homework for this, haven't you?"

It annoyed him that she doubted his sincerity. Still, what else should he expect? She was as skittish as a new colt, and he sensed her tension, her wariness. "You don't give yourself enough credit, Summer," he murmured, then straightened slightly. "Look, we're going to pass the other car."

Rumbling and rattling, the car they rode moved to one side as the track split into a section of two small parallel tracks halfway up the mountain. Based on the principle of cuckoo-clock weights, the twin cars were joined by a cable pulled through the machine room at the moutaintop terminal. When one came up, the other went down, and halfway between they met for a moment. The other car flashed past them, then the degree of the incline rapidly increased as the uppermost car began the final ascent.

Summer tilted her head back against Ryder's arm and gazed into the starry skies above their heads. The city lights spilled across the Tennessee River valley below in a golden splash of illumination.

"This is marvelous," she said, trailing the rose across her lips. "Very imaginative."

"It's different, at least. Do you think you're getting your money's worth?"

Summer smiled into the darkness, her eyes searching out the darker profile that was his face. "Absolutely. You really know how to show a lady a good time." A thought struck her. "I get it now. This is the part of the date that's supposed to be a trip to heaven, isn't it?"

"No," he muttered on a strange note. "This is."

His mouth on hers was more than a surprise. It was a revelation. Summer had never guessed this hard, decisive man was capable of such gentle wooing. His lips were warm and pliant and persuasive, and she felt herself melting, dissolving, opening to him. Seconds passed before he pulled away, their lips clinging, their breaths mingling in an erratic whirlwind.

"You—you have a pretty high opinion of your abilities, don't you?" she said unsteadily, her fingers clenching the rose stem as if to draw strength and sanity from the blood-red blossom.

"You're not the only one who's taking this trip." He nibbled along her jawline, and she shivered uncontrollably. "I'm along for the ride, too."

He gently bit the tender lobe of her ear, and she gasped. Her hands were against his chest, resisting. "Ryder, please. You don't have to do this to prove to me what a hot date you are."

He jerked back, and his large hands framed her face almost angrily. "I told you I never do anything I don't want to. And right now I want very badly to kiss you again."

"But—"

His voice was a ragged murmur. "For God's sake, Summer, for once will you just shut up?"

His mouth dammed her reply most effectively, then she forgot entirely what she meant to say in the consuming magic of his kiss. Skillfully his lips plied hers, tantalizing her, sparking a need deep inside her. His thumbs etched the sensitive corners of her mouth in a delicate stroking, and her lips parted. Groaning, he deepened the kiss, seeking with his tongue all the moist, secret places while he gathered her close against his heart. Her hands slid up around his neck, slipping inside his collar to trace the strong cords of his neck and feel the pulse that thundered in time with her own.

There was no time, no place; just the two of them, suspended somewhere between heaven and earth. Which made the return to reality all the more shocking when the railcar lurched to a screeching halt, and the lights came on. Blinded by the glare, breathing hard, they separated, scorched by the brief but violent flare of mutual passion. Ryder stood, and Summer saw him swallow. Nervously she licked her lips. The taste of him was ripe and full against her tongue, and she nearly whimpered. Grabbing her hand, Ryder hauled her to her feet.

"End of the line, honey. Let's go."

He led her up the staircase of the car, out onto the concrete platform that formed the terminal and overlook, through the wide hall past the darkened gift shops and snack bar, past the unmanned video games and twenty-five-cent kiddie rides so tempting to the unwary tourist. The hall led directly to the street, a narrow two-lane highway that circled the mountain. Ryder paused on the deserted sidewalk, then turned uphill.

"Where are we going?" Summer asked. His kiss had robbed her of most of her breath, and now this forced march up the sidewalk was taking what little remained.

"My car's parked in the lot of the gift shop across from Point Park," he said, referring to the national park where the famous Civil War "Battle Above the Clouds" was fought. "Feel up to a constitutional?"

"I don't have much choice, it seems."

"It's only three blocks."

"Uphill. And you're not wearing high heels," she complained, puffing. "What's the hurry?"

He stopped so suddenly she slammed into him, then his arms were around her. "Lady, you've got to be kidding," he muttered, and kissed her hard, almost desperately. Her head was swimming when he finally released her. Arm circling her waist, he half led, half carried her up the sidewalk past the darkened homes lining both sides of the street.

"I wish you'd stop that," she said fretfully. "I can't think when you kiss me like that."

"So don't think." His voice was a dark, husky chuckle. "That's nothing new for you, is it, sweetheart?"

"Beast."

"I love it when you talk dirty."

"You're impossible!" She laughed, excited and exhilarated.

"That's me. Here we are." He stopped beside a dove-gray Mercedes Coupe. On the other side of the street the crenellated stone towers of the park entrance rose like sentinels against the faraway illumination of the city. His dark head bent again, and he placed a brief kiss against her soft lips. He pulled back, muttering, then grabbed her waist and lifted her to sit on the hood of the car. "You're such a midget. Get up here where I can reach you without breaking my neck."

She squirmed and gasped when he nuzzled the side of her neck. His hands were warm and firm against her waist, his thumbs mere inches from the underside of her breasts. Things were happening too fast. "Don't, Ryder."

"Why?" His voice was muffled. "Don't you like it?"

"No. Yes. Oh, stop!" she said, batting him with the rose she still clutched. Her tone held a note of desperation. "It's getting complicated."

"Don't I know it."

He drew back and looked at her. Shadows played across her face, revealing her tremulous, exquisitely formed features, and her gleaming topknot was a golden beacon in the starry darkness. Carefully, as if she were a gossamer creation of the most delicate spun glass, he touched her hair and trailed his fingertips down the alabaster column of her neck. Unable to stop himself, he flattened his palms against the rounded curves of her shoulders, tracing the vee at the base of her throat, then down until his forefinger rested against her bodice and the gentle swell of her bosom. His finger moved slowly back and forth, following the satiny flesh, and he felt her quiver. Slowly he leaned forward and placed his lips where his fingers had been. She gasped, and her breasts rose to tempt him. He opened his mouth, testing the flavor of her skin, and her hands rose involuntarily to the back of his head, threading through his hair while her heart beat urgently beneath his mouth.

"I want you," he said.

"I know."

He felt a feather's whisper of a kiss brush the back of his lowered head. He straightened, and his jaw was tight with need. "I'll take you home."

She slid from the car's hood, looking up at him and biting her lip. "I think it would be best. But you mustn't come in."

He frowned, desire and frustration warring within him. "Why?"

"It would change things."

Ryder used his keys to open the car door and watched her slip into the seat. "It's too late, Summer. They've already changed."

They drove back into Chattanooga in silence, the air filled with tension. Summer knew that it would be so easy to let the passion of the moment sweep her away. She was frustratingly aware of her body's throbbing secret places. Ryder would prove an astute and demanding lover, she was certain, but she was also certain that to allow that to happen would be a mistake, damaging to their working relationship and devastating to her personally. She couldn't make love without commitment, some emotional tie that transcended mere physical attraction. She'd learned that much from Clancy. He and Ryder were too much alike,

single-minded, ambitious loners—ruthless if need be—and
possessed of needs that she could not understand.

But Summer's needs were simpler. She wanted to love and
be loved, in the way that Aunt Ollie and Uncle Burton
loved, for today, but also for tomorrow. And Ryder had already said that he would move on one day, to the next challenge, the next town, the next woman. As badly as she ached
at this moment, Summer knew that it was nothing com-
pared to the pain she'd feel if she gave herself totally to Ryder, and he gave nothing back to her. She just couldn't risk
that kind of hurt again.

When Ryder turned in the driveway of her town house,
Summer was relieved. The silent tension was intolerable,
and she was afraid that in the face of a determined effort on
Ryder's part, she might be too easily swayed from a position she knew was both prudent and right. The best course
would be a swift good-night and then to disappear into the
haven of her own cozy home, to the comfort and security of
her brass bed where she'd sleep dreamlessly—alone. Then,
come Monday morning, neither of them would have to face
endless regrets.

Ryder escorted her to the front door, waited patiently
while she dug in her bag for her house key, then took it from
her. The metal key felt cool against his palm. Unable to help
himself, he lifted his other hand to her face. Her eyes were
violet pools, wide and uncertain, and he longed to replace
that uncertainty with the purple fire of passion—for him.

"Still don't want me to come in?"

She shook her head, and her voice was Jubilee's husky
whisper. "It wouldn't be wise. You know that."

"What I know doesn't seem very important when you
look at me like that." His thumb traced the lower curve of
her lip, and he felt her quiver. "If you were honest, you'd
admit it, too."

"I am trying to be honest, about what's best for both of
us." Her voice trembled, but her gaze was unflinching.

"We'll have to work out this thing between us eventually, half-pint. My bet is that it'll be in bed, so you're just postponing the inevitable."

"I—I've enjoyed the evening very much, Ryder, but let's not spoil it with complications neither of us really wants."

He drew a deep breath, and dropped his hand from her face. "I'm not accustomed to logic and reason from you." His mouth tilted. "You've picked a helluva time to start."

Her small laugh was relieved. This kind of banter was familiar ground. "You'll thank me in the morning."

"Don't count on it, partner." He dropped a light kiss on her lips, then turned and inserted the key. "Frustration makes my temper uncertain."

Summer smiled and stepped through the door, automatically reaching for the light switch. "I'm sure you'll get over—oh!"

The living room was a shambles. Books spilled from the shelves. Tables were upended, cushions scattered. The chaos continued through the dining area and into the kitchen, where drawers and cabinets stood open, their contents tumbled. Summer took a faltering, disbelieving step forward.

"Oh, no," she whispered. "What's happened?"

Ryder's hard hands closed over her shoulders. "Stop," he ordered curtly. "Don't move. Don't touch anything."

"Why? What—"

"Honey, you've been robbed."

CHAPTER NINE

"I'M SO MAD I could just spit!"

"Yes, ma'am," the tall blond detective with the battered face replied politely.

Summer gestured around her ransacked living room. "Will you just look at this mess! And what's the point? They didn't take anything important, not even the TV set or the VCR! I don't get it at all."

"I have to admit it's unusual, Miss Jones," Kent Ogden said. "Are you positive nothing's missing?"

Summer hesitated, frowning. "I'm not sure. Everything's such a jumble..."

"What about jewelry, Summer?" Ryder asked beside her.

"I don't have many good pieces. Maybe some of the costume jewelry is missing, a few old things. There's a little gold-filled locket I can't find, a few scarves. Nothing of any great value."

"I think we're dealing with a group of juveniles here," Kent said. "Probably just on a lark, and took a notion to go after a few souvenirs. What kind of scarves specifically?"

"All kinds, paisleys and dotted, and the jade silk one that I liked so well because it's the same shade of green as—" She broke off, sudden horror widening her eyes. "Oh my gosh! Lizabeth!"

Dodging swiftly past the two men, she rushed to a narrow coat closet located inconspicuously behind the front door, and flung it open. She sagged with relief.

"Who's Lizabeth?" Kent demanded. He came up short behind Summer, and his jaw dropped. Nefarious characters of all descriptions ogled him from the confines of the closet.

Ryder chuckled at his friend's stupefaction. "Meet Lizabeth Lizard and her troupe, Kent."

Summer tugged Lizabeth's green sequined body from the dowel supporting it in the shelf-lined closet. Each wooden ledge was crowded with brightly costumed puppets and marionettes. Fondly she stroked Lizabeth's pink feather boa, her relief at finding her inanimate friends unharmed more than evident.

"My puppets, Lieutenant. Big Duke, Hermione Hogg, Wallace the Whale, Lizabeth and the rest of the cast. Thank goodness they're all right."

Kent's mouth twisted quizzically. "You set great store in these toys, ma'am?"

"You bet your buttons she does, copper," Lizabeth quipped. Summer laughed at Kent's nonplussed expression, shrugged Lizabeth off her wrist, and carefully replaced her on her perch. "I do a lot of volunteer work with my puppets. Their loss would have been worse than anything."

"It's just too bad all those buggy-eyed creatures can't identify a suspect for us," Ryder said dryly.

"It'd make my job easier," Kent agreed as they moved back into the living room. "We just have to assume this was some sort of prank."

"But why me?" Summer asked, a perplexed frown pleating her brow. Wandering around the room, she automatically began to put things to rights, stacking magazines, replacing a basket of dried flowers on the butler's table. "I don't keep a lot of cash around, and we've never had any trouble in this complex with vandalism."

Kent shrugged, his shoulders lifting under the weight of a well-worn leather bomber jacket. "Sometimes a roaming gang moves into new territory." He pointed at the two uniformed police officers carefully examining the jimmied lock of her sliding glass door. "Whoever it was hopped your back fence, then popped this door, probably with a tire tool.''

Summer stooped to retrieve several dusty photo albums from the floor and carefully set them back in their slots in her bookshelves. ''I still don't understand why they picked me,'' she said, and her voice was almost plaintive. ''I'd even left a light on.''

''Maybe they were watching the house. Someone could even have seen that clip on the news tonight about the auction and known you'd be out. You're what we call highly visible in this town. It might have been a curiosity-seeker. You never know.''

Summer shuddered, and Ryder frowned. Their formal attire was an incongruous note in the plundered apartment. ''Cut it out, Kent. You're scaring the lady.''

''Whoa, now, Tex,'' Kent drawled. ''She's entitled to know the facts.''

''What facts?'' Summer asked.

''The truth is we'll probably never catch whoever pulled this, ma'am. The boys aren't having any luck lifting prints, and we've got no witnesses. I think you're just going to have to be glad they didn't get away with anything more valuable than a few trinkets.''

''Oh, I am, but I feel so...so violated.'' She made a face. ''Strangers going through my things—ugh!''

''It's perfectly natural, ma'am,'' Kent said. ''We'll beef up the regular patrols around here for a few days. I'll file the report, and if you think of anything else that's missing you give me a call, okay?'' He passed her a card with his name and number on it.

''Thank you, Lieutenant Ogden. And thanks for coming so quickly.''

Kent gave Ryder's shoulder a hearty slap. ''Me and Tex go way back together. It's been a pleasure meeting you at last, Miss Jones. I'm just sorry it wasn't under different circumstances.''

"I agree. And call me Summer." She offered her hand, and it was swallowed up by Kent's enormous paw. "And thanks again."

"No problem, Summer. Oh, and you should get that door fixed real soon."

"I will." She glanced toward the other officers. "Excuse me, I'd better see what they recommend." Summer moved away with a swish of her petticoats, sidestepping a pile of pillows and the remains of a smashed goose figurine with barely a glance.

Kent lifted a bushy, wheat-colored eyebrow. "Classy lady," he commented. "Tough."

"For a ninety-pound pip-squeak, she's got a ton of steel in her backbone," Ryder agreed. "And of course, she'd put on a good show, no matter what."

"Granted. But you might want to keep an eye on her for a while. Stuff like this can throw the best of them."

"I understand," Ryder said. The two men walked toward the front door, their voices low. "Thanks for bailing us out."

Kent grinned. "Just doin' my job, partner. Nothing gives me greater satisfaction than to pull your fat out of the fire."

"It doesn't pay to be too smug, hotshot. So, how was Phoenix?"

"Hot as hell." Kent grimaced and pulled a hand over his square jaw. "You really know how to hurt a guy, don't you?"

"What, no luck?"

Kent shrugged. "Minimal."

"A killer still on the loose, and now a break-in here at Summer's. I can't tell you what that does for my peace of mind," Ryder drawled.

"Hell, don't you start in, too." Kent's uneven features registered his frustration. "I'm taking enough flak downtown as it is. But don't worry about Summer. This is a simple burglary. Our killer doesn't work like that."

"Still, it wouldn't hurt for her to take some extra precautions." Ryder's lips twisted in self-recrimination. "Especially since I've done such a fine job of making her face recognizable in this town."

Kent glanced across the room to where Summer was listening intently to the uniformed officers. "I'd say this is an isolated incident, but..." He shrugged. "Precautions never hurt. Just to be on the safe side."

"Yeah."

"Speaking of saving your hide, have you heard the latest scuttlebutt from Atlanta?" Kent looked concerned.

"No, what?"

"Word is Grigorio's lawyers plan to file a motion for a new trial. They say there's new evidence that just surfaced."

Ryder bit out a single violent expletive. "That murdering scum will try anything! If there's a retrial, we'll have to testify again."

"Yeah," Kent drawled, "and we're two of his favorite people, aren't we? Especially since it was our testimony that made the jury throw away the key to his cell."

Ryder's jaw clenched, and his mouth was a grim line. "It wasn't half of what he deserved for putting out contracts on Bill, the D.A., and who knows how many others."

"Maybe nothing will come of it, but watch your back, buddy." Kent gave him an amiable punch. "Hey, I'm out of here. I know you'll keep an eye on the little lady, but you know where to find me if you need me."

Across the room, Summer's distracted gaze flicked over Ryder and Kent at her front door, then returned to the policeman at her side.

"We've secured it as best we can, Miss Jones," the officer said, gathering up a toolbox. "Best thing is to jam an old hoe handle or broomstick in the track. Then, an intruder would have to break the glass to get in."

"Yes, I'll do that," Summer said faintly. "Thank you again."

They wished her a polite good-night and left. Summer stared at the bent and scarred door handle, her thoughts churning. A righteous anger had held panic at bay until this moment, but now a tight knot of fear grew in the middle of her chest. Sudden hands on her shoulder made her gasp and whirl around.

"Easy," Ryder soothed. "It's just me."

She sagged against him. "Oh! Don't do that."

"You're as jumpy as a kitten."

Pushing away from him and the undemanding solace of his arms was very hard, but she forced herself. "No, I'm fine, really. Just furious, that's all." She tried to smile. "You wouldn't happen to have the number of County Security Systems handy, would you? Do you think they might give me a price break?"

"That might be a good idea. And I'm sure they'd be glad to give Jubilee a discount."

She stared. "I was just kidding."

"I wasn't." His measured look was deadly serious.

Summer clasped her elbows to suppress a shiver. "I—I'll think about it." She glanced toward the door. "Are they gone?"

"The cops? Yes."

"Your friend is nice."

"Yeah, Kent's all right."

"You're all right, too, Bowman." Her smile was a bit tremulous. "Thanks for staying."

"No problem."

She took a deep breath and squared her shoulders. "Well, I'll let you get out of here. I've got work to do."

He frowned. "Is there anyone who could come stay with you tonight? Your aunt?"

Summer shook her head. "No, they're not due in from their trip until tomorrow."

"Well, let me call Vanessa, then."

"She went with Merl to Gadsden to spend the weekend with his parents. Really, Ryder, I'm fine."

"The hell you are. You're spooked, lady."

"So what if I am?" she bristled, suddenly defiant. "I'll get over it. No stupid burglar is running me out of my home!"

"You don't have to prove to me how brave you are, okay?"

She glared at him. "Fine! Now, if you'll excuse me, I've got to clean up this mess."

"It'll take you all night."

"So what?" Her tone was flippant. "I've got nothing better to do."

He cursed under his breath. "Forget it, Summer. I'm not going to spend what's left of the night worrying if you're all right." He caught her arm. "Come on. You're coming home with me."

She sucked in an indignant breath. "Now wait a minute, you arrogant—"

Slipping an arm around her, he pulled her toward the door. "Look, you can have the guest room, and we'll both get some sleep. Then I'll help you tackle this tomorrow." His hand pressed between her bare shoulder blades, and his voice was throaty and persuasive. "Come on, honey, you're shaking like a leaf. Let me help you."

"I..." Summer faltered, then shut her mouth. She didn't want to be here by herself. She *was* spooked. It was too many hours until dawn, and she wanted someone to take charge, someone strong she could lean on just for a little while. Was it so terrible to show a moment of weakness? Instinctively she knew that Ryder would never use it against her. She trusted him, and she needed his strength. Mutely she nodded. Ryder gave her an encouraging squeeze.

"That's using your head. Grab what you need, if you can find it, otherwise I'll lend you something. Don't worry, it'll all look better in the morning."

Exhausted, Summer paid scarce attention to the drive to Ryder's place until they turned and began to climb the same road up Lookout Mountain that they'd so recently descended.

"You live up here?" she asked.

"Best view in town." He expertly took the steep curves and within minutes was pulling into the driveway of a rambling stone dwelling. A gaslight illuminated the arched front door. "Come on in."

Ryder led her into the large living room, flipping a switch that bathed the room in golden lamplight. Summer was overwhelmed with impressions of space, lots of glass, and distinctly masculine textures in the stone fireplace, beamed, vaulted ceiling, and understated gray carpet and streamlined furniture. An ebony baby grand piano gleamed proudly in one corner, and a painting of a schooner under full sail rode a crest of waves over the heavy mantel. The house curved around a flagstone terrace visible through the uncovered banks of long windows. Throwing his tux jacket over the back of a navy blue sofa, Ryder gave her a speculative look.

"Want a drink? You probably could use one."

She shook her head. "No, thank you. You have a beautiful place." Drawn like a bee to a blossom, she drifted to the piano, letting her fingers slide over its shiny black finish, then softly pressing a single key. "Do you play?"

Ryder shrugged. "Some. But the piano came with the house."

"Oh." She shivered slightly and rubbed her arms.

"Cold?"

"A little," she admitted with a small, tremulous laugh.

"It's catching up with you." He frowned. "You need a hot shower and some sack time."

"Not yet." Her teeth were chattering. She sat down on the edge of the sofa, holding herself, her face pale with fatigue and strain. "Talk to me a while."

Ryder studied her carefully for a long moment, but his reply was easy. "All right. I'll build a fire."

Summer watched him set the paper kindling in the wide fieldstone fireplace, add chips of heart pine, then logs of split oak. She admired the way he worked, meticulously, and the way his shoulder muscles rippled beneath the white expanse of his dress shirt. *He's good at everything he does,* she thought. When they'd walked into her town house, he'd reacted coolly, calling his friend first, then efficiently dealing with the police and her own near-panic.

"Why does Kent call you Tex?" she asked suddenly. "I thought you were from Pennsylvania."

"I am. And I went to school in New York." He struck a match, and the tiny flame caught, leaping and crackling in a reckless quest. Dusting his hands on his thighs, he stood and turned toward her. "It's a joke."

"I don't understand."

"We worked together. In Atlanta. It was a . . . precarious time, and I was pretty much a greenhorn. It was a way Kent had of reminding me to stay sharp, to keep on my toes."

"What do you call him?"

He shoved his hands into his pants pockets, and his lips twisted with humor. "Kent."

Laughing softly, she shook her head. "You have a real sense of adventure, don't you, Bowman?"

He sat down directly in front of her on the heavy walnut coffee table, and his gaze was penetrating, making her stir uneasily. His black hair fell in a wave across his forehead, and he'd rolled up his cuffs and removed several studs in his white shirt so that it hung open, revealing a slash of firmly muscled chest lightly thatched with dark hairs. His jaw was faintly shadowed, and it gave him a piratical air, compelling and infinitely dangerous.

"I like things laid out in front of me, straightforward, with no fancy names attached. Simple, clear-cut, accurate. I know what I want."

"Life is more complex than that," she murmured, chilled. "You can't always define it in those kinds of terms. Why overlook its beauty and emotion by trying to set limits on it?''

"I just like to know where I stand." He took her icy hand, then frowned. "You're still cold?"

"I can't seem to get warm." Pulling free, she hugged herself again, rocking back and forth. Her short laugh was half embarrassed, half rueful. "Sorry."

"Don't be silly. You've had quite a shock. Why don't I fix you some hot chocolate? It'll help you sleep."

She forced a lightness she didn't feel into her tone. "All this and he cooks, too!"

"I can handle a microwave, but don't press your luck, Jubilee." He rose and headed toward the kitchen. "Hang on, I'll be right back."

Summer stared at the flames in the fireplace and listened to the burning wood crackle and pop. Rising, she stepped in front of it, lifting her hands to warm them before the glowing orange embers, but the heat could not penetrate the soul-deep chill that consumed her. Every nerve felt taut, but it wasn't the earlier events of the evening, or even the burglary that plagued her. No, it was the subtle messages from Ryder that disturbed her. Messages that said he wanted her, but with a no-strings-attached clause to any unspoken contract. It was adult. It was civilized. It was so cold-blooded it made her heart ache.

She gave a short, miserable chuckle. It really was rather honest of him, she supposed, to make his position clear from the start, just as though he were negotiating a difficult business deal, but whatever happened to good old-fashioned romance? Maybe Ryder wasn't capable of the emotional commitment she needed, or maybe he just didn't think she was worth it. She longed for his strength, for someone who could assuage the loneliness she tried to hide even from herself, but she knew better. She was playing it smart, keeping herself inviolate, but she was tempted. The nights were long and empty, and she knew in her heart of hearts that he could fill them—at least for a time. Yes, she was tempted, but she wasn't crazy.

Realizing suddenly how bone-weary she was, she gave a sigh and kicked off her shoes. A small sound caught her attention, and she glanced toward the windows, then stifled a gasp. A pair of bright eyes gazed back at her.

Exhaling, she shook her head. "You're losing it, Summer," she chided herself. "It's just a dog."

The little black and white animal cocked his head and whined hopefully, and again scratched on the glass with his paw. Intrigued, Summer cast a glance in the direction of the kitchen, shrugged, then went to open the door at the end of the bank of windows. The scruffy canine immediately ran to meet her, his entire body wagging with delight.

"Hello, pooch. Do you belong here?" she murmured, offering her palm for inspection. A stiff breeze rattled dry leaves and dragged them across the flagstones, but Summer ignored the cold, her hands seeking the leather collar around the dog's neck. The flat license disk attached to it bore the name and address of John Ryder Bowman.

"Well, what do you know?" Bemused, she opened the door wider. The mongrel pranced inside, then curled up before the fireplace, perfectly at home.

Ryder returned and set a loaded tray on the coffee table. "Here, Summer, maybe something hot—" A welcoming yip interrupted him, and he frowned at the dog. "You little beggar, how'd you get in? Didn't I tell you I'd send you to the pound if you ever showed your ugly mug around here again? Come on, out you go."

"The jig is up, Bowman," Summer said with a smile. She accepted the hot chocolate from him and warmed her hands around the earthenware mug. "I read his collar. The pound, indeed," she teased. "You old softy."

Ryder scowled, reaching for his own cup. "He's just a stray."

"You paid for his tag. That makes him your dog." She sipped slowly at the richly flavored beverage, letting its warmth soothe her.

"So I hate to see a free spirit caged up. Is that a crime?" He was almost belligerent.

Summer hid her smile in her cup and sat down on the hearth. "I see."

Ryder gave a growl of disgust, grabbed a handful of miniature marshmallows from a bowl on the tray and tried to drown them in his mug. While he fished for the melting morsels with his spoon, Summer felt an icy place within her heart soften and melt, too. Despite the image he cultivated, Ryder Bowman wasn't completely made of iron, after all. If something as simple as a pet's undemanding affection could pierce his armor, maybe he wasn't as calculating and cold-blooded as she feared. Maybe, underneath the logical, hard-as-nails facade was a sensitive, caring man who just needed to learn that it was all right to experience the more tender emotions. It was something to consider.

Summer picked up a pecan cookie, broke it, and offered a piece to the little dog, who promptly gobbled it up. She laughed and gave him another piece.

"He's got your sweet tooth," she observed.

Ryder grunted. Hitching up his pant leg, he propped his foot beside her on the hearth and braced himself against the mantel. "Watch out. He's such a panhandler, he'll take you for all you're worth."

She ruffled the dog's fur. "He's adorable. What's his name?"

"Dog. Mutt. Hey, you."

"Come on, you're bound to call him something." She raised her cup again to sip.

"Well, actually..." He looked a bit sheepish.

"Hmm?"

"I call him Clancy."

Summer choked on her chocolate, sloshing the hot liquid down her chin and onto her breastbone. Hastily setting aside her cup, she coughed and grabbed a napkin, frantically blotting, fighting a wild desire to giggle.

"I knew I shouldn't have told you," Ryder grumbled, passing her another napkin. "But every time the little scoundrel showed up it seemed as though *Bayside Beat* was on, so—"

"Don't explain," Summer gasped, her voice strangled. Helplessly she began to laugh. "The way my life has been going lately I should have guessed. His namesake is a hound. Talk about typecasting! Oh, God, would that puncture Clancy's ego!"

The dog's ears perked at the mention of the name, and he placed his front paws on Summer's knees. Laughter pealing, she scratched his ears and crooned to him, "You're not much of a dog, but you're twice the man Clancy Darrell ever was. Yes, you are."

Abruptly she crossed the fine line between laughter and tears. Her breath caught on a sob, and her pansy eyes flooded. With a little sound, half horror, half despair, she buried her face in her hands.

"Summer, what is it?" Ryder knelt on one knee in front of her, his hands on her shoulders. She tried to wave his concern away.

"I—I'm just being silly," she choked. "I'm overwrought. So much has happened. Just leave me alone."

"No, tell me." He forced her to look up and absorbed the anguished expression on her face. "What's this about Clancy Darrell? Do you know him?"

She sniffled, and her lower lip jutted mutinously. "None of your business, Bowman."

"Don't try to play the tough broad with me, Jubilee," he warned, giving her a little shake.

Defiance flared briefly in her eyes, then died. "You must be the only person in Chattanooga who doesn't know I was in love with him."

Ryder jerked. A hot surge of something primeval seared him. He knew it was unreasonable, this primitive, possessive urge, this jealousy of things in her past. Ruthlessly he clamped down on the boiling emotion and forced coolness into his tone. "Clancy Darrell, the actor?"

"I didn't spend all those years in California for my health," she said bitterly. "Or even my career."

"You were married?"

"Don't be naive. It was an 'open relationship.' So he could find himself. Open for him, that is. I did my best to make it work." Furiously she scrubbed at the tears that continued to flow down her cheeks. "Oh, why am I telling you this, anyway!"

"So he ended it?" he asked quietly.

"Of course not. I did." Her smile was brittle with pride. "He couldn't be bothered to take the trouble. I was never that important to him."

"I'm sorry."

"Don't be," she snapped. "He got his big break, and I got out."

"Maybe you got the best deal." He smoothed the tendrils back from her flushed face, and his fingers plucked at the pins of her topknot.

"I know I did. So don't you dare pity me!" she said fiercely. "I've been over Clancy Darrell a long time."

"Then why are you crying?"

"I'm not crying!" But her piquant face crumbled, and a fresh flood of tears scalded her cheeks.

He sat down beside her on the hearth, pulling her into his arms and pressing her face against his chest. The heated moisture of her tears seeped through his shirt to touch him with an emotional baptism.

"Hush, darling," he murmured into her hair. "It's all right."

"I'm not crying for Clancy," she protested on a sob.

"No."

"It's just the dog...and my place turned upside down...and I'm tired..."

"Yes, I know." He tugged the remaining pins from her hair, and it fell around her shoulders like a golden curtain. Threading the fingers of one hand through the silky strands, he massaged her scalp, evoking a sigh of pleasure. "Feel good?"

"Uh-huh." She gave a watery hiccup. "I wish you wouldn't be so nice."

His thumb tilted her chin upward so that he was gazing down into her tearstained face. Half smiling, he brushed feathery kisses along the damp spikes of her lashes. "Why?"

"It makes it hard—" He lightly brushed the corner of her mouth, and her breath caught for an instant. "—to remember."

"Remember what?"

"That you're just like Clancy."

Ryder's rage was conceived and born fully formed in an instant of white-hot consummation. Fury made him reckless, hurtful, and he took her mouth, grinding his lips against hers, punishing her for her damning assessment. Plunging through her frail barriers, he probed with his tongue until there was no part of her mouth that he did not know, no particle of her breath that he had not consumed. And it wasn't enough.

He drew back, breathing hard, wondering if it might *ever* be enough. Never had he felt such fury. And *she* had done this to him. He'd never let anger rule his relationship with a woman, but with her he had no control. His hand tightened painfully in her hair, pulling her face up until there was only a breath between them.

"I'm not Clancy," he said between gritted teeth. "And lady, you sure as hell better remember it!"

And then she surprised him.

"How could I forget?" she whispered, twined her arms around his neck, and pulled his head down again.

This kiss was different, the hard texture of rage replaced with a softness, a sensuality that conquered where anger could not. Remorse was a bitter taste against his tongue that mixed with the sweetness of passion. His head swam, and desire superseded fury, gentled it, then burned anew with an even fiercer fire.

He stood without releasing her mouth, pressing her close, then impatiently stripping her short jacket from her shoulders. One hand found the nape of her neck under the weight of her hair, the other the small of her back. He pulled her into the cradle of his thighs so that she couldn't help but feel the burgeoning throb of his manhood against her belly. As one, they groaned together.

His hands made futile forays down her back, seeking the fastener of the gown. "Is this a scene out of *Gone With the Wind*?" he muttered against her mouth. "This damn dress..."

Her voice was faint and breathless. "Don't you like it?"

"It's been driving me crazy all night—ah!" The zipper slid down, and his hands were warm against her bare back. With a muttered exclamation, he realized she was naked underneath the structured bodice, yet he was too busy kissing her to take advantage of his discovery. Her hands were doing wicked, tempting things inside his open shirt, and her mouth was sweet, so sweet...

Unwilling to let her go for even a moment, he walked them both awkwardly around the coffee table, then eased Summer down on the plush sofa, half lying atop her. She jerked the tail of his shirt free, and the rest of his shirt studs popped loose and were lost in the dense carpet. She was wild, matching his hunger breath for breath, caress for caress. Excitement sparked in him everywhere she touched, and he shrugged from his shirt to allow her roaming hands better access.

Releasing her lips, he nibbled down the delicate column of her neck. Her fingers slipped through his hair, stroking the tense cords of his neck. He tasted her skin, skimming over the ivory flesh until, at last, he pushed aside the loosened bodice, revealing satiny mounds of her breasts to his fevered gaze. She was all woman, perfectly formed, as he'd known she'd be, velvet flesh and pale pink circlets of nipples already puckered into aroused buds. Cupping one breast, he savored the texture with his tongue, then reverently took the throbbing tip into his mouth to test her essence.

Her fingers convulsed in his hair, and she arched against him, gasping. He raised up, looking down in the bewildered, desire-clouded depths of her eyes. Her lips were tremulous, kiss-stung, and he could not resist them, though his hands continued to caress her breasts. The kiss was gentle, and their lips clung as he pulled away.

"Who am I?" he asked hoarsely.

Her lashes fluttered, and she looked up at him, startled, expectant. "Ryder."

His smile was very slow. "Right the first time."

Scooping her up in his arms, her skirts bundled askew, her hair a wild tangle, he strode purposefully down the long hall toward the bedrooms. He pushed through a half-open door. Shadowy outlines delineated bed, chair, chest. Then, without preamble, he dumped her unceremoniously into the center of the bed, and left her with a brief parting kiss.

"I'll see you in the morning."

She sat up, clutching the loose bodice of her dress, dismay and confusion written on her face. "Ryder? I don't understand."

"Half-pint, I'm not damned sure I do, either." He paused at the door. In the uneven light, his expression was wry and a bit pained. "All I know is that as much as I want you, I'm not going to take you like this, not when we're both punchy, not when there could be all sorts of excuses and rationalizations later. When it happens—and it will—I want nothing between us, not a single thing holding us back."

"You take a lot for granted," she protested.

"As Kent likes to say, 'just the facts, ma'am.'"

Crossing her arms, she lay back on the bed with a bad-tempered flounce and stared up at the ceiling. "Either you're crazy or I am!"

"The bath's through there," he said, pointing at a connecting door. "Just don't use all the cold water. I've got a feeling I'm going to need a lot of it."

"Your choice, Bowman," she said sweetly, still staring overhead.

His laugh was low. "Sweet dreams, honey."

She sat up, clutching her dress, and threw a pillow at him. "Oh, for heaven's sake, *good night*!"

She looked so beautiful, so tumbled and desirable, that it was nearly his undoing. Swallowing harshly, he held on to his resolve by the mightiest of efforts, and pulled the door shut behind him.

Leaning against the wall outside her room, he let out a deep, frustrated breath. Yeah, he had to be crazy all right. But somehow, with Summer he didn't want their first time to be a mistake of the moment. He wanted her to come to him with no reservations. He wanted their lovemaking to be special.

He shook his head, wondering how he'd become so damned noble all of a sudden. It was rather—inconvenient. His hand moved on impulse toward the doorknob again, then hesitated. The flat of his palm pressed against the paneled door, as if he could absorb something of the woman who lay seething on the other side. There was really no doubt about it. He was crazy. Resolutely he turned and headed for the shower.

CHAPTER TEN

"WELL, I HEAR YOU HAD SOME EXCITEMENT over the weekend," Merl said.

Summer jumped, and the coffee she was pouring splashed over the side of her cup. Muttering imprecations, she hastily set the pot back on the hot plate in the employees' lounge, and wiped her near-scalded hands on her jeans. She shot a harried glance at the bespectacled program director.

"Really, Merl! Are you trying to scare me out of a year's growth?"

He whistled. "Mighty jumpy for a Monday morning, aren't you, doll? Can't say that I blame you, though. What an experience."

Summer felt the heat rise in her cheeks and applied herself to the task of carefully wiping up the spilled coffee. Merl was referring to her being robbed, of course, but more hair-raising than that was the near miss she'd experienced with Ryder Bowman. Even now she was uncertain how she'd managed *not* to end up in Ryder's bed. Obviously the Lord took care of fools.

"It was something I'd rather not repeat," she replied truthfully.

"Did he get anything?"

"Only my goat," she muttered under her breath, pouring a second cup.

"Huh?"

Forcing herself to focus on the conversation, she shook her head. "No, the burglar didn't get anything of value."

"Good thing you were with Ryder, huh? It could have been pretty sticky if you'd walked in on the intruder by yourself."

"The grapevine around here is amazing! Why ask me if you know the whole story already?" she demanded, then frowned at herself. "That sounded bitchy, didn't it? Sorry, Merl, I guess I'm still a bit strung out."

"I'd be mad as hell, too."

"Well, I shouldn't take it out on you." She forced a cheerful smile. "So, how was your weekend? Was it nice and restful out in the country? How did Vanessa get along with your folks?"

"Oh, it was fine. I guess." His long face looked even longer, and he tugged distractedly at the hem of his striped knit pullover.

"Didn't you have a good time?" Summer inquired gently.

"Well, sure. I mean it was nothing special, just the farm Chickens, pigs, cows, tractors . . ."

"Your parents didn't like her," Summer surmised flatly.

"Oh, no, nothing like that. They thought she was great!" His crooked expression was wry. "Let's face it. They've about given up on this old bachelor. They'd take to any girl I brought home, even if she looked like Godzilla! No everything was fine that way."

"Then what's the trouble?"

"Nothing I can put my finger on. She was just preoccupied most of the time, like she was having second thought about everything, including me."

"Oh, I'm sure that's not it at all," Summer said staunchly. "Maybe she was just nervous. Maybe it was all too much family all at once."

"Yeah. Every time my three nieces came into the room she'd find some excuse to leave. And I thought she like kids!"

"She does! Why else would she be doing volunteer work with that little girl?"

"That's another thing I can't figure. Why the sudden interest?"

"That's something you'll have to ask Vanessa."

"I have, but she just clams up. I tell you, Summer, it feels like she's pulling away from me, and there's not a thing I can do about it."

Summer frowned uncertainly, wishing she didn't know Vanessa's secret. It made it difficult to know what to say to Merl. Vanessa's conviction that Amy Brown was her daughter was obviously preying on her mind and affecting her fledgling relationship with Merl. Since Summer couldn't tell Merl the real reason Vanessa seemed so distant, she tried to reassure him the best she could.

"I think you're reading too much into this. We all have problems, and we're all a little moody sometimes. What Vanessa needs is for you to lend her a little support right now. Don't worry. She'll shake those blues before you know it."

"Maybe you're right." Merl gave a lopsided grin. "I hope so, anyway. I'm crazy about that gal, you know."

Summer laughed. "It shows. Let me run, Merl. It was my turn to go after coffee, and you know how grouchy Ryder gets when he doesn't get his full allotment of sugar."

"Boy, do I. You ought to hear him growl if I'm late with the program logs. I almost have the computer programs under control, but just in case . . . here." He grabbed a couple of glazed doughnuts out of a box on the counter, wrapped them in a napkin and balanced them on top of her cups. "I don't want to end up a victim of Ryder's screwy metabolism. Just keep the boss man fed and off our backs, okay?"

"You got it."

"And hey, tell him I've scheduled that remote for Jubilee and Gulliver at the Chattanooga Choo-Choo Complex for next Saturday."

"Great!" Summer beamed, juggling her burdens. "I love that place. The gardens, the restaurants—it's a lot of fun."

"I'm glad you're so enthusiastic. You know you're going to be swarmed with fans."

"The better to wallop the competition with, my dear," Summer replied in her Big Bad Wolf voice.

"I sincerely hope so," Merl agreed. "At the rate you two are going, you'll even give ole Luther at WDES a run for his money."

Luther was practically an institution in the Chattanooga area. With continuous broadcasting since World War II, his morning radio show was the oldest in the nation.

Summer gave a mock shudder. "You're betting we'll last better than thirty years? Some marriages aren't that long."

"Call me an optimist, but you two really cook." He opened the lounge door for her, then followed her out into the teal-carpeted corridor. "I guess it's up to the boss, anyway."

Summer had to agree. And according to the boss, Gulliver would be moving on long before there was any chance of surpassing Luther's record. All the more reason to avoid any kind of intimate relationship with Ryder. She moved down the hall, gingerly balancing her load, and her face began to burn with chagrin.

Right, she told herself, she was really avoiding a relationship when she'd practically begged him to take her to bed. If Ryder hadn't had the presence of mind to refuse, she'd be dealing with more trouble than just a little embarrassment right now. Facing him again Saturday morning had been hard enough.

She'd awakened, to find the house quiet. Old habits were hard to break, and despite the previous late night, it appeared she and Ryder were both destined to remain early risers. The morning wasn't very old when she'd rubbed the sleep from her eyes, donned a ratty Atlanta Braves jersey she found hanging in the closet, and ventured out.

The kitchen was empty, but the coffee was perked. There was no sign of Ryder, so she sipped a cup and watched the antics of a fat red squirrel out the kitchen window, trying not to think about the shambles in her town house or what she'd finally say to Ryder when she saw him. Eventually she'd begun poking into the cabinets in search of sustenance. One thing led to another, and soon she had biscuits baking, ham frying, and eggs whisked into a froth ready for the pan. The least she could do to repay Ryder's hospitality was cook for him. Besides, it kept her mind off other things.

She was back at the window looking for the squirrel again when Ryder jogged into the driveway, followed by Clancy. The little mutt's tongue hung out practically to the ground, but he gamely followed his master. Ryder, in faded T-shirt and gym shorts, seemed oblivious to the crisp, cool morning air. He loped across the yard easily, stopping to give Clancy a scratch behind his scruffy ears and to throw a stick for him.

Summer took a quick, deep breath. Everything about the man called to the female in her—his long, lithe form, the way his damp ebony hair fell over his forehead, even the way he showed affection for his dog. She groaned softly. Ryder didn't even have to be in the same building for her to respond to him! How was she going to play it cool? Had she already made the mistake of falling in love with him?

No, it's impossible, she told herself firmly. Maybe she was a bit infatuated after a romantic evening and a traumatic robbery, and especially after being held close by a man as dynamic as Ryder—but she wasn't in love. She couldn't be! She heard him at the back door, and hastily grabbed the bowl of eggs, whipping them with the whisk for all she was worth.

"Well, good morning, sunshine," Ryder said. He stopped just inside the door to untie his sneakers and sniffed appreciatively at the delectable aromas emanating from his kitchen. "You've been busy."

Summer's smile was a bit diffident. "I hope you like your eggs scrambled."

"Love 'em." He kicked off his shoes, then went to the sink to wash up.

There was something terribly intimate about fixing breakfast for a man in his stocking feet. The faint, pungent scent of Ryder's sweat was a tantalizing reminder of what it was like to live with a man. Summer swallowed and turned away, busily pouring two glasses of orange juice. "Drink?"

"Thanks." He took the glass and sprawled in a lanky heap in a chair at the breakfast table. He took several hefty swallows. "Ahh."

Turning her back to him, Summer dropped a pat of butter into the frying pan on the stove and waited for it to melt. "Do you jog every day?"

"Just about. I do most of my thinking when I run."

"Oh." She wondered if he'd spent this morning's thinking time rehashing what had almost happened between them. She had to get this thing straight between them, however reluctant she felt, and, according to one of Aunt Ollie's precepts, there was no time like the present. She poured the eggs into the sizzling pan. Picking up a wooden spoon, she frowned down into the congealing eggs. "Ryder?"

"Yeah."

She took a deep breath and screwed up her courage, but she couldn't bring herself to face him, not with the rosy color burning her cheeks. "Uh, about last night. I'm sorry for... for throwing myself at you. I realize I was being unreasonable, and I want to thank you for being a gentleman and—"

"Do you know you look damned cute in that shirt?"

She swung around. The jersey she wore was old and soft, and so large she'd had to roll the sleeves up three times to reveal her wrists. It hit her just above the knees, covering her modestly, but it felt like something you'd wear around the house with someone you were comfortable with, someone you didn't have to impress with your glamor. From deep in her memory came the thought that she'd owned a wardrobe of peignoirs when she was with Clancy, and he'd never offered the slightest compliment. But she wasn't discussing her attire. She made a gesture of impatience. "Are you listening to me?"

"Sure. Every word." Ankles and arms crossed, he gave her the once-over from the top of her sunlit ponytail to the pink polish on her toenails. "I never realized what great legs you have, either."

"I'm trying to apologize!"

"For what?"

Her irritation and embarrassment made her huffy. She brandished the spoon at him. "You know for what! I made a fool out of myself, and I have to look you in the eye every morning, and you should at least have the manners to accept—"

"Summer?"

She glared at him. "What?"

"Your eggs are burning."

With a squeal, she whirled to rescue their breakfast, scooping up the scrambled eggs and serving them onto waiting plates. Muttering darkly, she added biscuits and ham slices, then turned with a plate in each hand. Ryder was right behind her. She came up short, giving him a wary look. There was a brief tug-of-war over his plate.

"Maybe we both got a little carried away," he said quietly. She saw something of her own wariness in the green-flecked depths of his eyes. "Let's forget it, okay?"

It was certainly what she wanted. "Okay," she agreed, releasing his plate, and relief softened the disturbed violet of her eyes to a clear amethyst.

They ate in silence for several minutes. There was a restraint between them that hadn't been there before, and Summer grew more uncomfortable by the minute.

"You're a good cook," he said at last, pushing his plate aside.

"Thanks. I'm glad I could return the favor." She rose and gathered up the used dishes, then made a production of looking at the clock on the wall. "Oh, horrors! Is that really the time? I've got to get going. Could I call a taxi? I'm supposed to pick up Aunt Ollie and Uncle Burton at the airport this afternoon, and I've got that mess to straighten up."

"Relax," he advised with a lazy wave. "Have another cup of coffee. I'll run you home later."

"I really can't. I've got a thousand things to do." She disappeared for a moment to retrieve her evening bag, then returned to the kitchen, digging for her billfold. She pulled out a slip of paper with notations on it. "Yes, here it is. Flight 2121 from Atlanta at three-thirty. Aunt Ollie will have palpitations when I tell her what happened, anyway. I can't let them see the shambles my place is in! Oh, where is that key?"

A look of sudden alarm crossed her face, and she dumped the contents of the little bag out on the breakfast table. "Oh, my God. My keys are gone. Were they stolen, too?"

There were extra sets at home, of course, at least she thought she'd seen them last night dumped with the contents of a drawer into the middle of the kitchen floor, but...

"Take it easy. I took them."

Her attention snapped back to Ryder. "You did? Why?"

"So my housekeeper could go over to your place to straighten up. Mrs. Mills is excellent, and she'll do a good job. I didn't think you'd want to face that again."

She was stunned by his thoughtfulness—and his presumption. "Now wait just a darn minute! You can't—"

"I already have. And by the way, the owner of County Security says they'll have your new security system installed before nightfall. They were glad to cut a deal in return for advertising."

It took a moment for Summer to catch her breath. "You take a lot on yourself."

His smile was confident and unconcerned. "Listen, sweetheart, Jubilee Jones is a valuable commodity to me. I'm just protecting my interests."

"How flattering," she said with acid sarcasm.

"Just don't take it personally," he warned, and headed for the shower.

And just like that, they'd slipped back into the banter and bickering the fans of Jubilee and Gulliver loved, as though the moments of shared closeness had never happened. Oh, he'd taken her home, helped her with Mrs. Mills and the new burglar alarm, and even driven her to the airport to greet her aunt and uncle, but it was as though an invisible wall had dropped between them. There were no smoldering looks, nothing to indicate they'd experimented with passion. There was a distance between them again, as though they were merely acquaintances, and adversarial ones, at that.

Summer told herself she was glad of it, for it made working together simpler. They knew where they stood with each other. Not enemies any more, but not exactly friends, either. It was definitely safer this way, she thought, and tried to ignore an inner quiver of hurt when she entered the control booth, set Ryder's coffee cup and doughnuts down beside his elbow, and received barely a glance and a curt nod for her trouble.

All right. If that's the way he wants it, all business it is, she promised herself grimly. She donned her headphones and got to work. "And here's a time and temperature check from WCHT-WROC..."

Ryder covertly observed his petite partner at work. She looked like a teenager in jeans and a sassy red and white striped sweater, but he knew to his frustration exactly what a passionate woman she was. Even now he could feel the familiar tightening in his loins. He shifted and cursed himself inwardly.

He'd been a fool not to press his advantage the other night. Maybe if he had made love to her, she would have been out of his system once and for all. But his head told him that was a dangerous course to take. If he ever experienced all she was capable of giving, it might not be enough. A rush like that could become addictive, especially to a man who'd placed himself on an emotional starvation diet.

Never had a woman gotten under his skin like Summer Jones. Without effort, she wrung him out, evoking the most fundamental emotions from him. With her, in the span of an evening, he'd felt rage, protectiveness, affection, desire, tenderness. She made him lose control of the most central part of himself, that portion he held aloof from the world. Bitter experience had scarred him, made him wary in matters of the heart, so he ruled his emotional core with an iron will and a cool head. Somehow Summer breached his defenses, and she did it with ease.

Face it, Bowman, he told himself. *She scares the hell out of you.*

And that was the bottom line. That was why he wasn't going to let anything happen between them, no matter how loud his libido screeched in protest. He refused to let the attraction he felt draw him into a relationship he didn't want and couldn't control.

Ryder slid the toggle and hit the button for the next cartridge on line, then slipped his headphones down to dangle around his neck. His eye caught on a folded newspaper, and he tossed it onto Summer's side of the desk. "We made the paper."

Summer shot him a cautious look, then glanced at the newspaper and groaned. Someone had snapped a picture of herself and Ryder standing arm in arm at the Bachelor Auction. "Good God! They call us an ideal couple," she said sourly, reading the caption below.

"So you believe everything you read?" he challenged, grinning inwardly. She was such fun to bait. He loved to match wits with her. That, at least, was one aspect of their partnership he could still enjoy.

"I should be grateful for the publicity, right?" Her too-sweet smile flickered, and her expression became serious. "Beryl told me you matched my bid. That was awfully generous of you. The kids at the Foundation will appreciate it."

He shrugged. "I couldn't let you upstage me, now could I?"

"No, I guess not." Unwillingly she grinned. "You don't fool me for a moment, you know. It was a caring gesture, but don't worry. I won't breathe a word that might spoil that hard-nosed image."

Before he could reply, she hit her mike button, and she charged into the next announcement with a determined cheerfulness. "We've got freebies today, Gulliver. A pair of tickets for the Fall Color Cruise coming up at the end of this month. You can ride the riverboat *Southern Belle* along the Tennessee River to the Folk Festival at the Shellmound Recreation Area for forty miles downstream. These are round-trip tickets, folks, so let's give them away to lucky caller number five."

"All right, caller number five," Ryder repeated. "While we're winding up this morning's edition of the Coffee Club, we want to again thank Angie Perkins from the Chattanooga Chamber of Commerce for visiting with Jubilee today and also those of you who phoned in with questions and comments. Well, Jubilee, who's on tap for tomorrow?"

"I'll be taking a call from a Mr. Paul Edwards, who's just won first prize in the National Biggest Cockroach Contest."

"You're kidding!"

"Tune in tomorrow to find out." Summer cut her mike as Whitney Houston's newest hit came on.

Ryder dropped his headphone again and reached for his coffee. "There's got to be a limit to how tasteless you can go with this interview thing."

"You said you wanted variety," she said, shrugging. "I'm just trying to give the boss man what he wants. Did you know the winning bug was over three inches long?"

"Spare me the gruesome details, please." He shuddered and reached for the napkin-wrapped pastry. "If you ask me, someone else has gone a bit buggy around here."

"Just be careful," Summer warned with a twinkle in her eye. "He used a doughnut as bait."

"Oh, for crying out loud!"

"And while we're at it," Summer continued, warming to her subject, "I seem to remember something being said about syndicating these interviews. I've kept tapes of all the shows and most of the question-and-answer stuff. Do you want me to edit it into a couple of sample spots and pitch it to you again?"

"Careful, Jubilee, your ambition is showing." He poked suspiciously at the doughnuts, then with a sigh, dropped them into the trash can.

"Are you so chauvinistic you believe a woman can't share your drive? It may be a man's world, but a girl's got to take care of herself." Her voice had taken on a hard quality he scarcely recognized. She pointed a finger at him. "This is my future we're talking about, and I'm going to hold you to your promise."

"Playing hardball now, are you?" Ryder felt his expression grow tight with annoyance. "As far as I'm concerned you're still on a trial period, and if you can't come up with something better than a roach contest—"

"The wire services picked up the story, and it made the front page of *USA Today*. That's the problem with you, Ryder, you're a stuffed shirt. I'm striving for balance with the serious stuff."

Before he could respond, the intro to the next recording began, and their phone buzzed softly, the little red light on top of it flashing like a miniature police car. Summer reached for the receiver.

"You're caller number one—oh, hi, Aunt Ollie. What do you mean he's pouting? Well, just tell him he can't go to the beauty salon with you. Yes, I'll talk to you later. Bye."

Summer hung up and Ryder raised an inquiring eyebrow. She shrugged. "Trouble in retirement paradise, I guess."

"I should live so long," he muttered, his hand moving automatically over the control board to keep the music flowing. The phone chimed again, and Summer picked it up.

"Sorry, you're caller two." She paused, frowning. "No, Uncle Burt, I don't think it's selfish of her. Well, only her hairdresser is supposed to know! Yes, I'll talk to her." Hanging up, she gave Ryder a sheepish look.

He switched on his mike. "We still haven't had a winner for those cruise tickets, so keep trying." Another tap of his finger and a pre-recorded advertisement began to play. This time when the phone rang, he grabbed it. "You're the third—" He looked disgusted and slammed the receiver down. "They hung up on me."

"Must be your winning personality," Summer quipped. She moved around the control booth with the computerized log in her hand, expertly pulling the next hour's song and ad cartridges off of their tall revolving wire racks. The control-room door opened, and Vanessa breezed in, a sheaf of the morning's headlines in one hand. She wore an ecru sweater dress and about a ton of bronze jewelry.

"News time, gang," she said, slipping onto Summer's empty stool.

Ryder eyed the red digital readout on the board. "Two minutes, Vanessa."

"Right." She nodded and rearranged her papers.

Summer stacked the tape cartridges on top of the compact disc player beside Ryder, then edged closer to Vanessa. Her attitude was surreptitious, and it piqued Ryder's curiosity.

"You've got Merl worried," Summer said quietly.

Vanessa looked up, startled. "What? Why?"

"He's confused about Amy." Her words were spoken in the barest undertone. Ryder pretended to ignore them.

"He's got no reason to be concerned," Vanessa answered stiffly. "Amy has nothing to do with him." Her expression softened. "I can't wait to see her again. We've got a date to go to the library after school."

"You've got to be careful. Someone could get hurt."

Ryder gave Summer a sharp glance, then looked away again. There was something about the tension in her voice that disturbed him. He pushed another switch on the console and tried to dismiss his niggling concern. If two of his employees shared a bit of gossip, it was no skin off his nose. Still, it annoyed him not to know exactly what was going on at all times, especially where Summer was concerned. If that feeling was a contradiction to everything he'd so carefully and logically worked out in his head, it didn't bear closer examination.

Vanessa's voice was brisk again. "Don't worry. I know what I'm doing."

The phone pealed again, and with a last worried glance at Vanessa, Summer snatched it up.

"You're caller number four, try again—oh, hi. Play Lionel Richie's 'Lady' and dedicate it to me? Well, thanks, that's sweet. Look, it's time for Gulliver and me to sign off. Yes, you can call me tomorrow." She hung up and raked her hand through her hair in a harried gesture.

"When are you going to can that character?" Ryder demanded. "He calls every day, and it's getting tiresome."

"You're just jealous 'cause nobody wants to talk to *you*," Summer said snidely. "I don't mind talking, and I don't want to insult a fan."

"Hey, everybody," Ron Kerry said, stepping into the control room. "How's it going?" The phone rang again.

"What is this, Grand Central Station?" Ryder groaned, and reached for the phone. "Congratulations, you're the winner!" he bellowed. "Who . . . ?" He passed the receiver to Summer. "Your aunt."

"Aunt Ollie, what—" She listened intently, frowning, then glanced at her watch and sighed. "Yes, of course, I'll come. Don't worry, he'll get over it. I'll be there in thirty minutes."

No sooner had she replaced the receiver, than she had to answer it again. "Hello? Are you caller number five?" she said with a blank look. "Oh! Yes, you are! Congratulations."

Ryder snapped his fingers, demanding the receiver. "I'll get this guy's name. Wind up the show so we can get out of this madhouse!"

Summer nodded, passed him the phone, and hit her mike button. "And that's it for today's Coffee Club. Next up is Vanessa Lauden with this morning's news. Until next time, this is Jubilee..."

"...and Gulliver..."

"...wishing you two sugars in your cup!" Summer cued Vanessa, and the reporter hastily launched into her report. Scooping up her folder of notes, memos and advertising spots, Summer made for the door.

Ryder was right behind her. "Take it away, Ron."

"Hey!" The burly deejay leaned over the trash can, muttering. "Who threw away two perfectly good doughnuts?"

The door closed behind them, leaving them to the blessed quiet of the corridor.

"Great balls of fire, I feel like I've been shelled," Ryder grumbled. "You attract chaos like a magnet."

She gave him an angry look. "A little chaos could do you a lot of good."

"From six to ten every morning is all I can stand."

"Well, brace yourself, Bowman," she said, gritting her teeth. "We've got that Chattanooga Choo-Choo remote Saturday afternoon, and I have the dubious pleasure of inflicting myself on you for three more hours!"

She stomped off down the hall, ducked into her office, and reappeared with her jacket and shoulder bag.

"Hey, where are you going?" he demanded. "We've got ads to record."

"Tough." She punched the button of the elevator and glared at him, all defiance. "I'm going home. Aunt Ollie's having a crisis."

"So you'll just drop everything and go? Highly unprofessional of you, Jubilee."

She stepped into the elevator and lifted her chin with un-conscious dignity. "The people I love come first."

Ryder stared as the elevator doors slid shut, cursing him-self for being a jackass. What was the matter with him? Everything he did these days was all wrong. He was losing his touch and acting like a jerk, not the way he thought of himself at all. Why—

His thoughts lurched to a halt. What had she said? A re-mote? Just the two of them with a table full of equipment, out in the open where anything could happen? If she thought he was going to put her at risk that way after what had happened to her apartment, she had another think coming!

He hit the elevator button, then muttered an expletive. He could head her off by using the stairs. Turning, he loped down the corridor past the rest rooms, then pushed open the iron door into the stairwell. His feet thudded rhythmically down the three flights of stairs. He burst into the reception area, getting a surprised look from Carol, then saw a flash of red and white out the bank of glass windows. By the time he reached the sidewalk, she was disappearing into the cav-ernous opening of the parking garage in the next block.

The chilly wind whistled down the long concrete ramps of the garage and hit him in the face. He jogged past the at-tendant's booth at the entrance, receiving a strange look from the man behind the glass. Straining to see through the dim, shadowy recesses down the long lines of silent cars, Ryder finally spotted Summer halfway up the first ramp.

"Summer, wait!" He didn't stop to think why it was so important to inform her of his decision; it just was. He was a bit winded when he slid to a stop beside her blue Mus-tang. She had just stuck her key in the lock, and her hand froze on the handle.

"What now, Ryder?" Her weary expression was re-signed, and somewhat apprehensive. "I'll be back later to record those spots, so—"

His gesture cut her off. "Forget that. My remarks were uncalled for. I'm sorry."

She blinked in surprise. "That's why you chased me down? To apologize?"

"That, and to tell you that you won't be doing the remote."

"What? Why not?"

"It's too dangerous, considering the robbery."

She gaped at him. "That's ridiculous!"

"It's only wise to take—"

"Precautions!" she snapped, suddenly incensed. "Yes, I know. But this is so farfetched, it's absurd. There's no earthly reason why I can't do my job unless you're trying to get rid of me."

"You know that's not true."

"Do I? All I know is that I let you take charge of things in a moment of weakness, and now you think you can run my life." She jerked the handle, flung open the door, and flounced into the seat, every motion furious. "Well, thank you for your help, but I'll be at work at the Choo-Choo whether you're there or not!"

"You seem to forget I've got the final word around here." He bent and peered into the car. "I can cancel it altogether."

"You just try it, and I—I'll quit!" she threatened impulsively, her eyes bright with fury.

"You have a contract."

"I don't care. What have I got to lose besides a royal pain for a partner?" she shouted. She threw her shoulder bag into the passenger seat and fumbled with the key to the ignition. "Now get out of my way, I've got—"

She broke off her angry tirade, a disconcerted look on her face. From the small crack between the console and the passenger seat she pulled a jade green scarf.

"What's the matter?" he demanded.

"This is the one I thought had been stolen," she murmured, distracted. "It must have been here in the car all the time."

"Are you sure?"

"Certainly I'm sure! Will you stop questioning every move I make?" she snapped. "You're not my father or my husband, so lay off."

"But I am your employer."

"Then do your job and let me do mine!"

"All right, have it your way," he said, irate that she should throw his well-meant concern in his face like that.

"Fine!" She ground the key in the ignition, and the Mustang coughed into life.

"Fine!" He stepped back and slammed the car door shut with a violence he didn't attempt to restrain.

She revved the engine, reversed, then drove off down the concrete ramps with an ill-tempered squeal of her tires. Hands on his hips, Ryder fumed, then rolled his eyes heavenward, disgusted at his lack of control.

God above! he thought. *She's done it to me again!*

CHAPTER ELEVEN

VANESSA'S NEIGHBORHOOD was a quiet collection of modest older homes inhabited by a mixture of retired couples and young families. The wide sidewalks and tree-lined streets denied the hustle and bustle of city life, and it was that soothing, hometown feeling that had appealed to Vanessa when she'd been looking for a place to live. The white clapboard house she rented had a large front porch, tall ceilings, a minuscule kitchen and a bath with an old-fashioned claw-footed tub. In the evenings, after mothers called their children in for supper and the older folks had their after-dinner strolls, very little activity disturbed the late-day tranquility. That was why Vanessa was surprised when her doorbell rang just as the eight o'clock station break came on the television.

She carefully set aside the scissors and construction paper she'd been using, checked that her Indian cotton caftan was decently buttoned, and went to the door. It was Merl.

"Hello, beautiful," he said, leaning forward to give her a light kiss. His crooked grin was engaging and almost beseeching as he held up two paper cartons. "Invite me in, and I'll give you the choice of sweet and sour pork or *moo goo gai pan.*"

Vanessa's hesitation was momentary, but Merl sensed it.

"Hey, just tell me if I'm out of line. I guess I should have called. If you've got a guest—"

"Don't be silly," she said with a smile. "Come on in. I'm working on some posters for Amy, and the place is a mess, that's all. And I get the pork."

"The lady drives a hard bargain." He paused in the doorway of the cozy living room and whistled at the sight of her posters, markers, stencils and clippings scattered over floor, coffee table and sofa. "You weren't kidding, were you? This kind of mess takes real talent."

Vanessa laughed, turned off the TV set, and led him into the kitchen. She reached for silverware and plates and set them on the small breakfast table in the window alcove. "It's a social studies project Amy's working on. Her Nanny Barb isn't feeling well enough to help her with it, so I said I would."

"You're really into this, aren't you?" Merl slid into a chair and began dishing Chinese food onto the two plates.

Vanessa brought icy tumblers of lemonade to the table and sat down next to him. Her dark eyes sparkled with enthusiasm. "She's such a sweet little girl, Merl. So eager to please, but she's got a feisty temper, too. And you'd hardly know she's hearing-impaired. She reads lips like an expert, Mrs. Oates says, and of course, with her hearing aids she's really able to hear almost everything anyway. Her speech is a bit monotone, but that's typical, I think. I've been doing some reading about the subject."

"Nothing like a model child," Merl mumbled around a mouthful of *moo goo gai pan*.

Vanessa frowned, then toyed with the sweet and sour pork on her plate. "I'd like you to meet her sometime."

Merl's reply was offhand. "Sure. Here, want a fortune cookie?"

Vanessa accepted the crisp golden cookie, then broke it open. She scanned the message on the slip of paper inside, and her lips twitched.

"What's it say?" Merl asked innocently.

"I believe it's an indecent proposal," Vanessa said, giggling. "Merl Morgan, did you doctor these cookies?"

He made an indignant face. "Who, *moi*?"

"If anyone's mad enough to bribe a Chinese baker, it's you."

He gave her a comical leer, and lifted his eyebrows Groucho Marx style. "You bet your life! So, what's your answer, dearie?"

She touched his hand where it lay on the table and gave him a sultry look. "I'll take it under advisement."

He sighed. "Well, how about a movie tomorrow night instead?"

"I can't. I promised Amy..."

He waved his hands to spare the explanations. "Okay, how about Friday?"

"That's the social studies fair at Amy's school."

"And I suppose Saturday is out, and Sunday, too," he said, letting his irritation show. "Aren't you carrying this volunteer work a little too far?"

Vanessa looked away, biting her lip. "It's important to me."

"I thought I was, too." Standing, he cut off her involuntary protest with a sharp gesture. "Look, Vanessa, if you don't want to see me any more, I wish you'd just say it, instead of making up these excuses."

She gasped in dismay. "That's not it, at all!"

He took a step away, turned, and leaned against the enamel sink. "Then what is it?"

Rising, she clasped and unclasped her hands uncertainly. "I can't explain it exactly. It's just something I need to do right now."

Merl reached for her, catching her shoulders, and trying to look into her averted face. "What you need," he said carefully, "is to get married and have babies of your own."

She flinched. "Merl..."

"You know how I feel, Vanessa. I'm in love with you. I thought...I hoped you felt the same way."

Her whisper was ragged. "I do."

"Then why—"

Her fingers pressed against his lips. "Don't ask questions I can't answer. Just hold me, Merl."

Pulling her close, he buried his fingers in her dark curls, then tilted her face upward for his kiss. Her arms looped around his waist, and she pressed against him, returning the kiss with desperate longing.

When Merl pulled back, they were both breathing heavily. "Oh, Vannie," he said shakily, "what you do to me! I—" The soft chime of the doorbell interrupted him. "Damn!"

"Doorbell," Vanessa murmured, feathering little kisses along his jawbone.

"Yeah." The bell pealed again. Reluctantly he released her. "Guess you'd better answer it."

Stepping back, Vanessa blinked and gave a tremulous smile. "I suppose so."

"Try to hold that thought," he advised with a wink.

Vanessa blushed and crossed the front room. "I'll do my best," she flung saucily over her shoulder. She opened the door, and her mischievous expression vanished. "Amy!"

A little dark-haired urchin with red-rimmed eyes and a trembling chin looked back at Vanessa. She clutched a bulging, red Scooby-Doo book sack. The sleeve of a pink sweater trailed out of one flap like a forlorn flag. Vanessa dropped to one knee before the little girl and grasped her shoulders.

"Amy, what are you doing here? Are you alone? How did you get here?"

"I rode the bus and I walked." Her face quivered.

"Oh, honey," Vanessa cried, as distressed as the child. "What's the matter? What's wrong?"

"Nanny Barb went to the..." She hiccuped wetly. "...to the hospital."

"Oh, no." Vanessa gathered the girl into her arms and carried her inside. She pushed a poster off the end of the sofa and sat down with Amy in her lap. A distant part of her mind noticed that Merl watched them from the door of the kitchen. "I'm so sorry about Nanny Barb, but I'm sure she'll be all right," she soothed.

Amy shook her head vehemently, flinging silky black strands of hair across hers and Vanessa's faces. "N-no. She's too sick to take care of me anymore, and Grampa Oates has to take care of her now."

Tears were dripping down Amy's cheeks. Vanessa vainly wiped them with her fingertips and then began to remove Amy's windbreaker. "I know you're upset," she said gently, "but running away doesn't solve anything. I'm sure they're very worried about you."

Shudders quaked through the child's slim form. "Mrs. Baines..."

"Yes? Who's she?"

"The social-worker lady. She said I had to go stay in the group home." Amy's arms went around Vanessa's neck, and she sobbed brokenly. "Please, Vanessa, can I come and live with you?"

Tears prickled Vanessa's eyes and she hugged the little girl tightly. "Oh, baby," she whispered against Amy's sweetly fragrant nape. "My sweet baby. Yes, you can live with me."

"Vanessa," Merl said quietly. "It's not a kindness to promise her that."

"I mean it," Vanessa said fiercely. "She's staying with me. I'll find a way to keep her."

The tension went out of Amy, leaving her limp with relief, and her insignificant weight was a welcome burden in Vanessa's arms. She rocked and crooned until the girl's weeping diminished.

"Better now?" Vanessa asked gently. Amy's head bobbed against her breast. "Why don't you go wash your face? I've got to call Mrs. Baines and let them know you're safe."

"Do you have to?"

"Yes. Don't worry, Amy. We'll work this out, I promise."

Amy impulsively pressed a soggy kiss against Vanessa's cheek. "Okay."

Merl watched the little girl leave the room. "Vanessa, you can't keep her here."

"Don't tell me what I can and cannot do, Merl Morgan!" Vanessa said. She stood and rummaged in a desk drawer for the telephone directory. "That little girl needs me, and I'll be damned if I'll let her down again! There's no reason on earth why I can't take Mrs. Oates's place and become Amy's foster mother."

"Foster mother? Vanessa, you must be out of your mind." Merl raked his hand through his yellow hair. "Even if they allow a single, unmarried woman to do that, think of the responsibilities!"

"There's got to be a way. I'll hire a lawyer. I'll—"

"But what about us?" he asked.

She gazed at him in wonder. "This has nothing to do with us."

"If we're going to be together, it sure does."

"But it doesn't change anything," Vanessa protested.

"The hell it doesn't. Don't you think I should be included in a decision like this?"

She shook her head in disbelief. "I've got to do this for Amy and for me."

"Great!" Merl's jaw worked angrily. "I want to be part of your life, but you keep shutting the door in my face."

"Merl!" Her astonished voice was faintly querulous. "It doesn't have to be this way."

"I want to marry you, Vanessa. And I want to raise children with you. *Our* children."

She blanched at the implication. "I see. And Amy doesn't enter into your plans. Then I'm sorry, Merl," she said softly, determinedly, "because she does enter into *mine*."

"If that's the way you want it." His face darkened, and he grabbed his jacket. He paused at the door. "I'll be seeing you around, then."

The door slammed behind him, and Vanessa swallowed hard on the wave of emotion. With an effort, she forced that particular pain into a far recess of her brain to be dealt with later. Much later. Right now, Amy had to come first. She picked up the phone and began to dial.

"AND THIS IS IN DENALI NATIONAL PARK. That's where we saw the moose," Burton Pierson said, passing yet another snapshot to Summer.

"No, dear, the moose was in that preserve outside of Anchorage," Olivia disagreed. She pointed at the picture laid out on the living-room coffee table. "See? I'm certain we saw the moose with that delightful young man who gave us the tour. Derrick something, I believe."

"You've contradicted everything I've told Summer," Burton said irritably. "I was there, too, remember?"

Olivia's mouth compressed. "It's not my fault you can't keep your facts straight—"

"It doesn't matter, does it?" Summer interrupted hastily. Invited for Aunt Ollie's famous Friday-night chowder and a photographic review of their trip, she'd spent most of the evening trying to keep the peace. *What's the matter with these two?* she wondered, then desperately launched into another diversionary maneuver. "Oh, look at the mountains in this one! They make our Cumberlands look like foothills! Did you take this one, Uncle Burt?"

"Sure did. Pretty good photography, isn't it?"

"Burton, dear, isn't that from the roll I took on the cruise ship?" Olivia asked.

"How the devil should I know?" he exploded. He shoved the stack of snapshots toward his wife. "Here, you show the rest of them to Summer since you know everything. I'm going out to the shed to tie some flies."

With that, he lumbered to his feet and left the living room in a huff. Olivia heaved a great sigh that lifted her bosom under the bib of her gingham apron.

"I just don't know what's the matter with that man lately. Ever since we got home, he's been so testy!"

"I suppose there's got to be a period of adjustment for both of you following retirement," Summer ventured, thumbing through the rest of the photos.

"Well, I wish he'd get on with it!" Olivia muttered. "He wants to go everywhere with me, and then he criticizes the whole time. It's like having a permanent shadow. Why, if you hadn't talked him out of it, he'd have gone to the beauty parlor with me, and he wanted to come to my bridge group, too!''

Summer laughed and propped her denim-clad legs on the coffee table. ''Not your Tuesday Ladies' Club? That's been just you and your girlfriends for years.''

''Just try to tell your uncle that. I don't know what to do, Summer. The man is driving me bats!''

Summer smiled at her choice of words, but then tried to think seriously about the problem. ''You didn't have this kind of trouble on your trip, did you?''

''No, but that was different. We were busy every minute.''

''Maybe that's part of the problem. Uncle Burt's retired from a job that filled his days too well, and now he's at loose ends. He's got to get involved with some other activities.''

''Would you talk to him? The state he's in, you know he won't listen to anything I say.''

Summer leaned over and kissed her aunt's cheek. ''Of course.''

''Thanks, dear.'' Olivia gave herself a little shake and put on a smile. ''Now, enough of that. Tell me all your news. What's going on down at the station?''

''Hard work, as usual.'' Summer set aside the stack of photographs, then crossed her legs Indian-fashion, and settled down for a chat. ''The most exciting thing that's happened is Vanessa's becoming a foster mother. I think I told you about her taking an interest in one of Beryl's Brownies?''

Olivia nodded. ''Yes, you did.''

''Well, Vanessa and Amy developed quite an attachment, so when Mrs. Oates had a minor stroke and had to be hospitalized, Amy ran away to Vanessa rather than go to another foster home.''

''Oh, dear. The poor little thing!'' Olivia sympathized.

"You know Vanessa, though. She can get things done. To make a long story short, since it was an emergency situation, she got the social-welfare agency to approve her as Amy's foster parent on a temporary basis. Amy's with her now, and they've even gone shopping for a new pink bedspread for her room."

"Oh, I love a happy ending," Olivia said, a smile creasing her plump cheeks. "And how is Mrs. Oates? I'm sure the little girl will miss her."

"According to Vanessa, Mrs. Oates is expected to recover completely, but she's not going to be able to resume care of Amy. An active little girl is just too much for her now. Vanessa took Amy to visit her in the hospital, and they all had a long talk. Amy's to come visit anytime, just like she would her own grandmother."

"Such a wonderful thing for Vanessa to do," the older woman commented. "I always knew she was more than a fashion plate."

"She's extremely close to Amy already." Summer's vague words held more truth than she could tell her aunt. Vanessa had already confided that her attorney was petitioning the juvenile court for permission to examine Amy's birth records. Vanessa was confident her belief that Amy was her natural daughter would be confirmed, but Summer was uncertain what would happen after that. She prayed her friend knew what she was doing. "I know she intends for this to be a permanent arrangement," Summer told her aunt.

"It's a big responsibility for a young single woman. I hope she understands that."

"I'm sure she does, Aunt Ollie," Summer said. "The disturbing thing is she and Merl seemed to be getting serious, and now all this has put him off."

"That's a shame, but it's a fact some men don't want the obligations of a ready-made family."

"His face is longer than an old hound dog's these days. Seems to me if he really cares for Vanessa, then he ought to be able to accept Amy, too."

"Now, Summer," Olivia warned, shaking her finger, "don't you go trying to arrange other people's lives for them. They'll have to work this out themselves."

"I know you're right." She grimaced. "I said practically the same thing to Ryder when he tried to cancel tomorrow's remote."

"Why'd he want to do that?"

"Oh, he had some wild notion that since my place had been burglarized, I ought not to do it."

"Well, maybe's he's right," Olivia began, her blue eyes clouding with worry.

"Now don't you start, too! There's no connection. In fact, I'm more and more convinced that it must have been a bunch of kids, as Lieutenant Ogden said. Yesterday, someone put a couple of pieces of costume jewelry that had been taken in my mailbox. It's just the kind of prank a teenager would pull."

"Well, I'm grateful you've got that alarm now. I can't help but worry, but that makes me feel better."

Summer grinned. "And I've only set it off myself twice this week. I'm practically on a first-name basis with the people at County Security."

"I wish you wouldn't joke about this, Summer!"

"I'm sorry, Aunt Ollie," she said contritely. "But I think you and Ryder are making too much of the whole thing. It happened. It's over. That's all."

"Mr. Bowman has only your best interests at heart, dear. You're getting along a lot better, aren't you? The Coffee Club runs so smoothly, and you're so amusing together."

If you only knew, Aunt Ollie, Summer thought with a deep inward sigh.

The past week had been difficult, with both she and Ryder so edgy and snappish that the least little remark was liable to set them off. Summer was glad to know that even someone with an acute listening ear like Aunt Olivia hadn't picked up on the tension that made the air fairly crackle within the control booth and their dialogue sizzle over the airwaves. And even when the verbal sparks weren't flying, Summer was always highly conscious of every move Ryder made, and she'd looked up more than once to find him staring at her with a strange ferocity in his hazel eyes. Summer wondered vaguely if part of the problem was similar to Burton's and Olivia's—just too much of each other's company. It was a good thing the weekend was giving them a break, except for the three-hour remote tomorrow.

"Thanks for the compliments, Aunt Ollie. Working with Ryder is always a challenge," Summer said, her tone dry. "I'm looking forward to working at the Choo-Choo, and however well-intentioned Ryder's motives, he's not going to stop me. We do it for the fans as well as the sponsors. Besides, as I recall, they have some of the best barbecue in town."

"Always thinking about your tummy, aren't you, dear?" Olivia teased.

"I wouldn't say no to another piece of that pecan pie we had for supper."

Olivia laughed at Summer's hopeful expression. "All right. Come on, and I'll cut a piece for your uncle, too. Maybe it will sweeten his disposition."

"IT'S A BEAUTIFUL FALL AFTERNOON here at the Chattanooga Choo-Choo Vacation Complex, folks, and Gulliver and I want to invite you to come out, and bring the family to visit with us. We've got lots of goodies to give away and you're sure to have some fun."

"Right you are, Jubilee," Ryder said into the mike connected to the tabletop of remote equipment set up before them. "We're just outside the huge Trans-Continental Restaurant enjoying these beautiful formal gardens, built right between the old tracks where people boarded their trains when this was a working depot. Everything's trains, trains and more trains around here, and there's even a trolley ride for the kids. So come join us. We'll give away a prize to the first person who comes up to us and says 'I love the Coffee Club.' What's the prize for this half hour, Jubilee?''

"Two passes for the railroad movies inside the Choo-Choo Theatre, an assortment of taffy from the Choo-Choo's Candy Store, and a six-pack of albums from WCHT-WROC."

"All right! So whatcha' waiting for? Come on down! Now back to Roy Wiggens at WCHT-WROC for some more music!" Ryder expertly made the necessary adjustments to switch the feed back to the main station.

Summer removed her headphones with a sigh and reached for her soft-drink cup. For the first time in the little over two hours that they'd been here, there was a lull in the crowd, and she was grateful for the break. She took a long sip from the cup, and lifted the weight of her hair off her damp nape. The crisp October day had warmed up considerably, and she was regretting the calf-length wool skirt and high-necked Victorian blouse she'd chosen to wear to their outdoor location. She looked enviously at Ryder's checked shirt and lightweight slacks and repressed a sigh.

Ryder picked up a clipboard and ran his finger down the list of attractions within the thirty-acre complex. "Let's see. We've plugged the indoor pool, the choice of three different hotel accommodations, and the Imperial Ballroom banquet facilities."

"Right."

"The Diner Dining Car, the trolley and the model railroad exhibit."

"Check."

"The Choo-Choo memorabilia at the Depot Store, and the freshly pulled taffy at the Candy Store."

"Check again."

He looked up, frowning. "So what's left?"

"Fourteen—count 'em!—specialty shops. I'm doing my best to personally investigate each one."

"Is that where you got the pink fuzzy?" he asked, pointing toward the sack at her feet. Furry mauve ears poked from the bag. "Is that the newest addition to your menagerie of marionettes?

"Most of them are puppets, for your information," she retorted. "And no, it's not for me. It's a welcome present for Vanessa's foster child."

"Amy, isn't it?"

Summer glanced curiously at him. "That's right."

"Well, don't look so surprised," Ryder grumbled. "I had to give the social-service people the lowdown on Vanessa's job security, you know. Pretty gutsy of her to take on a handicapped kid."

"Oh, I don't know. She loves Amy. And that makes all the difference."

"I suppose it does." He became brisk again. "Okay, what else haven't we mentioned?"

"The manager's bringing the singing waiters by to perform in a while, and if you talk about the Penn Station dance club I think that will just about cover it."

"Right. Whew! I had no idea all this was here," Ryder said with a gesture at their surroundings.

A brightly painted steam locomotive stood on display on one side of the large area where they sat, forming an open-ended rectangle with the restaurants in the main depot building and the row of specialty shops down the other side. In the center sat the dining cars used as another eating establishment and the sleeper cars that could be rented by the night like regular hotel rooms. In this same section, unloading dock tracks had been removed, replaced by regular rows of formal flower beds filled with brightly colored mums, spaced by gazebos and fountains and the covered walkways. A bell clanged as the trolley made its circular trip from the side entrance of the restaurant to the hotel rooms at the rear of the complex and back again.

Ryder set down the clipboard and pointed toward a large sign over the shops that proclaimed Model Railroad. "I'd like to see the model trains myself," he admitted.

Summer's mouth tilted. "No! Never say there's a touch of kid left in Ryder Bowman!"

He tilted his chair back and gave her a wry grin. "All right, I'll admit it. But don't quote me on it."

"You're enjoying this, aren't you?"

"Sure." He shrugged. "Brings back memories. I picked up extra bucks doing this kind of thing in college. Management has its challenges, but it's nice to get out of the executive suite occasionally."

"I think it's fun, too," she said. "And amazingly safe."

"All right, I get the point. I guess I overreacted."

"I guess I did, too."

Ryder's dark eyebrow lifted in surprise. "So we're both apologizing. Again."

"It looks that way."

Ryder's gaze darkened, and he caught her hand under the table. "It's been a rough week, hasn't it?"

Her indrawn breath was shaky. "One of the worst."

"So, what are we going to do about it?"

The warmth and texture of his skin against hers was a distraction she couldn't afford, so she pulled free, a wry little smile curling her lips. "I think, Bowman, that we'll just have to tough it out."

Easier said than done, half-pint, he thought, his gaze locked on the tempting curve of her mouth. Despite all his qualms, he ached for her. He couldn't shake the memory of how soft her breasts were, how delicate her nipples. All week long, he'd wondered how it would feel to bury himself in her softness.

"Personally," he drawled, "hanging tough would be very low on my list of viable options."

"All right, Mr. CEO, what would you suggest?"

"We could finish what we started last weekend."

Her eyes widened, the violet irises darkening to a deep, roubled purple. "Could we? I thought we'd agreed an affair wasn't a good idea, for many reasons."

His voice was a low, hungry rumble. "It's difficult to remember even one good reason when the thought of holding you again makes me so hard I hurt."

She gave a little gasp, and involuntarily her eyes dropped o the bulge of his manhood straining against the fabric of his slacks. "Ryder, don't."

"You think it's that easy?" His chuckle was humorless. "Honey, the only remedy I can think of is checking us into the Choo-Choo's victorian sleeping car and making love to ou until neither of us can walk. Maybe then I could get you ut of my system."

"That's exactly why it won't happen," she said. "I won't ake risks again with a man who's afraid to let me get too lose."

"What? I just said—"

"That you'd use a physical release to keep me at an emotonal distance, so you could leave me without a second hought." She shook her head, and her golden hair bounced nd cascaded in her effort to negate his denial of his feelings. "No way, Ryder. If it ever happens, you're not going to get off that easily. I'll see to it."

"You're mighty sure of yourself."

"Yes, I am." Her smile was feminine and feline. "So beare, or the thing you fear most might come to pass."

His eyes narrowed, and his lips quirked in an indolent alf-smile as he enjoyed their repartee. "And what might hat be, half-pint?"

Her eyes were limpid, a mixture of innocence and seduction. "Why, you'll fall in love with me, of course."

The humor vanished from Ryder's expression, but any eply to her challenge was forestalled. A new group of admirers came up to the table, and with one last triumphant ook, Summer turned to greet them.

"Oh, Jubilee, I just love the Coffee Club," gushed a miniskirted teenager, and Summer promptly showered her with the promised prizes. Laughing, asking questions, signing autographs, she was the epitome of charm. Only Ryder had seen her claws.

Encouraged by the laughter, tourists and guests strolling through the grounds began to crowd around the table, and soon Ryder was just as busy doing his part. By the time the next live broadcast arrived there was quite a throng ready to be entertained by a chorus of singing waitresses and waiters from the Station House Restaurant.

"You both have been terrific today," Bob Peale, the advertising manager said to Summer and Ryder as they listened to the strains of "I've Been Working On the Railroad," "Sentimental Journey," and the perennial favorite, "Chattanooga Choo-Choo."

"It's been a good day," Summer replied. "I hope you'll ask us back again."

"You can bet on it," Bob replied. "Just one more favor. We'd like to advertise our photo studio. Would you mind putting on a period costume and posing out here for us?"

That was how they found themselves some minutes later making an entrance before the applauding crowd, Ryder in a blue Yankee Colonel's uniform, and Summer in a lilac and lace off-the-shoulder Civil War-era ball gown. The photographer quickly set up his tripod and motioned them into place before the many-paned windows of one entrance. To get a good view, people in the rear of the crowd perched on the walkways, climbed on the shed braces and scrambled over the locomotive itself. Out of the corner of her eye Summer even noticed a figure on top of one of the sleeping cars.

"I do declare, Colonel, suh," Summer drawled in her best Southern-belle accent. "Ya'll wouldn't be contemplating taking advantage of 'lil ole me?"

"My dear, such a thought never crossed my mind," Ryder intoned stenoriously.

In an aside to the audience, Summer snapped her fingers and whispered loudly, "Oh, drat!"

The crowd snickered appreciatively.

"Get a little closer now," the photographer instructed. "That's right, take his arm, Miss Jones."

Obediently Summer stepped closer and threaded her hand through the crook of Ryder's arm. He tried to position himself, succeeding only in banging the heavy sword hanging from his belt against his ankle. "Ouch!" he said under his breath. "How the hell did they ever manage these things?"

"Watch your image, Gulliver," Summer murmured.

"Okay, smile," called the photographer. He studied them standing decorously together and shook his head. "No, no, no. Can't we have some action here? Take her in your arms or something."

Ryder doffed his plumed hat and grinned. "With pleasure." There was a devilish gleam in his eye, and Summer took a skittish step backward.

"Now, Gulliver, what are you up to?" She laughed nervously.

For answer, he grabbed her arm and pulled her against him, evoking catcalls and whoops from the crowd. "Like this?" he asked.

"Great! Keep it up," the photographer shouted, clicking his camera madly.

Laughing, Summer pushed against the immovable wall of Ryder's chest. "Now, Ryder..."

"Quiet, woman. I'm in character," he growled, and suddenly bent her over his arm.

"Ryder!" she gasped, unnerved by the crowd's reaction, the unexpected closeness of the embrace, and the lambent desire shining deep in his eyes. "Remember, you're not Rhett, and I'm not Scarlett!"

His grin was devilish and devastating. "Frankly, my dear," he said, "I don't give a damn."

And then he kissed her, holding her firm and wooing her with such expertise she couldn't hide her response. When he released her, and set her on her feet again, she felt light-headed. Their audience applauded uproariously, the photographer gave a thumbs-up signal, and Ryder took a bow.

"Thank you, my friends, thank you."

There was a pop, and glass tinkled. Summer glanced around curiously, frowning at a shattered pane in the wall of windows behind them. She wondered if someone had thrown a rock. Then she heard another loud pop and sudden screams.

In that second she was falling, pushed down under the impetus of Ryder's lunging form. She hit the ground hard in a sprawl of skirts and blue uniform. The wind went out of her lungs. Ryder covered her, his weight pinning her to the hard concrete.

"What the hell are you doing?" she wheezed in protest. Struggling, she pushed against him. Her hand came away wet with crimson. "Ryder!"

"Stay down!" he gritted. "Someone's shooting at us!"

CHAPTER TWELVE

"I'M ALL RIGHT, I tell you!"

"Mr. Bowman, please," the nurse said. "You'll have to wait until the doctor releases you..."

Ryder's voice was low and ominous through the examining-room door. "Where the hell are my pants!"

Lt. Kent Ogden grinned at Summer and shook his shaggy head in disgust. Rapping sharply on the door, he pushed into the narrow cubicle with Summer at his heels. "Geez, Tex, can't you hold it down? We heard your caterwaulin' all the way down the hall."

Ryder sat on the edge of a gurney, bare-chested, a sheet over his middle, and a tidy white bandage circling his left upper arm. "Kent! Will you tell this battle-ax—" He broke off, frowning when he saw Summer's white face. "Why'd you bring her in here? She's liable to pass out!"

"I am not," Summer said faintly. The lilac ball gown she still wore was splattered across the ruffled bodice with Ryder's blood. She ignored everything except the man on the gurney. "Are you all right?"

"It's just a scratch," he answered dismissively, and glared at the inoffensive nurse. "Everything will be just peachy— if only someone would give me back my pants and let me get out of here!"

The nurse passed Ryder's missing slacks to Kent. "It was the only way we could keep him still," she explained. "Don't let him have them until the doctor okays it, Lieutenant." She cast a disdainful look in Ryder's direction. "Some people," she sniffed, and sailed out of the room.

"You've got a real way with the ladies, Tex," Kent drawled. "So, what's the doc say about that arm? Are your handball days over?"

"You wish. One good arm's all I need to beat your tail all over that court, anyway. It looks messy, but it didn't even need a stitch. What beats me is why they take a man's pants away to fix up his arm." Ryder's tone was aggrieved.

"To torture innocent victims, no doubt," Kent said.

"Well, the bastard just grazed me. Did you get him?"

"Nope."

"Hell, Kent!" Ryder stopped himself with a glance at Summer. "Hand me my pants, partner," he said grimly, "and then you can tell me how a gunman got away in broad daylight."

"We had a unit on the scene two minutes after the call came in, but maybe you were too busy bleeding to notice," Kent returned sarcastically. He tossed Ryder his pants. "There was quite a panic, and we can't come up with even one eyewitness who saw anything."

"Except me," Summer said softly.

"Except Summer," Kent amended. "She saw someone on top of one of those old railcars just seconds before all hell broke loose. The lab people are there now, and all signs indicate that's where the gunman was."

"I thought it was just somebody trying to get a better look at us clowning around," she said, swallowing hard. "I guess I was wrong."

"How could you know?" Ryder slid from the gurney, dragging the sheet with him. Clutching his pants, he looked pointedly at Summer. "Do you mind?"

"Oh!" Twin spots of color flagging her pale cheeks, she turned her back, staring between the slats of the venetian blind out the narrow window. The sounds of clothing being adjusted kept her eyes averted.

"So what's the next move?" Ryder demanded. "We can't let some lunatic go around taking potshots at Summer—"

"They weren't shooting at me," she said. She swung around, and her eyes were wide and scared.

Ryder reached for his shirt, a frown knitting his brow. "What?"

"Don't kid yourself, Tex, those bullets were meant for you."

"I don't get it." Ryder's voice was flat, the shirt forgotten in his hands.

"After taking the measurements and looking at the angles, the lab boys say it's ninety percent certain you were the gunman's target. I think it might be a good idea to place you in protective custody, considering the state of mind of our ex-friends down in Atlanta these days."

"Oh no, you don't!" Ryder snapped. "You're grasping at straws, Kent."

"You made any new enemies lately? I'd be glad to entertain any other notions."

"Maybe I said something on the air, and somebody got mad. Maybe some nut wanted some publicity. How the hell should I know?"

Kent frowned. "You better—"

"All right, Mr. Bowman." The young, curly-haired resident breezed in, interrupting them. He held a medical chart in one hand and a small bottle of pills in the other. "How's that arm feeling?"

"Fine, just fine," Ryder said impatiently. "Can I get out of here now?"

"Absolutely. Just keep the dressing changed. You might drop by and let me take another look at it in a couple of days. Oh, and here's a few painkillers." The doctor dropped them on the gurney and began to scribble rapidly on the chart.

"Don't need 'em," Ryder said shortly, shrugging into his bloodstained shirt.

"Take them, anyway. You're full of local anesthetic, but when that wears off, that wound is going to ache like the devil. It'd be a good idea to have someone stay with you, too. It isn't likely to start bleeding again, but you never know."

"Oh, for crying out loud," Ryder snapped. "I'll be fine if I can just get out of this joint!"

"He doesn't handle pain well, does he?" Kent asked Summer conversationally.

"All men are babies when they're hurt. I suppose I'd better take these." She picked up the pill bottle and turned to the doctor. "I'll be staying with Mr. Bowman, doctor. Don't worry, I'll take good care of him."

"Fine, young lady. You call me if you need me." The young doctor took one look at Ryder's thundercloud expression and decided to make a quick exit.

"Now, wait a minute," Ryder began. "I don't need a baby-sitter."

Kent folded his arms and pulled thoughtfully at his lower lip. "The way I see it, Tex, you got two choices. You can check into the hospital or you can go home and let Summer stay with you a few hours. Personally I'd go for my own place, but if you've got a yen for bedpans and—"

"Okay, I get the picture. I'm being rousted by my best friend and my partner. Thanks a heap."

"Don't mention it," Kent said with a grin. Then his rugged face took on a serious cast. "I want you to go home and get some rest. You and me got some serious thinking to do in the meantime. Just in case we are dealing with our 'friends' here, I'm going to place a couple of extra patrols in your neighborhood."

"Yeah." Ryder grimaced and supported his left elbow with his right palm. "Whatever you say."

"Better move him quick, Summer, while he's so docile," Kent remarked.

"It's rather a remarkable sight, isn't it?" Summer held open the door. "Let's go, Bowman."

"Everybody's a comedian," Ryder muttered. "And you'd better watch it, Ogden. One of these days you'll get yours."

"I'm looking forward to it," Kent said, laughing. He touched Summer's arm. "I'll give you a call later, okay?"

"Sure." Her long skirt swishing around her ankles, Summer followed Ryder down the corridor. In minutes, she was unlocking her Mustang and ushering Ryder into the passenger seat.

"Should I trust you to drive?" he asked, sinking down low on his spine and cradling his arm.

"Don't be insulting." She climbed in her side, then noticed the betraying tightness around his mouth. "Hurting already?"

His head rested on the back of the seat and his eyes were closed. "A bit."

"Don't be a hero," she said, digging into her purse. She passed him the pill bottle the doctor had given him. "A painkiller will help you from getting so stiff, too. Can you take them dry?"

"Yes, nurse." He swallowed the pills. Satisfied, she started the car and headed into traffic. "I've got to pick up my car," he muttered.

"Kent's having someone bring it home."

"And the equipment . . ."

"I called Merl. He'll take care of it."

"Look, there's really no need for you to stay. Your aunt—"

"I've already called them to tell them we're safe. Relax, Ryder. For once in your life, let someone else take charge."

"Looks like I don't have much choice."

For the first time since she'd heard those awful shots, she smiled. "Ain't it the truth?"

She was the picture of efficiency, chauffeuring Ryder home, letting them in his house with his keys, greeting Clancy and ordering Ryder straight to bed. Surprisingly he made no objection.

"I am bushed," he admitted, stifling a yawn.

"You lost a lot of blood, and those pills are probably making you drowsy. Are you hungry? I could fix something."

"Later. Don't bother about it, Summer. Mrs. Mills usually leaves something in the freezer. Look, you go home. I know you want to get out of that costume. I'll be all right after I've had forty winks."

"I've got a change of clothes in the car." She bit her lip. "Let me do this for you, please. Besides, you know Kent will skin us both if we don't follow orders."

He chuckled. "You've got that right." Cupping her cheek with his palm, he smiled. "All right, half-pint. If that's the way you want it."

"Yeah. So toddle off to beddy-bye land, and quit hassling me, okay?"

"Okay. See you later." Yawning widely, he ambled toward the bedrooms.

Satisfied, Summer got busy. She retrieved a set of gym clothes she kept in the car, and exchanged the ruined gown for shorts and a T-shirt. The gown went into a plastic bag and then back out to the car to be returned later, but she had scarce hope that it could be salvaged. Rummaging in the freezer, she found a package of homemade stew and popped it into the microwave to defrost. She made a pot of coffee, and fed Clancy. It seemed imperative that she stay busy, so she took some stale bread out on the patio to feed the birds and then sat watching the sunset until the increasing chilliness of the air drove her back inside. She grabbed the phone on its first ring, and spoke quietly to Kent. When she hung up again, she decided it was time she checked on Ryder.

Creeping down the carpeted hall, she peeked into the darkened bedroom. Ryder was sound asleep, sprawled on his stomach, the puffy geometric comforter pushed down to his waist and one bare foot poking out from under the cover. The stark white bandage around his arm stood out in the dim room like a beacon, and Summer felt her mouth go dry

and her stomach tumble as she gazed at it. Just a few inches
more to one side and . . .

She tore her gaze away, and noticed a discarded heap of
clothing at the foot of the bed. Tiptoeing, she gathered up
the clothes and left the room. She intended to drop them in
the hamper in the laundry room located just off the kitchen,
but Ryder's checked shirt, the one he'd been wearing under
the Union officer's jacket, was splotched with patches of
dried blood. She knew it would be ruined unless it was
washed soon, so she took it to the kitchen sink.

Summer twisted the faucet, letting the cool water run over
the shirt, then rubbed detergent into the stains. White bub-
bles churned, filling the sink, then turned rusty brown. Determinedly Summer scrubbed the fabric, rubbing it between
her fingers. There was a lot of blood. She hadn't realized
how much.

She stared at the pale brown river swirling down the drain
and swallowed harshly. Nausea churned, but she fought it
back, just as she had the shock and near-panic when she'd
realized he'd been hurt. She'd been frantic to help him, but
he'd held her still, covering her with his own body until he
was certain the shooting had stopped. Only then had he allowed her up, dragging her inside the building while security men and policemen cordoned off the area and calmed
the terrified crowd. A napkin hastily wrapped around his
wound was all the first aid he'd allowed until Kent had arrived and forcibly sent him to the hospital.

Summer's fingers found the frayed and ragged section of
sleeve ripped by the bullet, and she shuddered. She'd been
functioning on nerve alone, trying not to think, trying to do
the proper thing, but with the evidence of violence clutched
in her fists, she was consumed by the chill horror and abject fear she'd held at bay until this moment. There was no
denying the facts. Someone had tried to kill Ryder. Someone had nearly taken from her the most precious thing in her
life—the man she loved.

A sob escaped her, and her hands twisted in the soggy, stained shirt. What a fool she'd been, to deny what was in her own heart! From the very first, she'd felt the tug of his powerful attraction and known how dangerous he was. That was why she'd instinctively fought him on every level. But as she'd grown to know him, had seen all the fine qualities of his personality, the humor, the inner strength of character, her defenses had been stripped away one by one, until there was nothing left but the truth. She'd fallen in love with Ryder, only she'd been too blind and too scared to risk getting hurt. Now that cowardice seemed so petty and small. What was life without risk? The greater tragedy would have been losing Ryder today, without ever having told him how she felt. Hot tears fell into the cool suds. Summer collapsed against the edge of the sink, and pressed her forehead against the cold porcelain. Her wrists hung limp under the running water, and she wept and thanked God for a second chance.

"Hush, honey," Ryder said, his voice husky with sleep. His hands were warm and comforting on her quaking shoulders, turning her around and pulling her into his embrace. "For God's sake, Summer, don't cry so."

"I—I can't get all the blood out of your shirt," she sobbed, her cheek against the burgundy velour of his robe, her wet hands cinched tightly around his trim waist.

"It's all right." He reached behind her and turned the water off. His fingers slipped underneath the golden curtain of her hair, found and massaged the tense muscles in her neck and shoulders. "It's just a shirt."

"I woke you up."

"No, you didn't. I got up to get something to eat."

"Oh, I'll get—" She made an abortive move that he stilled easily.

"Stay right where you are a minute." He breathed in her scent, the light floral fragrance she always wore mixed with the wonderful woman smell that was uniquely Summer.

"It's a delayed reaction, that's all. Not surprising, considering what a hardy little trooper you were this afternoon."

"I've never been so scared in my life," she choked, burrowing closer.

"Me, too." His chin grazed the top of her head, and he drew a deep, shuddering breath. How could he describe the feeling he'd experienced when he'd thought *she* was in mortal danger. It was much worse than being a target himself.

"I didn't know what was happening," she murmured brokenly. "The shots—I didn't know what they were."

"Believe me, once you've heard it, it's a sound you don't ever forget."

"You—you've been shot at before?"

"Yeah."

She couldn't contain the sudden trembling, nor the tears that slid down her cheeks. "Those people in Atlanta. Are they really trying to—"

"Shh. Nothing's for certain. Just try to forget about it."

She jerked, leaning back against his arms to stare dumbfounded at him. "Forget it? How can I?" Her hands framed his face, as though to convince herself that he was indeed whole and safe. "I couldn't stand it if anything happened to you."

"Or to you." Catching one of her hands, he placed a gentle kiss in the sensitive palm. "Take it easy. Nothing's going to happen."

"Something almost did! We have to do something."

He studied her solemnly, wiping the dampness off her cheek with the pad of his thumb. The corner of his mouth twitched. "You look like a tigress ready to pounce. Are you going to take on all comers to protect me?"

"If I have to." Abruptly her eyes overflowed again, tears like glistening diamonds on a field of rain-drenched pansies. "Don't tease me, Ryder. I'm in n-no joking m-mood!"

His arms tightened, pulling her close, and he placed small kisses on her brow, her lashes, the corner of her mouth.

There was an element of indulgent laughter in the words he murmured, "I'm sorry, half-pint. What's the problem?"

"You infuriating man," she complained. "Can't you tell I'm in love with you?"

The hand smoothing her tangled hair faltered, and his expression was suddenly deeply troubled. "Oh, Summer."

She placed trembling fingers against his lips. "Don't search for words. I don't need them. All I need is you. I've been stubborn and prideful, and I could have robbed us both of something rich and generous, but after today I realized that some things are worth the risk."

He smiled faintly. "You're an incredibly brave woman."

A sudden thought made her voice quaver. "You—you're not turning me down again, are you?"

Green fire flared in the depths of his hazel eyes. "Not a chance, half-pint," he muttered, and his mouth found hers.

She was as sweet and fiery as he remembered, yet more so, her very flavor enhanced by the completeness of her surrender, the unbridled wildness of her passion. She tasted of salty tears, but she gave her mouth willingly, and Ryder groaned, deepening the kiss to capture her essence. Their tongues darted and played while hands roamed, caressing, trying to get closer and closer.

Releasing the belt on his robe, she explored the hair-dusted expanse of his chest, arching against him in mute invitation. Her fingers teased his dusky nipples, then traced the channel of his spine and slipped beneath the elastic of his briefs to explore the indentations in his muscular hips. She pressed closer, reveling in the heat and warmth of him, the musky male odor of skin and soap and piney after-shave. After a brush with death, he was so very much *alive*, so absolutely what she needed, she thought her heart would burst with wanting.

His lips trailing down her throat, Ryder paused at the base to count the pulse that jumped there. "You're heart's beating so fast," he murmured.

Her palm found the center of his chest. "So is yours."

Ryder tugged at the hem of her shirt, finding the bare skin of her back, so smooth and silky. Impatient for her, he pulled the shirt over her head, then cupped the fullness of her breasts beneath the lacy covering of her bra.

"All week long, I'd look at you and think about touching you. Here. And here." His index finger slipped under the lacy edge of the garment, stroking the soft flesh, the rosy hint of nipple already hard and pouting.

She gasped softly at his touch. "You did?"

Kissing her ardently, he grabbed her by the waist, and sat her on the kitchen counter. Standing between her knees, he reached around behind her to unclasp her bra, sliding the filmy garment down her arms and releasing her breasts to his heated gaze. "So soft. Like velvet," he muttered, bending to taste each creamy globe. His tongue flicked out to test one crest. "And so hard here."

Her hands grappled with the collar of his robe, peeling it off his shoulders so that it dropped to the floor. Head thrown back, she exulted in his exploration, her fingers twining through his dark hair to pull him even closer. But it wasn't close enough, and suddenly, they both knew it. Ryder picked her up, arms under knees and shoulders.

Summer gasped, looping her arms around his neck, and protested. "Your arm! Ryder, don't!"

Ignoring her he strode purposely toward the bedroom, kicking open the door, then lay her down among the tumbled bed clothes. He followed her down, covering her as he had earlier that day, but this time she welcomed his weight, sighing with pleasure at the tactile brush of hairy skin and smooth muscle against softer tissue. His kisses were hot and demanding, and she matched him sigh for sigh, demand for demand. Eagerly they helped each other off with their remaining garments, then, with the luxury of time, allowed the pace to slow while eyes drank their fill and hands explored in leisure.

"You're very lovely," Ryder murmured, lying on his good side. His hand tangled in the golden skein of her hair, tugged free to caress the curve of her hip, then drifted to the juncture of her thighs.

Her breath caught, and her lashes fluttered. It was sweet torture, a game her own hands now played. "For a man who's supposed to be hurt, you're rather, er, ardent."

"Lady, a man would have to be dead not to respond to what you're doing," he growled.

A shadow crossed her face, and he cursed himself. He did not want to remind her of that, not when her eyes were shining and she was liquid with desire. She was too precious, too perfect to hurt, and an overwhelming tenderness consumed him. He was drowning in a sea of emotion, like nothing he'd ever experienced, and she was at once the tide pulling him under and his only hope of rescue.

"Don't think of that," he said, rolling her beneath him and nudging her thighs apart with his knee. Looking deeply into her amethyst eyes, he watched her as he probed between her feminine petals. "Think of me," he ordered, gritting his teeth against the pain growing in his arm. "Think of us. Think of *this*."

"You're hurting!"

He pulled back. "Honey, I'm sorry. I know it's been a while for you."

"Not me, macho man. You!" Her soft laughter held a vast amusement. She pushed him onto his back, and in the space of a heartbeat positioned herself and helped him glide into her heated depths. Dual moans of pleasure echoed in the dark. "Rest your arm, hero," she panted. "I'm not into kinky sex. Pain and pleasure don't mix in my book, so just lie back and let me take charge of things for a while."

He was amazed at her generosity and the graceful way she'd made herself a true partner in this act of love. Few women in his experience had such giving natures, fewer still the freedom of spirit to call upon it during a first encounter. And he had to admit to a great relief now that he was no longer placing strain on his injured arm, as well as a powerful surge of renewed desire for the violet-eyed hoyden joined so intimately with him. Pleasure etched his features, but he still couldn't help teasing her just a bit.

Clasping her hips, he managed a wry grin and groaned. "You know what they say, 'no pain, no gain.'"

She smiled and began to move. "Here's where we prove them wrong."

By the time they both came to rapturous fulfillment, and collapsed together in a tangle of dewy limbs and pounding hearts, Ryder had to admit he'd never gained so much in all his life, and it was due entirely to a little lady called Summer Jones.

SUMMER WOKE SLOWLY, climbing up out of the depths of slumber reluctantly, yet drawn by the echo of some forgotten melody. Before she opened her eyes, she knew she was alone in the big bed. She was immediately lonely. Dragging the sheet free, she wrapped it sarong-style around herself, and hastened through the dark house in search of Ryder. She found him in the den, sitting at the piano in a shaft of moonlight, playing softly.

His expression was closed and introspective, though the music he played was evocative, romantic, emotional. His shoulders flexed beneath the burgundy robe he wore. Pale blue light slanted through the window, highlighting one side of his face, but leaving the other in shadow. He played beautifully, if absently, moving from one melody to another with ease—Chopin, McCartney, Gershwin—only favoring slightly his left side.

Mesmerized, Summer listened and watched. Why hadn't he told her he played when she'd been curious about the piano? His skill was obvious. Did admitting such a little thing make him too vulnerable? It was just another example of how he withheld himself, how he kept his distance, as if knowledge like this could somehow be a threat.

She looked at him, and her heart ached with love. Beneath the steely facade was a man with deep needs, a sensitive man revealed to her in brief glimpses of surprising tenderness, warm humor, even a melody played in moonlight. He needed her, though he'd be the last to admit it, or even realize. Flippantly she'd warned him she wouldn't make it easy for him, that coming to her carried risks, too, but she'd meant every word. She'd do everything in her power to open him up to the love he could feel. Becoming his physically was a small part of what they could be together, but it was a start. Somehow, she must make herself indispensable, as much a part of him as breathing. Then, maybe he'd understand that it was all right to love her back. Filled with new determination, she went to him.

Gliding through the pale rectangles of light, she appeared like a wraith, slipping onto the slick ebony bench beside him almost before he realized, almost before he could pull his thoughts back from that faraway place of hopes and dreams. The melody flowing from his hands became a halting glissando.

"Don't stop," she said softly, her fingers searching for and finding bass chords to match the song. She scooted nearer, struggling with the sheet that swallowed her petite form, then smiled so beautifully, so expectantly, he felt the notes take form again. They were so attuned, in such rapport, they played together as one, a rare experience, a duet almost as pleasurable and intimate as making love.

"Magic," she murmured in awe. "We're magic together, though you're much better than I am. Where'd you learn?"

"My mother." His left hand was tiring and the rhythm slowed. Summer nudged his hand aside, and he lifted it, trying not to grimace at the sharp twist of pain, then draped it across her back at her waist. His right hand toyed with a simple one-note melody, and Summer leaned against him, using her left hand to chord a basic counterpoint.

"She must be a very talented lady," she said.

"She is."

"Where is she?"

"Myrtle Beach. She bought a retirement home there after my father died. She's still teaching piano, too."

"That's the most you've ever told me about your family."

Ryder stopped playing. The notes died away. "Is it?"

She hit a final sharp, staccato chord, showing her impatience, then turned to him. "Is it so hard to share yourself?"

"It's the way I am."

The moonlight made her bold. "Is there a reason?"

"Summer, leave it alone. You know who I am. What do you want to hear? That a woman I thought I loved hurt me? Sure, it happened. You don't have a monopoly on failed relationships."

"I know that," she said quietly. "But it's important to me to understand."

"Did you read my book?" he asked abruptly. Mystified, she nodded. His voice was flat. "Then you know everything already. Her name was Elise."

Summer stifled a short gasp. "Not—not the woman who was Grigorio's mistress?"

"The same. She came to Bill and me with a story about organized crime, and I fell hard for her damsel-in-distress routine. We'd been getting too close to Grigorio with our investigation of Joe Simitall's 'apparent' suicide. She used me. Fed everything she could learn from us back to her lover, then set us up. They killed Bill, and if it hadn't been for Kent, I wouldn't be here, either."

"Oh, God, Ryder," she whispered. "I know that hurt. Is that why you find it so hard to trust your own feelings?"

"Maybe. No matter what you think, I'm hardly invulnerable."

"I know."

He caught her upper arms, his voice suddenly rough. "Do you? Don't look at me through those rose-colored glasses. Elise didn't make me the way I am. It isn't in my nature to trust or give freely. I'm not an easy man, never have been."

"Am I complaining?"

"You want more from me than I can give."

"Maybe not." There was a hint of a smile hovering around her lips.

"Dammit, Summer!" He shook her. "I'm trying to be fair. I want you, but I can't make promises."

"Have I asked for any?"

Ryder's voice was ragged. "I don't want to hurt you, but I can. You ought to run away as far and as fast as you can."

She leaned closer and pressed her lips against his collarbone. "I've never been very good at running."

"And I've never been very good at self-denial," he said hoarsely.

He kissed her hotly, his hands pushing aside the restrictions of the sheet, smoothing the lush fullness of her breasts, measuring the slimness of her waist. His tongue delved deeply into her mouth, staking his possession, letting her know the depths of his passion. Her response was complete and immediate, her hunger just as avid as his own, and the knowledge that she wanted him as badly as he wanted her pushed him over the edge.

Somehow they were on the thickly carpeted floor, and the pale squares of moonlight played over her lissome form in an erotic way. The ache in his arm forgotten, he worshiped her, adoring her breasts, teasing the quivering flesh of her inner thighs, touching and stroking her intimately until she was gasping with want and his own need rode him so hard he thought he'd explode.

Finally he positioned himself between her thighs. Her fingers dug into the lean muscles of his hips, urging him onward, but he held back, watching her face in the grid of light and shadow, and the play of emotions that told him far more than any words what this meant to her.

"Ryder!" Her voice was the lovely, throaty rasp that touched his core. "Feel how much I need you. Whatever comes, just love me now."

He could not deny her—or himself.

"For now, for tonight," he grated, then plunged into her softness and gave himself up to the madness. When she gasped and arched against him, she called his name, and he groaned with his own release, losing himself within her, and forgetting for a time that she was everything he'd come to fear.

CHAPTER THIRTEEN

"ALL RIGHT, BEAUTIFUL, rise and shine."

Summer lifted one heavy eyelid and tried to focus on Ryder's roguish grin. It was impossible. "Uh-uh."

"Hey, the early bird gets the worm. It's almost six-thirty. Daylight's burning."

Summer pulled the pillow over her head. W. C. Fields's rather muffled voice came from beneath it. "Go 'way son, yer bother me."

Ryder's sudden sneak attack, tickling her under the covers, made her shriek in protest. "Stop, Ryder!" Laughing, she tried futilely to fight him off. "You fiend! Wounded or not, you're going to get it!"

Rolling like playful puppies, they tumbled over and over, Summer doing her best to mete out equal punishment, and ending up flat on her back, hands pinned beside her ears. Panting, she grinned up at him, loving the way his dark hair fell across his forehead and the devilish glint flickering in his eyes. His gaze dropped to her lips, and he kissed her.

When he raised his head at last, she heaved a deep sigh of satisfaction. "I see you're feeling better."

"Just fine, honey. A bit stiff, that's all." He traced her upper lip with his index finger, and his voice dropped to a husky rasp. "And how are you?"

Her expression was languorous, her voice pure Mae West, pouty and provocative. "Umm, so how do I look, handsome?"

"Like you spent the night being thoroughly ravished."

Laughing softly, she wrinkled her nose and dragged her tangled tresses back from her face. "A hag, huh?"

"A gorgeous hag. But I thought you'd be above fishing for compliments this early in the morning."

"All I want is a little extra sleep. I had a hard night."

"So did I." He chuckled and moved his hips against hers. Summer's eyes widened. Beneath his cotton briefs the hard ridge of his arousal pressed against her thigh. Her breath caught, and the tip of her breasts, crushed beneath the weight of his muscular chest, began to throb.

"Animal," she accused with a shaky laugh.

"You make me crazy." He shook his head. "I can't get enough of you."

Her hand found the side of his jaw, and she stroked the bristly texture of his early-morning stubble. "Good."

"I forget everything when you look at me like that, but—" Groaning regretfully, he eased away. Plumping several fat pillows, he sat Summer up and pulled the covers to her breasts. He sat on the edge of the bed, facing her, his thigh pressing against her hip. "Much as I hate to say this, maybe we'd better not. You're probably sore, and we've both forgotten a very important detail."

"What detail?"

"Birth control, Delilah." His mouth twisted. "Lord, we were like a couple of hot-blooded teenagers, but I was a selfish bastard not to think about protecting you."

Her face suffused with rosy color, but she reached out for his hand. "It's okay. The timing isn't right."

"Shall I take care of it from now on?"

"No, I will," she murmured, looking away. The implicit assumption that they would be together filled her with a tremulous joy. His fingers caught her chin, turning her face up, revealing the faint tremor of her lower lip and a suspicious sparkle in her violet eyes.

"Hey," he said softly, "you didn't think I'd be satisfied with a one-night stand, did you?"

"You know I don't think." She flashed a shaky smile. "I leave that to you."

He frowned. "Are you sorry it happened?"

"Oh, no!" Her hands clasped his neck, stroking his nape lovingly. "I'm very glad."

"Sometimes it's hard for me to know what you're feeling."

She looked surprised. "I thought I was all too easy to read. What I feel now is . . . well, I'm scared stiff that someone took a shot at you, but I still love you."

"Hell, Summer!" He raked a hand through his dark hair.

"Does that make you uncomfortable? I can't promise to hide how I feel, Ryder, but there are no strings. I just want to be with you."

"Good." His eyes burned. "Because I still want you so much I'm not going to let you out of my sight. It's good between us, half-pint, and you don't throw away something like that."

She smiled. "I'm glad that's settled."

He studied her for another moment, then kissed her lightly. "You know, you're quite a distraction. I thought you might be hungry. Of course, I've already eaten all the stew—"

"For breakfast? Ugh!" She made a face.

"What if I offered you a cup of coffee?"

"Great." She pushed at the covers. "I'll get up and—"

"No, stay where you are. I'll get it, and then we can decide what we're going to do with the rest of the day."

"But I should be waiting on you," she protested. "That arm—"

He paused at the door, a mischievous smile twitching the corners of his mouth. "Nurse, all the TLC you gave me last night has resulted in a miraculous recovery. Now stay put. Ryder's back in charge."

He disappeared, and Summer sat on the edge of the bed, bemused. The early-morning chill made her shiver, so she picked up Ryder's robe from the floor and put it on. It swallowed her, but it was warm and redolent of Ryder himself, and she buried her nose in the lapel to inhale his scent. Sighing with contentment, she began to pick up the scattered scraps of clothing lying around the bedroom and pile them on a chair. She picked up one of Ryder's discarded blue socks, and a thought made her giggle.

Crawling back among the bed pillows, Summer stuck her hand in the sock, made a few adjustments, and suddenly had a puppet.

"Lizabeth? Is that you?" she asked.

"I'm incognito, sugar. Who were you expecting? The Prince of Whales?" Lizabeth replied in her sultry contralto.

"Wally hasn't got the chutzpa to invade my boudoir, unlike a certain reptile I could name."

"As a killer whale he's a wimp," Lizabeth said disdainfully.

"I don't know," Summer murmured, tucking in the hem of the sock, "he's rather a gentleman. Reminds me of that fellow who calls the station all the time..."

"Do you carry on these kinds of schizophrenic conversations often?" Ryder demanded from the doorway. He held two steaming mugs of coffee, and his expression was quizzical.

The puppet's "head" came up, ogling the nearly nude man at the door. "Whoa! Hunk alert!"

"Watch it, Lizabeth," Summer rebuked with a grin. "This one's spoken for."

"Weird, Summer. Definitely weird." He passed her a cup and sat down on the bed beside her.

Summer dimpled. "Better get used to it, Bowman. Lizabeth and I are very close."

Lizabeth undulated up Ryder's bare arm, and spoke in a sexy whisper. "That's right, sugar pie. We share and share alike." Summer made the sock puppet peek over his shoulder, then down at his lap. "But the more I see of you, sugar, the more I realize Summer's been holding out on me!"

He snorted, trying not to laugh. "Raunchy dame, aren't you?"

Lizabeth drew herself up in affronted dignity. "I'm a star! Didn't you catch me on *Animal Alley*?"

"Sorry. Guess I missed it."

"You've done it now," Summer whispered to Ryder, setting her cup aside. The puppet, nose in the air, made a production of looking exactly where Ryder *wasn't*. "You've insulted her. You'd better turn on the reruns quick, or your life will be hell. Go ahead, they're on now."

"You're cracked, you know that?" Ryder asked, shaking his head, but he rose and switched on the small portable television in the built-in entertainment center, all the same. Discarding his empty cup, he twirled the dial until he found the right station. Beeps, music and assorted sound effects blasted into the room as the inhabitants of *Animal Alley* experienced various misadventures. It was disconcerting to hear Summer's throaty Mae West imitation coming from the set.

"There I am!" Lizabeth chortled. "What a performance! I was robbed of that Emmy!"

Ryder lounged across the bed, glancing between the set and Summer. One large hand crept under the edge of the robe and stroked her calf and the sensitive area behind her knee. "I never guessed you led this kind of secret life. Have you considered intensive therapy?"

"Pay attention," Summer ordered, suppressing a smile. "This is Lizabeth's best part."

Ryder watched attentively until the program went off. "Not bad," he commented. "Pretty good, in fact. I like a story with a moral."

The puppet preened and gave him a come-hither look. "I see you recognize quality entertainment. Okay, sugar, you've redeemed yourself. I'm ready to kiss and make up."

"You've got to be kidding!" Ryder held up his hands to fend off Lizabeth's amorous advances. "No way am I going to kiss my own smelly sock!"

Giggling, Summer continued the assault. "You're insulting Lizabeth again."

Ryder caught her in his arms and rolled across the bed, grappling with the sock-clad hand. "Time to lose this lizard," he said, then stripped the sock free and tossed it across the room.

Summer went perfectly still, her hand still upraised. "Uh-oh."

"What?"

"Now look what you've done."

"What? It's just your hand."

"Don't think of it as a hand, sugar," drawled Lizabeth's voice. "Think of it as a naked puppet."

Ryder's mouth twitched, and Summer's face worked. Suddenly, they both dissolved into carefree laughter.

"I'd rather think of the little naked wanton in my arms, if you don't mind," Ryder managed finally. "You lunatic. Didn't you ever grow up?"

"Call me Peter Pan, I guess." Summer nuzzled his neck. "I like to make you laugh. You don't do it enough. Anyway, as you've pointed out so often, I'm no bigger than a kid. Maybe that has something to do with it."

"Lady, what you do to me is all grown up," Ryder growled. "And you play hell with my good intentions." With a groan, he stood up, hauling her up with him. "It's a beautiful Sunday morning. Let's spend it together. We can't stay holed up in this room all day long."

"We can't?" Her eyes were wide and innocent. "How disappointing."

"Smarty pants. Okay, just tell me what you had planned for today, and we'll do it."

"Really?"

"You name it."

"Hmm, well, there was something..." She glanced at the clock on the nightstand and made a decision. "We might be able to make it if we hurry. Okay, Bowman, get your gorgeous buns in gear, because we'll have to stop by my place on the way so I can get some clothes.''

"The way where?"

She shoved him toward the bathroom. "You'll see. Just hurry. Oh, and one question.''

He poked his head around the bathroom door. "What's that, half-pint?''

She grinned at him. "Do you get seasick?''

"I THOUGHT WE WERE going someplace we could be alone," Ryder grumbled into Summer's ear a couple of hours later.

"Whatever gave you that idea?" she shouted over the roar of powerful engines.

"Maybe the way you looked lying naked in my bed. Or on the rug or—ouch!" He rubbed the spot on his rib cage where her elbow had just connected. "What was that for?''

"Never mind. How's the arm?''

"Sore, but tolerable. Don't worry about it.''

"Just as long as you can still hold me.''

"Count on it. Now if we could only find a place to be alone...''

Smiling, she leaned back against Ryder's broad chest, bracing her hands against the railing of the riverboat, *Southern Belle*. They'd just managed to catch the eight o'clock excursion of the Fall Color Cruise, and now sailed the Tennessee River, headed thirty-nine winding miles downstream for the Shellmound Recreation Area on Nickajack Lake and the annual Folk Festival.

The crisp wind whipped rosy color into her cheeks and tugged at the collar of her short plaid jacket, but she was cozy and warm, sheltered by Ryder's bulk. On each side of them the gorge rose in steeply ascending banks. Crimsons and oranges and russets mingled to form a feast for the eye and the soul. Summer turned her face up toward the brilliant sunshine, reveling in the day, and the man beside her, and her own happiness. She waved at the fall foliage covering the mountainous banks. "Isn't that view worth the trip?"

"Yes, it is, but I didn't know every friend and acquaintance you had would be joining us!"

"What's the use of having all those complimentary tickets if no one gets to enjoy them? Besides, it's only Beryl and Larry and their kids, and Vanessa and Amy."

"And Merl."

"Yes, that's kind of amazing. Vanessa said he practically invited himself. Maybe there's hope yet."

"Hope of what?" He nuzzled her ear, making her shiver. His arms were crossed in front of her, pulling her tight against him so her jeans-clad bottom fit snugly, intimately against the front of his own denims. She was an armful of sheer delight, all vibrant life and shimmering light, from the top of her sunlit head down the thick cat's tail of her single golden braid to the tip of her red Reeboks.

"That Merl and Vanessa will get together," she murmured, in answer to his question, arching her neck with pleasure. His tongue lightly flicked her earlobe. Arousal arced through her middle. She drew a sharp breath, and her teeth caught her lower lip. "They're in love, you know."

"And you know the management frowns on office romance," he said, mock-sternly.

"Is that so?" She folded her arms over his, rubbing her fingers up the backs of his hands and slipping them under the knit wristbands of his navy windbreaker. She felt his arms tighten and smiled. "Then we're in big trouble, Bowman."

"Living dangerously is my life, half-pint."

She was silent for a long moment. "I wish we didn't have to make jokes about what happened, Ryder. What's so terrifying is not knowing who or why."

His voice was deep and calm. "I know. But that's Kent's department, and he's a good cop. Maybe it has something to do with the people we nailed in Atlanta, and maybe it was a freak incident. I can't let myself get paranoid about it."

Summer tried to be nonchalant, but her voice had a betraying quiver. "So maybe it really was a good idea to get you out of the city today."

He turned her in his arms so that he could see her face. Her hands slipped inside his windbreaker and circled his waist. Everywhere she touched felt warm and alive, as if his entire being had lain dormant until she woke him with her smile. His hands closed on her shoulders, and he longed for the power to erase all her fear, every apprehension. Under the electric blue dome of the cloudless sky, it should be easy to pretend that all was right with the world—at least for now.

"It was a good idea," he said. "So forget everything else. We're just a guy and his gal, out to enjoy the day and each other. Don't let anything else spoil it for us."

"All right." She lifted her chin in a gallant gesture. "Nothing will spoil it, I promise."

"That's my girl," he murmured, brushing his lips over hers. He forgot they stood on the crowded deck surrounded by camera-toting tourists, forgot everything but her and the need to taste her again. Groaning, he deepened the kiss.

"Aunt Summer! Aunt Summer!" Allison Hatcher's reedy voice interrupted them. "Aunt Summer, me and Amy and Rich are going down to see the engine rooms. Wanna come?"

Blushing, Summer pulled away from Ryder. Her half-smile was rueful. "Well, almost nothing will spoil it," she muttered, then turned to Allison. "Sure, I'd love to come."

"Yippee!" Allison hopped up and down, swinging Amy's hand. The two little girls were dressed almost identically in blue jeans and puffy pastel jackets, but Allison's short curls contrasted to Amy's ribbon-bowed ponytail and dual hearing aids. Allison grabbed Summer's hand and dragged her toward the companionway. "Come on!"

Summer gave Ryder a helpless look over her shoulder. "Come rescue me if I'm not back by the time we reach port."

"You got it, partner," he promised with an indulgent grin that made her heart melt.

Summer dutifully followed the little girls down several flights of metal stairs and made the tour of the engine rooms with Rich leading the way. The noise was earsplitting, and they all laughed when Amy solved the problem for herself by simply turning down the volume on her hearing aids. Finally Summer lured the children back to the relative silence of the large enclosed passenger decks with the promise of cold drinks and popcorn from the snack bar. Summer paid for the treats, and the kids raced happily off to find the adults.

"Yo, doll. What's cookin'?" Merl materialized in line beside her, ordering coffee. His scuffed boots, wool CPO jacket, and wind-mussed yellow hair gave him a farm-boy appearance, but his mouth was straight and morose, and his eyes behind his glasses were guarded.

Summer smiled hello and munched a handful of popcorn. "Having fun, Merl?"

"Yeah, sure." He stirred cream into his cup, his blue eyes speculative. "I see that peace has broken out on all fronts. Was it a bilateral agreement or total surrender?"

"What?" She was disconcerted by the bitterness in his tone.

"You and the boss man look pretty cozy. Did his near-miss have anything to do with it?"

She crumpled the half-eaten bag of popcorn, and threw it in a waste bin. "As a matter of fact," she said coolly, "it certainly did. What's it to you?"

Merl's long face was immediately contrite. "Oh, hell, Summer. I'm sorry. I didn't mean it that way."

"What exactly did you mean, Merl?"

"I don't know." He stared down into the murky contents of his cup. "Look, I'm sorry. You and Ryder have been spitting and sparking for so long—"

"We have not!" She was indignant.

Merl grinned. "Look, doll, even an old country boy like me knows that where there's smoke, there's fire. Seeing the two of you all friendlylike after all those fireworks, well... I guess I'm just jealous, that's all."

Summer's ire faded immediately. She touched Merl's arm. "I don't know exactly where Ryder and I are headed, but we're taking it one day at a time. Can't you do that with Vanessa?"

"That's why I'm here. At least, I thought it was." They walked over to one of the large windows and stood gazing out at the passing scenery. Merl sipped his coffee, grimacing at the acrid taste. "I don't know what to do about Vannie. I'm so crazy about her I'm sick with it, but I can't compete with an eight-year-old."

"It's not a question of competition, Merl." Concern darkened Summer's eyes to the color of hyacinths. "Vanessa cares for you, I'm sure. There's room in her life for both you and Amy."

"But what about me? Don't get me wrong, I don't have anything against Amy. She's a spunky kid. But, well, hell! It's taken me thirty years to get ready for a wife, and I don't know if I can handle the responsibility of a child, too." He shook his head. "I always thought things came in order— you get engaged, you marry, then you have kids. Call me a hick, but that's the way I was brought up, and that's the way I always thought it would be for me."

Summer gave a faint sigh. "Things aren't nearly that simple any more."

She bit her lip and thought of her own relationship with Ryder. She'd promised herself after Clancy that she'd steer clear of strong-willed, ambitious men with commitment phobias, but fate had thrown her a double whammy in the person of her hotshot rival deejay, Gulliver, and the dy-

namic radio magnate and former journalist Ryder Bowman. Everything about him from the minute she'd met him
had attracted her, infuriated her, compelled her in ways she
was still trying to understand. Was it any wonder she'd
fallen like a ton of bricks? She hadn't stood a chance. And
now she compromised her promises to herself and risked
heartache all over again on the merest hope that Ryder
would someday return her feelings.

"Sometimes you have to make adjustments," she said to
Merl, knowing he had to learn this lesson for himself.

He shrugged impatiently. "I can't help feeling that this
foster-mother thing is just a passing fancy for Vanessa. She's
going to come to her senses and realize that Amy would be
better off in a family with a real mother and father."

"She seems very committed to Amy," Summer murmured. "If you can't accept this part of Vanessa's life,
maybe you ought to bow out, Merl."

"I've already tried that," he said glumly. "It didn't work.
I can't stay away from her. I suppose I'm just a glutton for
punishment, but I guess I'll hang around for as long as she'll
let me. Sooner or later she's got to realize what's best for
Amy and for us. I know I have to keep trying."

"Be careful," Summer pleaded. "I'd hate to see either of
you hurt."

Merl smiled wryly. "Thanks, doll. I'll do my best. Want
to join the others? This tub ought to be docking soon, and
I don't know about you, but my tummy alarm went off for
lunchtime a while ago. I'm ready to eat!"

Summer laughed. "I'm with you, pal."

They climbed the companionway to the upper deck,
joining Larry, Beryl and Vanessa sitting in the wire-mesh
deck chairs. Merl took up a position slightly behind Vanessa's chair, and she gave him a tentative smile. He winked and
placed a hand on her shoulder, squeezing it through the
layers of her fringed Davy Crockett suede jacket.

Ryder stood at the rail, chatting easily, and Summer
couldn't help but admire the charming way he fit in. He

might be a mover and a shaker in the executive office, but he was one of the group today. When she approached, he caught her hand and drew her close beside him without pausing in the conversation, as if it were a natural and unremarkable occurrence, but Summer saw Beryl's swift, assessing glance and her tiny, pleased smile.

Shortly after noon, the *Southern Belle* docked at Shellmound. The rest of the day was a blur to Summer. The group separated and reformed several times, walking through the many craftsmen's and artists' exhibits, applauding the dancers at the clogging demonstration, lunching on southern fried chicken and sugar-dusted funnel cakes. Summer talked a long time with a man tying fishing flies in one booth, amazing Ryder with her knowledge of fishing and lures in general. They watched another craftsman building a dulcimer, a traditional stringed instrument of the mountain people, and listened to the "pickin'" and "fiddlin'" of a real bluegrass band.

A carnival atmosphere prevailed, and a warm glow pervaded Summer's mood, especially when Ryder held her hand or draped a casually possessive arm over her shoulders. As the sun moved toward the west, they strolled the teeming grounds, and she did her utmost to keep her promise to forget everything but having a good time.

"You know," she said, just after he'd bought her a primitive hand-carved whirligig to add to her country decor, "I've always wanted to do this kind of thing."

They loitered near the entrance waiting for the others to appear. The air was thick with the odor of crushed grass, a sun-warmed crowd and the assorted tantalizing smells of cotton candy, mustard and barbecue. Ryder's eyes crinkled at the corners with humor. "What thing? Spend money?"

She twirled her new toy at him, laughing at the mechanical antics of a wooden hen and chicks pecking on a green board. "No, silly. Walk around, hand in hand with my beau, the envy of every girl in sight. We could be a scene out of *State Fair*."

"The movie? Pat Boone, wasn't it?" Ryder grinned. "You mean I get to be the good guy for a change?"

Summer raised up on her tiptoes and kissed the end of his nose. "Mister," she whispered, "I have it on the best authority that you are very good, indeed."

His arms went around her waist. "Just wait 'til I get you home, and you'll see," he growled.

"Cut it out, you two," admonished Beryl, coming up beside them. She had the slightly harried look of a tired-out mom, shoulder bag weighed down on one side with purchases and a shopping bag in the other hand bulging with discarded jackets, half-eaten hamburgers and half a dozen sticky napkins. "Have a little propriety, if you please. There are old folks and babies present."

"Spoilsport," Summer said. "What's the matter? Have you run out of steam?"

Beryl wrinkled her pert nose. "Yup. I think this old body has had about all the fun it can stand for one day. Are you two ready to take the bus back?"

Summer caught Ryder's eye, and the thought of being alone with him again soon made her feel light-headed. "Yes, that's fine." She fought to remove the rather breathless quality from her voice. "Where is everybody?"

"Here they come," Ryder said, nodding at the approaching group. Vanessa held Amy's hand, Larry carried Allison on his shoulders, and Merl and Rich brought up the rear.

"Ready to call it a day?" Larry asked. He swung Allison down to the ground.

"My feet hurt," Allison complained.

Larry rubbed his daughter's neck. "I think the troops have had enough, and the heavier Beryl's shopping bag gets, the lighter my wallet is!"

"Just for that, you carry them both," Beryl retorted, shoving the bag at her husband.

"Oops, sorry, hon," Larry said. He dropped a kiss on her indignant nose and took the bag. "Take away her funds and she gets nasty."

"Oh, you!" Beryl giggled.

They all meandered wearily toward the bus stop, falling onto a couple of wooden benches to wait. A chartered bus would take them back to downtown Chattanooga where they'd begun their sojourn earlier that day.

"Did everyone have a good time?" Summer asked.

"Yeah!"

"Did we!"

"Kids, what do you say to Summer for giving us the tickets?" Beryl prompted in proper motherly fashion.

Rich and Allison dutifully chorused their "Thanks, Aunt Summer," complete with hugs and kisses. Amy shyly hung back, until gently urged by Vanessa, then added her thanks.

"I had a good time, Miss Jones." Amy's voice was strangely lacking in inflection due to her hearing disability, but her expression, tired but still animated, said it all. Summer gave the little girl a warm hug.

"I'm glad you did, Amy. Maybe we can all do it again sometime."

"Yeah!" Rich agreed. "What about next weekend?"

"Oh, no, you don't, young man," Beryl said firmly. "Don't get any bright ideas. Once a year is enough. Besides, next weekend we'll have to be getting your Halloween costume ready."

"I'd forgotten Halloween is just around the corner," Summer commented. Allison and Rich sat between their parents, and Amy was perched in Vanessa's lap. "So, kids, what are you going to be for Trick or Treat? Bats? Ghouls? Merl always comes to the office as Count Dracula."

"I vaant to drink your blo-o-od," Merl responded with an appropriately fiendish expression.

"Oh, yuk!" Allison said, with a eight-year-old's honesty. "That's old stuff."

"Gee, I always thought I was pretty spectacular," Merl said, feigning hurt.

"Maybe this year you'll get lucky," Ryder drawled, leaning against the back of a bench. He tugged gently on Summer's braid, his eyes hooded to hide a teasing gleam. "Maybe Vanessa will let you nibble her neck."

Vanessa blushed, and the adults snickered, but Allison wasn't to be deterred by grown-up foolishness.

"Aunt Summer, if you really want to know," she said earnestly, "we've got it all figured out. Rich is going to be the Wizard of Oz, and I'm the Wicked Witch of the West."

Summer nodded her approval. "Cute idea. And what are you going to be, Amy?"

"I think...maybe Glinda the Good Witch of the North," Amy replied.

Vanessa's dark head bent closer to the little girl on her lap, automatically adjusting her position so that Amy had a clear view of her mouth to facilitate lipreading. "But I thought you wanted to be Dorothy?"

"No, I've changed my mind," Amy said. Her brown eyes were quite serious. "Dorothy just wanted to go home, but now I've got a new home, haven't I? Forever and ever?"

"Yes. Yes, you do." Vanessa's voice was thick, and her dark eyes were suspiciously bright. "Shall we tell them?"

Amy nodded, pressing her cheek against Vanessa's, and her dark ponytail was virtually indistinguishable from Vanessa's brunette locks. Vanessa looked up at the curious faces around her and took a deep breath.

"Amy and I were keeping it our secret, but we've had such a special day, with all the people we really care about." Her eyes searched out Merl, mutely begging for understanding. But his face was closed, and her gaze fell away. She licked her lips, and plunged on, finishing in a rush. "We wanted to tell you that I—I've seen the lawyers, and—and Amy and I are adopting each other."

CHAPTER FOURTEEN

"I TELL YOU I'M WORRIED," Summer said, fitting her key into her town house door. "Did you see Merl's face when she told us? It was like he'd been stabbed in the heart."

"You're making too much of it, honey," Ryder said. The setting sun cast peachy light across his face. "Sure, it was a big announcement. A single gal doesn't adopt a child every day, but he'll accept it. He's got no other choice."

"I don't know. He looked so...betrayed. Why didn't she talk it over with him first? She shouldn't have sprung it on him like that, not if she loves him—"

The phone pealed within, and she broke off. Pushing open the door, she threw her jacket on the sofa and hurried across the dim living room to pick up the receiver. "Hello?" She blinked, then held it out to Ryder. "For you."

His jacket joined hers, and he took the phone. "Yeah?"

"Where the *hell* have you been?" roared Kent Ogden through the line.

Ryder frowned. "Shellmound. Summer and I went to the festival. We just got in."

"God! I've been trying to find you all day. Why didn't you check in with me?"

"I didn't know I was under arrest, ole buddy."

"Ignorance ain't much of a defense, Tex, especially if it gets you wasted!"

"You want to tell me what's going on?" Ryder growled, scowling. He was aware that Summer hovered nervously nearby.

"If I knew, then there'd be no problem." There was a two-second silence, and when Kent spoke again his voice was modulated, his anger clamped under control. "Ballistics says the gun used on you yesterday was a typical Saturday-night special. Not what we'd expect from a professional hit."

"Should I be relieved?"

"I don't know. Maybe it was an amateur, and then maybe we're dealing with some very clever people. People devious enough to choose a misleading weapon."

Ryder shook his head. "Sounds a bit farfetched to me. You're stretching for it, Kent."

There was a moment's hesitation, then Kent's words came, low and hard. "Grigorio's lawyers are petitioning to have him released. They'll be in court first thing tomorrow morning."

Ryder's curses were obscene, explicit. He looked up to find Summer's eyes locked on him, her face pale and frightened. A giddy instant of déjà vu threw him back in time to another place, to another terrified woman caught up in a dangerous situation. But no, this wasn't Elise, planning to betray him to protect her lover, it was Summer, his own Jubilee, and what scared him was the danger he'd put her in by his mere presence.

"Give it to me straight, Kent," he said grimly. "How are we going to stop it?"

"Any way we have to. Can you be ready to leave for Atlanta within the hour?"

"Yes."

"Meet you at the Delta counter at Lovell Field."

"Right." Ryder dropped the receiver into its cradle.

"Tell me," Summer demanded. Tersely Ryder repeated what Kent had told him.

"Pack a bag," he ordered.

"Yes. It won't take me a minute. And we need to change the dressing on your arm. When we get to Atlanta—"

"Not *we*, honey. *Me*."

Confusion clouded her eyes. "But—"

"I'm taking you to your uncle's, and you're going to stay there until this mess is cleared up. As of right now, the Coffee Club is off the air, and Jubilee is on vacation. Jack or Ron or somebody can pick up the slack. I don't care."

"Well, I do!" Hands on hips, she faced him belligerently. "I can work. This has nothing to do with me! So if you won't take me with you—"

"Not a chance!"

"—then I can take care of the Coffee Club."

"Forget it!" His expression was implacable, unyielding.

Frustration and fear made her angry. "But—"

"Dammit, Summer!" he roared. "Don't argue with me!"

The outburst made her take an involuntary step backward, and her lower lip quivered. Cursing, he hauled her into his arms and buried his face in her hair.

"Don't you understand, sweetheart?" he groaned, holding her tight. "Those bastards play for keeps. Anyone I'm close to is at risk. I can't do what I have to do unless I know you're safe. Okay?"

She nodded, swallowing hard, clinging to him. "What—what will you do?"

He gave a faint, mirthless laugh. "Don't worry, I'm not going down there packing a six-gun, if that's what you're thinking. Haven't you ever heard that the pen is mightier than the sword?"

"Yes, but—"

"The public wrath, when it's aroused, can be a fearsome thing."

"And you're going to make the tiger roar," she guessed.

"If it's not too late." His fingers bunched in her hair.

"I'll go to Uncle Burt's," she said in a raw voice. "Just promise me you'll be careful."

"I promise." He lowered his head, and his mouth found hers, taking her breath, drawing out all her sweetness. She was soft and pliant and willing, and desperation drove him. He wanted to brand her, to mark her in some way as his own, so that even if the unthinkable happened, she wouldn't forget this moment or him.

His hands cupped her breasts, kneading them through the fabric of her shirt, and he swallowed her moans like a man dying of starvation. Feverishly he found the snap of her jeans and jerked it open. Sliding the zipper down, his hand followed, and he palmed her feminine mound. Beneath the silk of her panties he found her hot and damp and ready, and his manhood surged in response. With a growl of desire, he scooped her up and carried her to the bedroom.

With frantic hands and halting breaths, they pushed aside the minimum of clothing, then he sank himself deep, deep into her glorious, pulsating depths, nearly dying with the ecstasy of it, of her. His mouth was open against her throat, and his thrusts were hard, swift and driven. She half sobbed, arching in response to his power, reveling in the wildness of their passion. She stiffened, then cried out, a soft, untamed sound he caught with his mouth and inhaled. Her convulsive inner contractions milked him, and he shuddered with his own powerful release, his hoarse shout to the deity neither a blessing nor a curse, but a paean of thanksgiving.

There wasn't anything he could say after that, nor time to linger. All too soon, they stood on Burton's front sidewalk saying goodbye.

"What do I tell them?" she asked tremulously. She clutched a small suitcase, but he knew she had no real idea what she'd packed.

"As little as possible." He gently rubbed a knuckle down her cheek, and she turned her head to press her lips to it, making him shudder anew. "Take care, half-pint. I'll call you as soon as I can."

"Be careful," she ordered, fighting the quaver in her voice.

His jaw twitched, then he kissed her once, lightly, got into his car and drove away. Ryder's hands clenched on the steering wheel, and he fought the urge to watch her through the rearview mirror. She hadn't bargained for this kind of thing when she'd fallen in love with him, he knew, and he hated leaving her like this, when things between them were too new to be settled. Resolutely he locked away the welling sensations of tenderness and regret. He had work to do, and he'd do it better now knowing Summer was safe. When this was all over, then they'd see where this would lead.

"I THINK YOU OWE ME an explanation."

Vanessa looked at Merl's haggard expression and gave a resigned sigh. She'd known it would come to this sooner or later. It was Monday, a week and a day since the excursion to Shellmound, but the tension between her and Merl had become nearly unbearable at work, especially since Ryder and Summer's week-long absence had deprived her of her usual buffers. Merl's unannounced visit this crisply cool and sunny late afternoon was not totally unexpected. She'd known that resentment had been brewing in him all week, and it hurt that she'd been the cause of it. Maybe it *was* time for truth. Merl deserved that much, even if the truth killed whatever feeling he still had for her. Wordlessly she opened her front door wide and let him in.

"Where's the girl?" he asked abruptly.

Vanessa stiffened. "Her name is Amy. And she's in the kitchen putting glitter on her Glinda costume. We can talk in here. Just keep it low."

"Dammit, Vannie!" Merl jammed his hands in the front pocket of his jeans. "If you'd talked to me, I don't think we'd both be feeling so miserable right now."

She sat down on the sofa and looked at her hands in her lap. "I'm sorry, Merl, truly I am. I never meant to make you unhappy. I care for you a great deal, but Amy needs me."

He perched on the arm of the sofa. "What she needs is a family with a mother and a father."

"Are you volunteering for the job?" He was taken aback at the blunt question, and her lips twisted. "No, I guess not."

Frustrated, he ran his hands through his yellow hair. "Am I such a bastard to admit I don't know if I could handle it? There's bound to be a family out there begging to adopt a cute kid like Amy."

"They've had eight years to surface. No, Merl, at Amy's age, and with her hearing impairment, there's little chance she'll ever be adopted. Why do you think my application is going through with so little hassle? I'd like her to have a father, but I'm doing the best I can for her under the circumstances. And..." Vanessa drew a deep, shuddering breath, and her voice dropped to a whisper. "...and no one can love a child like her natural mother."

Vanessa stared intently at Merl, holding her breath. His shaggy brows drew together in a puzzled frown, and he automatically shoved his glasses up on his nose. There was a flicker of movement beyond the door leading to the kitchen, but her concentration on Merl was so complete it didn't register.

"What are you saying?" he asked slowly.

"She's my daughter." Vanessa's chin quivered, but her dark eyes held a fierce glitter. "It's a story you've heard a hundred times. I made a mistake with a boy I thought loved me when I was seventeen. But he couldn't handle it, and when my baby girl was born, I put her up for adoption because I wanted a better life for her. By the grace of God, she's come back into my life now. And nothing and no one is going to take her away from me again."

She waited defiantly for the censure she knew would come, but his expression was stunned. His lips moved, but nothing came out.

"She's yours?" he finally croaked.

"My own flesh and blood. My lawyer persuaded the judge to open the records, and there's no doubt. She even looks like I did at that age. Can't you see the resemblance?"

"My God." His Adam's apple bobbed. "Your illegitimate daughter. That certainly explains a lot."

Vanessa tried not to cringe, but she knew Merl, she knew his background, and she knew this was something he couldn't lightly overlook. Still, now that he knew, she felt a deep sense of relief. He might never accept the situation, but at least now there was no tangle of lies between them. Maybe he could begin to understand, perhaps even in time to forgive. If he loved her... but no, there was nothing of that in his blue eyes, and Vanessa felt her feeble hopes wither and die.

"You understand now, don't you?" she asked woodenly.

He dragged his gaze and his thoughts back to her with a visible effort, standing up hastily. "Yes, of course. Thanks for telling me." He broke off, gulping. "I've got to go."

Disappointed beyond all measure, Vanessa could only nod, struggling with the burning lump in her throat.

"I'll see you tomorrow," he said. She nodded again, and he made for the door as if pursued by the devil himself.

The door slammed behind him with a depressing finality. Vanessa dropped her forehead onto the back of the couch and let the hot, silent tears fall.

"I WISH YOU'D GIVE the fellow a call, Uncle Burt," Summer said. "I talked with him a long time, and it sounds like something you'd really enjoy."

Burton Pierson pushed his supper plate away. If he'd been five years old, Summer would have sworn he was pouting. "I'm not a joiner, never have been," he said gruffly.

"But this is different! This is a fly-fishing club. They go around giving fly-tying demonstrations, and they organize fishing trips. This Mr. Huston had a whole booth of flies and lures for sale he'd made himself, and none of them held a candle to yours, Uncle Burt. Why, you and Aunt Ollie might enjoy going around to all the different festivals with a booth like that."

"Don't waste your breath, dear," Olivia advised. "You know your uncle's mind is made up. He'd rather sit around and vegetate—"

"Now wait just a minute!" Burton sputtered. "You two are ganging up on me again."

"That's because we love you," Summer said earnestly.

"Burton, I've had just about enough of this," Olivia said in her no-nonsense voice. "Either you find a way to start enjoying your retirement, or I'm going to go out and get a job myself just to get away from you!" She stood up, threw her napkin into her chair, and stalked out of the kitchen.

"Don't you threaten me, woman!" Burton shouted after her. "You know you've never worked a day in your life, and I won't have it now!" He shot Summer an anxious glance. "She doesn't mean it, does she?"

"You'd better pay attention. I think she does." Summer stifled a sigh. "Retirement takes some adjustment. She's not accustomed to having you around the house all the time any more than you are being here. And what difference does it make if she does want a job? She could work part-time just for the change, or volunteer for Foster Grandparents or tutoring. You're going to have to come up with some priorities for the two of you, things you enjoy doing together and alone. Whatever happened to that fishing boat you wanted to buy?"

"Too expensive. When we pass on, I want your inheritance—"

"Uncle Burt!" Summer surged to her feet with a sound of irritation and began gathering up dirty plates. "You didn't work all your life to scrimp and save now. I'm going to be very angry if you say another word about something as silly as leaving me an inheritance. In fact, as long as I'm off, I'm going to take you shopping tomorrow and *make* you buy that boat!"

Burton looked somewhat disgruntled. "You're serious about all this, aren't you?"

"Yes, Uncle Burt, I am." She set the plates in the sink, then walked over and placed a kiss on his balding pate. "I just want you and Aunt Ollie to be happy."

"Maybe I should give this Huston fellow a call."

Summer breathed a sigh of relief. "I think you'll be glad you did."

"All right, I will." He got to his feet. "Just as soon as I finish the evening paper."

She picked up the Monday afternoon edition of the newspaper from the cabinet and passed it to him. "Here. I'm finished with it."

"You're following that story in Atlanta pretty closely, aren't you?"

"Yes." She ran water in the sink. The mundane talk did little to relieve the fear and worry that had hovered over her since Ryder left.

"Heard from Ryder?"

"Not since last week."

Ryder's two phone calls had been brief to the point of curtness, and vastly unsettling. She'd longed for some word of reassurance, yet his natural reserve made him reticent. At least, she prayed that's what it was. She tried not to worry that he'd already begun regretting their time together. Maybe he didn't want the emotional entanglement involved. Maybe she shouldn't have been so free with her feelings. Maybe—she forced her tumbling thoughts to a standstill. It wasn't productive to speculate this way. It would only drive her crazy.

"You said he's working with the media to keep this story before the public?" Burton queried.

"Yes, that's what he told me." It was what he hadn't told her that frightened her. She could only guess at what he and Kent were up to. But there was no question that whatever they were doing, it was producing results. "Ryder and Kent's efforts got the D.A. a continuance on the Grigoric matter," she told her uncle, "but it was supposed to come up in court again today."

"They must be making some officials mighty uncomfortable," Burton remarked. He slapped the front page with the back of his hand. "Did you see these headlines? People are up in arms about the thing. Imagine, trying to free a killer like that on a technicality."

"It's awful." What was more awful was the terrible certainty that Ryder and Kent could end up targets of the mob again. She pushed the thought aside. There was no use brooding. All she could do was trust that Ryder knew what he was doing, but oh, how she missed him.

"When are you going back to work?" Burton asked. "Not that your aunt and I haven't enjoyed having you this week," he added hastily.

"I'm not sure." She shrugged, rinsing a soapy plate. "Ron tells me the station's gotten a few calls demanding Jubilee's return. One or two of them even got rather nasty. I hate to upset my listeners, but I suppose I'll have to wait until Ryder gets back."

"It was wise of him to insist on your taking a vacation and staying here to avoid persistent reporters. Just as well, too. I can't tell you how concerned I was when they called about the alarm going off at your place. I'm glad you weren't home at the time."

"Whoever was prowling around probably wouldn't have even attempted getting in if I'd been there with my lights on and all," Summer said dismissively. "It might even be those same kids again. At least the alarm scared them off this time."

The phone rang, and Summer hurriedly dried her hands, hoping it was Ryder.

"Hello? No, what... Slow down, I can't...yes, I'll be right there." She hung up, gnawing her bottom lip.

"What is it?" Burton demanded.

"It's Amy. Vanessa thinks she's run away."

"What!" Burton shook his head. "Kids!"

"I'm going over to help look for her. She can't have gone far. Would you call some more station people? The more of us out there, the sooner she'll be found." She grabbed her purse and headed out the back door.

"Okay," Burton called. "Phone me as soon as she's located."

Within ten minutes, Summer pulled her Mustang up to the curb in front of Vanessa's house. Vanessa opened the door even before Summer climbed the porch steps. "Has she come home?" she asked.

Vanessa's face was white, distraught, tear-streaked. "No. I've looked *everywhere*. Oh, Summer! My baby! What am I going to do?" she wailed.

"Stay calm first. Why would she take off like this? I don't understand. Did you two have a disagreement?"

"No, she was working in the kitchen on her Halloween costume, and then Merl came by—" Vanessa's eyes grew wide as a thought struck her.

There was a rap on the open front door and Merl barged in. His face was a pale mask of concern. "What's happened? Did you find her yet? I came as soon as Mr. Pierson called."

"It's all your fault!" Vanessa cried.

Merl froze in his tracks. "What are you talking about?"

Vanessa wrung her hands and groaned in an agony of self-recrimination. "She heard us this evening! She must have, it's the only explanation!"

"Heard us?" Merl parroted, confused. "She wasn't even in the room, and we were talking so low she couldn't have heard anything, anyway."

"She *lipreads*, you idiot!" Vanessa screamed. "She must have watched from the kitchen door. She could make out every word! Oh, God, she knows. How will she ever forgive me for deserting her? No wonder she ran away, she hates me!"

"Oh, no, Vanessa, of course she doesn't," Summer said in a soothing tone. "We can't panic now. Think. Where would she go? Would she go to Mrs. Oates?"

Tears ran unchecked down Vanessa's cheeks. "I've already called her, but Amy's not there."

"What about her best friend?" Merl suggested, the muscle in his cheek twitching wildly. "Isn't it Allison?"

"I'll call Beryl," Summer began, but was interrupted by the phone. Vanessa leaped toward it, snatched it up.

"Hello? Who—Beryl? Oh, thank God!" She sagged weakly. "Yes, I'll be right over." She hung up, buried her face in her hands, and began to sob. "She's all right...she's all right."

Merl looked as though he was doing his best not to cry, too. "Come on, Vannie. I'll drive you over there."

"No!" Vanessa's head snapped up, and her dark eyes blazed. "You've done enough! She's *my* daughter, and I can take care of her by myself!"

Vanessa grabbed her purse and rushed out of the house.

"Go after her, Summer," Merl said, his eyes bleak. "She's in no condition to drive."

Summer obeyed, catching up with Vanessa on the street. She was trying to unlock her car, but her hands were shaking too much. She made no objection when Summer relieved her of the keys, swiftly unlocked the vehicle, and pushed her into the passenger seat. They said little during the twenty-minute drive to Beryl's. Vanessa spent most of the time staring out the window to regain her composure.

Beryl was waiting for them. With her plump face creased with compassion, she led them inside, then to the glass door leading onto the rear deck. In the gathering twilight, they could see a small, lone figure sitting on one of the swings hanging from the play set. Vanessa looked helplessly at Summer and Beryl.

"I don't know what to say to her."

"Go ahead, honey," Beryl said with an encouraging pat. "You'll find the right words."

Vanessa licked her dry lips, nodded, then squared her shoulders and went outside. Crossing the backyard, she came up to the little girl and squatted in front of her. "Hi."

Amy's expression was impassive, almost indifferent. "Hi."

"I was very worried about you," Vanessa said softly. Her heart felt torn to shreds, and she longed to hug Amy tight, but held back, fearful of the shifting sands of their relationship. Instead, she took her hand, folding and unfolding her daughter's fingers with her own. "You—you overheard me talking to Mr. Morgan, didn't you?"

"I think I want to go live at the group home," Amy announced. Her expression was stoic, distancing.

"You don't really mean that, do you?" Vanessa murmured painfully.

"Yes. I do." There was a scared defiance behind the monotone of Amy's voice. Vanessa's lips hardened.

"Well, you can't," she said flatly. "You're my daughter, and you're staying with me, and that's all there is to it. And if you ever run away like this again, I'll tan your bottom, young lady."

Amy's eyelids flickered. "I don't want to stay with you any more."

"Tough."

Disconcerted, Amy's lower lip trembled. "You don't want me! You're just saying that! Mr. Morgan won't marry you if I'm around, will he?"

"Oh, honey!" Understanding dawned, and Vanessa was staggered and humbled by the sacrifice Amy was trying to make for her sake. "Is that what this is all about?"

"Well, he won't!" Amy said defensively.

"It doesn't matter." Vanessa's hands clasped Amy's thin shoulders urgently. "Are you doing this because you think it's want I want?"

"You were crying."

"I was upset, because I like Merl very much, but Amy—I love you, more than anything else in this world." She peered into her daughter's dark brown eyes, willing her to comprehend. "I know you don't quite understand everything, but we'll talk, and I'll answer all your questions.

What's important now is for you to know that you and I are a family. If I get married some day, or if I never do, nothing is going to change that again.''

"Really?"

"Really. I promise." Vanessa solemnly drew an X on her chest. "Cross my heart."

Amy looked up at her shyly through her thick lashes. "Are you really and truly my real, live mother?"

"Yes." Vanessa's voice shook. "I couldn't take care of you when you were a baby, but now I can. And I want to so badly, Amy. Will you let me?"

A tear rolled down Amy's cheek, and she smiled tremulously. "Okay... Mama."

Vanessa gulped and pulled her daughter into her arms.

"Look at those two," Beryl said from the house. She sniffed once, shot Summer a wry look, and let the curtain fall back into place. "Kids! Lord love 'em! They'll give you gray hairs, but what would we do without them?"

"I don't know," Summer murmured, struggling with a thick lump in her own throat.

"I'm going to tell the kids and Larry they can come out of the back of the house now that the crisis seems to be over," Beryl said. "How about a nice cup of spiced tea while we wait for Amy and Vanessa?"

"That sounds good."

"Okay. Be right back." Beryl bustled off.

Summer couldn't help but take another peek out the window at the two figures embracing in the backyard. A wave of something akin to envy washed over her. How lucky Beryl and Vanessa were, to have children to lavish their love upon! Summer had never really considered the possibility of children of her own in any great detail. It had always been something in the future, but now a deep hunger burned, a longing to hold a babe to her breast. In her mind's eye she saw a little boy with ebony hair. Not just any child, she knew. Ryder's child.

Abruptly she was angry with herself. It was her fatal flaw to want too much, to depend on another for her happiness, hoping for more than he was capable of giving. Ryder had said nothing about wanting a future with her, and she was wrong to read any special tenderness into anything he'd done. He was a generous and demanding lover, but he'd made it clear from the beginning all he wanted from her was an affair. To expect more was only to set herself up to be hurt later—just as she'd done with Clancy.

Not this time, she promised herself fiercely. She loved Ryder Bowman, but until he was ready to gamble on a future with her, she couldn't depend on him. She had to stand on her own two feet and take care of herself. Wasn't that what she was doing when he'd come into her life just a few short months ago? And she could do it again. If he didn't have sense enough to realize she was the best thing that ever happened to him, then to hell with him! She had her career, and she'd prove to everyone, including herself, that she could be self-reliant. And the first thing to do was to stop hiding from shadows and go back to the thing she did best.

"Tea's ready," Beryl said, appearing with a tray loaded with a teapot and plates of Halloween cookies. "Do you think we can lure Vanessa and Amy inside?"

"Let's give them a few more minutes," Summer suggested, accepting the cup of orange- and cinnamon-flavored tea Beryl offered her.

"Maybe you're right. Say, how's the vacation going? Tired of loafing yet?"

"As a matter of fact, yes." Summer's voice was firm with quiet determination. "I'm going back to work tomorrow." *Whether Ryder Bowman likes it or not!*

"... THIS IS JUBILEE ..."

"... and world-renowned Ron Kerry, sitting in for Gulliver..."

"... wishing you two sugars in every cup!"

The station jingle sped out over the air, and Summer removed her headphones with a tired sigh. *Dammit!* she thought irritably. *It's just not the same without Ryder.* It was just as well she'd decided not to take calls today. She just couldn't be perky Jubilee with only Ron for inspiration. She made herself smile warmly at the deejay to make up for her uncharitable thoughts. It wasn't his fault he couldn't outshine Gulliver.

"That was great, Ron. Thanks."

"No problem, Jubilee. When's Ryder going to be back?"

She shrugged, changing places as Jack Maxwell and Vanessa appeared to take the next shift, then pausing in the hall with Ron. "Can't say. I suppose he'll let us know."

"You want me to set up that interview with the mayor for tomorrow?"

"I'll do it."

"Want to come downstairs with me for coffee? I'll buy the sweet rolls." Ron looked like a hopeful grizzly bear.

"Thanks, I can't. I've got a week's worth of mail to dig through before I can even begin recording commercials."

"Okay. See you later." Ron ambled down the hall, whistling tunelessly.

Summer walked into her office, grimacing at the triple stacks of mail that leaned in precarious piles on her desk. The listening public sure had a lot to say this week! Determinedly she picked up a letter opener and slit the first letter, beginning in chronological order with the oldest.

There were the usual fan letters, the requests for autographs, the inquiries regarding public appearances. And as always, there was the ubiquitous love letter. She smiled at the flowery and romantic language of her unknown admirer, then frowned in puzzlement. The tone of this one was somewhat different than usual, almost desperate, containing a plaintive passage about missing her. Checking the envelope and bottom of the letter was still no help. There was no return address, and it wasn't signed, so she couldn't even respond with an autographed picture.

There were more letters from the admirer. The next two were frantic pleas for her to return to the air, blaming Gulliver for her absence. The fourth one was a heavy envelope. When she ripped it open, the golden chain of a necklace slithered out and fell on her desktop. She picked it up curiously, then froze. Hanging from it was a tiny locket with an engraved *S* just like the one Aunt Ollie had given her for her fourteenth birthday, just like the one that had been . . .

" . . . stolen," she wheezed. Shivering, she clutched the necklace and re-read the fourth letter. It was almost incoherent, a frantic plea. " . . . can't stand not hearing your sweet voice," she read aloud. " . . . realize how much I need your friendship, your love . . ."

Shuddering, she dropped the letter, thinking furiously. Was her secret admirer also the thief who'd ransacked her town house? There seemed to be no other explanation. But it went against the grain. His letters had always been so sweet, so shyly devoted. Had he written more? She searched through the rest of the mail, and discovered the final envelope on the bottom of the third pile. She read the scrawled missive, and her breath stopped and her blood congealed with growing horror.

Her admirer wrote,

I know why you are so unkind to me. I failed you. My golden one, forgive me. Gulliver still holds you in bonds. Do not fear, my sweet. I will free you from his contagion forever. I will not fail again. The next time Gulliver will die.

CHAPTER FIFTEEN

THE AIRPLANE BANKED LOW over the outskirts of Chattanooga, lining up for its final runway approach. Ryder tightened his seat belt, flexing his stiff shoulders under his oxford-cloth shirt and tweed jacket. He glanced at his rangy companion who'd spent the better part of the flight staring out the window in pensive contemplation.

"So what's eating you?" Ryder asked.

Kent's wandering attention snapped into focus. "Say again, Tex?"

"I said you've been awfully quiet. What's the matter? Aren't you pleased with the way it all came out?"

Kent grimaced and shifted, making his leather jacket creak. "Can't complain, I guess."

"What's not to like? Grigorio still behind bars, the motion for a new trial quashed, and nary a rat hole or rat we didn't shake down. Everything's clean."

"It's coming up empty there that worries me."

"You've just got a naturally suspicious nature, my friend."

The plane touched down on the runway with a slight bump, and the roar of the aircraft braking filled the cabin. Kent's mouth was a thin, grim line. "I'm just a cop trying to do my job. There's still that little matter of your attempted murder. We can't link it to any of Grigorio's people, so what we're dealing with here, Tex, is some kind of wild card. And that makes me very nervous."

"Yeah, me, too," Ryder replied sardonically. "You going to go out and try to round up all the psychos in the city?"

"It might come to that. Until then, well, you know the drill."

"Stay out of the limelight, watch my back, and look out for suspicious characters carrying heavy munitions."

"Funny. Just be careful or you'll find yourself laughing all the way to the hospital again—or worse."

The plane taxied to a stop at the gate, and both men rose, grabbed overnight bags from the overhead lockers, and joined the line of disembarking passengers. Within minutes they were through the terminal and on their way to their cars parked in the long-term parking area.

"I'll be in touch," Kent said with a final wave.

"Right."

Ryder unlocked his Mercedes and got in. It was good to be home. The matter of Grigorio had been settled to his satisfaction, and unlike Kent, he felt that the Choo-Choo shooting had been an isolated incident. He knew there'd be a logjam of work piled on his desk, and he was ready to get back to the business of running the Bowman Network. But mainly, he was crazy to see Summer again.

Although he'd been concentrating on other things in Atlanta, the separation had been sheer hell, especially considering that they'd had such a short time to be together. Missing her had been an ache phone conversations only made worse, and after a couple of unsatisfying calls, he'd had to avoid such distractions. He only hoped she'd understood. Now he was eager to hold her again, to test her softness and taste her unique flavor. In fact, he couldn't wait.

He started the car and the radio came on, filling the confined space with Jubilee's sultry tones, chatting over the air with Ron Kerry. Ryder frowned, somehow jealous that she shared even that much with another man. And what was she doing at work, anyway? Hadn't he told her to stay away? God, she was a hard-headed little number! He listened to her sign off the Coffee Club, his irritation growing in league with his desire. Pulling the car into traffic, Ryder headed for the heart of the city. He had a few choice words planned for his number-one employee, and then he was going to kiss her until they were both breathless!

He pulled his car into a slot in the parking garage next to Summer's blue Mustang. The sandy-haired attendant behind the glass booth at the entrance barely looked up when Ryder hurried past. Within minutes, he strode into the WCHT-WROC lobby, greeted Carol, and admired the bright orange ceramic jack-o'-lantern on her desk. More Halloween decorations were in evidence in the office when he got off the elevator. Honeycomb paper ghosts, wart-nosed witches, and even a black rubber bat or two graced the halls with the appropriate holiday "spirits." Ryder nodded to passing staff, but did not allow himself to be detoured from his path straight to Summer's office. He rapped sharply on the door, entered, and shut the door behind him.

Summer whirled around, gasped, and sat down abruptly in her chair, a paper crushed between her fingers. "Ryder! You're back."

"Hi, half-pint."

He grinned slowly, savoring her appearance. She'd pulled her hair back from her face with a clip on each side of her head, and she wore the pink fuzzy sweater he favored so much. She looked sweet and adorable, like a sugarplum, with two bright spots of color dotting her cheeks. Greedily he couldn't wait to taste her.

Forgetting his former irritation, he stepped behind the desk, pulled her to her feet, and folded her against him. His mouth was avid and hungry on hers, and it took him a moment to realize there was no answering response. She hung stiff as a stick within his embrace, her lips immobile and cool. He frowned and lifted his head. "Summer, honey? What's the matter?'

"Why should anything be the matter? I'm just surprised to see you, that's all." She stepped back out of his arms, turning her head away and jamming the piece of paper she held into her jeans pocket.

"That was hardly the welcome I was hoping for."

"Oh?" she glanced up at him, unconcerned, then down at her cluttered desk. She swept the assortment of envelopes and mail into an untidy pile. "Well, welcome home."

Ryder watched her, his brows drawn in a fierce line. She fluttered here and there over her desk, stacking and restacking. "What are you doing?"

"Working." Her attitude was distracted. "I've got a lot to do, Ryder, so if you'll excuse me?"

Her words were so unexpected that for a moment he was dazed. Then he came to his senses. "What's going on? Dammit, talk to me!"

"Nothing." Her tone grew shrill. "Nothing at all. Just leave me alone!"

His eyes narrowed. Things didn't add up. She was upset, but why? Beneath the plastic front she had erected, he felt her tension, her fear. She was in a panic about something, and trying to bluff her way through.

"You've got to go," she said, and her voice cracked slightly, something Ryder had never heard before. "I think the best thing—"

"The best thing is for you to tell me what the hell is wrong!" he roared.

She blanched. "Nothing."

He lost his temper. With a curse, he grabbed up her bag and jacket, and hauled her toward the door. "Come on."

"Ryder, no." She hung back.

"We're going someplace quiet to talk. Now do you come like a lady, or do I haul you out over my shoulder? I've done it before and I won't hesitate to do it again."

"Maybe it would be better to leave." There was a sudden, feverish light in her violet eyes. "Yes! We should go. Now."

Her abrupt turnaround unbalanced him for a moment, just enough so that he found himself following in her rapid wake out of the building. Her footsteps were quick, and he was forced to lengthen his stride to keep up with her. He threw her jacket over her shoulders, and she shrugged into it, casting him a fearful glance. He swallowed harshly, ripped apart by that look.

I've got to get to the bottom of this! he thought with a mixture of fury and fear.

He took her arm and turned her toward the parking garage. Weekday traffic zoomed down the street as people headed for an early lunch hour. That was it. He'd take her to his house, and they'd sit calmly over lunch to hash out whatever was bothering her. She didn't demur when he tucked her into his car, left the garage and headed for Lookout Mountain.

Ryder negotiated the heavy traffic carefully but swiftly, his own agitation revealed by his white-knuckled grip on the steering wheel. Summer didn't say a word when they turned onto the two-lane highway that climbed up the side of the mountain. She stared out the window as if the "See Rock City" and "Visit Ruby Falls" advertising signs were the most important messages of her life.

He couldn't stand it. Reaching over, he touched her cheek with his fingertips in a gentle, soothing caress. He felt her tremble, and his heart lurched. Was she afraid of him?

"Summer, tell me what's going on. Please, half-pint. This is killing me."

Her strangled laugh dissolved into a sob. She caught his outstretched hand and pressed it to her face. "Oh, Ryder, I'm so afraid! I—I don't know what to do. You're—you're in danger."

Thoroughly disconcerted by her words, Ryder pulled the car into a narrow lay-by, released both seat belts and dragged his weeping lady into his arms. She clung to him, her arms circling his neck, her tears seeping into his shirtfront.

"Shh, sweetheart, don't cry. Whatever it is, I'll fix it, I promise. What's made you so afraid? Tell me."

She lifted her tearful face. "Oh, Ryder, someone insane—insane and evil!—is trying to kill you, and it's because of me!"

"What?" He shook his head, mystified.

She dug in her jeans pocket, pulled forth the crumpled letter, and thrust it at him. "See for yourself. It was in today's mail."

He scanned the page. "Sounds pretty crazy."

"But we've got to take it seriously. He's already tried once!"

"Who sent it?" He flipped the page, looking for a signature.

Summer's mouth twisted bitterly. "My secret admirer. There are other letters. One of them contained my locket. He's got to be my burglar, too. Things that were taken have been turning up, and a prowler set the alarm off this week. I think he's...obsessed with me or something, and sees you as a threat."

"Why didn't you tell me this at the office?"

"I wasn't thinking! I'd just read the letter, and then suddenly you were there, and all I could think of was that as long as you were near me you'd be in danger!"

"Baby, that scared me worse than a dozen ax-murderers!" He dragged her against his chest and lowered his mouth in a hard, demanding kiss that left them both gasping. His eyes glittered with green fire when he raised his head. "Don't ever do that to me again."

"No, I won't," she said weakly, her expression bemused and faintly slumberous. "I promise."

"All right, then. From now on, we'll fight this thing together. No more going it alone, is that clear?"

"Yes, Ryder."

"Woman, you don't fool me a minute with that docile act," he said, chuckling. He kissed her lightly, then released her. "Okay, buckle up. I think the best thing we can do right now is go talk to Kent. Maybe he'll be able to come up with some answers. Suit you?"

"Yes." She let out a deep breath and smiled. It was wonderful to share the burden and the hope. Ryder took a look up and down the highway, then made a U-turn, and headed

the Mercedes back into the city. Adjusting her seat belt, she
sat back, much relieved. The greenery covering the side of
the mountain flashed past.

"What will Kent do?" she began.

Ryder's low curses and suddenly ferocious expression interrupted her.

"Ryder, what—"

He pumped the pedal to the floor, then jammed the gearshift into a lower gear, eliciting a grinding protest from the
tortured engine. His swift glance toward Summer was grim.

"Hang on to your hat, kid—we don't have any brakes!"

Ryder fought to control the speeding vehicle, but the incline was steep and their velocity snowballed. He pulled the
emergency brake, filling the car with the smell of scorched
rubber, but still they streaked down the side of the mountain like an out-of-control express. Only his skill kept them
from leaving the winding highway altogether. Leaning on
the horn, he rammed the right front fender against the side
of the cliff again and again in a desperate effort to slow them
down.

White-faced, Summer fought down the urge to scream
and braced herself on the dashboard, lurching against her
seat belt each time the car slid into the rock face. The shocks
made the vehicle vibrate, rattling them around like peas in
a tin can. Metal shrieked, and rocks and debris attacked the
car like a barrage of artillery. The window on her side shattered into an icy pattern. She was too frightened to close her
eyes, too afraid she was going to die. She said a wordless
prayer.

Ryder grunted. The road was flattening out, houses and
sidewalks appearing on each side, but they were still going
much too fast, and headed for the major intersection at the
base of the mountain. If they plowed through that . . .

"Get down!" he barked to Summer. The intersection
loomed ahead. Ryder jammed the gearshift into the lowest
gear and killed the engine in a desperate move. The car
bucked and his shoulders strained to control the now-

powerless steering wheel. Struggling, Ryder steered the car over the sidewalk, and it plowed across a front yard to come to a lurching, bumping standstill in the middle of a tall privet hedge. The silence was deafening.

Ryder unclenched his hands from the steering wheel and reached for Summer. "Are you all right?"

"I—I think so." She gasped for breath.

"Let's get out of here." He freed them from the seat belts, kicked open his door, and dragged her out after him. He realized vaguely that he was drenched with sweat. They stumbled away from the wreck, clinging to each other, bruised and shaken, but alive. An elderly man from the nearby house hurried toward them, and in the distance a siren wailed.

Some time later, after the police had arrived, and after they'd inventoried their bumps and bruises and found no serious injury, and after they'd agreed with Kent that they had been very lucky indeed, Ryder made a surprising comment.

"*Now* I'm mad."

"Accidents happen, Tex," Kent drawled. He'd arrived on the scene minutes after the city police car, a little white around the mouth, but willing to joke and tease Ryder and Summer to ease the tension once he'd seen they were safe. They stood in the yard watching a tow truck being hitched to the partially demolished Mercedes.

"I'll bet you a beer that your people are going to find my brakes were tampered with," Ryder said. "And before you tell me I've got a case of paranoia, look at this."

He gave Kent Summer's letter and filled him in. His hand gripped Summer's waist as he talked, holding her possessively close. "My car's been at the airport all week—plenty of opportunity to sabotage it. I'm sure this fellow didn't count on Summer being with me when I wiped out. You're the detective. How are you going to find this nut?"

"Jesus." Kent whistled, and his eyes narrowed. He handled the letter by the edges, and a closed expression clouded his rugged face when he looked at it.

"Hey, Lieutenant!" A uniformed officer gestured, radio mouthpiece in hand. "Call for you from downtown."

Kent went over to the car, and when he came back there was a fierce, grim light in his slate blue eyes. "How's this for timing? Your station and one of the local TV stations received anonymous calls just minutes ago—pleading for Jubilee to stay away from Gulliver's car!"

"Golly, our would-be killer has a soft streak," Ryder said sarcastically.

"What are we going to do?" Summer rubbed fingertips against her throbbing temple. Now that the adrenalin surge was over she was weak and shaky, and her knees felt like jelly.

"*We* aren't going to do anything," Ryder said firmly. "You are going to your uncle's. You're done in, and I want you someplace I won't have to worry about you." He turned to Kent. "Can one of your patrolmen give her a ride?"

"Sure," Kent said easily. One eyebrow lifted. "Planning on covering this investigation personally, are you, Tex?"

"You got it, partner."

Kent gave a long-suffering sigh. "Thought as much. Well, come on. I'm going to give this letter to the boys in the lab, and then we'll go review our anonymous caller's message."

"You mean they *taped* it?" Ryder asked, surprised.

"The TV station did, at least some of it."

"Then what are we waiting for?"

"Ryder!" Summer looked at him in exasperation and disbelief. "There's someone trying to *kill* you. Shouldn't you make yourself scarce or something?"

"Don't worry, Kent will protect me," Ryder said with a grin that died when met by her worried expression. His arms went around her, and he buried his nose in the shining mass of her flower-fragrant hair. "You just sit tight, half-pint. I'll be back as soon as I can."

His kiss was exquisitely tender, and, shaken as she was, she couldn't fight him. He sensed her acquiescence, and smiled, then whisked her into the waiting patrol car.

"You got it pretty bad, ain't you, Tex?" Kent asked softly as the police car pulled away. Summer's face was a pale oval visible through the rear window.

"Yeah." Ryder's voice was faintly surprised. "I guess I do."

"PUT YOUR FEET UP, DEAR," Olivia urged. "Can I bring you anything? Would you like a brandy? How about some hot milk?"

"Don't fuss, Aunt Ollie," Summer said, stretching out on the chair and ottoman. She stifled a groan, already stiff and sore from the battering she'd taken. Even a hot shower hadn't helped much. Forcing a reassuring smile for her aunt's benefit, she said, "I'm all right, really."

"When I think what could have happened...!" Olivia raised her clasped hands in thanksgiving. "Thank you, Lord!"

"It's the rest of this matter that's bothering me," Burton interjected. His normally jovial countenance was creased with worry. He held the remote control for the television, flipping through the successive channels in an absent manner. "A man who'd stoop to murder to dispose of an imagined rival isn't sane. Summer, are you certain you have no idea who this secret admirer of yours could be?"

"No, I'm just as baffled as you are." She shivered. "I can't imagine what I've done to inspire this kind of obsession."

"Now don't you be thinking this is any of your fault!" Olivia admonished.

"But what if I did something or said something that caused it?" Summer bit her lip, agonized with guilt. "Ryder's in danger, and I can't help feeling responsible."

"He's very important to you, isn't he, dear?" Olivia asked.

Summer blinked back a prickle of moisture. "I'm in love with him."

Olivia perched on the arm of Summer's chair and stroked her niece's hair. "Well, I'm sure that everything is going to work out."

"Quiet, you two," Burton ordered. He touched the button on the remote control that increased the television's volume. "Here's a news report. I want to see if they'll play that taped phone call again."

Summer frowned at the set. Tony Keatchum smiled back at her, his deep voice reporting the mysterious warning the TV station had received almost simultaneously with the near-fatal accident on Lookout Mountain.

"Police officials are presently conducting an investigation," Tony intoned. "They're most interested in the message this station received. Here's the audio playback."

There was a faint crackle of static, as though through a phone line, and another voice blared from the set.

"Stop Jubilee. Get her away from Gulliver. The car's... not safe. I fixed it good. I won't miss this time like I did before..."

Summer's eyes widened, and she leaned forward, straining to hear. There was something...

"W-warn her... can't let her go w-with him..."

"Oh, my God!" Summer gasped and her feet hit the floor. "Oh my God, OH MY GOD!"

"What is it?" Burton demanded.

"I know that voice!"

"SUMMER, ARE YOU CERTAIN?" Vanessa asked.

"Yes. I think so. I'm not sure." Summer drew a deep breath and passed Vanessa another reel of tape.

"Is that a multiple-choice answer?" Merl demanded, feeding tape through a reel-to-reel recorder. The table in the production room of WCHT-WROC was littered with dozens of other spools, most of them marked "Jubilee—Interviews."

"I can't be positive, but I've got a feeling..." She made a face. "Maybe I'm just going crazy, but I swear the fellow who calls me here nearly every day is the same guy that phoned that warning! He called in questions so often that I finally quit recording him, but I know that he's got to be on some of the first interview tapes—if I could just find them."

"Well, you keep listening, and we'll keep digging them out," Vanessa said firmly. "Here, Merl, go through this box."

They worked without a break. Summer punched buttons on the tape recorder, playing snatches of her interview programs, then fast-forwarding the tape, listening again, fast-forwarding again. The production room was filled with high-pitched garble mixed with deep voices, high voices, twangy voices, educated voices—but not the voice Summer was looking for. Frustrated, she fed yet another tape into the machine, punched a button—and froze.

"...don't need to use Retin-A, Jubilee, you'd be beautiful even w-with w-wrinkles..."

"That's him!" Summer rewound the tape and listened again. Merl and Vanessa crowded closer to hear. The voice repeated its message, and Summer shuddered uncontrollably. "I know that's him. I always thought he sounded a bit like Wallace, the Prince of Whales, with that faint stutter on his *W*'s. If I could only prove it!"

"Can't the police do one of those voice prints?" Merl asked. "Maybe they could compare this tape with the one at the television station."

"Merl, you're brilliant!" Summer planted a kiss on the side of his long face, then turned back to the recorder, rapidly removing the tape. "I'll call Kent. Only...I don't know what good it will do, really. There's still no way of knowing who the man is."

"Let the police figure out an angle, doll," Merl advised "They're bound to come up with something."

"I hope you're right," Summer said fervently. "This is too scary."

"You said it," Vanessa agreed. "I don't care if tomorrow is Halloween, this is giving me the creeps."

"Me, too. Thanks for your help, you two. I'm going to get in touch with Kent right now." Clutching the precious reel to her chest, Summer gave a worried half-smile and hurried out of the production room.

Merl and Vanessa were alone for the first time since the previous evening's disastrous conversation, and there was a moment of awkward silence. Vanessa turned away, busily returning the discarded reels of tape back into their rightful places.

"Vannie..." Merl began, then stopped, swallowing harshly. "Vannie, I just wanted to tell you I'm sorry about what happened yesterday."

"It's all right," she said shortly.

"You know I never wanted to do anything to hurt you or Amy."

"I know." Nervously she shoved tape reels into the storage racks, not meeting his gaze. "It wasn't your fault, and I shouldn't have said what I did. Actually, it had to happen sooner or later, and Amy and I have had a long talk. Everything's okay."

Merl's deep sigh of relief was heartfelt. "Great. I mean it. Really, I—"

"Oh, stop, Merl! It's hard enough without all this forced sentiment," Vanessa said, her tone brittle. Her eyes were huge and nearly black in her pale face.

"Nothing's forced about the way I feel about you."

She made a small negative gesture and turned away. "Sure. You're thanking your lucky stars you didn't get involved with a woman with an *illegitimate* kid! Think of what your folks would say! At least you spared them that shame!"

"Now wait a minute!" His voice was angry. "My parents don't have anything to do with this. And anyway, they're not so bigoted they'd hold a mistake against anyone, much less you! They're crazy about you, and they'd love Amy, too.''

"Well, they aren't going to get the chance, are they?" She shook her head. "Never mind. Amy and I are family enough, and we're going to make a new life for ourselves."

"What?" Merl grabbed Vanessa's shoulders and turned her to face. "What do you mean by that?"

She looked at him with a bright defiance. "There's an opening at Ryder's Knoxville station, and I've decided to take it."

"What!" His fingers tightened on the soft flesh of her upper arms, and his face was suddenly pasty. "You can't!"

"I can't stay here any longer," she choked. "It hurts too much."

"Why?"

Crystal tears formed on the edge of her lashes, and she quivered. "Don't, Merl. Leave me my pride, at least."

He shook her, his lips pulled back in a snarl. "For God's sake, woman! I'm not going to let you do this to us!"

The tears spilled down her cheeks. "What else can I do?"

"You could marry me."

Vanessa's mouth made a silent "O," and Merl hauled her into his arms. His voice was a husky rasp in her ear.

"I'm just a country boy, Vanessa. No one ever accused me of being an intellectual giant, but there's one thing about me. Once I learn something, it stays learned."

"It does?"

He nodded, rubbing his big-knuckled hands across her back. "Yeah. And I've finally learned that a family is what you make it. The only important thing is love. And I know I've got enough love in me for you and Amy, if you'll only let me try."

"Oh, Merl." Her shoulders shook.

"Don't cry, Vannie. Oh, honey!"

"I'm sorry, Mel," she snuffled against his shirt. "I'm sorry I'm not what you wanted."

His hands tenderly smoothed her dark curls. "You're wrong, sweetheart. You're brave and sexy and compassionate and beautiful and loving. You're *exactly* what I want, only it took me a while to get it through this thick skull. I can make you happy, I know I can. Just give me a crack at it. What do you say?"

She drew back to look up into his earnest expression, a brilliant smile shining through her tears. "You lunkhead. I love you. What else can I say but yes?"

"You will?" His blue eyes lit up. "Well—well, swell!"

"Swell?" Giddy laughter tinkled from her throat. "Oh, Merl! Summer's right. You really have a way with words."

His smile grew into a crooked grin. Deliberately he took off his glasses and tossed them on the table, then pulled her close. "Maybe so," he murmured, lowering his head, "but you'll find I'm a whiz at nonverbal communication."

"HOW COME YOU NEVER STAY where I put you?"

Summer turned her back on the banks of high-tech communications equipment that made up the dispatching nucleus for the Chattanooga Police Department and gave Ryder a relieved smile. "I guess that's because you never put me where I want to be. But that's typical for a male chauvinist pi—"

"Watch it!" Kent interrupted with a grin. "You've got to be careful what you say about S-W-I-N-E in a place like this." His glance about the large room included a bevy of uniformed officers, plainclothes detectives, stenos and dispatchers, all busily going about the business of keeping the residents of the city safe.

"Oops. Sorry." Summer laughed but the sound was strained.

"Come on in my office," Kent said, leading them into a glass-partitioned cubicle along one wall. "You said on the phone you recognized the caller's voice?"

She sank down in a wooden chair facing his battered blue metal desk. Ryder took up a protective position behind her.

"Yes," she said. "They already took the tape I had to your crime lab. I know you think I'm probably imagining things, but my ear is trained to hear things like inflection or a particular cadence. That's why I'm able to do my character voices and impressions. I swear my persistent caller is the same man who gave that warning."

Kent nodded, taking a seat behind the desk. The spring in the caster chair screeched a protest at his weight, but he ignored it, leaning backward and staring up at the ceiling with a frown between his wheat-colored brows. "It fits the scenario. I'm willing to bet on your instincts, Summer, but we'll get the lab to confirm it."

Ryder crossed his arms over his chest. "It doesn't do us much good either way."

"That depends." Kent glanced at Summer. "You think your caller could be persuaded to phone in again?"

She grimaced wryly. "The problem has been to keep him off the lines. That was one reason Ron and I didn't take calls at all today. Why?"

"How'd you like to try your hand at police work? If you can get him to call in and keep him talking, then we could trace the call. I'm pretty sure I can get an arrest warrant for probable cause. Then we haul this sucker in and see what makes him tick."

"I'll do anything I can to protect Ryder," Summer said, her expression suddenly fierce. "He's been lucky twice. We've got to stop this guy before he tries to strike at Ryder again."

Ryder's hand closed over her shoulder and squeezed. "You didn't know you'd recruited a pint-sized vigilante, did you, Kent? Still, I don't want her doing anything that might put her at risk."

"You've been the target so far," Kent pointed out. "Besides, she can't come to much harm talking over the phone." A polite rap on the glass booth had him gesturing a uniformed policewoman to enter the booth. She handed him a report folder and several flat plastic bags containing sheets of paper.

"McGinty says you've got a perfect match."

"All right, Randi. Thanks."

The policewoman left, and Kent flipped through the report, frowning to himself.

"Do the tapes match?" Summer asked urgently.

"Yeah. The voiceprints jive. The odds are against both the letters and calls threatening Ryder coming from two different people. I'd say we're dealing with one man here." He looked up, and his blue eyes were chilly with determination. "And something else."

"What is it?" Ryder demanded.

Kent placed two plastic-bagged letters on the desk. Pointing to the first, he said, "This is Summer's letter."

"So?" Ryder asked impatiently.

Kent lifted the second letter, but his eyes never left Summer. "And this is the letter Cleva Wagner received the day before she was stabbed to death. They were written by the same man."

CHAPTER SIXTEEN

THE SCREAMS of the helpless victims jangled Summer's overstretched nerves. With a small, angry sound, she dropped the edge of the window drape, covering the back-alley panorama of trash dumpsters and hazy streetlights. She crossed the nondescript motel room and flipped off the Wolfman and Dracula Halloween double feature pouring from the television screen. The sudden silencing of a terror-ized shriek in midyelp was worse. She shivered and rubbed her palms up and down her arms, then picked up a stale cracker from the tray holding her half-eaten dinner. Perch-ing on the edge of the faded blue bedspread, she nibbled the cracker.

So far, she decided, protective custody wasn't all it was cracked up to be.

Kent had explained it all to her. She understood that he had to protect the only lead he had, and he wasn't going to blow perhaps his only chance to put Cleva Wagner's mur-derer behind bars. Of course, Ryder hadn't exactly seen eye to eye with his friend. Using Summer as "bait," as he termed it, was both unethical and dangerous, to his way of thinking. And *he* wasn't going to let her take such a risk! She'd never seen either of them so furious, Ryder's eyes snapping green, Kent's normally placid temper flaming al-most out of control. They'd roared at each other like two caged lions. Summer had been afraid they would come to blows. They might have, too, if she hadn't grown tired of being ignored and intervened.

"I'll do whatever you want, Kent," she said firmly, refusing to acknowledge Ryder's protests. "He's got to be stopped. I think maybe somehow it's my fault."

"That's ridiculous!" Ryder snapped. "You're no more at fault than Cleva Wagner was. If anything, I'm the one that ought to be horsewhipped for pushing your face into the public eye. Now this madman's fixated on you! I still think you ought to leave the city until this is over."

"She can't. I need her," Kent said tersely. "It won't *be* over without her."

"Listen, you—"

"Oh, stop!" Summer cried, appalled at being caught in the middle between two best friends. "I know what I've got to do. Ryder, I appreciate your concern, but you're scaring me. Kent, Ryder's got firsthand knowledge of how deadly this man can be, so he's got a right to be concerned. But all I have to do is talk to this guy on the phone, right?"

"Right."

"Then we do it in the morning." She looked at each man in turn, a determined, stubborn one-woman dynamo—more than a match for the both of them. "End of discussion."

And that was how she'd come to be spending the night in a second-rate motel on the eve of the most important broadcast of her life. She'd placed a reassuring call to Aunt Ollie, and there was a very polite policeman stationed at the end of the corridor, but it didn't change the fact that she was alone with her thoughts.

She wasn't really afraid. After all, the killer was faceless. *But not voiceless,* she thought. Remembering the soft, shy voice of her overzealous caller, she shuddered to imagine the terrible violence concealed within. How could he have committed such an awful crime? Cleva had been the object of a similar obsessive devotion, Kent said, and somehow it became twisted and violent. The darkness of the human psyche was fathomless, and the knowledge that she'd been watched by a man with an innocent woman's blood on his hands made her queasy.

Someone knocked on the door, and she gave a little gasp, her hand covering her fast-pumping heart. The cracker made her mouth dry, and she had to swallow twice before she could answer.

"Who—who is it?"

"Ryder."

She let out a shaky breath and hurried to the door, fumbling with the lock and chain, flinging the door open with a relieved smile.

His face was a black thundercloud. "Dammit, Summer! You're supposed to check who's outside before you release the chain." Stepping inside the room, he closed and relocked the door.

"I knew it was you," she said, her tone defensive.

"Well, don't take such a stupid chance again, is that clear?" Ryder's features were hard and cold, his movements jerky with tension.

"Why the dickens are you mad at me?" she asked hotly, then nearly groaned at her own belligerent words. *Oh, Lord, why do we have to fight now?* It was a difficult situation for both of them, but didn't he realize how badly she needed for him to hold her? Pride made her lift her chin. "What are you doing here, anyway?"

"We finished setting up for the phone trace at the station, and Kent wanted me to stay away from my place tonight, too. They checked me into a room down the hall." He pulled a key with a black plastic tag from his pocket and tossed it carelessly on top of the dresser. "You know what I told them?"

"No, what?"

"That they ought to save the taxpayers' money." He hauled her against him, finding her lips with his, plunging his tongue deep in her mouth to steal her breath. When he raised his head, she sagged weakly against him.

"I'm staying here tonight," he said, his voice thick. "There's no way I'm letting you out of my sight until this is over."

"You feel responsible," she accused shakily.

"You're damned right I do." His mouth tilted in a half-grin. "I've got to protect my investment."

There was a sharp twinge of disappointment in the region of her heart. She didn't want him to come to her out of a sense of duty, but she might have realized he'd take this tack. Someone was endangering his top deejay, threatening the success of his business, and producing a bundle of potentially adverse publicity. Not to mention two uncomfortably close calls on his own life. Of course he'd stick with her to the finish, but then what? Her feeble hope that one day he'd come to love her enough to make a permanent commitment seemed as ephemeral and fantastic as a child's fairy tale. But she didn't want a white knight, she wanted a partner, someone to face all of life's possibilities with her. She gave a resigned sigh, placing both hands against his chest.

"The only one who's responsible for me," she said in a low voice, "is *me*. It's time I learned that once and for all."

He lowered his head. "Let's talk philosophy later."

"Stop, Ryder!" She turned her face, and his lips grazed her cheek, sending ripples of seductive pleasure across her skin. His skill and her own response made her angry. It was the only defense she had.

He wound his hands through her pale hair, sliding them through the glossy skein to rest on the curve of her neck and shoulder. Massaging the tense muscles with his fingers, he murmured in her ear. "You're tight all over. Everything is getting to you, isn't it?"

"Yes," she said. Pulling free of his embrace was the hardest thing she'd ever done. She walked to the dresser and leaned her hands against it, staring at herself in the mirror. "Everything."

She longed to take the warmth and solace he offered, yet she knew in that moment that she had to stand on her own two feet. Her relationship with Clancy had been one of dependence, and she was afraid circumstances were pushing her in that direction with Ryder. She'd always let her empathy for others guide her actions, sometimes even to the detriment of her own happiness. She had to face the fact that she might never to able to reach Ryder. He might be satisfied with just a physical relationship, but she knew she could never be. The present situation suddenly became a symbol for everything that stood between them. He feared true intimacy, and in the end she would be alone again. For her own future, her own peace of mind, she had to prove to herself that she could meet him as an equal, on her own terms, even if it meant giving him up.

Ryder moved behind her, pushing her hair aside with one long finger, pressing his lips to the nape of her neck. Beautiful, sweet and vibrant Summer, he thought. In this storm, she was the only calm center, and his need for her burned.

"Let me take care of you tonight," he murmured against her skin. Slipping his hands beneath her sweater, he filled his palms with the warmth and fullness of her breasts, pulling her backward to rest against his length. "Lean on me for a while."

"I can't." Her words were a breathless whisper, but nothing could disguise the raw agony lurking in her hyacinth eyes. "I'm afraid of leaning too far and then falling flat on my face when you disappear."

"I don't understand, half-pint."

She met his gaze in the mirror, then turned in his arms to stare full into his face. "Do you love me, Ryder?" she asked baldly.

He studied her while panic crawled through his gut. What had gotten into her tonight? Hadn't he shown her how he felt? "I care for you very much."

Her short laugh was tinged with bitterness and regret. "Always the cautious answer. A thinking man's solution to a sticky problem." She stepped away from him. "You'd better go."

Exasperation mixed with an equal part of frustration, and he raked unsteady hands through his hair. "I've got a feeling I've missed part of the conversation here. Would you mind running that past me again?''

"I guess it's a question of trust," she said, her words slow and thoughtful. "You don't trust me enough to love me, but if you don't love me, I can't trust you to be here when I need you. One of those vicious circles you read about."

"That's clear as mud," he said angrily.

She was moving away from him, he could feel it in his bones. This whole situation was filled with potential disaster, yet he hadn't foreseen this! Had the threat to her life made her reflect on their relationship, and had it come up lacking? He knew the inadequacy was his, and the realization made him feel guilty and uncomfortable. The thought of losing her froze his very core, yet he didn't know how to reach out and pull her back.

Not since that time in Atlanta had he felt so helpless. A killer stalked Summer, and his inability to do anything to protect her was hauntingly reminiscent of Elise's betrayal. That misjudgment, that failure of faith made him cautious, distrustful of the turbulent gamut of emotions Summer evoked from him without even trying. He felt as though he had been swept into the vortex of a tornado. He would be lucky to come out of the thing alive, so why waste time worrying about which way was up, which down—as long as they were together?

"You're just upset, and rightly so," he said tightly. "Try to relax. It'll all be over soon." But his placating words only served to incense her more.

"Don't you dare patronize me, Ryder Bowman!" she snapped. "What's clear is that I can't count on you, so I've got to face this alone, and not depend on anyone but myself."

"You don't know what you're saying," he said between clenched teeth. "I'm here for you, and you know it!"

"I'm talking about feelings, Ryder," she said. "Those real emotions that you're so afraid to experience. Love and commitment. That's what counts, not numbers in a ledger, not points on the giant scoreboard of life."

"I thought I'd been fairly clear that I wanted a relationship with you," he said, tension vibrating in his deep voice.

"Yes, you have, and that's what's so chilling. The very words you use to talk about us put everything on an impermanent basis, rather like a business deal with an option clause that allows both parties to bow out gracefully if the going gets tough. I guess I was wrong to let it go this far, but I hoped..." She took a deep breath. "I wanted forever."

She saw his face freeze up and despaired of reaching him. His coolness was an understandable defense. After all, it was better not to care, not to feel. That way you never got hurt. She understood, but it didn't stay the pain that lashed her heart. Her voice shook.

"I know you care for me. I even believe that you love me a little, but logic and caution and fear hold you back. You're afraid to risk everything emotionally because that would mean losing control of a part of yourself. But I can't settle for less—not this time."

"What do you want from me? Should I go down on one knee and promise undying devotion?" His mouth curled with cynicism. "Honey, that's not the way my world is made. I learned that lesson a long time ago."

"I think you only know about the pain, not the promise of love, so you keep your innermost self unfettered. You're free, Ryder, but at what price? Your cocoon of self-protection is as much a prison as a shield. It's frightening to reveal yourself completely. It makes you vulnerable. But sometimes it's worth the risk. This isn't Atlanta, Ryder, and I'm not Elise! Don't you understand that I'd never betray you?"

"Then what are you doing now?" His face was hard.

"Trying to survive."

"Alone?" he sneered.

"Not by my choice, but out of necessity."

He grabbed the key from the dresser. "Then I wish you joy in your solitude. But just remember you threw away something special because of a disagreement over semantics."

"Perhaps." She shrugged, and tears sparkled on her sooty lashes. "We'll never know for certain, will we?"

"So you're going it alone again?"

"Yes." Her smile was brittle. "Isn't that amazing, Ryder? Now I'm just like you."

"WHAT IF HE DOESN'T CALL?" Summer asked the following morning. Throwing her braid over the shoulder of her gold and black plaid flannel shirt, she shot an apprehensive glance at the clock of the control booth. "The Coffee Club's nearly over."

"Then we'll keep at it until he does," Kent replied. He lounged in a folding chair in one corner, his long legs extended, his eyes deceptively sleepy. A new temporary phone sat on the floor beside him. "As long as it takes."

"Don't worry," Ryder interjected, working the control board automatically. He wore a bright red shirt and faded denims. Summer was reminded sharply, poignantly, of his powerful physical attraction, yet his expression was unrelentingly grim. "He'll call. I'll see to it."

"How are you going to make him call?" she asked nervously. "Nothing we've done so far has worked."

"Let's play a little game." The song playing came to an end, and he hit his microphone button. "That was 'The Monster Mash' and before that 'Spiders and Snakes,' in honor of the holiday. Jublilee, since today is Halloween, I wondered what kind of costume you'd chose for Trick or Treat?"

"Gulliver, that's for kids."

"You're such a shrimp, you could get away with it. I think you ought to go as a hot-air balloon."

"Are you calling me fat?"

"If the shoe fits...actually, the balloon reminds me of your brain."

"So now I'm an airhead!"

"Flighty is the word I'm looking for. On second thought, maybe a gorilla mask to match those hairy legs of yours."

"Thanks a bunch!" She glared at him. "And you could shave your head and be Don Rickles!"

"Ouch! With a witch's tongue like that all you need is a broomstick."

"You're a meanie, Gulliver!" This repartee wasn't as much fun as it used to be, she thought with a pang, and tried to control the betraying quiver of hurt in her voice.

Summer hung on to her composure by the merest thread, the estrangement between them a consuming agony, yet determined to match his coolness in every respect. But the morning's work, even with the distraction of this plot, had taught her one thing. She wasn't so masochistic that she could endure working with Ryder any longer. She couldn't sit across the desk from him morning after morning, loving him, yet knowing he wasn't willing to give of himself in the way she needed. It meant the sacrifice of the Coffee Club and her career, but she had to get out of temptation's way, before she abandoned her principles and went back to him on his terms. And that, she knew, could only end in disaster and further heartbreak.

"But maybe our listeners don't agree with me," Ryder continued. "For a chance at a couple of free dinners from Mason's Barbecue, call in with your suggestions for Jubilee's costume and some words of comfort. I swear, folks, I think I made her cry!" The next song began.

"You did not!" she said indignantly, instantly on her mettle again.

Ryder's expression was veiled, unreadable. "Yeah, but your admirer doesn't know that. Maybe that will arouse his protective instincts."

"It might work, at that," Kent agreed. "Especially since he's got so much hostility for Gulliver already."

The tone on the phone pealed, and the banks of lights indicating the other lines began to blink one by one. Summer hesitated, paralyzed. Ryder picked up the receiver and handed it to her. "Go ahead, Jubilee. You're on."

It wasn't a shy, stuttering voice on the other end of the line. With the phone set on intercom, they could all hear the suggestions from a series of fans. There was a wide variety of voices, but not the one they were looking for.

"This is Jim. How about the tooth fairy?"

"...alligator..."

"...Mata Hari..."

"...bag of jelly beans..."

"...Statue of Liberty..."

"...Nancy Reagan..."

"Hello, Jubilee? W-why is Gulliver picking on you?"

Summer's breath caught, and her eyes grew wide. It was him! Wildly she signaled to Kent, who snatched up his phone and spoke quietly into it.

"Uh, hello," she said. "I—I haven't heard from you in a while. Don't worry about Gulliver. We're just having a little fun."

Ryder vehemently shook his head. He mouthed the words, "Keep him talking." Summer swallowed and took a deep breath.

"Have you got an idea for a costume for me?"

"A princess."

"I like that." Revulsion trickled down her spine, and she struggled to keep her tone friendly. "Why don't you tell me about it?"

"Cloth of gold, to match your hair. W-what do you mean, having fun with Gulliver? He's bad for you."

"Oh, I—I don't know," she stammered. Her beseeching gaze locked on Ryder's strong countenance. He grabbed her hand and squeezed encouragingly. His strength and purpose flowed into her, bolstering her confidence. Kent watched her intently, his jaw locked, shaking his head. *No luck on the trace yet.* He made a circular motion with his hand. *Keep it rolling.*

She took a deep breath. "Forget Gulliver. He's not important."

"He'll drag you down. Can't you see? You're just like the others."

"No, wait! Don't hang up! You've won!" she said desperately. "You had the best idea. You're so clever, that's why I like you to call in. I've missed our talks."

"Really? I w-won?"

"Yes. Two free dinners. You can drop by the station to get your prize. I'd really like to meet you," she babbled. "I feel as though we're old friends. Maybe we could use those dinners together."

"You mean it? W-well, okay. I'll come by today." He hung up.

Summer made a small sound of dismay, then raised anxious eyes to Kent. Ryder took the dead receiver from her limp hand and hung it up. Kent listened intently for a long moment, then slammed the phone down with a suppressed curse.

"Missed it."

"Oh, no," Summer moaned, slumping into her chair and burying her face in her hands. She felt completely washed out and enervated. "Now what? Oh, my God—he's coming here!"

"Take it easy, Summer," Kent said. "We can make it work."

"Jesus, Kent! This is going from bad to worse!" Ryder snapped. Through the whole thing, he'd automatically punched controls, keeping a steady supply of music piped over the air. "Get ready to sign us off, Jubilee. And tell him to call you back."

Numbly she nodded, then began the familiar spiel, ending with a request for her prizewinner to call her back. Vanessa and Ron appeared for the shift change, and gratefully, Summer stumbled from the control room, followed by Ryder and Kent. In the corridor, she leaned against the wall, taking deep breaths to fight the sickening churning in her stomach.

"Half-pint, are you all right?" Ryder asked, his voice deep with concern.

She drew herself up, swallowing on a wave of nausea. She could hardly bear it when he was kind to her. It made her want to throw herself into his strong arms and bawl like a scared baby. But she'd made her decision. A show of weakness wouldn't be fair to either one of them. "Give me a minute," she said tightly.

"All right." He turned and went into a low-voiced powwow with Kent. She had herself back under a semblance of control when the two men approached her again.

"Here it is," Kent said, laying out the plan. "You're to stay close to the phone. If our suspect calls back, then we'll try to trace the call again. In the meantime, we'll prepare for him to come visitin'. I'm going to call for some backup, and Ryder's sending all his nonessential personnel home for the day. I'll have a policewoman take the receptionist's place downstairs. Everything will be locked tighter than a barrel except for the front door. When he comes, if he comes, he'll have to ask for you. The policewoman will tell him he has to talk to you first, and have him call upstairs. You identify his voice, and we'll move in and make the arrest. You'll be separated by three floors at all times. You won't even have to see him. Can you go for it?"

"Yes. Whatever's necessary."

"Atta girl." Kent grinned encouragingly and pounded her on the back. "We'll make a cop out of you yet!"

"Don't give her ideas," Ryder said sourly. "All we need is for her to develop delusions of being Annie Oakley."

"Wa-a-al, pilgrim," Summer drawled as John Wayne, "she wouldn't be my first choice."

Ryder scowled. "If you can't take this seriously, maybe Kent ought to send you back to the motel."

"You can't. You need me," she pointed out flatly. "You might feel superior because you had to dodge a few bullets in Atlanta, but you're not the only one with the courage to do what's right. And if I can do anything to get this killer off the streets, then I will! Now I suggest you and Kent tend to business before our visitor arrives, otherwise I'm going to find myself with a dinner partner who carries his own carving knife!"

She had the satisfaction of seeing Ryder's face go white. "That's not funny."

"No, it's not, is it?" She felt her false bravado fade away to nothing. "I just want this over!"

But that was sooner said than done. Time dragged by. The office was nearly empty, only Merl and the current deejay on deck. Several policeman moved from floor to floor, finally taking up waiting positions on the second story, and displaying an impressive arsenal of weapons that made Summer's skin crawl.

"Is all that really necessary?" she asked Kent.

He shrugged. "Probably not. But better safe than sorry."

They ordered take-out pizzas for lunch, but no one but Merl ate much. The afternoon plodded by, and Summer jumped every time the phone rang. But still there was no phone call, and no visitor at the front desk for Jubilee.

"He's not coming," Summer said, watching the five o'clock traffic from Ryder's office window. "Any suggestions?"

"I guess he got cold feet." Kent shrugged. "You've got to learn patience in this business."

"You can have it," Ryder retorted. His fingers drummed on his desk.

"I'll say. This waiting is driving me crazy." Summer tucked her hands into her jeans pockets and looked at her two companions. "Now what?"

"I guess we'll just have to give it another go tomorrow." Kent's jaw hardened. "You can bet I'll have kicked a few rear ends at the telephone company. If we get another chance, they'd better not blow it again."

"It was my fault." Summer sighed and rubbed her tired neck. "I got rattled."

"You did fine. Don't be so hard on yourself. She handled herself like a real trooper, didn't she, Tex?"

"The Duke would have been proud," Ryder drawled, studying her carefully.

Summer stirred uncomfortably. It had been necessary to put all personal feelings aside during this long day, but now there wasn't anything to blunt the raw longing she felt. She looked away from the penetrating green gaze. "I just want to go home," she mumbled.

"Home, no," Kent corrected. "Motel, yes. Tex, you, too." He held up his big palms at their dual groans. "Just standard operating procedure. Take any complaints to the Captain, okay? I'll have a squad car deliver you. I guess we can call it a day. Are you ready?"

"Let me go wash my hands. I feel grimy," Summer said.

"Sure. There's no hurry," Kent replied.

It felt odd walking down the hall toward the ladies' room. There was a deep stillness in the rows of offices that was not normally there, as if the very walls and furniture sensed the uneasy tension that had haunted the station that day. Even the Halloween decorations looked forlorn.

Summer pushed open the door to the ladies' room, wondering how Allison, Rich and Amy looked in their Wizard of Oz costumes. She would give just about anything to be out of this nightmarish situation and back in her own cozy town house, handing out goodies to the neighborhood children. Usually she even dressed Lizabeth for the part and had as much fun as the kids. She washed her hands, laughing softly, imagining the look Ryder would give her and her puppet if he saw them in their matching peaked witch's hats.

She sobered, a sudden lump clogging her throat. Patting the long tail of her braid to smooth some stray wisps, she gave herself a long look in the mirror, then pinched some color into her pale cheeks. No, there wouldn't be any more good times like that, but at least she was proving to herself she could be strong, that she didn't have to depend on Ryder's or any man's strength. Why did that victory feel so hollow?

She wondered if there could still be some way to salvage her relationship with Ryder. Kent had talked of patience. Perhaps she had rushed things, scared Ryder off just as he was beginning to believe in the idea of them together. Maybe she'd unconsciously believed he was too much like Clancy, and had driven him away with her desperate grasping. Ryder had demons and failures, but then so did she. If she admitted that much to him, maybe they could talk things out together, sort out what they each wanted from this love affair. She knew she loved him. Wasn't it worth a try? Pushing open the door into the corridor, she resolved to make one last effort. When they got back to the motel, she'd go to his room and—

A figure stood in the open door of the stairwell opposite the ladies' room. Summer gasped in surprise, then relaxed.

"Oh, hi, it's you," she said smiling. The slight, sandy-haired young man in the attendant's uniform smiled back. He held a set of keys in his hand, and his pale blue eyes blinked owlishly. Summer read the embroidered patch on his shirt. "It's Bud from the garage, isn't it? Is something wrong with my car?"

"Everything is fine, Jubilee," he said in a soft, shy voice that froze Summer in her tracks. "I've been w-wanting to meet you for a long w-while."

CHAPTER SEVENTEEN

HE DOESN'T LOOK DANGEROUS, Summer thought.

There was an innocent air about him, a boyish hesitancy. Sandy hair and a smattering of brown freckles gave him a Tom Sawyer appeal—until she noticed his eyes. A transparent blue, they burned with a wild, unholy light that abruptly brought her to herself and the realization that Kent and Ryder were at the opposite end of the hall, totally unaware of this visitor!

For a terrible instant, she had the urge to giggle hysterically. Aunt Ollie had always said you had to be careful what you wished for, because you might get it. She'd wanted to prove she could stand on her own and—Lord help her!—here was her chance.

"Well, hi!" she said, infusing her voice with every ounce of warmth she could and forcing herself to offer her hand. "Gosh, it's nice to meet you, too."

A bit dazed, he shook her hand. "You're so beautiful. My golden angel."

"You say the sweetest things," she gushed, gently withdrawing her hand and trying not to shudder. "I've been waiting all day for you. I'll bet you want those free dinner vouchers." She began to edge backward along the hall. "Come on, Bud, and we'll see what I can rustle up."

"My name is Ernie. Ernie Polk."

"Well, Ernie, I can't tell you how much I enjoy having a fan like you." She was babbling, but he didn't seem to notice, following her like a moth mesmerized by a moving flame. They were past the elevators, halfway up the hall, and she began to think it might be all right, if only—

"Where are we going?" Ernie asked. "I don't want to go in there."

"Well, of course you do," Summer said reasonably. "I have to get the vouchers for you. You are taking me to dinner, aren't you, Ernie?"

That distracted him for a second. "You mean you'll go?"

"Sure," she began.

Ryder and Kent walked out of the office at the end of the hall, their conversation cut off in midsentence at the sight of Summer and her companion. Ryder took a step forward, his dark brows drawn together in a frown. "Summer, who . . . ?"

"That's Gulliver!" Ernie accused, his voice suddenly venomous.

Behind Ernie and Summer, the elevator doors slid open, and two uniformed police officers stepped out. There was a split second of mutual confusion, then Ernie went berserk.

"It's a trick!" he shrilled.

"Ernie, no!" Summer said, backing up.

"Summer, move!" Kent roared.

"You lied!" Fast as a striking viper, Ernie grabbed Summer's braid, jerking her back against him. A snub-nosed handgun appeared in his hand, then pressed against her jawbone. He looked back and forth between the men on each side of him. "Get back! Get back, all of you, or I'll kill her!"

Kent raised his hands, palms open. "Easy, man. Anything you say." He gestured to the two uniformed officers to back off. "Look, nobody wants to hurt anyone. Can't we just talk this over?"

Ernie glanced around, then backed awkwardly through an open office door, dragging Summer with him. His hands, surprisingly strong and wiry, tugged her braid unmercifully, making tears of pain spring into her eyes, but she was too terrified to even cry out.

"You little bastard! Let her go!" Ryder shouted, starting forward. Kent restrained him with an effort.

"Don't do anything crazy, Tex!" he snapped.

"Stay away from us!" Ernie screamed, and slammed the office door in their faces.

"DAMN! How much longer?" Ryder asked in a ragged voice.

There weren't words to describe the absolute hell he'd experienced the past forty-five minutes. He kept picturing Summer's face in the moment before the door had closed, terrified, her beautiful violet-blue eyes filled with tears. *If that bastard lays so much as a finger on her,* Ryder silently vowed, *I'll strangle him with my bare hands!*

"At least he's still talking to us," Kent replied, nodding at the police department's top hostage negotiator who was speaking quietly into the phone on Ryder's desk. They'd been able to at last prevail on Ernie Polk to pick up the extension in the windowless office where he'd taken refuge with Summer. Now Dr. Patterson was doing his best to find out just exactly what he wanted.

There was a knot of ice in the pit of Ryder's stomach. He and Kent had cleared out Merl and the deejay on duty, and for the first time on record, WCHT-WROC was off the air. Besides the negotiator, there was a SWAT team in readiness downstairs. Ryder dragged an unsteady hand through his hair. He hoped it wouldn't come down to that!

Nothing in his life was as important to him as Summer. Not his pride, his career, not even that part of himself he'd held aloof and inviolate. It wasn't important any longer, because somehow, without his even being aware, he'd given it all to Summer—only he'd been too much of a coward to tell her that heart and soul he belonged to her. She made him feel really alive, releasing a powerful array of emotions that sometimes frightened him, awed him, humbled him, but forever changed him.

Yes, he loved her. She wanted forever, and he'd been too stubborn to admit she *was* his forever. What foolishness of pride had made him hold that back? And yes, he wanted to be with her, now and always. Such a simple thing to say. Why had he left it unsaid? Now a madman's bullet might end her life, and he'd never even told her what was in his heart! There could be no greater tragedy. If only he were given another chance, he'd spend his entire life making it up to her.

Kent was watching Dr. Patterson, his fists jammed deep in his pants pockets. "You know, Tex," he said, "it's days like these that give a cop gray hairs."

Ryder knew his friend well enough to see that he'd taken the responsibility for this fiasco upon himself, and it was eating at him. He clamped a hand on Kent's shoulder. "It's nobody's fault. Stuff happens."

Kent's glance was wry. "I think I'm getting too old for this game. I'm losing my touch. I forgot Murphy's Law."

"If something can go wrong, it will," Ryder quoted. "How'd he get in anyway?"

"Unlocked the rear door with a key he must have gotten from Summer's apartment, then came right up the stairs. I feel like an idiot!" Kent's face took on the fierce, predatory expression that made him so feared and respected on the streets. "We're dealing with a psychopath, but I'm not going to let anything happen to that little lady."

"I know it." Ryder's expression was as grim as Kent's. "So what do we do?"

"Summer's safety comes first, so for starters, we give him everything and anything he wants."

"And then?"

"Then we nail his hide to the wall."

"W-WE'RE GOING TO BE SO happy together," Ernie Polk's soft voice crooned over Summer's bent head. His fingers gently stroked her hair. Shivering, she kept her forehead on her upraised knees, sitting on the floor with her back pressed against the wall. She'd kept this stoic position during Ernie's many telephone conversations over the past hour and a half. At her lack of response, he knelt beside her and moved closer. "My golden one, I love you so much."

Summer's head jerked up, and her eyes flashed. "If you love me, why are you keeping me here? You're frightening me, Ernie."

"It can't be helped." He smiled, a sly, calculating grimace that raised the hairs on the back of Summer's neck. "But soon. Soon, w-we'll have all we ever dreamed of. Because I love you."

"You don't love me! You don't even know me!"

"But you're w-wrong, my angel. I w-watched you in the garage, nearly every day. The letters, the calls. I even w-went to your house. You liked it when I brought your things back, didn't you?"

"Why, Ernie? Why did you tear up my place and break my things?"

"It was Gulliver's fault. I saw him on the television that night, touching you. I had to show you I was more important. I know your feelings are strong for me—only Gulliver keeps you from seeing it."

The avid light that shone in his eyes at the mention of Gulliver scared Summer more than anything he'd done so far. After all, he'd put away the gun, and hadn't done more than touch her hand or her hair with all the reverence of an acolyte approaching a sacred shrine. But she sensed his sickness and knew that his sanity was attached to a hairtrigger. The slightest wrong move could set off an explosion of violence.

"I think you've got the wrong woman," Summer said shakily.

"No, it's you I love, Jubilee."

"My name is Summer. How can you love me if you don't know that?" She saw a flicker of uncertainty in his expression, and pressed the advantage. "I'm a lot of people, sugar," she said *à la* Mae West.

"You're foolin' me," he said, disconcerted.

"Am I?" the high-pitched squeal of Hermione Hogg demanded. "Are you s-s-sure?"

"Stop it."

"Wa-a-ll, pilgrim, we'll have to call in the cavalry to do that," drawled the Duke.

Unexpectedly Ernie burst into relieved laughter. "I know John Wayne! So you like to play games! That'll be lots of fun on our trip." Still chuckling, he stood up.

Alarmed, Summer scrambled to her feet. "What trip? Where?"

"Away." He waved vaguely. "Out West maybe. I lived in Phoenix once. With my mother." His expression grew savage. "She's dead."

"I—I'm sorry," Summer whispered, staring.

Abruptly his face smoothed, and he smiled. "As soon as w-we're away from Gulliver, I know you'll see how perfect our love is meant to be. Not like the others. Not like Cleva."

Summer's mouth went dry. "What about Cleva?"

"She was a liar. And a w-whore. But she paid." His eyes were blank and stark with remembrance. "Oh, yes, she paid dearly. My mother paid, too."

Fear shot through Summer. "I can't go with you, Ernie."

"Yes, you can. I told them to put the keys in your car— you like your little car, don't you?—and lots of money, too. We can go anywhere, do anything." The phone rang, and his face lit up with a broad smile. "That should be them, telling us it's all ready."

"But I don't want to go anywhere with you!" she cried.

His expression clouded, and his mouth tightened. Deliberately he pulled the gun from inside his shirt. "Sure you do."

Summer gulped and shut up. He spoke into the phone. His expression was again cheerful when he put down the receiver. "It's all set. Let's go, Jubilee."

Grabbing her upper arm, he pulled her up next to him, the gun pointed at her rib cage, then walked out of the office. The floor was deserted. They walked along the hall, through the stairway door, then down the three flights of steps. Their feet echoed in the stairwell, and Ernie nervously examined each turn before pushing her on. The rear emergency door opened out into an alley next to the parking garage. It was dark, illuminated by only a distant street lamp and the headlights of passing cars at the mouth of the alley. There was no one in sight.

Where is everybody? Summer thought desperately. Surely they weren't going to let this criminal kidnap her! Maybe Kent was afraid she'd be hurt if they tried to rush Ernie and overpower him. She began to consider the fact that she might have to devise a plan to escape on her own.

Ernie dragged Summer across the alley, then over the concrete balustrade to drop onto the sloping entrance ramp of the garage. Nearly running now, he pulled her up the ramp lighted with a row of bare bulbs, then around a curve, to slide to a halt at the rear of Summer's Mustang. He shoved her closer to the driver's door, never releasing her.

"Open it."

She did.

"Are the keys in it?"

She looked again. "Yes."

"Money?"

"There's a suitcase in the back seat."

He released her arm. "All right, get in and scoot over."

A glimmer of an idea struck her. She took a deep breath and got in, grabbed the keys, rolled over the console, and bolted for the opposite door, pushing it open with the intention of jumping the railing and making a dash for it.

Ernie gave a roar and reached across the car for her, snagging the collar of her shirt. It ripped, slowing her down but not stopping her mad scramble out the partially opened door. There was a loud clatter of footsteps and muffled shouts, and Ernie jerked up. She half fell onto the pavement on the passenger side, skinned and gasping. Ernie pivoted, swinging his gun around over the angle of the open car door. A tall figure materialized from the shadows in front of the car, leaning negligently against a concrete pillar.

"You creep," Ryder said. "What makes you think I'll let you take my woman?"

"Gulliver." Ernie's voice was a low growl of hatred.

"Ryder, no!" Summer started to get up.

"Get back, Summer!" he ordered, his eyes never leaving Ernie's face. She subsided, inching backward away from the car on her hands and knees. "This is between us. I'm the one you really want. It's me you hate, isn't it?"

"You should die." The gun in Ernie's hand wavered, and his eyes took on a brilliant light of madness. "You tried to corrupt my angel."

"Your angel is in love with *me*," Ryder taunted. His gaze flicked to where Summer crouched beside another pillar, then back to Ernie. "And I love her. She sleeps with me, touches me everywhere, in a way you'll never know. You can *never* have her, and you know it."

"I'm going to kill you," Ernie choked. His gun hand shimmied wildly.

Summer smothered a frightened whimper behind her hands, the keys she held digging painfully against her lips.

Ryder's laugh echoed off the concrete battlements. "You poor stupid jerk. You've tried twice. I just won't die, will I? Haven't you figured it out? You *can't* kill me."

Ernie fired. Summer screamed and surged to her feet, but Ryder didn't fall. He merely smiled and took a step forward.

"See?"

Ernie's eyes bulged in terror. He raised his gun again.

Summer pitched the keys with all her might. Whitey Ford would have been proud. They hit the side of Ernie's head in the same instant a marksman's rifle cartridge blasted the gun and Ernie's hand into bloody pulp. He fell to the ground, screaming. Armed police officers swarmed out of nowhere, Kent in the lead.

Ryder dashed around the car, kicking the mangled gun away from the writhing killer. Their eyes met. Ryder held his side, but his smile was feral. He stripped his shirt up to reveal the heavy orange mesh of bulletproof body armor, and his lip curled. "Trick or treat, you scumbag!"

"Ryder!" Summer launched herself at him. "Oh, God, are you all right?"

He winced slightly, but clasped her to him, drawing her away from the injured killer. Police with first-aid kits worked over the moaning figure, and in the distance an ambulance siren shrilled.

"Take it easy, half-pint," he murmured, kissing her tenderly. "I'm okay. Bruised a rib, that's all."

Her hands moved over him, proving for herself that he was indeed hale and whole. "I was so afraid you'd been shot! All those crazy things I said last night—it doesn't matter."

"Shh." His thumbs gently rubbed her cheek. "Yes, it does. My life isn't worth a plugged nickel without you. I'm only sorry it took a madman to make me realize it. I meant what I said back there, Summer. I love you."

An almost unbearable joy swelled her heart. "Then that's all that counts, isn't it?" she whispered, her voice husky with love.

They were interrupted by a very irate police lieutenant bearing down on them.

"Jesus! You took ten years off my life with that stunt," Kent bellowed. "I'm definitely getting too old for this job!"

"So retire," Ryder said unkindly.

Kent threw up his hands. "Summer, you've got my sympathies. I tell him to stay put, and the next thing I know he's playing hero."

"You wouldn't make a move, so I had to. I wasn't letting him take her out of my sight again." Ryder's arm tightened on Summer's shoulder. "I knew I had him rattled. I'm surprised he hit me at all."

"Yeah? Well, you stuck yourself right in the line of fire, did you know that? My marksman couldn't get a shot off until you moved." Kent wiped the sweat from his forehead with his big fist, and his tone modulated to a medium roar. "It's a wonder he didn't blow your head off! Don't you ever do anything that *stupid* again, Tex, or I'll—I'll shoot you myself!"

Summer couldn't help it. Kent looked so disgusted she began to chuckle. The next thing they knew, all three of them were laughing hard enough to split their sides.

"Don't worry," Ryder finally managed, gasping for breath. "I don't ever intend to repeat the experience. Once is quite enough."

"Me, too." Kent glanced at the approaching ambulance. "Get out of here, will you? Some of us have got to earn a living, and it looks like it's going to be a long night. I'll bet ole Ernie's gun will be a match to the Choo-Choo incident, and there ought to be plenty of hard evidence in whatever rat hole he's been living in."

"He's sick," Summer murmured. They watched the attendants load Ernie into the ambulance. "I feel sorry for him."

"Don't worry, he'll live, which is more than can be said for most of his victims," Kent said, suddenly grim again.

"We're probably going to link him to a couple of similar murders in Arizona, too. He'll be given psychiatric help, and put somewhere he'll never hurt anyone again."

"Just make sure they throw away the key," Ryder muttered.

Summer pressed closer to Ryder, reveling in his strength, but there was an unfamiliar hardness. She shivered. "I know this thing probably saved your life," she said, her fingers working on his shirt buttons, "but do you think we could dispense with it now?"

"Yeah, good idea." Ryder shrugged out of shirt and armored vest, handed the vest back to Kent, then stuck his arms in his shirt again. "That thing weighs about a ton."

"Bitch, bitch, bitch." Kent grinned and slapped Ryder on the back. "Take the lady home, will you, Tex? I'll get official statements from you tomorrow."

"*If* you can find us," Ryder said. The look he gave Summer made her blush. "We've got some serious talking to do."

Arm in arm, they walked into the Halloween darkness, unafraid.

"I THOUGHT WE WERE GOING TO TALK."

"Hmm?"

"Ryder, you lied to a policeman," she said with a sigh. A slim finger of moonlight illuminated the room. Her cheek was pressed against his chest, and she was caught tight in the circle of his arm. Replete, satiated with passion, they lay naked in Ryder's big bed, basking in the afterglow of love. It was wonderful.

From the foot of the bed came a small, hopeful yelp.

"Aghh, Clancy, not now," Ryder grumbled. "I'm too comfortable."

The dog barked again and bounced.

"It sounds important." Summer laughed.

"All right, all right." Stretching and groaning, Ryder readjusted Summer's position, planted a shivery kiss on her shoulder, then got up.

Summer snuggled deeper in the covers, half listening in drowsy contentment to the small murmurs of conversation between the dog and his master. After a while, she felt the bed shift under Ryder's weight again.

"What kept you? I missed you," she murmured, then gasped as his air-cooled skin met her warmer flesh. He pulled her against him, spoon-fashion, soaking in her body heat, his hair-dusted thighs pressed against her bottom, his hands making tantalizing forays across her stomach and breast.

"You know what I feel like?" he growled, nuzzling her ear.

"A Popsicle?"

"Clever, Jubliee. Guess again."

"I don't have to guess." She wiggled slightly, teasing him.

"I feel like—some music, smarty."

"You want to play the piano now? Don't you ever play it in the daytime?"

"Ask a simple question," he groused, then reached for a button on the nightstand. "This kind of music."

The late-night sounds of Jack "Mack the Night" Maxwell flowed from the bedside radio.

"Oh! We're back on the air," she said, excited. Turning toward him, she began to draw subtle patterns in the silky hair on his chest. "How'd you manage that?"

"I kicked both Jack and Merl out of bed before we left the station and told them to hop to it."

"The boss has spoken," she mocked softly.

"What's the use of being the boss if you can't crack the whip occasionally? Besides, Merl couldn't complain when I told him it was a station manager's job."

She lifted her head. "What? You gave him a promotion?"

"Sure. I'd planned it anyway. I've got to have more time to devote to the Bowman Network, now that we're on firm ground at WCHT-WROC. I've decided Chattanooga makes a perfect location for a centralized corporate office. Besides, Merl will need the increase in salary to support his new wife and daughter."

"Ryder, he didn't!" she gasped.

"He did. In all the excitement, he didn't have a chance to tell us, but he and Vanessa are getting married."

She hugged him. "Oh, that's great! I can't wait to tell Beryl and Aunt Ollie."

"Speaking of Olivia, do you think she bought all those reassurances you were giving her over the phone?"

"She was upset, naturally, but Uncle Burt will calm her down."

"Did you tell her you were with me?"

"I think she knew. She likes you, Ryder, for some strange reason."

"My charm extends to women of all ages," he teased. "She and your uncle are fine people, Summer. I like them both a lot."

"I'm glad. I think the rough patch they went through following Uncle Burt's retirement is just about over. He's going to buy a boat, and Aunt Ollie says as soon as he does, she's going to learn to fish!"

"Just what I like, a happy ending." He laughed, threading his fingers through her hair. "Maybe there's one here for us?"

"It might be arranged," she whispered.

"I love you, Summer." He shook his head in amazement. "I can't believe how hard it was for me to admit it. Now it seems the most natural thing in the world."

"It makes me very happy to hear it." She brushed the dark hair back from his brow. "I love you, too."

"You were right. I was afraid to let go. I had to trust enough to really feel for the first time, and you showed me the way."

"And I won't be so scared of leaning on someone's strength, now that I know you're the right someone. We complement each other, Ryder, balancing our strengths and weaknesses."

"It makes a good partnership," he said seriously. "Professionally, personally, we have a lot to give each other."

"I think you're right."

"What? Have Gulliver and Jubilee finally agreed on something?" he asked.

"Kiss me, and let's find out, big boy," Summer drawled in her Mae West best.

Ryder didn't need a second urging, but just as things were beginning to get interesting, he drew back.

"Ryder...?"

"Wait. Listen," he said.

"And for all our late-night listeners on this All Hallow's Eve," announced "Mack the Night" from the bedside table, "we have a very special series of oldie dedications. A three in a row special, from Ryder to Summer, with love. Just for you, kids, here's 'Me and Mrs. Jones,' 'You Are the Sunshine of My Life,' and 'Having My Baby.' Enjoy!"

"Oh, that's beautiful!" Summer's eyes prickled with moisture, and she blinked and sniffled quietly as the first song warbled over the airwaves.

"Don't cry, half-pint," Ryder said. "And don't keep me in suspense. The musical question is, will you marry me and make this a permanent duet? I want it all with you—wife, kids, a scruffy dog, a forever where we can build all our dreams together. What do you say? I can promise you a prominent position within the Bowman Network. *Very* close to the chief executive."

She arched an eyebrow. "Do the perks include a syndicated interview show?"

He threw back his head and laughed, showing that dimple she doted on. "You got it, Jubilee. You know you've earned it."

"A duet, hmm?"

Eyes met, and souls entwined. Ryder's husky words were a solemn vow. "For the rest of our lives, half-pint."

"How many love songs do you know?"

"About a zillion."

Summer heaved a contented sigh and pulled his head down to meet hers. "That ought to just about do it."

Harlequin Superromance

COMING NEXT MONTH

#362 WORD OF HONOR • Evelyn A. Crowe
As a child, Honor Marshall had witnessed her
mother's death in an air disaster. Years later, when
she found out it was murder, she vowed to seek
revenge. Special agent Travis Gentry agreed to help.
But his price was high.

#363 OUT OF THE BLUE • Elise Title
When a wounded Jonathan Madden showed up in
Courtney Blue's bookstore, it was like a scene from a
thriller—and Courtney had read plenty of those!
Jonathan was no mere professor, as he claimed to be.
But he was definitely hero material....

#364 WHEN I SEE YOUR FACE • Connie Bennett
Mystery writer Ryanne Kirkland couldn't allow
herself to think of a future with Hugh MacKenna,
the charismatic private investigator from Los
Angeles. Firstly she was blind, and secondly there
was a possibility she'd have to live her life
on the run. Hugh only wished he could make her
understand that his life was worthless
without her....

#365 SPRING THAW • Sally Bradford
When Adam Campbell returned to her after a
twenty-year absence, Cecilia Mahoney learned the
meaning of heaven and hell. Heaven was the bliss of
love regained, hell the torment of being unable to
find the only child Adam would ever have—the one
she'd given away.

Have You Ever Wondered If You Could Write A Harlequin Novel?

Here's great news—Harlequin is offering a series of cassette tapes to help you do just that. Written by Harlequin editors, these tapes give practical advice on how to make your characters—and your story—come alive. There's a tape for each contemporary romance series Harlequin publishes.

Mail order only

All sales final

TO: *Harlequin Reader Service*
Audiocassette Tape Offer
P.O. Box 1396
Buffalo, NY   14269-1396

I enclose a check/money order payable to HARLEQUIN READER SERVICE® for $9.70 ($8.95 plus 75¢ postage and handling) for EACH tape ordered for the total sum of $_____ *
Please send:

[ ] Romance and Presents   [ ] Intrigue
[ ] American Romance   [Temptation
[ ] Superromance   [ ] All five tapes ($38.80 total)

Signature_____
                                        (please print clearly)
Name:_____
Address:_____
State:_____ Zip:_____

*Iowa and New York residents add appropriate sales tax

AUDIO-H

Your favorite stories with a brand-new look!!

H A R L E Q U I N

American Romance®

Beginning next month, the four American Romance titles will feature a new, contemporary and sophisticated cover design. As always, each story will be a terrific romance with mature characters and a realistic plot that is uniquely North American in flavor and appeal.

Watch your bookshelves for a **bold** look!

ARNC-1

Coming in June...

Harlequin Presents...

PENNY JORDAN

a reason for being

We invite you to join us in celebrating Harlequin's 40th Anniversary with this very special book we selected to publish worldwide.

While you read this story, millions of women in 100 countries will be reading it, too.

A Reason for Being by Penny Jordan is being published in June in the Presents series in 19 languages around the world. Join women around the world in helping us to celebrate 40 years of romance.

Penny Jordan's *A Reason for Being* is Presents June title #1180. Look for it wherever paperbacks are sold.

PENNY-1

Harlequin Regency Romance™

Romance the way it was *always* meant to be!

The time is 1811, when a Regent Prince rules the empire. The place is London, the glittering capital where rakish dukes and dazzling debutantes scheme and flirt in a dangerously exciting game. Where marriage is the passport to wealth and power, yet every girl hopes secretly for love....

Welcome to Harlequin Regency Romance where reading is an adventure and romance is *not* just a thing of the past! Two delightful books a month.

Available wherever Harlequin Books are sold.

REG-1R